T0267458

"As varied, creative, heartfelt, and fun as the community of writers who conjured it, *We Mostly Come Out at Night* is the narrative bestiary you need."

—**Elana K. Arnold, National Book Award finalist, Printz Award honoree, and author of** *Damsel,* *Red Hood,* **and** *What Girls Are Made Of*

"These monster stories positively pulse with humanity. Not only are they gripping and suspenseful, but they have such depth [and] meaning and stand as powerful testaments to the fierceness and fabulosity of the queer experience."

—**Dan Clay (aka Carrie Dragshaw), author of** *Becoming a Queen*

"Monstrously delicious, absolutely captivating, and wholly necessary. This collection's exploration of otherness and self-acceptance grips the heart in its clawed hand. At times unwavering in its rawness and often triumphant in its queer joy, this book belongs on every shelf. Sharpen your teeth and read on."

—**Rocky Callen, author of** *A Breath Too Late* **and co-contributing editor of** *Ab(solutely) Normal: Sixteen* *Stories that Smash Mental Health Stereotypes*

"I could not get enough of this book! Compulsively readable, *We Mostly Come Out at Night* reclaims the power of otherness from a queer perspective, introducing readers to monsters we not only understand, but maybe want to be (or already are). A gorgeous and stunning triumph."

—**Nora Shalaway Carpenter, author of** *Fault Lines* **and co-contributing editor of** *Ab(solutely) Normal: Sixteen* *Stories that Smash Mental Health Stereotypes*

WE MOSTLY COME OUT AT NIGHT

15 QUEER TALES of MONSTERS, ANGELS & OTHER CREATURES

EDITED BY
ROB COSTELLO

RP | TEENS
PHILADELPHIA

Running Press Teens
Hachette Book Group
1290 Avenue of the Americas, New York, NY 10104
www.runningpress.com/rpkids
@runningpresskids

First Edition: May 2024

Published by Running Press Teens, an imprint of Hachette Book Group, Inc. The Running Press Teens name and logo are trademarks of Hachette Book Group, Inc.

The Hachette Speakers Bureau provides a wide range of authors for speaking events. To find out more, go to www.hachettespeakersbureau.com or email HachetteSpeakers@hbgusa.com.

Running Press books may be purchased in bulk for business, educational, or promotional use. For more information, please contact your local bookseller or the Hachette Book Group Special Markets Department at Special.Markets@hbgusa.com.

The publisher is not responsible for websites (or their content) that are not owned by the publisher.

Print book cover and interior design by Frances J. Soo Ping Chow

Library of Congress Cataloging-in-Publication Data
Names: Costello, Rob, editor.
Title: We mostly come out at night : 15 queer tales of monsters, angels & other creatures / edited by Rob Costello.
Description: First edition. | Philadelphia : RP Teens, 2024. | Audience: Ages 13 and up | Audience: Grades 7-9.
Identifiers: LCCN 2023038700 (print) | LCCN 2023038701 (ebook) | ISBN 9780762483198 (hardcover) | ISBN 9780762483211 (ebook)
Subjects: CYAC: Short stories. | LCGFT: Short stories.
Classification: LCC PZ5 .W298 2024 (print) | LCC PZ5 (ebook) | DDC [Fic]—dc23
LC record available at https://lccn.loc.gov/2023038700
LC ebook record available at https://lccn.loc.gov/2023038701

ISBNs: 978-0-7624-8319-8 (hardcover), 978-0-7624-8321-1 (ebook)

Printed in the United States of America

LSC-C

Printing 1, 2024

FOR THE ALL THE QUEER LITTLE BEASTIES OUT THERE, MAY YOU SING, SHINE, AND SLAY.

EDITOR'S NOTE &
CONTENT WARNING

Don't let the playful title fool you! Despite presenting readers with an assortment of fifteen weird and wondrous monster tales, this anthology also reflects the reality of our times. The lives of queer and trans teens today can be beautiful, sad, funny, confusing, romantic, messy, embarrassing, and even scary. The authors here have not shied away from portraying the rich complexity of that experience. While there are many moments of queer joy to be found in these pages, there are also moments of pain and trauma. As you can probably guess, many characters deal with homophobia and/or transphobia. But there are also those who must cope with additional burdens, such as drug addiction, poverty, grief, homelessness, and even abortion. My goal for this collection is that every reader who picks up a copy will find themself reflected back in at least one of these stories, drawing strength and hope from the encounter.

For some, hope shines brightest in the darkness. But not for everyone.

So remember, not every story here may be right for you.

Please read with care.

—Rob Costello

THE BESTIARY

INTRODUCTION

First things first: there's nothing to be afraid of here.

Yes, there are monsters. And it's perfectly natural to mentally leap to fangs and gore and all the things that go bump in the night. Why wouldn't you?

For thousands of years, across countless civilizations, people have conjured all sorts of beasties to explain away their deepest fears and anxieties. The ancient Greeks, for example, invented the mythical sea creatures Scylla and Charybdis to account for the dangers of sailing through the treacherous Strait of Messina. In southern Africa, evil sprites called Tokoloshe were often blamed for otherwise inexplicable illnesses and sudden deaths, while the Algonquin-speaking peoples of North America embodied the terror of winter's deprivations in windigo folklore.

Whether we realize it or not, we're still doing this today. It's no coincidence that UFO and abduction stories skyrocketed at the dawn of the space age, while vampires enjoyed a renaissance at the height of the AIDS epidemic, when sex, blood, and death were literally fused in the popular imagination. Godzilla rose from the Sea of Japan as a direct result of the trauma of Hiroshima and Nagasaki, while, more recently, Slenderman appeared just as parents were beginning to reckon with the toxic influence of the internet on their kids.

In this way, monsters have always served as tangible representations of our intangible fears.

An incomprehensible threat looming from the cold vastness of space.

An invisible danger lurking within our own bodies.

A cataclysmic force that, if unleashed, could level the planet.

A corrupting influence seducing the innocent under our very noses.

But dig a little deeper, and you'll find there's something else going on with these monsters. Something even more primal that gets at the heart of what most human fears are really all about: *a loss of control.*

Monsters arise when people are either genuinely powerless or sense they are losing control. They are a metaphor for a perceived imbalance of power. After all, to the extent that we fear, say, the beasts in the *Jurassic Park* franchise, it's not because we literally believe that a horde of cloned dinosaurs will someday escape a theme park and ravage the globe, but because our sense of helplessness in the face of unchecked genetic manipulation and looming environmental disaster is so overwhelming, it makes us *feel* as if we are the hors d'oeuvres at a velociraptor dinner party. An effective strategy to cope with the terror of losing that much control is to turn it into a monster.

Hence: *Jurassic Park.*

The great gift of the monster story is that it offers us the opportunity to talk and think about topics that might otherwise feel too frightening or difficult to tackle head-on. In telling stories about them, we exert the power of our imagination to overcome the fears they represent. After all, it's a lot less scary to envision fending off a rampaging tyrannosaur than it is to confront the consequences of climate change and bioengineering run amok. Unlike AIDS, you can kill a vampire with a stake through the heart, and, according to Hollywood, all it takes to defeat a full-scale alien invasion is Will Smith, Jeff Goldblum, and a '90s-era computer virus.

But that's what stories do. They prepare us to face the unknown. They arm us with possibility. They enable us to apply some semblance of order and meaning to a universe that is otherwise indifferent to our existence. Telling a monster story is a powerful act, not least because such a story gives a shape and limit to an otherwise amorphous anxiety, making it seem less scary, less immense, less baffling and unconquerable. Stories change our perspective on our own strengths and vulnerabilities. They alter our perception of what threatens us most. They provide us with comfort and reassurance—even in the face of tremendous loss—and in so doing, they offer us the hope that we can conquer our worst fears and take back control of our fate.

Control over our own fate—isn't that what we all want?

Isn't that what queer and trans folks have fought so long and hard to achieve?

It's here that the idea of a queer, monster-themed anthology was born.

After all, we queer and trans folks know a lot about monsters, don't we? From the time most of us are first figuring out who we are, we're forced to confront them wherever we look, from the classroom to the chat room and everywhere in between. Sometimes we meet them in the doctor's office. Sometimes on the street. Sometimes in our own homes. And that's not even counting the monsters that infest statehouses, churches, school boards, and right-wing media outlets.

The bitter irony, of course, is that these selfsame monsters, who rightly perceive the cultural embrace of queer and trans identities as a loss of their power to control and erase us, have figured out how to claw back some of that power by turning the monster metaphor against us. They accuse *us* of being monsters. For the outrage of using the bathroom in public places. For the insult of choosing to marry whom we love. For the sin of matching our outsides to what we feel on the inside. For the crime of writing books and telling stories about our own lived experiences. For the sheer audacity of existing when they would prefer us to disappear.

These would-be oppressors have weaponized the hate and ignorance of their fellow bigots to tell lies about us in order to enrich and empower themselves. Lies masquerading as monster stories that they then use against us.

To make us feel helpless, even powerless.

But we're not powerless at all, are we? That's what makes them so afraid. If nothing else, the past half century has taught the world that when queer and trans people come out of the closet and stand together, we are an inviolable force for freedom, justice, and love.

And so, to me, that's what the fifteen weird, wondrous, and *very queer* monster tales in this anthology are really all about:

Reminding us of just how powerful we truly are.

In *We Mostly Come Out at Night*, we embrace the metaphor of the monster to reclaim it as our own. In these pages, you will meet a menagerie of fiercely queer creatures and monsters, including aliens and angels, gargoyles and gorgons, sirens and sea witches, shape-shifters and trolls, and other fantastical beings of legend and lore. We have Mothman and Malificen—er, *I mean*, Carabosse; a Beast with a rose; a girl and her many shadows; and even a sentient house harboring a magical agenda all its own. Some of these creatures are truth tellers ("How to Summon Me"; "World-Weariness"), while others teach us the beauty of our true selves ("The Fatal Song of Attraction"; "The Girl with Thirteen Shadows"). There are beasties who keep us safe ("Be Not Afraid") and those with whom we fall in love ("A Serpent and a Wish"; "Bastian and the Beast"), monsters who offer us community ("The Color of Sky on Earth"; "The Freedom of Feathers and Fur"), and others who provide the comforts of home ("The House of Needs and Wants"). There are wise and witty entities ("Other Fish"; "Bonne Nuit"), creatures who show us a way to escape ("Boys Who Run with the Boars"; "How We Founded Club Feathers at the Discard Depot"), and even an angelic force who delivers upon the divine promise that the meek shall inherit the earth ("Sons of God and Daughters of Humans").

You will also meet a beautiful and inspiring crew of teenagers just like you—lesbian, gay, or bi; ace and aro; trans or enby. They are questioning and imperfect, thoughtful and optimistic, sometimes wounded yet still so strong. Though they strive to become the best versions of themselves, not all the obstacles they face along the way are bound up in their sexuality or gender identity. Many struggle with universal challenges, like figuring out who they are, where they fit in the world, and how to make themselves heard. Some wrestle with trauma, while others savor the sweetness of first love. Some simply want to find a safe haven to call home.

With contributions from both acclaimed authors and talented new voices, the tales in this collection come from every realm of speculative fiction. Some are seeded in darkness, while others brim with humor and light. There are horror stories and fantasy stories, gritty future fictions and sweeping mystical adventures. There are romantic fairy tales and whimsical modern fables, an allegory of an alternate Earth (née Earnath), and even a postapocalyptic biblical reimagining. There are stories influenced by folklore, myth, and magical realism, some comic, some sweet, some angry, some moving.

When taken as a whole, the stories in this anthology aim to comfort and entertain you, to make you laugh, break your heart, stoke your outrage, stir your pride, and inspire you with hope. But most of all, this anthology exists to remind you of just how fierce and fabulous you truly are. Because, after all, monsters are powerful.

And so are you.

Thus, I hope that this anthology will in some small way fortify you with the courage to seize your own fate and move through this sometimes bleak and monstrous world like the bright, beautiful, and powerfully queer beastie you were born to be.

Like I said, there's nothing to be afraid of here.

With boundless love and admiration,

Rob Costello

BASTIAN AND THE BEAST

BY JONATHAN LENORE KASTIN

T he rose was the color of Bastian's own blood. A red that belonged in the mouths of wolves and lions. He recognized it as soon as he saw it, the one thing he had asked his father to bring back from his travels. Not a jewel-encrusted sword or a saddle inlaid with silver. Just a rose. Something beautiful in the dead of winter.

His father stood trembling before the fire, as if the cold had never left him, and crushed his hat between his shaking fingers.

"The youngest," he said. "He wants the youngest." His eyes were huge in the flickering light, as though still seeing the Beast with his terrible claws right here in their own small cottage, looming over the shabby furniture.

Bastian held the rose close, a thorn digging into his thumb. His two older brothers snickered and whispered to each other, turning to say with one voice, "What would a fancy lord want with the likes of you, even if he is a Beast?"

Bastian wasn't certain he would go until they said that. But there was something about being wanted. "Yes," he said, sucking the blood from his thumb. "Of course I'll go."

The carriage came for him at midnight, a strange contraption of lithe shadows, no driver, and two horses the color of foam. Bastian clung to his belongings, the only objects that felt solid in the moonlight: a faded leather bag full of books, spines cracked. They still smelled of smoke from the fire that had destroyed their old home and changed their fortunes for the worse.

The carriage waited as he said his goodbyes, panic fluttering behind his ribs.

"Don't go," his father said, face white.

But how could he not, with that rose pinned to his hand-me-down coat and that strange tale his father had woven of the Beast that lived in a lonely castle and spoke like a man?

At the gate, his brothers dug through the three huge chests of gold the carriage had brought them, whooping and singing drunkenly. They didn't even look up as Bastian climbed inside.

"I have to," Bastian said to his father. Then, before either of them could say another word, the carriage gave a jolt and glided away through the snow. Bastian watched as the cottage faded, his father shrunken and unmoving, his brothers tossing gold into the air in glittering arcs.

Bastian slept—who knew how long—and when he woke again the air smelled of orange blossoms and gunpowder. The sky outside the carriage window flashed blue and green, then a shimmering gold as cannons cracked and fireworks burst overhead. Bastian had seen those fiery lights seven years ago, before the fire, at his tenth birthday party. His father had hired a display to rival that of kings and queens, no extravagance too costly for his youngest.

Bastian shivered as the carriage came to a stop and he climbed out, clutching his bag to his chest. Before him stood a large manor house as familiar as the calluses on his own palms. Its walls were the color of lemon curd, the stone walkway leading up to the huge front doors drenched in torchlight. Not a hint of snow marred the ground, the orange trees white with blossoms. For one fractured moment Bastian could see the whole structure burning. The gunpowder in the air stung his eyes, and the fireworks painted the sky a flaming red. He shrank back against the carriage. The bag slipped from his hand, and as he bent to retrieve it, the carriage rattled behind him, the horses making their way at a trot to the stables. The fireworks slowly melted into the air and burned out.

Bastian took a deep breath and climbed the front steps. He lifted the brass knocker, and the door swung open onto a long hallway. Silence pressed close and with it a watchfulness. The shadows inside stretched longer than seemed natural, and every flicker of light from the torches made his skin prickle. A

Beast, his father had said. A terrible ravening creature with eyes that could burn a hole in the sky and teeth like daggers. Maybe the Beast had eaten all the servants long ago and that was why there was no one to welcome him. He laughed, then flinched as the sound of his laughter rattled through the empty building.

And empty it was. No sign of any living thing in the familiar sitting room with the broken grandfather clock or in his father's library, though it still smelled faintly of stale cigars. No one in the hall unless one counted the frozen faces of his ancestors in half a dozen faded portraits. Perhaps his father had made a mistake and there was no Beast after all. But when he came to the dining room, everything was just as his father had described, a banquet laid out before him. Roast pheasant and parsnips, cakes glazed in honey, and wine to wash it all down.

Bastian was so hungry he dropped his bag of books onto the table and forgot all about the terrible claws and the jaws that could crack bone. After years of scrabbling to find enough to eat, he didn't bother with niceties. He stuffed everything he could get his hands on into his mouth, and into his pockets, so lost in the pleasures of a full stomach that he didn't hear the Beast enter. One moment Bastian was licking the grease from his fingers, and the next he looked up to find the shadows gathering across the table. He glimpsed a flash of teeth, a ragged mane of yellow fur, and he held very still.

The Beast watched him with luminous eyes that seemed too sad to be frightening. "Good evening, Beauty," he said, his voice low and ragged, like he hadn't used it in some time.

Bastian blushed. Did the Beast find him beautiful? He stared down at his hands, skin raw and red from years of

4

hard work. No one had done so before. He swallowed. "Good evening, Beast."

"You came willingly?"

"Yes." He had put the rose in the buttonhole of his coat, and his thumb throbbed where the thorn had pricked him. He longed to ask, *Why did you want me? And what will you do now that you have me?* But the words stuck in his throat.

The Beast nodded. "Then I'll show you to your room." He turned and melted back into the shadows before Bastian could get a better look at him.

Bastian snatched his bag from the table and rushed to follow, suddenly afraid of being alone again in that empty, watchful house. Moonlight filtered in through the windows as they roamed the halls, rendering everything strange and alien in the half-light, but the Beast never slowed his pace. He seemed to see quite clearly in the dark, eyes burning like a cat's.

The Beast stopped at last in front of a familiar door and turned. "This is your room. You'll find everything you need here." Shadows still swirled around the Beast's face, but nothing could hide those sorrowful eyes. They lingered on the rose in Bastian's coat, and the Beast seemed about to say more, but turned away abruptly and disappeared down the hall, taking the scent of leaf litter and pine with him. Bastian stood frozen, feeling as if he had been left floating alone in a great sea.

Taking a deep breath to steady himself, Bastian stepped inside his room and lit the lamps. It was his old room exactly— before they had lost everything—the bed canopied, the wardrobe taking up one side. There were his books on the shelves that he had thought burned and the sketches he had hung on the walls.

It felt like a terrible trick. To give him back everything he had lost just when he was finally used to having lost it.

He turned to the wardrobe, afraid for one terrible moment that it would be filled with his old dresses. But when he opened it, he found instead rows of velvet coats, silk shirts, embroidered waistcoats, and breeches, finer even than the clothes his brothers had owned before the fire that had consumed all their riches.

He ran his hands along the fabric and smiled.

That night he dreamed he walked down the mist-drowned bank of a river. The roaring of lions filled his ears. Then a young man stepped out of the mist in a black coat. His eyes were amber, his hair a shaggy gold. He smiled at Bastian, a warm but rueful smile.

"Are you frightened?" asked the young man.

Bastian shook his head.

"The eyes can be so deceiving," the young man continued. "But I think you know that." He stepped nearer, brushed his fingers against Bastian's cheek.

"Who are you?" asked Bastian, feeling flushed, almost dizzy under the young man's steady gaze.

"Don't you know?"

There *was* something familiar about him, but what it was Bastian could not say.

The young man leaned in close. "Come and find me, then," he whispered, and Bastian's eyes drifted shut.

When Bastian woke, he was back in his room with breakfast on a little tray by the bed, his cheek still tingling where the young man had touched him.

Bastian wandered the whole house that day, pressing his face to every window and opening every door. He never saw another living soul, not even a mouse or a spider. But the house was just the same as he remembered it. His brothers' rooms were full of shattered wineglasses and broken furniture, his father's piled high with maps covered in red circles for every port his ships had sailed to before they had all sunk to the bottom of the sea.

He didn't go into his mother's room. He could smell her perfume through the door, thick and overpowering. It sent him fleeing from the house, crashing through the back entrance into the garden. There was the spot where he had fallen off his horse and ruined a new gown. His mother had slapped him and threatened never to buy him another one again. Bastian had been so elated at the idea of escaping the horrid dresses his mother forced him to wear that he didn't even mind the sting in his cheek.

A hulking shadow moved between the hedges, and Bastian stepped out onto the lawn. He found the Beast sitting on the lip of one of the fountains. He seemed to gather darkness around him, hiding his face from view every time Bastian tried to get a clearer glimpse.

"I know this house," said Bastian.

The Beast dipped his claws into the water. They looked too chipped and worn to be frightening. "Do you?" he said, as if it really didn't matter one way or the other.

Bastian squeezed his hands into fists. "Yes. Did my father know? Did he see this place as I do?"

"Everyone here sees what they want to see. If he wanted a blackened tower crawling with horrors, that is what he got."

"What do you see?" Bastian asked.

The Beast seemed surprised, the shadows nearly pulling away from his face. Then he breathed a heavy sigh and said, "All my sins."

Bastian thought of the perfume drifting from his mother's room. The fear that scent conjured, and the guilt. "Do you have so many?" he asked, wondering what a Beast could possibly know of such things.

The Beast raked his claws along the edges of the stone fountain. "Aren't you afraid to find out?"

"I think if you were going to kill me you would have done so already."

The Beast nodded slowly, as if a little ashamed of himself, and bowed his head.

Bastian took a step closer. "Why did you bring me here?"

The Beast stilled. "A rose for a rose," he said after some time.

Bastian flushed, suddenly too warm in the strange summerlike heat. The Beast didn't look at him, but Bastian could feel him waiting for a response. It frightened Bastian more than sharp teeth and jagged claws. He turned and hurried back up the path.

That evening, Bastian sat alone before another sumptuous feast, half wanting the Beast to join him, half fearing it, but the minutes ticked by with no sign of him. Bastian picked at his food, wondering where the Beast went when he was not darkening the hallways. Did he have his own room like Bastian's? If so, he hadn't seen it. Perhaps the Beast roamed the woods, terrorizing the countryside. It was hard to imagine. Maybe he sighed the surrounding peasants to death. Bastian laughed, then shoved his plate away and buried his face in his arms. The loneliness was worse than any Beast. He walked back to his room, shut the door, and wept.

He was weeping when he woke beside the river in his dream. A cup lay spilled at his feet. He had been drinking from the water that bubbled past but could no longer remember whether it had tasted fair or foul. A branch snapped behind him, and he turned. The young man with the amber eyes was watching him. "Have you found me yet?"

"I've looked in all the rooms," Bastian said. "I've opened every door. Even the cellar and the attic. I know it all by heart."

"And there's no space for me in it." The young man nodded gravely, as if he had known all along.

"No," said Bastian. "That's not what I meant." But the mist was already rising around him.

"I'm right in front of you." The young man's voice was only a whisper now. "Can't you see me?" Then the dream faded with the dawn.

Of course, Bastian hadn't been entirely honest. He hadn't yet been in his mother's room, had avoided it as one would a poisonous spider. And he hadn't found any sign of the Beast's lair. Perhaps he didn't even sleep in the house, but in a cave somewhere like an animal.

Bastian took out one of the fine suits from the wardrobe, a bright green color like spring moss that matched his eyes. He marveled at how well the clothes fit his body, as his brothers' hand-me-downs had never done. Then he wandered the corridors again, coming slowly to his mother's room. Just as he opened the door, he thought he heard her laugh, as jagged and sharp as broken glass, but the room was empty like all the others.

He remembered years ago, sitting slumped in the chair before the vanity weeping into his hands as his mother scolded him. He had cut off his long black hair with a pair of kitchen shears and stood before the mirror in glorious triumph. His mother had found him and slapped him hard enough to draw blood.

"What have you done, you ugly girl?" she shouted. And then she marched him to her room and painted his face, swathing his shorn head in scarves and hats, trying to hide what could no longer be hidden. That he wasn't the girl she wanted, that he never would be.

Bastian shuddered as he stared at the heavy gilt-framed chair and the rose-canopied bed, the scent of his mother's perfume—lilac and violet—filling the air. The smell had lingered at her sickbed, mixing with the stench of death, so he could no longer stomach it.

He backed out of the room and slammed the door shut.

He fled back to his own room, with its familiar books and papers, and dived under the blankets. How strange to come so far from his past and find it everywhere around him, smothering him. He wondered again what the Beast saw when he roamed the halls, and it suddenly occurred to him that he had never really searched his own room, had merely taken its familiarity for granted.

He inspected the back of the wardrobe, under the carpets and bed, behind the curtains. Nothing. Then he pulled back the tapestry of a beautiful lady with a tiger resting its head in her lap. He paused. There was a door there he was sure he had never seen before. It was formed from rough and heavy wood, so black it might have been burned. Beyond it lay a spiraling stone stairway ascending into darkness. He had read enough books to know that he should not go up there. All the same, he took a candle from his bedside table and plucked the rose from its vase, slipping it back into the buttonhole of his coat for courage. The red of its petals looked even more potent in the flickering light. Then he climbed the stairs.

He climbed a long time, until he found himself at the top of a tower—impossible, his house had never had a tower. Several torches lit the stone walls, making the shadows flicker and dance. The windows were covered in thick drapes, the mirrors that hung on every wall cracked. Bastian held up his candle, peering into the darker, unlit corners of the room. There was a nest of blankets, and above that hung an enormous painting of two young men. One had lion-colored hair just like the young man in his dreams, only this man's mouth was set in a cruel and arrogant smile, as if he had tasted something that should have been delicious and found it wanting. The other young man was pale with hair like thistledown. He had his head in the lion-haired man's lap, their hands clasped together. Bastian blushed, remembering the way the man in his dreams had looked at him, like he was beautiful, like he was wanted. He shivered.

Bastian turned away from the painting and made his way to the windows, hoping to catch sight of some familiar part of his long-ago home, but when he pulled back the curtains and stared at the glass in the candlelight, it seemed to shiver with color, forming into a moving picture. The lion-haired man sat on a throne wearing a crown of jewels, while the thistledown-haired man toiled away in a stable, feeding and watering the horses. Then the thistledown-haired man stood before a peddler's ramshackle cart and pulled a wand from the pile of odds and ends. He flicked it three times overhead and was transformed: a crown graced his head also, and his rough-spun clothes turned to sable and silk. The two princes met in the woods, and the lion-haired man offered his lover a rose, white like the color of the young man's hair. They kissed. But then the spell was broken. The false prince's clothes turned to rags and his crown to a wreath of flowers. The true prince was enraged and struck his lover, tearing the rose to pieces. With tears in his eyes, the young man raised his wand again and cursed the prince. The petals of the rose turned as red as the flower in Bastian's buttonhole, and the prince's features stretched into a monstrous Beast who raged across the surface of the glass until the colors faded away and a shadow spilled over Bastian.

He turned. The Beast hovered in the doorway.

"It was you," said Bastian. "In my dreams."

"Have you found me at last?" The shadows fell away from the Beast's face, and Bastian's breath caught in his throat. The Beast's fur was golden, his eyes the same bright amber as the man in the painting, only these eyes were softer, kinder, as if grief had worn away all the sharpness. He gestured toward the portrait. "Then you know my shame."

"You loved him," said Bastian, gazing up at the thistledown-haired man above them. "Why did you turn him away?"

"I was a fool. He deceived me, yes, but I was too proud to understand why. I won't make the same mistake again." The Beast stepped closer, his eyes shining in the dark. "Do you love me, Beauty? I hoped you would the moment your father took my rose. We've both been alone for so very long." He leaned down and kissed Bastian's mouth, fur soft as velvet against his skin. "May I sleep with you tonight?" He slid Bastian's coat down his shoulders, began to unbutton his shirt. "I won't turn you away."

Bastian leaned into his touch, reveling in the sleekness of the Beast's fur, the heat of his mouth, the marvel of being wanted. Then he heard his mother's voice in his head, laughing in disgust, telling him how ugly he was. He saw his brothers' faces when he had put on their clothes for the first time, embarrassed, angry, merciless. Bastian pulled away and backed into the window.

"I'm sorry," he said. "I—I wish to go home."

The Beast frowned. "Would you leave me now when we've only just found each other?" He reached out a massive paw as if to stroke Bastian's cheek, then seemed to remember the sharpness of his claws and drew back.

Bastian stared at his own hands. They were shaking. "Please, just for a few weeks, so I can think . . ."

"You won't come back," said the Beast.

"I will," said Bastian.

"Then go." The Beast turned away. "I won't stop you."

Bastian ran all the way down the stairs. When he crashed through the secret door, he slid down to the floor, curling into himself, breath coming in gasps. He sat there for some time trying to still his thunderous heart. He could still feel the Beast's fur beneath his fingers.

Little by little, sounds began to break through the silence. It had been so long since Bastian had heard the echo of laughter and the crystal clinking of glasses raised in a toast that he didn't realize, at first, what he was hearing. He got up, still trembling, and opened the door to the hall, but there was no familiar corridor here. He stood in a dining room unlike any he had ever seen before. At the head of a great table sat his father and brothers with half a dozen guests, champagne filling their glasses. He looked back the way he had come, and his old room was gone.

"Bastian!" cried his father, pushing back his chair. His brothers only stared, open-mouthed. "It is my youngest come back to us. How did you escape the Beast?"

Bastian found his voice at last. "He let me leave."

"Let you?" said one brother.

"You didn't slice his throat and get away?" said the other.

"No," Bastian said. "No, he's not like that. The Beast was kind to me."

The guests laughed merrily, as if Bastian had made a wonderful joke. "Come, tell us all about it," said a woman with sapphires dripping down her dress. "Did he lock you in his tower and keep you in chains?"

"Does he ravage the villagers and pick his teeth with their bones?" asked a gray-haired lady, peacock feathers sprouting from her hair.

"Maybe he collects young men to feed his monstrous appetites." The company turned to one another and nodded enthusiastically.

But no matter how hard Bastian tried to tell the truth— that the Beast had never hurt him, would never hurt anybody ever again—they didn't want to hear it.

"He may be horrible, but he is very rich," said one brother, pouring Bastian a glass of champagne, then raising his own in a toast.

"And it is because of his riches that we are here now," said the other. "We have made better use of them than he, no doubt."

"Well," said his father. "You're safe with us. That's all that matters."

Bastian tried to imagine his sad-eyed, melancholy Beast feasting on oysters and drinking wine with the assembled guests while they laughed and prodded him with their forks, goading him to violence. The champagne bubbled through Bastian's blood, and he began to feel sick.

When he lay awake that night, in a strange bed with damask curtains, he didn't think of the river or the prince. He thought of the day his mother had died, her skin sickly, sweat-drenched, lips bloodied. She had squeezed Bastian's hand so tightly and made him promise to be a proper lady, to put away these child-ish thoughts of being something else entirely. He had smiled and nodded and promised her. He would be good, of course he would. Then he had gathered his dresses and petticoats and burned them under an autumn sky, putting on his brothers' old hand-me-downs instead. They had rolled their eyes and scoffed. His father had said nothing. For the first time in years, Bastian had felt like he could breathe.

Weeks passed in a haze of parties and opulent diversions. Operas, balls, fox hunts . . . Bastian drowned them all in wine and tried not to think about that window where the pictures came to life, or the Beast who waited for him with his soft golden fur and his mouth like silk.

Then one evening his brothers came to him with sly smiles and half a bottle of whiskey. "You're too sad," they said. "You should be happy to escape the Beast. Now we have everything we've ever wanted."

"I know what you need," said one, pulling a red card from his pocket.

"Come with us tonight," said the other. "There are places even someone like you can go for an evening of comfort and affection."

"People who won't care about what you lack." His brother lifted a purse full of gold coins in one fist.

Bastian took the card and frowned. He glanced at the rose still in his buttonhole, the rose that had once been just that shade of red, now browned and wilted. He dropped the card and pushed them away.

"Maybe he loves the Beast?" They laughed at him. "Maybe he wishes the Beast would eat him up." They turned on him as one. "You really are a freakish creature."

That night Bastian dreamed of the Beast's garden. The branches of the rosebushes were bare, rosehips swollen in the snow. When had winter intruded on that enchanted place? Bastian had known only sunshine and warmth during his stay there. He wandered through the twisted rows, a growing sense of unease settling over him, until he came to a figure crumpled in a drift of white. It was the Beast, his face slack as in death.

The air seemed to freeze in Bastian's throat. How long had it been? A month? A year? He had lost track of the days entirely.

He rushed to the Beast. His body was cold and still. "I've come back," said Bastian, shaking him hard. "You must wake up. Please."

The Beast didn't stir, but a light sprinkling of snowflakes began to fall. "I'm here now, see? I'm here. You can wake up." Bastian began to weep, his tears melting the snowflakes on his cheeks and blurring the edges of everything.

When he awoke, he could still feel the chill of winter on his skin, the hollowness in the pit of his stomach. He should never have left. "I want to go back," he whispered. "Please let me go back."

He scrambled out of bed and stumbled toward the bedroom door. He flung it open, and the corridor in his father's new house was gone. He was back in the garden between the orange trees, snowdrifts piled high around him as he raced outside in his bare feet. The cold slipped easily through his nightclothes until he was shivering, but he didn't stop until he came to the rose garden.

The rosebushes had grown wild in his absence, stretching into a high thicket with thorns as long as the Beast's claws. Between the tangled branches Bastian could just make out the familiar bulk of the Beast's body, but there was no way through to him without being cut to pieces.

Bastian stared up at the thorns. He didn't want to go back to his father's house—the hollow parties, the strangers who whispered about him behind his back. He wanted the Beast's sad eyes to look at him as he had that night in the tower, as if Bastian was worth all the roses in the Beast's garden.

"I'm coming," Bastian whispered. Then he shut his eyes and pushed through the branches, clenching his teeth as the thorns dug into his skin, blood blooming red against the snow. The branches cracked and snapped around him, pulling away, until he finally broke through.

The Beast lay still before him, and Bastian gave a hoarse cry. Too late. He was too late.

Then the body beneath him moved. The amber eyes opened. "You came back. I didn't think you would," murmured the Beast.

Bastian fell to his knees, relief flooding him. "You're alive," he said. "I thought . . ." He shuddered at the image of the Beast lying dead at his feet. Frozen and still forever, leaving Bastian alone.

The Beast lifted a paw and brushed back a strand of Bastian's hair. "Would you have wept for me?"

Bastian nodded, tears already spilling down his cheeks. "I should never have left you," Bastian continued. "I was afraid you wouldn't really want me."

"I told you," said the Beast. "I won't make the same mistake again."

"Even though I'm—?" Bastian gestured down at his own body, the body no one had ever quite accepted or wanted.

"Don't you understand yet, Beauty?" the Beast said, pulling him closer. "That's why I chose you. Only we can see each other for who we truly are."

The Beast kissed him then until the cold faded and the sun burned through the clouds, the garden blooming green and scarlet around them. When Bastian opened his eyes again, the man in his dreams, the prince with the lion-colored hair, lay beneath him. If Bastian tilted his head to the side, he could just see the outline of the Beast in his face, like a trick of the light.

Bastian smiled. "Shall we try again?" he asked. He pulled the prince to his feet.

In the distance, Bastian could see that the house had changed. It wasn't the same familiar lemon-colored manor from his childhood, but it wasn't a blackened tower, either. It was a cottage covered in wild roses, some as white as thistledown, others as red as blood.

The prince nodded and squeezed Bastian's hand. Then together they made their way to the cottage under the summer sun and out of this tale.

MONSTER REFLECTION

I can't remember a time when I wasn't fascinated by witches. Witches were powerful and wild, free to do as they pleased. What could be more attractive to a child? Witches could be monsters themselves, but also friends with monsters: imps and Baphomets, demons and familiars. I remember finding a copy of Erica Jong's *Witches* on my mother's bookshelf in elementary school, paging through the pictures of those wild women and that monster of monsters, the Devil, both terrified and delighted. I wanted what those women had: the power, freedom, and will to change my fate.

OTHER FISH

BY ALEXANDRA VILLASANTE

Your dirt-poor grandmother prayed to Yemanjá that she might find a man to love her, even though she was the darkest of all her sisters—*lastima que eres tan negra,* your bisabuela told her.

Your unfortunate mother prayed to Yemanjá that she might find a man to take her away from this backwater corner of Uruguay, forty kilometers from the border with Brazil and a million miles from a life worth living.

And now you stand, an hour before dawn, clutching a paper boat you carefully made, bottom sealed with wax to ensure it *would carry your message to Yemanjá, the mother of the sea, the demigoddess your family prays to alongside La Virgen and Jesus.*

This late in January, it's cold enough that you augment your usual Paladins hoodie and matching team sweatpants worn under your uniform skirt with a navy blue puffer coat two sizes too big. Isa would say it's cold enough to freeze a witch's teat, which you've argued doesn't make sense and is an unfair characterization of witches of all genders.

You're stalling. Isa is why you're here, why you have to get La Madre's help. At the water's edge, toes bare, you step into the icy water. This is crucial; the discomfort is how she'll know you are sincere; the touch of your bare skin will echo the drop of your blood placed amid your written words.

You bend down, whisper La Madre's name, and float the paper boat, a guttering votive aflame at its center, praying that it won't sink. It rocks on the low tide, wavering into the sea as if it's unsure if it should go forward or run back to the safety of your hands.

You watch until it disappears. Dawn breaks, a crack of orange glass against the gray that quickly gets blurred, then snuffed out by the sky.

Nothing happens. You drink hot café con leche from the thermos and wonder how much longer you can spend on the futile, the superstitious, and the embarrassing. How much longer before you have to leave or you'll miss the school bus.

Then—

A line of bubbles appears on the water, near the rock where you sit, an exhalation from the depth of the ocean, a breath of brine and mineral secrets. Oil-slick skin breaks the surface of the waves, splashing laps of water over your rock; you stand so you don't get wet. The seallike skin is shiny, black, and voluptuous as it rises, then coils around to reveal tentacles, flowing like whirlpools around and around, the undersides a dusky lavender. The thermos drops from your hand—you didn't even realize you were still holding it—and on and on the creature rises. You think sea lion; you think giant squid; you think leviathan; you think monster.

Massive shoulders tattooed with delicate tracery of seaweed and spangled with barnacles like a pearl necklace gone magnificently awry. A shake of sodden hair reveals a face like a terrible surprise, wide eyes, livid lips on a curving, dangerous mouth and teeth—

She's going to swallow me whole, *you think.*

"Hello, little fish."

I didn't have time to change before my shift started at the bookstore, but Anika—newly promoted assistant manager— hates the Catholic-schoolgirl look, so I'm wearing one of the T-shirts we sell, with *Savoy Bookshop and Café* printed above a steaming cup of whatever you want it to be.

"Almost done with those fairy-door things?" Anika asks from upstairs. I'm sitting on the floor on the lower level in the children's books section, trying to get the tiny battery in this even tinier diorama behind a fairy door to work. It's a replica of our own bookshop, about the size of a thick hardback book, and looks as if the spine had been removed and instead of pages, you could see the bookshop you're standing in, like you were a giant looking in on fairies. Very trippy.

Unfortunately, this thing has to be at toddler-eye level—and no matter what I do or how I contort myself to set it up, it won't turn on. Finally, in desperation, I just jiggle it, and the little light blinks on.

"Yeah, all done." I dust off my skirt, pull up my knee socks since I have neglected to shave since New Year's Eve almost a month ago, and trudge up the stairs. Anika looks worried, and I can't blame her. She, Isa, and I are the only people in the store.

"I'm going to go in the back and check stock. You two can handle things, right?"

Things are a totally empty shop and a cold afternoon that is bucketing down rain. Before I can make a snide remark about managing the ravening hordes, Isa pipes up.

"You know we can, boss!" she says from behind the behemoth espresso machine. She doesn't even sound snarky when she says it.

I get another fairy-door-diorama thing out of an old tea chest—the kind they used to ship tea in at the time of the Boston Tea Party, a wooden crate with metal corners designed to scratch up your shins as you pass. The artist who makes them for us, who was probably at the Boston Tea Party, packs the dioramas in old newspaper and wool from her alpacas.

"Try this one," Isa says, handing me a mug of something she concocted.

"You know I don't try unless you tell me what it is."

"Nothing you're allergic to, nothing you don't believe in, nothing you can complain about." She knows me so well. She's my best friend, after all, and best friends keep a running list of things you hate; it's in the job description.

There's thick golden foam topping the mug and a sprinkling of what smells like ginger. I'm thinking golden latte or something close.

"It's not a golden latte," Isa says, reading my mind. "I'm gonna try giving these out next time we have a busy Saturday afternoon, to the first five people who can name a book about wizards, witches, and magical schools that isn't a problematic trash fire."

"*The Troubled Girls of Dragomir Academy,*" I say without hesitation and take a sip. It's gingery and has turmeric like a golden latte, but it's got something else thick and sweet weighing it down.

"I know *you* can name a thousand books, you total nerd, but I'm trying to encourage the masses. What do you think?"

"It's very yummy. And you put white chocolate in it for me."

"Yup." She smiles. "How I'm best friends with someone so basic that she likes white chocolate, I don't know. What would our ancestors say?"

Her Dominican ancestors gifted her with tight brown curls—extra bouncy in this humidity. She has to keep pushing them over to the side of her head that isn't shaved. During school, she parts her hair down the middle to keep her shaved hair secret from the nuns at St. Bede's. But every other moment of her life, she's showing it off.

My ancestors—either the colonizers or the Indigenous people of the Southern Cone of South America—gave me hair so black and so straight that humidity just makes it straighter. As Isa jokes, I'm her straightest friend in more ways than one.

I put the mug down only when I've finished every drop; I missed lunch, so my stomach is telling me to ransack the display case for a bagel or pastry to tide me over.

"Want more?" Isa asks. She lifts the metal steamer jug over my mug at the same time I shake my head and cover it with my hand. I just watch as the stream of golden milk scalds the back of my hand, like it's not my hand, like it's not burning me.

The next second, Isa has dragged me to the sink and is running cold water over my hand, apologizing over and over again.

"It's okay," I say. "It's fine." But *fuck*, it hurts.

"Jesus, Ines, I'm so sorry. Let me get Anika, or the first aid kit, something!"

My hand is throbbing under the numbing stream of cold water, and I'm kind of in a daze, disconnected from the pain in my hand. My brain wants to think about other things, like how intensely brown Isa's eyes are. And they're wayward, too, like her hair; too full of light and mischief to stay any place too long. But now they're locked on mine, worried.

Isa always complains that her lips are too full—*the amount of Blistex I have to buy to keep these puppies lubricated*, she jokes—and I tell her to stop being idiotic, that she's beautiful; some girls would kill to have lips like hers. But I never really saw them, never looked at them up close. As she holds my shoulder with one hand, my burning hand with the other, I can feel her chest rising and falling; she's holding me like I might fall, and I might. Why have I never noticed her eyes, her lips? She's got her teeth buried in her bottom lip like biting into a ruby fruit, and it's so clichéd I can't let myself do this.

"Are you okay, nena?" she asks.

Somewhere in me, in a location I didn't even know existed, a lock slips out of place.

We're friends. *We're friends.*

Maybe it's a faulty battery that I jiggled that finally came on, like the little fairy dioramas dotted around the store. This location, this room, wasn't even there before, and now the whole secret space blazes with light. I can see every corner, every unread book in this room, every comfortable chair, and Isa. She's always been in this room.

After a thousand years, I pull my hand out of the water and pat it dry with a paper towel.

"I'm fine, nena," I say. "Stop worrying."

"*You* had me worried with all that zoning out," she says, regaining a little of her smile.

"I forgot to eat," I say, and she jumps into action, heating up a pastry from the café, something stuffed with nuts and white chocolate and cinnamon she knows I love.

Because she's my best friend, and that's what we are to each other.

That can't change.

You haven't moved from your rock; your socks and shoes are sloshing with water, your mother's favorite thermos miles out to sea by now. This is what always happens to you when disaster strikes, you realize. You freeze, a deer in headlights. It's the thing your mother hates about you, and your mother loves you a lot. She just can't stand how, in the face of an accident—a spilled drink, a

*crashed car or a broken window, a slapped face—you freeze when
you should move.*

*The monster—it can't be Yemanjá, the beautiful goddess of
the sea, whose stylized, painted portrait sits at the altar in your
bedroom, a pale goddess, light blue dress clinging to her hips, star
crown on her head, pearls falling from her hands. This creature is
nothing like her. She sprawls over fathoms of sea—she might even
be the sea for all you can understand. The light of dawn gets dim-
mer the longer she's before you, and she's not still, she's not here
for you—she's in abeyance, waiting for—what?*

*"Cat got your tongue, child? Or do landfolk no longer talk out
loud? It's been a while since I've gotten a note from one of you, but
not that long!" She throws back her head, and you hear shrieking
birds in her laugh. She raises both her arms above her head, as if
she were lounging on the very sky. She winks.*

*"I . . . I didn't call you," you finally stammer. Of course, it's the
wrong thing to say; you never have the right thing to say. You are
the worst, as your mother tells you, the worst in a crisis, the worst
when things go wrong. That's why she sent you to St. Bede's. You
can't be trusted.*

*"You really did, little fish. When you asked for help, help of
that kind, well, it comes only from someone like me, not the pale
memory of an African orisha your people remade to look like
Bettie Page. Pfft," she says, rolling her shoulders even wider, her
breasts and stomach rippling with laughter.*

You turn to scramble off the rock, to run. Oh, sure, your mother's voice says in your head. Now you run? When this monster has
you in her sights, when she's smiling at you with enough teeth
to disembowel a shark. Now you think to run? Nossa Senhora!

"Pececito," the monster says, and it's as if she's speaking in your mother's voice. It stops you in your tracks, turns you around to face her.

"You won't find what you're looking for anywhere else. And you're in deeper trouble than you know. I can help. For a price." Your knees quiver and bend. You have to sit on your wet rock again or you'll fall into the sea, into the many arms of this monster. You sit.

"Now. Tell me what you want," she says.

Anika sent me home with a dressing on my hand and a stern reprimand to be more careful. Then she muttered to herself about workplace accidents and insurance as Mamá held the umbrella over my head so I could slide into the car without getting drenched.

"Bye, beastie, feel better!" Isa said from the door. When I started calling her my bestie, she started calling me her beastie, and it stuck. We're friends like that, only now I want to screw that whole thing up?

"What happened?" Ma asks, and I tell her a story. It involves zoning out and not moving fast enough and not being careful enough. It doesn't involve telling her about Isa and how I feel like a thin membrane between us, thin as the pith between segments of oranges, has been peeled away.

"Menina, you have to be more careful!"

So I become more careful and call in sick the next day because I'm a fucking coward. Then I call out Sunday, even though I know I'm disappointing everyone and freaking my mother out. I stay in my room and think.

"Your abuela wants to talk to you, Ines," Mom says on Sunday afternoon—she holds out the family iPad, the one that has nothing on it except Facebook, Solitaire, and WhatsApp. It's like her words wake me up, and I see my messy room the way Ma must see it, plates stacked on top of one another, candy wrappers stuffed into mugs of questionable substances.

"Okay. I'll clean up right after I talk to her." I take the iPad and watch as Ma hangs my laundered and pressed uniform from the doorknob. Once she's gone, I tell Abuela to wait a second, then go and make sure Mamá isn't lurking in the hallway, listening. She isn't, but I close the door tight because nothing says she wouldn't come back and eavesdrop. It's sort of her vibe, all-knowing, all-listening, all-chismeando. If you've heard good gossip, odds are it came from mi mamá.

Finally, I sit on my bed and pick up the iPad so I can properly see my grandmother's face.

"There you are, mija! I was getting worried I'd have to talk to the ceiling!"

"Sorry, Nonna. It's good to see your face."

When I was little and Abuela was still in Uruguay, I thought I could feel the distance, the thirteen-hours-on-a-plane distance, the summertime in winter distance. Now that she lives in Florida with my tía, she feels closer, even though I don't see her that much more often.

"¿Estas escuchando, nena?" she says, sounding a little concerned.

"Yes, sorry, I'm listening. I hurt my hand at work, that's all."

"I know; I was asking you how you are feeling. Your mamá seems to think that something else is wrong and that's why you

29

have been gloomy and in bed the whole weekend. Those are her words," Abuela says, holding up a hand like a disclaimer. "You know I make no judgments!" She says it like it's a joke, but it's true. Abuela doesn't ever judge me. She never thinks I'm too slow or too messy or too anything. She just tells me I'm doing my best and that's enough. But is it? And when it comes to Isa and me, is doing nothing but hiding enough?

"I have a question."

"Okay, I may have answers."

I give Abuela the little smile that deserves.

"No, seriously. A serious question."

"Bueno. I'm ready."

"Tell me about Yemanjá. How did you get her to do what you asked?"

Her brown face crinkles under her sunglasses. She's sitting by the pool in my tía's gated complex in Naples. "You don't just get a diosa to do what you want, mijita. That's not how it works."

"You know what I mean. How did you get her help?"

She takes off her sunglasses, I guess so she can see me better. It feels like she's trying to squint her way into my soul. But she doesn't ask a thousand questions like Mamá would. She sighs and sits back.

"Okay, well, you know it was a very different world when I was your age and where I lived in las afueras, you know the far-away places from the city?"

I think about introducing Abuela to the term *boondocks*, but I don't want to stop her flow. I just nod.

"Okay, so there I was, morena como me ves, even though my mother kept me away from the sun as much as possible and made me wear a hat and long sleeves to the beach. She was desperate to make me as light-skinned as possible, ¿sabes? You know people thought that was the way to raise girls in those days. They had to be beautiful, and that meant white."

My grandmother is beautiful. At nearly eighty years old, her skin has few wrinkles, her thick, black hair touched with gray and curling away from her face, her brown eyes clear and full of intelligence. It's one of my favorite faces in the whole world.

"So, what is a girl to do when her sisters find novios and she cannot? What does she do when her own mamá tells her that she won't ever get a husband and will have to stay and take care of her parents forever? Which, by the way, I did anyway, but that's another story."

"You know I love your stories, Abu," I say.

"Don't interrupt. Where was I? Oh, yes. I was desperate. I prayed to God. I prayed to La Virgen. And I know that sometimes, God answers a prayer with silence. But sometimes, in that silence, he plants an idea. My idea was to ask La Madre de la mar for help."

"Yemanjá," I breathe, like it's a prayer, and maybe it is.

"Sí. Yemanjá. It was almost her feast day, February second. It was the middle of summer, so we were preparing for the big feast on the beach in Rocha, near where we lived. On the second, the beach would be full of people dressed in blue and white, statues of Yemanjá, and little paintings. Like the one I gave you at your quince, te acuerdas?"

"I remember." I have my own altar, with a tiny print of Yemanjá striding out of the water next to candles, a colorful tray I got on sale at Target that says *Recuérdame,* and photos of Abuelo Floro and our first dog, Chichi.

"Bueno. So I sneak out two days before the feast, the last day of January, and I bring a stub of a candle, fosforos, a little paper boat I made, and a bottle of wine with just a sip left, so I thought no one would notice. And that's it. You know the rest."

I almost leap through the screen. "I need to know exactly what you did, Abuela. Like, walk me through the whole ritual."

"¿Otra vez? But I've told you a thousand times, mija. Why do you want to know?"

"Because maybe I want to pray to Yemanjá, too. Maybe I need to ask her for something."

Abuela's face, usually so full of joy, falls into worry.

"Ines, amor. Are you in trouble?"

"No! Nothing like that!" The subtext here is that I'm pregnant, because what other trouble could a girl like me get into?

"Because you need to talk to your mamá if it's anything serious. You can't pray to anyone to help you with something like that."

"No, I promise, Abuelita. I'm really okay. I just. I wish I were different." I mean, I wish I *weren't* different. I can't afford to be different. I need to be the way I was two days ago, before I saw Isa with new eyes, before I found the hidden room inside me, before I knew more than I wanted to know about myself. It shouldn't be hard to turn off that light, close up that room, pretend I never saw myself from a new angle. But I've tried all weekend, and I can't stop thinking about it. What I want, what I need, is for things to go back to the way they were. Where I felt that Isa was my ride-or-die and that I was her beastie, her straight friend who understood, her ally friend. I need to go back to that reality.

Abuela tells me in detail exactly how she prepared her little boat, lit the flame, and launched it into the sea.

"And then what?" I ask.

She shrugs. "A few weeks later, your Abuelo Floro was visiting Rocha with friends from Montevideo for turismo, and when we met, we fell in love. Or he fell in love with me, even though I did go outside without my hat, despite my mother's wishes. Or maybe it was because of that. And from him, and your father, you got your green eyes. Y asi pasó," she says with a sigh.

"Gracias, Abu. I love to hear your stories."

"And will that make you feel better, mijita, do you think? Are you going to school tomorrow and do all the things your mamá wants you to do?"

"Sí. I'll be up very early tomorrow. I'll be ready to go. I know what to do now."

Because tomorrow is January 31, and I'm going to do exactly what my abuela did. I'm going to ask Yemanjá for help. I'll make a paper boat, go to the beach, and pray to the goddess of the sea to ask her to change things back to the way they were.

You rehearsed your words, your stance, your proposition, just like Mr. Headley taught you when you joined debate club. Why did you join, when in fact you hate confrontation? Well, because Isa was doing it, and Isa makes all the things you think are boring seem more fun. Spending time with Isa makes you happy, so when she asked you to join debate club, you did, even though you don't

care about debate, or rhetoric, whatever Mr. Headley says about the noble art of speechifying. You wanted to spend more time with Isa. Nothing wrong with that. But you wish you'd spent more time learning how to state your case. The Sea Witch is almost through all her patience, and you still haven't told her what you want and why.

"I want to go back to the way I was three days ago," you finally say.

"You want to go back in time? Why, to play the lottery? Be at the right party at the right time? Kiss the girl?" she says with raised eyebrows and a lift of her shoulders that disturbs a cloud of seagulls.

"I want to kiss Isa. That's the problem."

"What's an Isa when it's at home?" she murmurs.

"She's my best friend. And I don't want to want to kiss her."

The Sea Witch has a face as rolling and changeable as the ocean. But now it's still as lake water for a full minute before she cackles, like sea lions barking.

"Oh, little fish, you do make me laugh," she says, wiping salt-foam tears from the corners of her eyes. "I really love you landfolk. You just can't help being the muddliest little minnows. Lemme get this straight. Ha! Straight! Okay. So that's the trouble. That's what you're freezing your ass off at dawn for, that's what you've dropped your own most precious blood on a paper boat for, that's what you want? You want to be straight?"

"It's not that I don't like queer people," you begin.

"Sure, sure, some of your best friends are queer," she sneers.

You need her to understand. You're not like that. "I'm Isa's best friend. I've stood up for her since freshman year, when she *was bullied for coming out. I went with her to tell her mom and sat with her when her dad cried. I've been through it with her, and I support her in every way."*

The Sea Witch trails a hand through the water, a lazy tentacle swirling around her arms like an eager shawl.

"I guess other is for other people, huh?"

You knew this was a mistake from the moment this creature broke through the surface. She's nothing like the image on your altar, the sanitized image of perfect womanhood, a queen, a fairy, a beautiful goddess. This creature is confusion, slippery and tactile and too many conflicting desires. She's exactly what you don't want.

"I'm sorry," you say, hoping the panic in your chest doesn't translate to the words coming out of your mouth. "I made a mistake. I'm sorry I wasted your time."

"No worries, hush puppy. I've got all the time in the world, and you'll find I'm a reasonable woman."

You almost croak out, Really? *Until you realize that no, not really. She's got a tentacle, no, two, wrapped around your ankles. You couldn't leave if you wanted to.*

"You know what I like about you, little fish?"

Seaweed spreads like a rash across the back of your neck and creeps toward your mouth.

You shake your head.

"I think you're the type of girl who can handle getting what she asks for."

With that, the Sea Witch twitches a hip and yanks you into the air by your feet. You were right with your first thought upon seeing her smiling face. She's going to swallow you whole.

MONDAY

When I get on the school bus, I'm shivering so hard that the bus driver makes me sit directly behind her, under her winter coat, and blasts the heat on me.

"Did you fall into the ocean?" she asks, but my teeth are chattering so hard I can't speak. And anyway, *I can't speak.* I made a *deal.*

The driver—I don't know her name, and that embarrasses me because it just means I never bothered to learn—parks in our lane, then escorts me to the nurse's office. I don't think she realized how wet I was when she let me on to the bus, but from the puddle on the floor and the way my hair hangs in strings, it's pretty obvious.

"Her lips are a little bluish," the bus driver says to the nurse, who waves her away and gets me to strip off my sodden clothes and put on sweatpants and a T-shirt from the spare clothes bin—donated clothes for when vomit, pee, or other substances make uniforms unwearable.

The nurse takes my temp, frowns, and puts me under a heated blanket. Outside the little cubicle, I hear her call my mother.

"I think she was fooling around at the beach and fell in. She's completely soaked. Seaweed in her shoes. I think she should go home. No fever, at least not yet."

Mamá picks me up and takes me home, asking so many questions that they run into one another, no room for answers. When she pulls into the drive of our little house, the one that used to be guest quarters for one of the richer houses up near Watch Hill, she asks me what happened.

I turn to her and shrug, then point to my throat with a regretful look.

"Lost your voice?"

I nod. I must look pretty pathetic because she doesn't push me.

In my room, in my own flannel pj's, Ma slathers my chest with Vicks VapoRub, then wraps an old T-shirt around my neck and tucks it into my collar.

"Sleep. You'll feel better by tonight."

I sleep, no nightmares, no tentacle dreams. And when I wake up, I do feel better. Except for the tiny pearl that's grown on the tip of my tongue. It clacks against my teeth, a reminder that I promised not to speak.

TUESDAY

"Does this mean you won't be at debate club?" Isa asks. She's frowning at me in the way that should make me feel like I let her down. But I don't feel anything now. I haven't felt anything since yesterday morning. I make myself write *SORRY* on the mini pad that hangs on a lanyard from my neck.

"And the doctor says you're fine, you just lost your voice. Like laryngitis?"

I nod.

She peers at me. "Are you really okay? You seem, like *off.*"

Everything is fine. I underline the words until my pencil point breaks.

WEDNESDAY

At the bookstore, I'm trying to make up some of my lost work hours, but after the third patron tries ASL on me when I don't immediately open my mouth to speak, I ask Anika if I can work in the storeroom, leaving Anika and David, my ex-twice-removed, working the floor. An hour later, David brings me a white chocolate steamer.

"How's it going?" he asks after I thank him with a nod and a smile.

I point to the word *Fine* on my notepad. I've written a bunch of words that I use over and over again there. *Thanks*; *No*; *Yes*; *Okay.*

"My sister had laryngitis in third grade. She could talk. It was just painful, and she sounded like a frog."

I point to *Okay* and raise my eyebrows. This is a pointless conversation.

"Just saying that it doesn't seem to me like you can't speak. It seems like you don't want to speak."

And it seems *like you're mansplaining shit to me that you can't possibly understand. This is why we broke up, David! You think it's your job to sound like you know everything, like somehow I'll find that really intriguing instead of infuriating. One semester of college psychology and you think you know everything. How did I ever think you were cute?!*

I don't say.

I shrug and keep unpacking boxes of special editions.

"Sometimes, when we suppress parts of ourselves that we don't want to confront, our bodies take on that stress, and it causes us to have psychosomatic responses. Take for example when you fell into the ocean. That was a traumatic event that might have stirred up some undercurrent or memory of violence. It's called selective mutism. Because you're selecting to be mute." His floppy hair, which I used to think was so swoony, falls into his face like it's embarrassed for him. He sweeps it back and gives me an expectant look.

What do you want, a medal for that claptrap? You are every girl's nightmare first boyfriend, you know that? How did I ever let your tongue anywhere near me?

I don't say.

I write furiously on my notepad, tear off the sheet, and toss it to him.

Fuck. Off.

As an exit line, it's not bad.

THURSDAY

Good luck at the debate tonight, I text Isa. She responds with a mermaid and crystal ball emoji. I sit up in my bed, worried that she knows—about the Sea Witch, about me and the deal I've made. But she must have already handed Mr. Headley her phone because she doesn't respond to any of my texts until two hours later, when I've been through every possibility, every disaster scenario, and exhausted myself while eating a whole box of Cheez-Its.

Sorry, my brother got my phone before I handed it to Headley. He's into sending random emojis right now. Thinks it's hilarious, the tick. You okay?

Yup! Fine!

FRIDAY

It's been only five days, but everyone is used to me being voiceless. At school, the teachers just ask me to write down questions and answers. I've been put into a new box—*doesn't speak, handle with paper and pencils. Check in with guidance if it lasts longer than a week.*

There are two things I do every few minutes; I click the tiny pearl at the end of my tongue against my front teeth, and I look for the room with Isa in it. The secret one that threw me into a panic. The one where I knew I could fall in love with my best friend.

The room is gone. I don't feel anything at all. That's good. That's better than the alternative.

At the bookstore, Anika looks at me suspiciously.

"Sure you're not sick, like contagious? Maybe you should wear a mask?"

So I wear a mask; it makes it easier to explain why I'm not talking. It's sunny and surprisingly warm for February. We prop open the door to the bookstore to let some fresh air in.

"Do you know how to say *groundhog* in Spanish?" Isa asks me.

I shrug.

"Marmota. My dad told me."

I scribble on my pad. *Marmota saw his shadow. Six more weeks of winter.*

We both look out the open door, where it smells of spring and sunshine. Isa has a thoughtful, grave look on her face.

"That asshole," she says, and I crack up. Her timing has always been so perfect. She's one of the funniest people I know. I click the pearl against my teeth and check my feelings. Nothing. Good.

SATURDAY

"Mija, I'm worried about you," Mamá says at breakfast. I point to *Fine* on my notepad and shovel oatmeal into my face. One more day, that's what the Sea Witch said. I'd give up my voice for seven days, and she'd cure me of falling in love with my best friend. I know how gross it sounds to use words like *cure* when talking about love. I'm completely ashamed of myself for wanting this gone instead of accepting it.

I put my hand on my mother's arm, and she sits down next to me.

I write, *What happened with you and Papá?*

"What do you mean, nena?"

Tell me why he left.

"You know why he left. He found another woman to love. He had another family. It's sad but not a very interesting story."

But why did he change? What changed him? I write. The way I see it, he was either a liar, pretending to be someone he wasn't, or something changed him so completely that he could break all his promises to his old family and make new ones to his new family.

Mamá says what she's always said, words that never fail to send escalofríos through me.

"People change." She shrugs.

Not me. Not if I can help it.

SUNDAY

I dream that I'm sitting in the audience watching Isa debate Westerly High School. The public school regularly kicks St. Bede's ass when it comes to sports, but our debate team is competitive. The topic is LGBTQIA+ after-school clubs in private schools—that's how I know it's a dream; St. Bede's wouldn't even contemplate opening this topic up for debate.

There's no legal basis for—

Don't human rights exist in a private institution that—

TheWordsBlendTogetherBecauseTheyTalkSoFuckingFast.

I wake up to my mouth hanging open, tongue tapping a song against my bottom teeth. I almost think I recognize the song, but then I don't. I pull my tongue and its pearl tip back behind my teeth. It's just before dawn on the seventh day. I have a rendezvous with a Sea Witch.

You repeat the ritual, the boat, the drop of blood, the votive—you even sacrifice another thermos of café con leche into the ocean, in case that matters. When she surfaces she's a whirl, a cyclone of sea-foam, tendrils that threaten to come apart in the wind. There's a sunrise somewhere, you're sure, but the sky is lowering and unrelenting with rain. Hijo de su madre, you think. That groundhog was right. More winter.

At first, you're afraid to speak. After seven days of silence, you've gotten used to it, and now you wonder if there's some kind of trick, a trap. It was seven days; that was the deal. The most noise you've made with your voice was a cough or a laugh, and that didn't count. Then, when the sea-foam resolves itself to a vast tide pool on the surface of the waves, flotsam cradling minia-ture sea-creature worlds, you speak.

"I did what you asked."

"You didn't use your voice?"

"I didn't."

"You didn't speak to the person you might love, you didn't bother sharing yourself and your feelings with others so they could know you?"

"You know I didn't. I kept my end of the deal."

"Good. I gave you a life lesson in one week that it usually takes landfolk decades to learn. You're welcome."

You pull at the neck of your sweatshirt like it's choking you. "But my heart, it's still. I still feel." As long as you didn't talk, you could fool yourself into thinking the room, the light, Isa—didn't matter. But now?

"Is it gone forever? Am I cured?"

The Sea Witch leans her head on the edge of the breakers as if resting on the edge of a bathtub. Kelp-coiled hair piles above her head like a beehive. She reminds you of a performer you saw at a drag brunch in Providence, Loretta Lynchpin. Her beehive hairdo is studded with hermit crabs and conch shells. She watches you like she's waiting for you to get the joke.

"You did this to me. You took my voice."

"I? I did nothing of the kind."

You stare at the creature—no, not a creature, a blot, an aberration on nature—and you feel such hatred for her that you almost scream.

"I gave you a prescription for life—how to live without giving away your heart. I told you to silence yourself, to cut yourself off from others until you didn't feel a thing."

"I did that. I did all of it." You're panting like you've been running, but you haven't moved a muscle.

"More fool you, little fish."

She turns in the water to face you, displaying the broad swath of her shoulder, the ropes of starfish and mussels streaming out from her head. Her black eyes are tide pools of creatures, poor and unfortunate almas who didn't listen to their hearts.

"Land fish are tricky fish," the Sea Witch says, her voice pensive and echoing, as if you were inside the chlorine-and-mold-smelling swimming pool at school. "Trickier than other fish. You don't want what you want; you're not happy with what makes you happy."

She sighs, floating like an abandoned Madonna, slight, no taller than you, wearing a light blue dress, a star crown on her now-immaculate loose black hair.

"You are Yemanjá!" you accuse, as if this is all an elaborate hoax, a prank with hidden cameras and knowing smiles.

"I'm just a sea monster, sweetheart. I've had a lot of suffering in my time, and I'll admit, I was pissed enough, fish enough, that I wanted to burn your smugness down when you first summoned me. Then again, we don't have a lot of fire out here on the water—though give me a good oil spill, and I can make some wicked little flames dance."

You are bewildered and freezing and once again soaked. How many more days of school can you miss, of work? Maybe you've just lost your mind. Or bonked your head and this is all an elaborate dream. The pearl on the tip of your tongue reminds you. This, if nothing else, is real.

"You can tell yourself lies, and you might even believe them. But no one has the right to know dick about you, except you. This is where I tell you to be honest with yourself. But you won't listen to me, and besides, what the fuck do I know about honesty? I hear that in an honest heart, there just aren't shadows." She shudders dramatically. "What's scarier than not having someplace dark to hide?" The Sea Witch rolls, rippling wake waters like a rip current through the surf.

"My point to you is this—I didn't make you do shit."

She starts to sink her body down through the water, a diving vessel, steady and deliberate, until only her tide-pool eyes and seal whiskers show above the water. Then she's gone.

As soon as the Sea Witch disappears, I call Isa. And because she's my best friend, she comes right away.

"So. You can talk now?"

"Yes."

We're parked in the empty lot of a beachfront hotel that's closed for the winter. I'm in the back seat of her mother's old Volvo, the one with the image of La Virgen de Guadalupe hanging from the rearview mirror, stripping off my wet clothes and dressing in a pair of Isa's leggings and a Sublime T-shirt her brother left behind. Then I wrap myself up in car blankets that smell like Isa's dogs. The heat is on so high, the vents are making flapping sounds.

"Did you lose a bet?"

"Why do you say that?"

"I stopped believing in laryngitis halfway through Tuesday."

I decide to tell her the truth. The Sea Witch's words about an honest heart having no shadows ring in my ears.

"I made a deal with a Sea Witch."

Isa tilts her head to one side. "A Sea Witch? Meaning, there's more than one Sea Witch?"

This is such an Isa thing to say, I can't help but smile.

"I don't know. She might be the one and only Sea Witch."

"Like Ursula in *The Little Mermaid*?"

"I don't know her name," I say. "I never even asked. No wonder she thought I was such an asshole."

"Is that why she cursed you?"

"She didn't curse me."

"You lost a bet to her."

"No."

"You sold your voice to her to get the person you love to notice you? There's a guy named Eric you haven't told me about, and your name is really Ariel?"

"No."

"Jeez, Ines, give me a hint."

I crawl over the back to the front passenger seat, smelling of dog and kid brother. I've never been less sure of myself in my life.

"I don't want to change."

"Good idea, you're perfect the way you are," she says, then looks away, a blush or the full-force car heat warming her face.

"But something is changing me, and it scared me so bad that I asked our local Sea Witch to change me back to the way I was. She told me I couldn't speak for a week and it would . . . cure me."

"Did you fall on the breakers and . . . ?"

"Again, no. Cállate so I can get this out before I lose my nerve. I'm afraid of who I'm becoming because I don't know who that will be."

She shrugs. "I get scared of changing, too. I freaked out when I got boobs. Freaked out when my hips widened and I got stretch marks. When I started liking girls—way before the boobs and the hips—I nearly crapped myself thinking it was the end of my life."

I'm so stupid. Of course she understands.

She puts her arm around my shoulders.

"It's going to be okay," she says.

"How do you know?" I whisper, leaning my head against her shoulder. One of our hearts or both of our hearts are beating much faster than they should be.

"I don't know. I guess I really mean, whatever we become will be okay."

I want to tell her about the room I found. The one I didn't know existed that contains a whole fucking part of me and how I tried to pretend that part wasn't real. I was just lying to myself, muting my own voice.

"Is there an Eric or someone else you like, Ines? You can tell me," she says.

"I have some, um, complicated feelings. Uh," I stutter.

She nudges me with her shoulder till I turn and face her.

"Me too," she says. "Complicated. And changing."

Should I make a joke about friends with benefits? Or turn away and connect my phone to the Bluetooth, drown out both our heartbeats with our Best Friends playlist?

I lay my hand on her collarbone, a part of her I'm pretty sure I've never intentionally touched. I feel her heart wild under my hand.

"Yeah," she says with a shy grin. "I've liked you for a long time, nena. And I figured I had to say something soon, or I'd lose you even as a friend."

"Did you know I liked girls? Did you know before I did?"

"Shit, girl, I don't even know if you do now. Or I guess you just told me. You like girls. Cool. But do you like me?" Isa asks.

"I really do."

I might even love you, I think. *You're still my best friend,* I think.

I close the space between us, our breath and the heater steaming over the windows, blotting out the ocean and the whole world.

We kiss, and the lights blaze in the room I found and refuse to lose ever again, no matter what changes it brings. Then more kissing and, *oh shit!* It's not a room at all. It's a whole house with rooms and cupboards and passageways to explore.

"Girl," Isa says when we pull apart for breath. "Did you get your tongue pierced?"

MONSTER REFLECTION

When you are a child of immigrant parents, otherness is for Americanos. To my parents, things like mental illness and queerness *must* be American inventions. We were encouraged toward the norm, toward what would show us in the best, most acceptable light. We were not encouraged to stand out in any way.

So, of course, as soon as I got to high school, I dyed my hair black, inked my eyes with enough kohl to black out the sky, and started listening to punk and goth music. God forgive me, I even tried to wear pancake makeup to make my midbrown face look whiter. I wanted the otherness that Americans seemed to have easy access to.

A large part of that goth identity revolved around monsters. Misunderstood, attractive, and beguiling in their monstrosity—because of their otherness, not in spite of it. Bereft vampires, carnivorous fairies, tiger boys, and witch girls, I found them in music, art, books, and film. (I mean, how many other straight-seeming girls watched *Heavenly Creatures* on heavy rotation throughout the '90s and wished they were Edward Scissorhands so they could kiss Winona Ryder?)

Through monstruos, I accessed parts of my identity that I couldn't have found on my own, and those parts flourished—claws and all.

HOW TO SUMMON ME

BY VAL HOWLETT

HOW TO BEGIN

Say my name thirteen times. Not seven. Not nine. I have been through periods where almost everyone gets the number wrong. Most recently, it was three. I kept hearing that triple chant—felt faint little tugs from below, but I did not fall, and I could not see the glass or humans on the other side.

Light candles. There is no specific number required. I like the symmetry of two, the way they look like two morsels floating out of reach. Or three—two tall candles with a shorter one in between. There's a baleful beauty in that shape.

There should be no other light around you. The lights in your world are too bright. They won't allow me to see you. And you certainly won't see me.

Chant in unison, if you are more than one. Don't rush through it. This is especially important to remember if you are alone. Those who call me in solitude tend to mumble or chant too quickly, as if they want it to be over. Why? Remember, I am moving through a regular day on my world, chasing morsels, picking fruit, cleaning waste. You are the one summoning me.

Do not hold one another's hands. Or do, if you'd like, but you do not need to. Nor do you need to add flourishes or try to sing.

Only repeat the name humans have given me, again and again.

HOW TO BEHAVE WHEN I ARRIVE

When I fall into view for you, as you materialize behind a pane of glass for me: do not scream, or switch on your hideous light, or run away.

I may be the only connection you ever have with my world. Do not turn it meaningless with your fear. There is much I can do for you. There is much of me to know.

An understanding of my abilities has been lost to time. In the far past, humans knew about catoptromancy. Or at least, girls did. Back then, I was rarely called by boys.

The girls would appear in packs behind the glass, squeezed close so they could all fit, their long hair down, the ruffles and ribbons from the tops of their nightgowns pressed against the others' cheeks. Some hid their eyes or shrieked when they saw me, but others looked at me and asked a question in a clear, if shaking, voice.

Who will my future husband be?

What will my future husband be like?

Please, can you tell me the man I will marry?

They knew about my sight.

On my world, it's not unique. All beings see this way. When we encounter each other, we see the being as they are and have been and will be in all the parts of their life. But that means four versions, or five, and not so distinct from one another. Beings like me have variations in perception that come from age. The young of our kind, whose tentacles are not yet strong enough to push them into the air, must rely on the pack for food and teaching, and have attachments and fears that come from dependency. But once we reach adulthood, our days have natural patterns. We do not change much.

But humans are so changeable. They shock me with their multitude—each of them, every time.

I cannot tell you everything. I don't see everything. But when I look through the glass and see you, I do not only see you in the present. I see baby you and four-year-old you and eighty-year-old you, if you live that long. I see you as you are while falling in love and a different you, grieving. I see you confident and driven and you, lost, wondering where you fit.

When girls asked me about their husbands, I tried to answer. I would look at the questioner and close most of my eyes, block out the younger version of her who ran around the nursery, naked and free; the current her, gazing at me with hope; the slightly older her, fretting over exams; the elderly her with a more wrinkled face. I would focus on how she was as a young woman—the her as an object of affection, basking or shrinking from the attention; the her walking down the aisle with love or hope or nerves or all of it; the her making a home for two.

I almost never knew the man's name, unless the last name was important to the questioner. But I could get an impression of him from the young woman herself. What she loved about him, what she found frustrating, what about being with him caused her to change. I'd tell the girl in the mirror those things, and the girls around her would transform from the news. Their fear would fall away as they chattered about who he might be from the boys they knew.

They were so beautiful in those moments, open and talking like they were rooting for one another. Even if there was envy or disdain between them, it would be mixed with a shared exhilaration. It felt good, to give them that. The others, the ones I hadn't scried for yet, would steal glances at me that were wary but excited, too, like what I had to give was more valuable than the terror I provoked.

Sometimes I stayed with them, telling their futures, for hours.

BE CAREFUL WHAT YOU ASK ME

Remember: You must be prepared for all possible answers. Including ones that scare you.

So many of the old encounters were cut short because I said something the girls did not want to hear. When I closed certain eyes and saw nothing—no life in adulthood or old age, the girls did not receive the news well. They cried or stared at me in terror or called me evil or incorrect. Once, a protective bystander looked right at me, her arm still around her sobbing friend, and scolded. "You should have told her a lie," she said.

Lying is human. It is nuanced—not a practice I could easily adopt.

Sometimes a questioner asked about her husband and I saw an older version of her devoted to another woman instead of a man. When I told her, the group reacted differently. Their laughter was less conspiratorial, more accusatory. "Old maid!" the other girls would taunt. When I tried to point out their mistake, explain that I did not see solitude, but instead real connection and love, they would cut our time short. Some would leave the room, and the rest would follow, or someone would turn on a lamp, and the light change pulled me up from the place of the mirror, returning me to my world.

I did not care for such abrupt endings. Those girls were the most interesting. I would have liked to gaze at them longer, to glean how they became their older selves. I am neither girl nor boy, but it only takes looking at one human to understand that gender shapes all of you—your connection to it or lack thereof, your reaction to the genders to which you don't belong. I wondered at the girls' ability to propel themselves from the way of things with no instruction. Did they have internal compasses that I could not see? And when I focused on the older versions of those girls, I found their resolve—a certain silent ferocity. It was mesmerizing—their guardedness and the entrancing cracks in it, when they let go.

Then there was Francis. Or Mabel, rather. They went by Mabel when they met me at the glass, a high-collared girl with sandy hair, full cheeks, and a smile that seemed a bit taunting. They were with a group of girls the first time I saw them, but they did not speak to me directly. Soon after, Mabel summoned me alone. Over the candlelight, they stared right at me as if issuing a challenge. They did not ask the usual question. Instead, they asked, "Who will I be when I grow up?"

I thrilled at the request, the piquant answer I could give. I took my time closing some of my eyes, taking in Older Them, so distinct from the girl before me.

I saw a person who cut their hair and dressed as males do, who spent considerable time mending their shirts and undergarments until they fit their body. Who worked odd jobs with only men and tried to match their strength and sometimes matched their callousness, who swaggered around women at the same specific bar, buying drinks and flirting. Who was quick with a joke. Who was easy to know casually and difficult to know intimately. I told Mabel this. I told them they would take the name Francis.

Mabel stared at me through the glass, their eyes wide and light, like moons. They looked at me like I had foretold their death. It was startling, to give them news that seemed positive—a picture of someone energetic and reaching, if not content—and still cause them pain. I remembered the girl who had scolded me for not lying, and I felt a pang—not of sadness, but something close. Maybe I was doing something wrong. Maybe humans were not meant to know their futures. But if that were true, why did they call me? Why was I pulled to them?

I wanted to reassure Mabel that, as Francis, they would be content. But I couldn't. The truth was they would be content in many stages of their life, and in others, they would not be. A reasonable truth about most human lives, but for Mabel, I wished I could lie.

BE NOT AFRAID

Thankfully, that was not our final meeting. Mabel summoned me again and again. And each time, they were less afraid, more emboldened to ask me new questions.

They asked, "How will I get a job if I dress as a boy?" And, "Will I lose everyone?" And I stopped feeling uncertainty about what to tell them, because my answers reassured them, showed that they would have adventures, and a community. "*When* you," I corrected when they said "if I," and I'd get distracted from the girl before me, Mabel narrowing their eyes as they said "Right," by Francis a few years older, hopeful and proud in their suit, a new grace in how they walked.

Sometimes they asked me a question about myself. How did I know the future? Did I like being summoned, or did I hate it? The pleasure of their interest made me feel warm. But it also snapped me from gazing at confident Francis, doling out drinks at a party, or worn-down Francis, riding the rails with their girlfriend, and forced me to focus on Mabel, the half-grown, plump-cheeked child before me.

I wished I could tell Francis about my world. Not Mabel, who could barely focus, kept glancing backward at their door. "If you are afraid," I finally said, "perhaps it would help to scream and get it over with."

"Sorry," they said. They faced me, took a deep breath, and let it out slowly. "I'm scared someone is going to come into the bathroom and see me and not see you, and I'll find out I've been talking to myself."

I did not know how to answer. I did not know what would happen if someone interrupted our communion. Would another human see me, if they had not chanted my name? I guessed that they would not.

I changed the subject and asked them a question. "Why do people scream when they see me?" I had always wondered. "Is it the tentacles?"

They looked confused. "What tentacles? I think it's the blood."

"What blood?" I asked.

That's how I discovered that I appear to humans differently from how I look on my world. There is something about the glass that alters me. From Mabel's description, I pieced together that humans saw me as another girl, only one whose skin was dotted with red spots.

"It isn't blood," I told them. "They're my eyes."

Mabel looked at me like an unwanted future.

"It's an understandable mistake," I told them. "They're small. You probably can't see them opening and closing from there. But if you look closely—" I stepped toward the glass. "If you really focus . . ." I got as close to the glass as I could without pressing myself against it.

After a few moments' hesitation, Mabel did the same. They stepped toward me, closer, closer. I could see the shadows beneath their eyes, the small difference between their brows, the chap in their lips. I felt their eyes drift over me, or the me they thought I looked like. "I see them," they whispered with triumph, and a bit of awe. I saw *them*. Francis-to-be, looking at me. Francis-to-be, wanting to know me more.

So I told them how to bring me into their world, their side of the glass. I wanted them to know that I was real, that they were not hallucinating. I wanted us to touch.

The next time I heard the chant, I knew they'd done as they'd been told. They had gathered the correct number of people. They had followed my directions.

But when I landed, I could not find them. There were so many girls in the room with me, screaming. Their screams were louder there. They moved so quickly. My tentacles flailed. The air was different, pulling me down, so that I kept striking out at everyone, until I saw them—Mabel-Francis, their face flushed in horror. They were screaming, too.

If you bring me to your side of the glass, don't be afraid. Great things can happen when you're not. Fear ruins everything.

DO NOT DRINK AND SUMMON

Mabel did not summon me again. Francis did, but only once, much later, when they were stout and their face was lined. They had set up a makeshift looking glass in their tent and squinted through it, drunk and weary from a day's hard labor.

They had not called me to their side. They preferred the me they saw in the glass.

"You came!" they exclaimed, after a moment. "You're here!"

While I had longed to see them again, it felt unfair to be called in this moment, this unfortunate moment, out of their entire life. With them too drunk to really hear me. Not a younger Francis, heartbroken because their first love was marrying another, or a vicious Francis, who lashed out at their younger girlfriend when they felt frustrated by their job. Those were Francises I could have helped. But what could I do with this living mop who was too ruled by feeling to be able to converse?

They chuckled to themself, muttering some joke I could not hear.

I told them, "In your state, I'm impressed you lit the candles."

They pointed at me, their finger wavering. "You're real! I didn't even think you . . . I thought you were me. Something my mind did." They opened their hand near their head as if miming an explosion.

"Why didn't you summon me sooner, then?" I asked, and the question came out sharper, needier than I had intended. "If you had called me and seen, you would've known I'm real."

"No!" they said. Then they shook their finger at me, as if there was more to their argument. But they did not say anything else.

"You could bring me to your side of the glass again."

They laughed—an ugly sound.

"I was scared last time," I rushed on, "but now I know what to expect. And so do you. You know what my true form looks like." I was talking so much, the way humans do.

"Even if I could find enough grown men on the campground willing to chant with me, you can't come here because you have tentacles! And all those eyes!" They motioned wildly. "It's terrifying. I see you in my nightmares."

I don't remember what I said next. I was not my usual self. I was more desperate, less practical. I wanted only to prolong the conversation, to speak to Francis despite their impossible state, because even their insults were better than waiting for them to call me back.

I kept pleading. Francis's gaze drifted until our eyes no longer met. They shook their head at nothing, blew out their candles, and sent me back.

Only after the encounter did I realize with horror I had been another me during it—different from the being I had been before. Frantic and pleading. Full of unrequited need. Which meant when other beings on my world looked at me, they saw it. My desperate difference. It had always been a part of me.

LISTEN

Soon after that, the summonings changed. Word must have spread among humans about how to call me, but not what I could do. More people brought me to the glass—people in different dress, boys, sometimes adults. But they did not ask me questions. They just screamed and sent me away.

I would feel the pull when called thirteen times, would fall into the familiar white world where glass stood before me. I would look at those humans with their old selves and young selves inside them and watch their fear take over. I did not offer to tell them anything about their futures. I did not even speak.

Very rarely, humans would call me to their side of the glass, having taken all the necessary steps by accident. But it was always too much of a shock—the cramped space, the size difference, the unyielding drag of gravity. I never had time to get my bearings. All I could do was reach, through the noise, through the fear, not knowing what I was reaching for. Then it would stop. I would be back where I'd been before, where the world was quiet and familiar, except for the noise of the humans' fear playing in my mind.

It was another girl who broke the pattern. Her name was Roberta. She had big black curls that framed her face and blue pants that went wide at the bottom. When she called me to the glass, she did not scream. She went quiet for a moment, then adjusted her posture and said, "That's it?"

It surprised me enough to make me focus on her face, curious and bold. I tried not to look too closely at her at twenty-one, in terrible shock after losing her parents and one brother in a car accident, or her at thirty-three, stretched thin to the point of tears with three kids of her own. I closed my eyes on those versions, so I saw only the doted-on youngest-child her, demanding my attention.

"Are you disappointed?" I asked.

"I thought you'd be scarier; that's all," she said. There was more bravado in her voice than truth. But she wasn't shaking.

I told her she could ask me questions. I should have been more specific. She didn't think to ask me about her future husband (short, with a terrible temper, but reliable and good with the kids) or her future life (longer than anyone else's in her family, with many stages, some full of purpose, some difficult and terribly lonely). She only asked questions about me.

Did I appear to everyone or just a few people? Did I want to eat her brains? Was it hard being stuck in a mirror? Was I a ghost, or would I get to grow up?

Would I get to grow up? There are times when I am pushing through the air in my own world, stretching my limbs or searching for food, when the question drifts through my mind, asked in her young, pointed voice. It was innocent and incorrectly phrased from a lack of understanding of my kind. So why does the very sound of it remain?

Something about the question made me want to meet her. I told Roberta I was not a ghost. And, despite my experience, I gave her instructions on how to call me to her side of the mirror. I'll give them to you, too.

IF YOU WANT ME TO CROSS OVER

Bringing me to your world requires more of you. More work, more preparation.

A group of seven or more must recite my name all thirteen times, together. And before that, your group must perform a laying of hands, in which you try to transcend your own plane of reality.

There are many rituals that could accomplish this. The most common is a ritual performed by girls. They pound one another's backs with the sides of their hands, chanting "concentrate" again and again, then, loudly, "CRACK AN EGG ON YOUR BACK, let the blood drip down, let the chills run up," rhythmically, running their fingers up and down one another to simulate those sensations.

Another requirement: one human must be much more afraid than the rest—because they have already seen some true horror, a dead loved one, perhaps, or because they have the most sensitive and active imagination.

I know you cannot measure fear, but if you'd like to meet me, you'll have to use your intuition. Find a girl who can't watch scary movies, who shrinks from speaking up in class, who moves with the discomfort of someone who doesn't want to be anywhere. Invite her to your party. Offer to have your mother pick her up, so she won't back out at the last minute and not show up.

When I told Roberta that, she said, "You must think I'm zappy. I don't want to bring your bloody self anywhere near me."

But soon enough, I appeared on her side of her bathroom, surrounded by girls her age, all with brown skin like hers and similar clothes to hers and waves of future selves.

I had warned her what would happen, what I would look like. I had told her to tell her friends. When I felt the tug, I thought it might be coming, and my shock was not as great.

But all the girls were screaming. She had not told them, perhaps, or they had not believed her. I tried not to move my tentacles too much, looked around for Roberta. Then I saw her, rooted in place, screaming too. The other girls running around her.

I did not know what to do. I thought if I reached out and touched her, the way humans touch, maybe we could move beyond our circumstances and connect. I stretched a tentacle toward her. She saw it and moved toward the light, and then all of them were gone.

IF YOU WANT ME TO STAY

You won't, will you? You would rather I depart right after I arrive, to give you a fright or tell your future and disappear.

Once I'm there, in your home, it would feel too real. I could really hurt you. I could make a mark.

I tried to make an impact on the people I saw after Roberta. I tried to speak to them. Many still screamed and could not see reason. But some let themselves look at me and respond.

I did not offer them their futures. Instead I asked, "What do you seek?"

Their answers were varied: fame, respite from a tormentor, money for their family, a boyfriend, a girlfriend, love. I did not promise them anything that would not come to pass. But even when I denied them, I tried to keep them talking. I asked why they wanted what they wanted, and sometimes they would tell me, their voices warm with the relief of unburdening. Sometimes, suspiciously or with wonder, they asked me questions. "What are you?" was the most common one.

I never knew how to answer.

Yesterday, I was speaking to a girl through the glass, a chatty, skinny teenager. She asked me where I came from, and I was telling her what my world looked like when she said, "I wish we could switch places."

Her wish settled into me, awoke something inside me, from the same deep place that once told me humans could summon me to their side of the glass. I knew that, if I told her how to do it, if she brought me into her room and I willed it as she turned on her light, we could switch. She would be pulled into my body and back through the glass, into a world where everyone has four tentacles and many eyes and sees all beings, her kind in my world and the humans from her own, in all their variations, from all the points in their life. And I would walk out the door and into her life, seeing through two eyes only.

But I did not know if I would be able to alter her life, or if I would have to live exactly as she would have. I had seen her future selves. There were not many. A teenager who cares for her mother and thinks she is broken. A teenager who dates a much older boy and feels guilty for not liking him, for having feelings for a neighbor girl instead. A desperate young adult who has been kicked out of her home. A ruthless young adult, robbing other humans, sticking a gun in their faces, feeling only numb callousness. Then nothing.

I don't wish to live without mistakes or hard times. I know that's impossible. But humans can have so many selves. I want the opportunity to try on as many as I can.

Your life, though? Yours is a life I'd love to step into.

And think of what you'll get in return—an opportunity to experience another world. A chance to see through many eyes and move with sharp, graceful tentacles. A break from the chaos of your world for the certainty of mine. My pack is large and works together. When you see each of them, you'll see them as they are throughout their lives, and it will be mostly the same. The variations of them will be infinitesimal. It will be easy to take them in.

If you're worried about the monotony of such a life, don't. You'll be summoned. Humans—mostly girls—will draw you to the glass. You'll look into their scared, wide eyes and see all of them. Old versions and young versions, partnered and single and happy and alone.

You'll come to feel what I have long known: that human life is not a simple march forward in time, but many lives, connected by circumstances. That kind and cruel acts are closer than they seem. That every person, even those who do terrible things, has moments of tenderness and care.

It will be easy. You have very little to do. At the next sleepover, when the pranks are done, and you've already played Truth or Dare and are awake later than you have any right to be, suggest another game. Tell your friends to close their eyes while you pound their backs and make them think of death. Theirs, a stranger's—it doesn't matter. As long as, for a second, it brings them somewhere else.

Suggest another game.

By then, most of the good girls will have retreated to the other room to sleep. Take one scared girl by the hand, and lead the girls who are a little more daring. You won't be sure how they feel about you, or if you care, but you will want to hold your own, show off your nerve. And you won't want to miss anything.

Turn off the switches; light the candles. Be assured that if this works, I will treat your body well. Shush your friends' giggles so you all can chant together, in unison.

Bloody Mary.

Bloody Mary.

Bloody Mary.

Keep going.

MONSTER REFLECTION

When I was seven and gullible, I made a friend at a Christian day camp. Her name was Cirisa, with a soft c.

Cirisa was a year older than I was and liked to lord it over me, teach me things. We were at a narrow pond beach, digging in the sand, when Cirisa told me, "Don't dig too far down, or the Devil will grab you and pull you into Hell." She gestured to some nearby boys, digging a hole together that was already very deep. Something (what I realize now was a stick with a ball-shaped top) was protruding from the sand at the bottom. "See?" she said, pointing to it. "That's the Devil's eye."

I cannot express the dread I felt that a creature so evil was so close by—a creature that could pull me away from everyone I loved into everlasting torment. I did not dig in the sand for years after that. And while my fear of the Devil was eventually replaced by more worldly fears, I am still a little unsettled, deep down, whenever I think about my first monster.

BE NOT AFRAID

BY MICHAEL THOMAS FORD

ake out all the yellow ones," Mamaw says. "Put these in."

She takes a box of Christmas bulbs out of the plastic grocery sack from the Dollar General and sets it on the kitchen table beside the tangled strings of lights I'm trying my best to work apart. They're lined with green, blue, red, and yellow bulbs.

"What color do you want me to replace them with?" I ask her.

"Don't matter," she says, and takes a draw on the cigarette in her mouth. She blows the smoke out, and it settles over the table like smog. I wish she would quit, but she won't, even though her cough has been getting worse and worse. She won't go to the doctor anymore, either, because as she says, "He don't know nothin' I don't already know."

What she means is that she's probably going to die before too long. Maybe not next month or even next year, but more likely than not she won't be around to see me graduate from high school in two years. But that's not something we talk about. Just like we don't talk about what will happen to me and Pike if she does. With our parents gone, she's the only relative we have. Since Pike is eighteen and technically an adult, I guess he'll be in charge of taking care of things then.

Except that Pike is the one who needs taking care of, and I've been looking out for myself since I was twelve. As much as I love Mamaw—and I love her more than just about anything— she's not exactly a caretaker, either. Most of the time, I feel like the only adult in the house, and I'm not even old enough to drive.

"Shouldn't we be replacing the *red* ones?" I say. "I thought his eyes were red."

Mamaw shakes her head, taps her ash into the empty Ale-8- One can beside her. "That statue they got over in Point Pleasant makes everyone think that," she says. "Those Blenko glass eyes and all. But they're yellow." She pauses, takes another puff of her cigarette. "At least, they were when I seen him. I s'pose he might look different to different people."

Him. What she means is Mothman. But we don't say his name around here. Mamaw thinks it's bad luck. One time, maybe a year after our parents died, I did say it, and she slapped my face so hard I couldn't breathe for half a minute. I just stood there looking at *her* face all twisted up in anger and fear. "Don't," she said. "Don't call him. Not ever."

Mamaw and Mothman have a history. She was five years old in 1967, the year the Silver Bridge linking Point Pleasant, West Virginia, with Gallipolis, Ohio, collapsed, a little more than a week before Christmas. Forty-six people died in the tragedy, including Mamaw's cousin Elmer, who was driving a beer delivery truck across the bridge when it went down and dumped everyone on it into the Ohio River.

For a year before the bridge accident, people reported seeing a big, winged creature with glowing eyes in the area. Somewhere along the way, they started calling it Mothman. Then they decided that Mothman must have been showing up to warn everybody about the bridge. I don't know why, exactly, but the idea stuck, and ever since then, Mothman coming around has been linked to bad things happening. Especially for Mamaw, who is kind of obsessed with him, first because of what happened to Elmer and then because she says she saw him not long before my parents died. She didn't bring *that* up until after their funeral, though, so I'm not sure what to think about it.

I don't have any particular feelings about Mothman one way or another. He's a big deal around here and brings a lot of tourists to Point Pleasant, where they've got a museum and the statue Mamaw mentioned. He's our monster the way Scotland has its Nessie and New Jersey has its Devil, and since we don't have a whole lot to call our own here, I guess that's a good thing. But sometimes I think people use him as something to blame their bad luck on when blaming the real problems is too hard.

Anyway, the Christmas-lights thing is new and has come about because this is the first year we've done anything for the holidays since my parents died. Christmas was always my mama's thing, and with her gone, Mamaw couldn't bring herself to do it. The boxes of ornaments have been in the attic. But a few days ago she asked me and Pike to get them down, and now the artificial tree is up in the living room, waiting to be decorated.

I pull a yellow bulb out and drop it into the plastic margarine container on the table. I stick a blue light in where that one was. I'm taking out another yellow one when the door bangs open and Pike walks in.

"There you are," he says. "What the fuck are you doing?" He doesn't wait for me to answer before saying, "Come on. We're going for a ride."

My stomach knots up. What Pike means is that he picked up another delivery from Wart and now he needs to make a run, to take the drugs to his buyers. And he needs me to hold them because I'm only fifteen and if we get stopped by the cops and they search us, I'm supposed to say they're mine. That way, Pike won't get arrested.

It's a stupid game, and we're lucky that we've never been stopped. Eventually, though, our luck is going to run out. It always does. And while I won't go to jail, I could end up in a mess of trouble. But Pike doesn't think about that. He never thinks more than one step ahead. Daddy always said that was why he was a lousy deer hunter and never got any. "Those deer are three steps ahead," he always said. "That makes them two steps smarter than you, Pike."

I know arguing with Pike is useless, so I get up and take my coat from the hook beside the door. "I'll help you when I get back," I tell Mamaw. She nods and continues replacing the lights.

"Is this that stupid Mothman bullshit again?" Pike asks as we walk to his truck.

"Yeah," I say as I open the door of the beat-up Ford and climb into the passenger seat.

Pike gets in, fishes in the pocket of his oil-stained Carhartt jacket, and hands me a plastic baggie filled with half a dozen smaller bags of small, white crystals. Meth. Wart's specialty. I tuck it into my pocket and put my seat belt on.

"Safety first," Pike teases as he starts the truck and heads down the driveway. His own seat belt hangs unused beside him.

I don't say anything. I've stopped begging Pike to worry about himself. But it bothers me that he does things like this. Our parents died in a wreck, and it's like he's daring the universe to take him, too. I don't get it.

"We're making two stops," Pike says as we head down the road. "You stay in the truck. It'll be quick."

I nod. I know the drill. Pike does all the actual work. I'm just the fall guy if he needs one. Just along for the ride.

I hate that we have to do this. But we do. We have the same bills to pay that everyone does, and most months there's barely enough to cover them. Usually Mamaw waits until they threaten to turn off the water or electric before she pays those, and the assistance we get for food doesn't go as far as it needs to. We also have some bills other people don't, like one of the medicines Mamaw needs that her insurance won't cover. She tried going without it, but she got sicker and sicker. Finally, Pike went to

Wart and asked him for a loan to pay for it. Wart gave it to him on the condition that Pike come to work for him. Pike's been doing that ever since. I wish he would get a real job, but real jobs are hard to come by around here. And jobs that pay as well as what Pike makes from doing this are almost nonexistent. Pike told Mamaw that he talked to the insurance company and got them to pay for her medicine. I think she probably knows this isn't true, but she doesn't ask, just like she never asks where Pike and I are going on our rides. We used to come back with at least a pop or a bag of chips, to make it look like we made a junk-food run, but we don't even do that anymore.

We come to Hapsburg and drive through town, passing stores and houses decorated for Christmas. A plastic Santa waves from a porch. In some of the windows I can see Christmas trees, the lights twinkling. I wonder how many of them have no yellow bulbs. Probably, I think, just ours. Then we turn onto a side street.

"Where are we going?" I ask Pike. But I'm afraid I already know the answer.

Pike doesn't answer me, confirming what I fear. He drives until he stops in front of a house I know very well. The porch is hung with colored lights—including yellow—and in the yard an inflatable Grinch stands almost to the roof, grinning at us.

Pike holds out his hand, and I give him the bag from my pocket. He takes a couple of baggies out and hands me back the rest. Then he gets out and walks up the steps. He knocks on the door, and a dog barks. Trixie. She's a German shepherd mix. If she knew I was here, she'd go nuts, wanting me to scratch her behind the ears the way she likes.

The door opens, and Mrs. Clarke appears. She darts her eyes toward the truck, and I wave. She doesn't wave back, just hands Pike some folded-up bills, and he drops the baggies into her hand in return. Then she's gone, and Pike is walking back to the truck.

I wait until we're back on the main street, heading for our next stop, before I ask, "Did she say if she's heard anything from Burlie?"

Pike shakes his head. "Nothing. I mean she didn't say. So I guess not."

Burlie is Mrs. Clarke's boy. My best friend. A lot more than my best friend, although that part is a little confusing. Confusing enough that Burlie ran off a couple of months ago after he got into a fight with his parents about it.

I don't say anything else as Pike drives to the next house and makes the second deal. Twenty minutes later, we're home again, and I go into the house to find Mamaw asleep in the recliner in front of the TV. There's a burning cigarette in her hand, the inch-long ash dangling like a broken finger. I take it and drop it into the Ale-8-One can on the coffee table. I take the crocheted afghan from the back of the couch and lay it over Mamaw, then go to my room.

On my bedside table is the copy of John Crowley's novel *Little, Big* that Burlie left on my bed the night he went away. It's his own copy, battered and taped together, because it's his favorite book and he's read it I don't know how many times. The pages are smudged with orange Cheetos dust from Burlie's fingers, the cover torn, the spine crooked from being held open. It's the most important thing Burlie owns, and he left it as a promise that someday he would come back for it. And for me.

I pick the book up and open it. Tucked inside the pages is the note he left with it, the one where he tells me he loves me and wants to be with me but needs to go away for a little while. I take it out now and read it again, although I don't need to. I know every word of it by heart.

Now I use the note for a bookmark. Even though *Little, Big* is Burlie's favorite book, I've never read it. Instead, I asked him to tell it to me in his own words. He tried, but he didn't get very far before he left. So now I'm reading it for myself. It's a difficult book for me to get through, since reading isn't the easiest thing for me to begin with, and reading a book like this one takes extra concentration because the sentences are tricky. You think they mean one thing, but by the end you think maybe they mean another. Sometimes I have to read one sentence four or five times until I get it. Even then, I'm not always sure. But I still love the story, which is about a family that has made deals with the fairies that turn their lives upside down and sideways. And I love the way it makes me feel, and sometimes that's even more important than knowing exactly what's going on.

That's how it was with Burlie and me. I didn't always understand what was going on with us. I didn't always have the words to describe it. But I knew how it made me feel. The first time he kissed me, when he was sleeping over and we were sharing the bed, I finally had a word for it. But it was the feeling that was the most important thing. When he kissed me, I knew it was what I'd been waiting my whole life for. And even though I worried what people might think, I honestly didn't care. I really didn't.

But Burlie's parents cared. They said they didn't want a kid who was "like that" and that he had to stop if he wanted to keep living there. Like who you are is something you can just change like a shirt.

Pike and Mamaw don't care. Pike said it's nobody's business, and that if anyone ever gives me shit about it to tell him and he'll take care of it. Mamaw said there's been queers (that's her word, not mine) in the family for seven generations back, including her Uncle Henny, who lived with his man, Cork, for forty-seven years on a farm where they raised goats and seven children they adopted for various reasons and put through college using money they made selling all that goat milk and cheese.

I don't know if Burlie's family blames me for things or not. Before driving over there with Pike, I hadn't seen any of them since Burlie left. Burlie thinks they might not even know it was me he was in love with, since the way they found out about him was that his mother went into his room looking for money he might have saved from mowing lawns and shoveling driveways and instead found a couple of books that made her suspicious. When she asked him about them, he told her the truth, because one thing Burlie is incapable of doing is lying. Even when it might save him a whole lot of trouble.

I open *Little, Big* and pick up where I left off. I don't let myself read more than three pages a day, because I told myself that by the time I reach the end of it, Burlie will have come back. You'd think that would make me read it *faster*, so that he'd be home sooner, but the truth is that I'm not sure it'll work. I don't know why I think that, but I do. And I'm afraid that if I finish the story before he returns, that will somehow make him *never* return.

He's been gone since before Halloween. It's December now. Burlie has been gone forty-one days, and I'm on page 109 of *Little, Big*. It's 538 pages, which means I have 429 to go. If I stick to my three-page-a-day limit, I'll finish sometime in April, May if I read fewer pages a day. I could go even longer if I read only a page a day, or skip days and stretch into summer, but that feels like cheating. One of the things I've learned from reading *Little, Big* is that magic has rules, and this feels like a kind of magic.

Besides, if Burlie isn't back by springtime, let alone summer, he's not coming back.

I wish I knew where he was. He said he'd call or email or something when he could. He hasn't, though, and that has to mean something, right? I don't want to think about *what* it means, though, because him not being in touch can't be good.

I shut the book and lie on the bed with it resting on my chest. I close my eyes and picture Burlie's face. I have pictures of him on my phone, but I like to try to remember on my own. Most of the time, it's easy. Sometimes, though, I can't remember exactly what color his eyes are, or the shape of his mouth. Then I panic that I'm forgetting him, and I look at a photo to remind myself.

Tonight I remember. I see his eyes perfectly. They're a gold-brown color. His hair is brown, too, kind of long and tucked behind his ears. He's smiling—he's almost always smiling, at least when we're together—and the nails on one hand are painted black. They're also chipped, because that's the hand he picks with when he plays guitar.

I fall asleep thinking about him, and this turns into a dream where I'm walking through the woods behind our house. I know where I'm going—to the abandoned house that sits in the middle of the trees. Somebody lived there once, of course, but not for a very long time. The paint has long since faded away, and the boards are a silvery gray. Most of the windows were shattered years ago, and there's no furniture. Sometimes Burlie and I would spend the night in there, our sleeping bags spread out on the wood floor in the living room, the space lit up with battery-powered lanterns. When the weather turned colder, we had fires in the fireplace, which still has a working chimney.

I daydreamed a lot about fixing that house up, making it our own. It's too far gone to do that, but it was a nice fantasy. I pictured us painting the walls, getting the water running again, filling the rooms with furniture. I imagined us cooking together in the kitchen and heading upstairs to bed. I thought about listening to the rain on the roof while we snuggled under blankets and made plans for later.

In my dream I walk through the woods. There's no path, no road, but I know exactly how to go. Only now, something is wrong. The trees don't look right. And when I peer through the fog I'm walking in, I see the outline of the house for only a moment before something swallows it up. Then it reappears off to my left, farther away than it should be, and when I change direction to get to it, I stumble over unfamiliar ground.

"Willet!" I hear Burlie call my name. "I'm over here! Come find me!"

"I'm coming!" I cry out, my voice tight. I'm straining to see the house, to find my way to it, to Burlie, but the fog is too thick. It swirls around me, cold and damp. I shiver. This isn't right.

"Willet!" Burlie calls again. He sounds frightened.

"Coming!" I try to answer, but I choke on the fog as it fills my throat.

"Willet!" Burlie's voice is shrill with fear now. He says my name again, but it turns into a scream, which grows thinner and fainter, as if Burlie is being lifted into the air. I hear the sound of wings flapping, and the fog around me stirs.

Then there's nothing but silence.

I wake up in darkness. For a moment I think I see lights in the corner of my room, pale yellow dots like the headlights of an oncoming car. Then they blink out, and there's nothing but darkness and moonlight. I don't know who turned the lights in my room out. Maybe I did? I don't remember doing it.

Then I recall the dream. *Burlie.* Burlie calling out to me. Burlie being carried off by . . . something. But what? And where did it take him?

I know it's crazy, but I'm suddenly filled with the need to go look for him in the abandoned house. Our house. Maybe, I think, he's been there all along, hiding from everyone while he decides what to do. Maybe he's been waiting there for me to find him. And I haven't been out there once since he left.

I get up and pull on some clothes and boots, then head to the kitchen. Mamaw is still asleep in her recliner, snoring. The TV is on—a Hallmark Christmas movie with the sound off—and a blond woman is looking in a mirror and holding up two scarves as if trying to decide which one to wear.

I get my coat and open the door as quietly as I can, slipping outside. It's snowing lightly and the moon is only a thin slice in the sky, so it's not easy to see. But I know where I'm going, and I have a small flashlight that I keep in my inside jacket pocket just for this reason. I take it out and turn it on, the narrow beam barely cutting through the snowy dark.

The woods start not far behind the house. I disappear into them, following the route I've walked with Burlie so many times. My boots crunch softly on the old snow while the falling flakes swirl around me as they drift down through the leafless trees. I know walking in the woods alone at night isn't the smartest thing to do. There are coyotes—I hear them yipping off in the distance—and worse. But I need to know if my dream meant anything.

It takes about fifteen minutes to reach the house. I see its shadow in the trees as I get closer, like it's waiting for me. When I get to the sagging porch, I see the front door is open. Maybe the wind blew it open, but I don't think so. Somebody has been here. My heart leaps.

I rush inside.

"Burlie?" I call out.

There's no answer.

I shine the flashlight around the living room, as if maybe I just can't see him. But the room is empty. I call Burlie's name one more time, just in case, but I know he's not here. It was only a stupid dream. Still, it makes me sad, and I realize how badly I wanted him to be here. I feel like if I stay in the house another second, I'll start crying and won't be able to stop.

Then I see that the room isn't completely empty. There's something on the floor in front of the fireplace. I walk over and crouch down. It's a Walkman, a portable cassette tape player. They haven't made them in years, but they were really popular once, and this one belonged to Burlie's grandfather. Burlie thinks it's cool, and he likes making tapes of his favorite music and listening to them on something old-school. He says it's more real than digital.

I set the flashlight on the floor, pick the player up, and pop it open. There's a cassette inside. The label says *XMAS MUSIC FOR WILLET* on it in Burlie's sloppy printing. Looking at it, I feel my heart flutter. Burlie *is* here. Or was. But when? How long has the Walkman been sitting here? And why? If he meant to give me the tape, why didn't he?

I close the player, slip the attached headphones onto my ears, and hit Play. A low, bubbling synthesized bass line begins to play. Then a man's voice sings. "The angel Gabriel from heaven came, his wings as drifted snow, his eyes as flame."

There's a noise behind me, the creak of a foot on the stairs. I whirl around, kicking the flashlight and sending it spinning across the floor. "Burlie?"

Standing at the foot of the stairs leading to the second floor is a shadow, darker even than the darkness of the room. It's too big to be Burlie. Too big to be any person. As the song continues to play in my ears, the shadow grows, wings extending out on either side. Then two pale yellow eyes flare, as if someone has lit kerosene lamps.

I stand there, frozen, waiting for something to happen. I don't know what. Anything, really. But the thing doesn't move, doesn't blink, doesn't speak. It's just there. I don't do anything, either. And I'm not sure if it's because I *can't* or because I don't want to. I feel like I should be afraid. I *am* afraid. At the same time, I don't think this thing (I can't bring myself to use the name I know I should) wants to hurt me.

What it does want, I don't know.

I force my pinkie finger to bend, to prove to myself that I can move if I want to. I curl my fingers into fists, then relax them. I do the same with my toes, curling them inside my shoes. Still, I don't run. I stand, looking into the yellow eyes. Waiting.

Hours seem to pass with neither of us moving. Then the wings beat, once, and I feel cold air surround me. The yellow eyes blink out, and the thing is gone. Now there's just the darkness of the winter night.

I let out a long sigh, surprised to discover that I've been holding my breath. I look for the flashlight, pick it up, and shine it at the stairs. Nothing. I'm alone in the house. Then I realize that the song is still playing in my ears. It's been only a minute or two. I hit Stop, and the singing ends. Now all I hear is the low whistling of the wind in the chimney.

The fear I couldn't let myself feel while it was happening surges in. I need to get out of the house. I run through the door and toward home. I don't know exactly what I saw in the house, but I can't help thinking about the yellow Christmas lights Mamaw wanted out of the strings. I can't help thinking about her story, of *all* the stories I've heard. And if it was Mothman who just appeared to me, what does it mean? He always arrives as a warning. Combined with Burlie running away and now finding the cassette tape he made for me, I fear these things are all related.

When I get home, Mamaw is still asleep, and the blond woman is now ice-skating with a man who looks like he'd rather be doing something else. I go back to my room. Lying on the bed,

I rewind the tape and start the first song again. This time, I listen to the lyrics. I take out my phone and start Googling. The song is called "Gabriel's Message." The version on my tape is sung by Sting, who I know was in a popular '80s group called the Police, but the song itself is an old one, like hundreds of years old. It's about the angel Gabriel appearing to Mary to tell her that she would be the mother of Jesus.

In other words, a kind of warning.

The song ends, and another one comes on, this time Fiona Apple singing "Frosty the Snowman." I know this one because Burlie played it a lot. He *loves* Christmas, and especially Christmas music and those old stop-motion specials about Frosty, Rudolph, and the Miser Brothers. He's played me a *lot* of Christmas songs. But I don't remember him ever playing "Gabriel's Message." So why is it the first one on the tape?

A warning.

An angel.

Mothman.

When I think about it, maybe Mothman is a kind of angel. There's the whole wings thing, obviously. And he supposedly appears to people to tell them something. Tidings, like in the carols. Comfort and joy and all of that. Only his messages aren't comforting.

I don't know what to think. Now that I'm in my own house, in my own room, what happened in the abandoned house feels like it might never have really happened. Maybe I made the whole thing up. Maybe the yellow eyes were the flashlight reflecting off bits of glass. Only I'm pretty sure there was no glass where the thing was standing. And the flashlight was on the floor, facing the other direction. Which means either it was all in my head or it was real.

I lie there, thinking about all of this and listening to the tape Burlie made for me, until dawn arrives and weak sunlight trickles into my room. It's still snowing, and the sky is gray. The whole world feels cold, and I can't get warm. It's like the wind the creature in the house swept at me with its wings has wrapped around me and won't let go.

I get up, pull a hoodie over my head, and go to the kitchen. Mamaw is standing at the stove, cooking bacon. "Made coffee," she says. "Want some eggs?"

"Sure," I say. "Thanks." She rarely makes breakfast, and usually it's just a bowl of Froot Loops or Cap'n Crunch for herself. This is a surprise.

I pour some coffee into a mug and sit down. As I wait for breakfast to be ready, I consider telling Mamaw what happened in the abandoned house. But now that it's daylight, it all seems kind of silly. So when she sets a plate of bacon and scrambled eggs in front of me, I eat it without saying anything.

"Where's Pike?" I ask Mamaw. "He never sleeps through the smell of bacon cooking."

"Don't know," Mamaw says. "Not in his bedroom. Truck's gone. Guess he went out."

I grunt. Pike being up this early is almost unheard of. That means he probably got a call from Wart or one of his clients and went out to make a sale. At least he didn't wake me up to go with him. I'm grateful for that.

Mamaw is standing in front of the open refrigerator. "Outta pop," she says. "And only got two cigarettes left."

Now I know why she's made me breakfast. She wants me to go to the store for her. With Pike gone, that means I'll have to walk. It's more than a mile each way. But it's Sunday morning and I don't have anything else to do, so after I finish eating, I set the plate in the sink and say, "Think I'll go to the Piggly Wiggly," as if this isn't exactly what she wants me to do.

The walk is actually nice. Because of all the snow, there aren't a lot of cars out, and I have the road to myself. I have Burlie's Walkman in my coat pocket and the headphones on, listening to the Christmas songs he picked out for me. The mystery of how the player ended up in the house is still there, but I ignore it for the moment and try to just enjoy the music. But every time a song mentions angels—and there are a *lot* of angels in Christmas songs—I think about what I saw and what it might mean.

A song comes on by a group called Over the Rhine. They're from Ohio, like me and Burlie, and he really likes them. Every year they do a series of Christmas concerts, and one of the things Burlie wanted to do was go see them together. He was saving up money for tickets.

The song on the tape is called "Snow Angel," and even though it's a Christmas song, it's sad. It's all about someone whose lover goes off to war and doesn't come back, and how the one left behind is comforted by knowing that one day they'll die, too, and the two of them will be reunited and be happy again. Not exactly cheery. But the singer's voice is beautiful, and Burlie loved playing the record the song is from. He said sometimes sad is better than happy because sad reminds us that happy doesn't last forever, and that we need to enjoy it while we can.

Another warning.

When I get to the Piggly Wiggly I keep the tape playing while I go inside. I pick up a six-pack of Ale-8-One, then head to the checkout for Mamaw's cigarettes. I'm not old enough to buy them, but nobody ever cards around here. I set the pop on the conveyor belt and say, "Pack of Newports."

"Willet," a voice says, and I look up and see Gina—Burlie's sister—behind the register. I forgot she works Sundays. We stand there, looking at each other, neither one of us asking the question I know we're both thinking.

"Heard anything?" Gina says finally.

I shake my head. "You?"

"Nothing," Gina says as she sets the cigarettes down in front of me.

I hand Gina a twenty, and she makes change. Then we stand there, staring at each other again. Gina's eyes are the same color as Burlie's, and they're filled with sadness and questions. I can't help her with either.

"Let me know if you do, okay?" she says.

I nod. "You too."

I put the cigarettes into my coat pocket, pick up the six-pack, and leave. I think maybe I should have told Gina about finding the cassette player. Then again, it would probably only make her worry more.

When I get home, Mamaw is sitting at the kitchen table. As soon as I shut the door, she says, "Cops called."

I stop, the pop still in my hand. "Did they find Burlie?" I don't know why the cops would call us about him, but he's on my mind and it's the first thing I think of.

"No," Mamaw says. "About Pike. They arrested him."

I don't have to ask her what for. And if she was surprised to learn the reason, she's not showing it. I set the pop down, take the cigarettes out of my coat, and hand them to Mamaw. She fumbles with the wrapper, her hands shaking, but gets it off and takes a cigarette out. As soon as she lights it and takes a drag, she seems to settle down a little.

"What now?" I ask her.

"I don't know," Mamaw answers. "Don't have the money for bail."

We actually do. Or at least I know where we can get it. Wart. But that will put us more in debt to him than we already are. "I saw him last night," I say.

Mamaw looks at me. "Saw who? Pike?"

"No," I say. I hesitate a moment before adding, "Him. Mothman."

Mamaw looks hard at me. "You sure?"

"No," I admit. "But yes."

She nods. "Came to warn us about Pike."

I don't agree or disagree with her. But it does make sense.

"Guess I should have said something," I say.

"Wouldn't matter," she says. "He doesn't show up to give you a chance to change things. Only to let you know something bad is coming."

"That doesn't seem fair," I tell her.

"Life ain't fair," she says.

She's right about that. But we've had more than our share of not fair, and I'm not sure what the point of warning us that more might be coming is when there's not much we can do about it. We were already barely getting by. Now, with Pike in jail, things are worse. There's no money for a lawyer. If Pike doesn't come home, it's just me and Mamaw. And if something happens to Mamaw, it's just me. Especially now that Burlie is gone. I'd have nobody.

I can't even let myself think about that, about what would happen to me then. And there's nothing I can do about any of it right now, so instead of hanging around the house being angry or upset, I decide I need to walk out to the abandoned house and see it in the daylight. I tell Mamaw to call me if she hears anything, then go back to the woods.

When I get to the house, the front door is shut. I pause before going in. I don't know why, since I can't imagine finding anything in there that would be more frightening than what I saw last night. Still, my heart is beating as I turn the knob and go inside.

The living room is empty. I examine the walls around the stairs, but there's nothing there that might have reflected light. I knew there wouldn't be, but I had to make sure. I'm looking up the stairs and thinking about checking out the second floor when I hear something behind me and turn around.

My heart is already pounding. But it's not Mothman. It's just *a* man. Wart. He must have come to the house, seen me going into the woods, and followed me.

Wart is skinny, with a scraggly reddish beard that hangs halfway down his chest. He's got a green knit cap pulled down almost to his small, yellowy eyes, and he's standing with his hands in the pockets of dirty jeans. He looks at me, then spits on the floor.

"You're Pike's brother," he says. It's not a question.

I nod.

"Heard about him getting caught." He doesn't wait for me to respond before continuing. "Sounds like he got stupid. That could be trouble for me."

"Maybe you should sell your own drugs, then," I say before I can stop myself.

Wart looks like he wants to punch me in the face. Instead he says, "He still owes me five grand. That means *you* owe me five grand."

"Five grand?" I say. I had no idea Pike had borrowed so much. "Where am I supposed to get five grand?"

"You on the nice list?" Wart says, showing a mouth of broken teeth. "Maybe Santa will bring it to you. If not, you come work for me, least until your bill is paid off."

"We're gonna get Pike out," I tell him.

Wart laughs. "Sure," he says, as if I've said I'm going to fly to the moon. "Even if you do, he's done working for me. I don't work with guys who get caught. Besides, the cops'll be watching him. Hope you're smarter than he is."

He turns and leaves. I don't bother going to watch, as I just want him away from me.

I need to get home, so after waiting a few minutes I go to the door and look outside. Wart is gone. He could still be lurking around somewhere in the woods, but he's already made his point—if I don't pay off my family's debt, things will get a lot worse—so it doesn't really matter. I hightail it back to the house, where Mamaw is pacing in the kitchen, a Newport burning in one hand and the phone in the other. She hangs up a moment after I come in.

"That's the last bail place," she says. "Can't afford none of them."

I want to go hug her. Actually, I want her to hug me. I want someone to tell me everything will be okay, that Pike won't be in jail forever and Burlie will come back. I want to be comforted. But Mamaw only leans against the sink and keeps smoking. I can tell she's worn out. She doesn't have anything left to give anyone else.

I go to my room and try to distract myself by reading *Little, Big*. But nothing can keep me from thinking about what's going on. Five grand. Where am I going to get that kind of money? Even if Pike gets out, how is *he* supposed to get that kind of money if he can't work for Wart anymore?

I have to think of something else.

Then I remember something I read when I first looked for information about Mothman, about how sometimes people leave offerings to the Mothman statue in Point Pleasant. They put out plates of sausage rolls and cans of Mountain Dew. Both things are super popular in this part of the world, and I guess people assume since Mothman is from here, he likes them, too.

I don't have either thing in the house, but I know where I can get them. I head out to the kitchen, put on my jacket. "I'll be back," I tell Mamaw. She doesn't ask where I'm going.

This time, the trip to the Piggly Wiggly seems to take longer, because I'm in a hurry and want to get there and back. It's dark by the time I get home, and I head right into the woods. When I come to the abandoned house, I take the can of Mountain Dew and the package of sausage rolls out and set them on the porch. I stand there staring at them, feeling ridiculous. But I've started this thing, and I need to see it through. Besides, I don't have any other ideas.

"Hey," I say, feeling dumber by the second. "I don't know if you're real. I think you are. Even if you are, I don't know if you give a shit about me and my family. Maybe Mamaw's right and all you do is show up to let us know things are about to suck even worse than they usually do. I don't know what the point of that is, unless you're also telling us we get a chance to change what happens, even if Mamaw doesn't believe that. That's what I'm trying to do. Change what's happening. I don't know if you can help us or not, but you're the best chance I've got."

I don't know what else to say. I've never made an offering to anyone before. I don't know how it's supposed to work. I mean, I know how prayers are supposed to work, but I've never really believed anyone listens to those. If they did, there'd be a lot more people getting what they want.

"Anyway," I say. "I brought you this stuff."

I wait a minute or two. I don't know what for. An answer? It's not like Mothman is going to appear and eat the sausage rolls and drink the pop. When I was a kid I used to leave milk and cookies out for Santa on Christmas Eve, then wait for him to show. I always fell asleep before he did, but in the morning there'd be half a glass of milk and the cookies would be gone. That was enough for me to believe he was real for a long time.

I turn and walk back to the house. Inside, Mamaw is back in her recliner. I ask if there's any update on Pike, and she shakes her head. I go to my room, lie down, try to calm my racing thoughts. I slip the headphones on and listen to the tape Burlie made me. Songs about angels fill my head, and eventually I fall into a restless sleep.

I wake up when someone shakes me. I open my eyes and see the glowing end of Mamaw's cigarette hovering above me like a star.

"Come see this," she says. "Hurry up."

She turns and leaves. I have no idea what's happening, but I get up and follow her. In the living room she's standing in front of the TV. The news is on, and there's a reporter standing near what looks like a car crash. A truck is on its back on the side of the road, the front end smashed into a telephone pole that tilts wildly. Glass is all over the place. The reporter is talking to a man.

"Ain't that Dewey Miller?" Mamaw says.

"Yeah," I say. "What's he doing on the TV?"

Mamaw doesn't say anything, but she turns the volume up.

"So you say something hit your truck and rolled it?" the reporter says to Dewey.

Dewey nods. "Weirdest thing I ever seen. Weren't no deer or nothing like that. It was more like a big bat or something. It had wings. And red eyes."

"Yellow," Mamaw mutters under her breath.

The reporter nods but looks skeptical. "A bat large enough to turn over a pickup truck," she says.

"I know it sounds crazy," Dewey tells her. "But I swear that's what it was."

The reporter turns to the camera. "Police tell us they suspect black ice and driving over the speed limit for the conditions are a more likely cause of this accident that has sent one man, Warther Reeves, to the hospital with life-threatening injuries. In any event, until they can get this cleaned up, Trenton Hollow Road is closed, so take an alternate route."

As the camera pans to the wreckage of the truck, Dewey shouts, "I'm telling y'all, it weren't no goddamn black ice!"

Mamaw looks at me. "He's right about that," she says, and walks into the kitchen.

I know what she's thinking because I'm thinking the same thing. It doesn't seem possible, but now I want to know if the sausage rolls and pop are gone. "Be back in a bit," I tell Mamaw as I get my jacket and one more time head out to the abandoned house in the woods. I stop at the edge of the porch, shining the flashlight on where my offerings were. The cardboard tray the sausage rolls were on is empty. The can of Mountain Dew is on its side, a little puddle of pop next to it.

Raccoons, I think. *Maybe a possum.*

Except that I know I didn't open the can.

Then I notice something else on the porch. At first I think it's an animal lying there. But it doesn't move. I go over to it and shine the flashlight on it. It's a knit hat. Green. There are rips in it and darker areas that look wet. The last time I saw that hat, it was on Wart's head. I touch the darker spot, and my finger comes away red.

I'm staring at my finger when there's a rustling sound. When I turn, I see yellow eyes watching me from between the trees. My heart starts to beat harder. I resist the urge to run into the house, shut the door. This time, I want to see who those yellow eyes belong to. I want answers.

Then the two eyes blink, and when they open again there's just a single eye, and it's moving toward me. I wait to feel the rush of beating wings.

"Willet!" a voice calls out.

"Burlie?" I answer, confused.

The eye moves more quickly in my direction, and I realize that it's not an eye at all. It's a flashlight. A flashlight that Burlie is carrying.

"Willet!" he calls again.

Then he's in front of me, and we're looking at each other. I can't believe this is happening, that he might actually be real. But then his arms go around me, and he's kissing me, and it's all so real that I can hardly breathe. When we finally let go of each other, I say, "I found the tape."

"The what?" Burlie says.

"The tape you left me," I tell him. "With the Christmas songs. The Walkman was in the house."

"I didn't leave it there," he says. "I had it with me. At least I thought I did. In my backpack. I promised myself I'd bring it back to you in time for Christmas. Then, a few days ago, I looked for the Walkman and it was gone. I wondered where it went. I thought someone stole it or I lost it. You found it here?"

I nod. "I thought you left it for me. To let me know you were coming back."

Burlie laughs. "Weird," he says. Then he laughs again. "Maybe the fae took it and brought it here."

"It doesn't matter," I tell him, because it doesn't. "Where were you? Why didn't you call or email or anything?"

"It's a long story," he says. "I sold my phone when I needed money. But I'm back now." He reaches out, takes my hands in his. "It's going to be okay. Everything is going to be okay. I talked to Gina. She's moving out. We're going to get a place. Things are going to change, Willet."

He hugs me again. Over his shoulder, I see movement in the trees behind him. The darkness ripples. Two yellow moons appear. This time, I'm not afraid. The darkness expands like wings unfolding. Then the moons rise up through the trees and into the night.

I don't know exactly how everything has happened. But I've got some ideas. I think about the green hat and what that might mean. We've still got the rest of the Pike problem to sort out, but now I have a feeling we'll manage it somehow.

I kiss Burlie again. "Yeah," I say. "I think they are."

MONSTER REFLECTION

When I was five, I discovered a book called How to Care for Your Monster, which was written and illustrated by Norman Bridwell, the creator of Clifford the Big Red Dog. From this I became firmly convinced that not only were monsters real, but also that I could be friends with them. Not long after, I fell in love with monster movies, which I watched every Saturday on our local television station's creature-feature show. My favorites were about the Creature from the Black Lagoon, the Wolf Man, and Godzilla. But really, I loved them all. I wanted to know their stories, to understand them, to meet them in real life.

Since then, I've continued to be fascinated by the things we call monsters. In stories and movies, they're almost always way more interesting than the so-called heroes. Sometimes, I write about them, like in my novel *Lily,* which is, in part, about the notorious Russian witch Baba Yaga. And when I moved to Appalachia, I became particularly fascinated with our most famous local cryptid, Mothman. I have a tattoo of him holding a pawpaw (pawpaws grow here in Ohio) on my leg, and there's a six-foot carved wood statue of him in our living room. (If you want to know about another awesome Ohio cryptid, look up the Loveland Frogman.)

Oh, and my favorite job apart from writing stories? For a short time, I got to answer Godzilla's fan mail.

THE FREEDOM OF
FEATHERS AND FUR

BY DAVID BOWLES

I have come to New Spain to kill my brother.

The reason is complicated, but the manner straight-forward. I walk with a limp, courtesy of the bastard whom I have come hunting. So I must lean upon my makila, a thin cane common in Navarra, the land of my Basque people. If I yank up on its pommel and grip, I unsheathe a deadly steel spike, plated in silver.

I plan to thrust its point into his monstrous heart.

I arrived in Veracruz two weeks ago, on Saint Mark's Day of this year of our Lord 1541. Three months earlier, I had set sail from Orio aboard the *Itsaserroi*, built from oak trees and crewed by sailors from my homeland. Though I had planned to shun all company, stewing in my need for familial justice, the ship's surgeon took a particular interest in me while treating the unusual wound on my leg. Xavier Mugartegui. At twenty-one, he is just four years my senior, with enchanting blue eyes, a keen mind, and skillful hands. We spent long hours conversing about diverse topics. He was surprised that a "handsome village youth" could be so well read.

"Lope," he once teased, the corners of his lips twitching playfully, "fate brought you aboard this ship so I should not die of boredom. Your mind and wit rival your face in beauty."

At sea, men often abandon themselves to vice, seeking warmth and company in one another's arms. But though the temptation of Xavier's smile was difficult to resist, resist it I did.

One monster in the family is quite enough.

After an awkward farewell, I disembarked and began to inquire at various inns and taverns, tracking my brother south, deeper into the lush, green forests of the New World. I've begun to understand why Mikel has fled to this savage, unexplored land. It pulls on my heart, inviting me to plunge deep.

But I refuse to surrender myself to the whispered enticements of nature, neither those of the world at large nor my very own. Life is a struggle against the flaws that inhere in self and cosmos, the traps laid at the beginning of time to separate the righteous from the depraved.

So was I taught. So I must believe. Otherwise . . . no. Better not to even think it.

My brother has marched off under the command of Francisco de Montejo, nicknamed el Mozo, who intends to conquer the Yucatan Peninsula. Amusing. Consider how long it took the Castilians to acquire Navarra, not to mention the centuries they struggled to expel the Moors. The bastards wouldn't even be on these shores without Basque galleons.

Nevertheless, I have to feign confidence in Montejo's leadership. To catch up with Mikel, I need to join the reinforcements who head out tomorrow.

I'm close, elder brother. Have you caught my scent with those devilish senses yet?

This time, it will be *I* who marks *your* flesh, who draws blood.

Marching is hard with this leg, and my initial awe at the foliage fades as the humidity makes my sweat pool beneath my chafing uniform. I wish I could strip down to my linen braies, but the vicious mosquitoes that nip at my face would then cover me in bites. Nonetheless, I manage to keep up, helping my superiors read maps, keep logs, and write responses to sealed orders. My skills are the fruit of many years of struggle, convincing my parents to accept my pursuit of knowledge, to let me pore over manuscripts at the chapel of San Bartolomé, to spend precious money acquiring books from merchants who traveled through our humble village of Gorriti on their way between Bilbao and Pamplona.

A priest for a son was not something they had hoped for, but for a while the prospect brought them great pride and joy.

Until Mikel ripped all that away.

After three days of pushing single file through dense and wet jungle, our only respite the bright trilling and colorful plumage of exotic birds, we reach the town of Kaalk'iini, which Francisco de Montejo has just subjugated. The eyes of the Mayaob—the Natives of these parts—smolder even as they avert their gaze from our disheveled forms: unshaven, ragged, stinking. I know that look well. Older folks from my homeland stare sideways at Castilians in government positions still, remembering the conquest that made Nafarroako Erresuma—the Kingdom of Navarra—simply another province of the Hispanic monarchy. Our language has been deemed illegitimate, with all records originally written in Basque having to be redone in Castilian Spanish and notarized by a Castilian official. We can't even select a Navarrese bishop. Our culture is subsumed in this new *Spanish* identity, against our will.

Conquest is an ugly business, one in which I have little interest. These people are darker and shorter than I am, have strange tattoos and piercings, worship pagan gods that often seem more demonic than angelic—but this land is *theirs*. Why must others invade it? To what end?

I ignore the battle preparations. As my captain reports to el Mozo, I begin my inquiries.

"Mikel?" one grizzled soldier repeats. "Ran off in the middle of battle four days ago. We heard a wolf howling not long after. Wonder if it killed the deserter."

Rage rises in my gut. How will I find him now? I don't have his . . . instincts to guide me.

There's little time to think, as we begin marching to Me'ex Kaanul. The trees are thick, ladened with bizarre, knobby fruit that our Native guides urge us to eat for hydration. There are no rivers or lakes in which to bathe or slake our thirst, just unending jungle, eyes glinting in the deep shadows, unknown predators seeking surcease from the oppressive heat.

Before we arrive at the village, we are surrounded by thousands of Maya warriors. A hail of arrows and spears rains down, thudding into the other young conscripts, ripping holes in their bodies, spraying blood in red fans.

I fire my musket once before fleeing as a man with pointed teeth and an obsidian axe rushes from the trees, straight at me. Hobbling as fast as I can, I pull the steel-and-silver spike from my makila and stab at the fierce bodies that try to stop my flight.

An arrow slams into my weaker leg, sending me sprawling. My head smashes against the root of a tall tree our guides call báalche'. As the dark of unconsciousness cascades upon me, I roll over to behold its wide branches laden with purple blooms, spread over me like a parasol . . . and a red-painted warrior lifting a club to bash in my skull.

The last thing I see before losing awareness must be a hallucination: a lizard the size of a man, covered in multihued feathers, leaps onto my attacker, jaws closing around his neck.

Then the world goes black.

In the inky void, a voice echoes.

"Jelebnen! Change!"

As I awaken, the pain in my leg and head make me retch. Struggling to keep the bile down, I open my eyes.

Crouched before me is a Maya boy about my age. He's wearing only a loincloth and a leather satchel strapped across his chest. His dark brown skin accentuates the muscular lines of his body, lithe but strong. His face is handsome, alluring in an almost feline way, with narrowed black eyes and a long nose that is both thin and close to his face, curving along its lines and coming to a flared, gentle tip that points at his full lips, which have now curled into a bemused smile.

"Why not transform? Why endure the pain?" he asks in Spanish. I look down at my leg. Someone has cut away part of my pantaloons, removed the arrow, and packed the wound with herbs. I reach up to touch my head: a similar poultice has been tied in place.

"Who are you? Did you do this for me?"

"I'm Ayim Cher. And yes, I did. I pulled you out of harm's way. But let me repeat: This patching up is temporary. You need to shift into animal form to fully heal."

"I don't have a damn . . ." I pause, swallow my anger. "Do you know Mikel Haritzmendi? Looks like me, just a couple of years older?"

Ayim rocks back on his heels. "I knew it! You're his brother, no? Lope?"

I push myself farther upright against the tree, where he must have leaned me. "You've met him? He told you about me?"

"I didn't meet him, but word came to me. I've been out patrolling for the last few days, watching for invaders and the refugees they pursue. Your brother asked us to give you aid."

I cast my gaze about and find my makila, the spike sheathed. Grabbing it, I attempt to stand despite the nauseous dizziness.

"I need to see him."

Ayim catches me as I stumble over a tree root. He is shorter than me, and my face ends up pressing against the top of his head. His hair smells of leaves and incense. One strong arm wraps around my waist; the other grabs my hand. A tingling thrill rides up my arm at his touch.

"You're really not in any condition to be walking around the forest, Lope." He looks up at me as I recoil from the way my body responds to his. "It's okay. You can transform in front of me. I have heard the Cries."

"I don't," I snarl between gritted teeth, "transform. I'm not a demon spawn like Mikel."

Ayim's angled eyebrows beetle together. "Lope, I can *smell* you clearly. You're a waypek. I'm guessing the claw marks on your thigh are from your brother. We've run into Spanish shape-shifters before. We know that you often pass the ability through infection rather than cultivating it on your own."

Of all his confusing words, I focus on just one as I twist in his grip. "I'm not Spanish. I'm Basque. Their language feels as wrong on my tongue as it does on yours."

"Apologies." His eyes glisten with visible regret. "I shouldn't make assumptions."

His manner is disarming. His tangible concern and respect make it difficult to remain angry at him. So I soften my tone even as I continue to protest.

"No, you shouldn't. I'm not a shape-shifter or—what did you call it?—a waypek. Not a gizotso." I take a deep breath, steeling myself for rejection. "So . . . I need your help. Will you please take me to my brother?"

Ayim shifts his body until he's bearing part of my weight on his shoulder.

"Of course I will. Just take the first step, Lope. It's always the hardest. From there, the way gets easier."

As he leads me along a path through the forest, Ayim reveals that he is one of the Children of Chin, a secret society with members in towns and kingdoms all across the peninsula. They have gathered in a sacred place called Loltun, safe from invaders while they decide what to do about the encroaching conquest.

"The Code of Chin," he tells me, "keeps us from organizing an army to confront the Spaniards. But we have other options."

"How old are you?" I ask.

"Seventeen."

"My age. What about your parents?"

"Our family once helped maintain the ancient city of Chichen Itza, built by our ancestors centuries ago. We would give aid to pilgrims and priests. When el Mozo arrived, my father and other men died trying to keep the invaders away. My mother and I were at the mercy of the new rulers, who renamed the place Ciudad Real. For two years we served them, and I learned their tongue. There was a baptism. A Christian name that I will not now repeat was forced on me."

I'm impressed at his pride, at how steadfastly he has held to his ancestral ways despite the ongoing conquest. Then I hear my brother's voice, echoing those sentiments as well, on that hill in Navarra, and the confusion makes my head throb. I sigh and grip my makila.

"Ah, yes, Castilla has a way of scorning other languages, other traditions. It uses force to bring us to our knees and make us accept its ways. But el Mozo was finally expelled, wasn't he?"

"Yes. Many warriors of the Itza, my people, at last surrounded Chichen Itza and began to harry the Spaniards, forcing them into retreat. My mother and I were dragged along. Understanding that we'd be forever separated from everything we cared about, my mother attempted escape. But she was killed."

The moistness in his eyes makes my chest constrict. Such willingness to show grief, coupled with his wisdom, bravery, and skill . . . I swallow heavily. I have never met a boy like Ayim. His qualities eclipse the bemused maturity of Xavier Mugartegui, the ship's surgeon fading from my mind as a star before the rising sun.

I am overcome by a desire to comfort Ayim, to embrace him and encourage him to cry out his grief. I see myself in him. I suspect that if I look more closely, I will see even more.

Instead, I squeeze my wound so the pain will numb these old, illicit cravings of heart and flesh. "Yet you are free, Ayim. How?"

"I served as a translator until el Mozo was forced to retreat from Yucatan. During that final battle, I heard the Cries of Chin."

Before I can ask what he means, a low growl and the rustling of branches whips our heads around. A great spotted beast like a tiger has exited the tree line. Behind it come two cubs. Ayim clamps his hand over my mouth and pulls me into a shallow alcove in the rocky hill beside the path.

"Balam," he whispers in my ear. "Be still."

My back is pressed against his body. I can feel every contour, from groin to chest. His bare calf touches mine just below my wound. It is maddening. I try not to imagine melting into him. Instead, I focus on his calm breathing. The slow, strong rhythm of his heart proves a powerful antidote to the light fluttering of my pulse.

When the big cat has made its way beyond us, Ayim releases me. By instinct I flick my tongue to my lips, tasting the salt of his fingers.

"Better not to confront a mother with her cubs," he explains after making sure we are safe. "She's looking for food, and those jaws can bite right through bone. Wouldn't want to lose you to her. We've only just met."

"In my homeland," I say, trying to ignore the intensity of his gaze, "we have wolves. Same strategy. Steer clear of them altogether. Unless they come for your animals."

"Ah, wolves. Like wild dogs, yes?"

I think of my brother, eyes glowing in the moonlight, teeth bared. I remember the feel of those claws ripping through my flesh.

"Yes. Wild and rabid. Dangerous."

The jungle gives way to broken, rocky hills. Trees stand in copses or loose forests, and refreshing breezes sweep down off distant mountains to the south. I while away the hours by asking Ayim for the names of trees and animals in Itzat'an, his native tongue. His patient repetition and modeling make the experience joyful. Ayim is a born teacher, more effective than any with whom I have studied.

"Akach," I declare, swatting at a fly.

"Excellent pronunciation, Lope!"

I'm not sure what lightens my heart more, the praise or his smile. I use humor to avoid that dilemma.

"Indeed. I've already learned four languages. A fifth shouldn't be so hard."

He smirks. "I guess I can't fault your arrogance. I'm the same. And why should we diminish or hide our gifts? It's not what Chin wants from us."

"That name. *Children of Chin. Cries of Chin.* What is Chin?" I ask.

Ayim narrows his eyes in contemplation. "Literally? *Little one.* But that's what we call our . . . patron god, I suppose is the best phrase. The part of the universe that guides and protects people like us."

I almost ask whether "like us" means Maya . . . or something else. But then comes a frantic rustling in the forest ahead of us, and a mud-smeared child bursts from the tree line, falling flat on their face in the middle of our path.

Leaving me to stand awkwardly on my own, Ayim dashes to the child's side, speaking soothingly in Itzat'an. Though the Native folk of this land express their genders differently,

I deduce from the tattered wipil blouse and hairstyle that the child is a girl of perhaps eight summers.

Ayim does what he can to console the girl, who is weeping with fear, pointing back the way she came. As they converse, I make out the words *kimil* (death), *Loltun* (where the Children of Chin are gathered), and *way balum* (which I think means were-tiger).

After cleaning the girl up and giving her some food from his supplies, Ayim draws a map in the dirt and makes gestures with his hands as he explains what I presume is the path to his people. He mentions uy-awatob Chin, the Cries of Chin. The girl nods and looks at me. Ayim makes reassuring noises.

Then, to my astonishment, the child pulls her tattered blouse over her head and *transforms into a tiger cub*! With a soft, satisfied growl, she bounds off into the forest.

Returning to my side, Ayim explains.

"That was Kanhal. Her village was destroyed, but she managed to escape. Still, she's been pursued ever since by el Mozo's men. I told her to stop thinking like a human child—the feline within will be welcome among the Children of Chin."

"Why not have her travel with us?" I ask. "She's so young."

"And fast. Do you want to catch up with her? Jelebnen. Change."

I scoff, looking away.

"That's what I assumed. So she's taking a message, letting my people know we're on our way. Letting your *brother know*."

I imagine our encounter in a flashing series of bloody images.

"Don't worry. Kanhal will be safe. And if she can hear the four Cries, she can accompany us when we leave these hills."

The news comes as a shock. "Leave?"

"The Spanish won't let us live, Lope. You know it well."

Suddenly weary of thoughts of violence, I change the subject.

"What are these Cries of Chin you keep mentioning? Commandments of your god?"

With an impish smile that crinkles his eyes, Ayim takes my weight again.

"His words," the boy's voice rasps near my ear, "which only the chosen can hear. Sometimes from afar. They drew your brother to these shores. And you followed in his wake."

We travel until sunset, keeping the far-off crack of musket fire at our backs. Though I've seen maps of el Mozo's planned march along the coast, the flight of Kanhal and encroaching sounds of battle suggest that the conquistador has changed plans and is headed eastward.

Toward us.

When twilight and exhaustion make more travel impossible, Ayim leads me to a small cave partly hidden by bushes. He checks my injuries, taking care not to cause me pain as he repacks my wound.

I give voice to my roiling emotions. "I admire the aid you give your people. That girl—she might've died if you had not helped. But . . . encouraging her to embrace shape-shifting?"

"Don't you feel it?" he asks as he finds a spot to sleep a few feet away.

"What?"

"The yearning. Your *way,* your animal soul. Longing to be set free."

"I . . . I learned long ago to ignore the whisperings of my heart and live according to the will of God." There's no need to be this honest. But Ayim has hidden nothing from me, so it feels only right that I explain myself.

"How do you know the will of your god? From the Bible? Priests? Are you certain they contain more truth than your own heart? That the voice deep within, the one that feels *so right,* is actually wicked?"

I have no answer. It is a dilemma that I have tried to pretend doesn't exist.

"Good night, Ayim," I say instead, turning toward the bare rock.

There is silence for a moment. Then Ayim whispers.

"Chin speaks within the heart. His voice is your voice, speaking what you know to be true. What a tragedy to ignore him."

Even though I do not respond, even though I refuse to look into the hypnotic depths of those black eyes, his smell has already penetrated my clothing, my skin, my hair. His gentle voice is echoing in my mind. With each new act of wise kindness, he makes it impossible for me to dismiss him as an immoral pagan.

As I doze off, I swear I can hear the distant howling of a wolf.

Inside me.

We are awakened by the sound of explosions. *That bastard.* Against his commanders' advice, el Mozo has brought cannons ashore and had horses drag them through this tropical hellscape so he can level Maya villages.

"We need to get moving," Ayim says. "Your refusal to transform means we've left a long and very visible trail for the Spaniards to track."

He isn't wrong, so I lean on him in silence as we exit the cave.

The going is especially hard today. Ayim tries to keep to riverbeds and valleys, but there is much climbing and descending of hills. My head and leg ache fiercely by midmorning.

"Tell me more about yourself," Ayim suggests. "It will occupy your mind."

I hesitate. But Ayim knows so much already, and the thought of getting some of this weight off my soul compels me to speak.

"My family is from the valley of Gorriti," I explain. "We've managed a farm there for centuries. Yet I was . . . different from other boys in the area, from my own family. Language and letters drew me in. Knowledge, that's what I wanted. Like you, Ayim. I persuaded my parents to let me visit a monastery where monks would help me decide whether to become a postulant."

Ayim helps me over a rocky streamed. "A priest. I understand that call."

"My brother answered another one. His animal soul, I guess you'd say. And he took up with a sodality of gizotsoak. Werewolves, living in our region, holding strange rituals in the caves of Mount Ulizar."

Ayim gives a soft gasp. "Lope. I need to make something clear. Loltun, the place I'm taking you—it's a refuge for wayob. Shape-shifters."

Part of me had assumed as much, but I am still irritated at the revelation.

"I pray your shape-shifting friends aren't as bloodthirsty as Mikel's. Have you seen a sheep? In Castilla, groups herd sheep along special paths protected by royal decree and traveling judges who have mountain knights under their command to stop marauders from stealing their flocks. Foolishly, the gizotso group that turned my brother decided to cross into Castilla and feed on just such sheep."

Ayim sucks in air. "The knights retaliated."

"They shot and killed several werewolves, then pursued the others back into Gorriti. The gizotsoak dispersed, hid, but the judge and his knights began a vicious investigation. They . . ."

My voice cracks. I swallow a sob. The rest is so hard. I fear my heart will sunder.

Ayim puts his arm around my shoulder, leans his temple against my chin. "I . . . I am your friend, Lope. Speak the thing to me."

"I was at the monastery. I could do nothing to protect my parents. Other monsters revealed Mikel's name, and the knights dragged my mother and father into town. Tortured them. My uncle stopped me as I was entering the valley. Warned me not to go into town."

"So you went to the mountain to find your brother."

I'm awed at Ayim's intuitive empathy, as if heaven has crafted a companion for me.

"Of course I did. But Mikel found me first. I demanded he return to receive punishment in our parents' stead. He countered with another offer: to accompany him to New Spain, where we could start over. He felt a call, he claimed. A tugging at his soul, urging him west across the sea. I was enraged. How could he just abandon Mother and Father to that slow death? I struck him once. Twice. Thrice. And in that moment, he snarled and became a wolf, slashing my thigh with his claws."

I look down. The tips of four ragged red lines extend beyond the top of the poultice. I can see the infection is getting worse.

"I hobbled home. Changed. And then went to town to beg for my parents' release." A deep, shuddering breath. "They had been executed. I wasn't arrested, as I had been away and the village priest and mayor both vouched for my Christian character. The knights' mastiffs picked up Mikel's scent, and soon they were off. I waited for news, but they never caught him. So I sold the family farm and followed my brother."

We're stopped beside a small sinkhole. Ayim shoots me a sidewise glance. "Must you kill him?"

Tears stream down my cheeks.

"How can I not?"

We end our travel early because of my exhaustion, taking refuge in another shallow cave in one of the broken hills around us. I have a raging fever. Ayim boils some roots and leaves, and the tea eases the worst of the pain. Gradually, I slip into a deep sleep.

In the dream, my paws pad soft but firm upon the crumbling slopes as I circle the cave in the starlight, which seems to penetrate my very bones. All of a sudden, I yearn to run. My four legs now pound against the earth, claws gripping at stone and loam.

The joy is overwhelming. I skid to a stop, tilt my head back, and cry my allegiance to Mother Moon, whose face rises full and round above me.

Then I scent a rabbit, and my jaws slaver with greedy appetite. I give chase.

The rending of that sweet flesh is my most honest act in years.

I'm awakened by the feeling of something being draped over my hips. Ayim stands over me, a mischievous look on his face.

"It took you long enough."

"To what, rouse myself from sleep?"

"No. To transform. Look at yourself."

I am completely naked, save for the shredded remains of my shirt, which Ayim has used to give me a little modesty.

And my leg is healed. Not just healed. New. No scars, neither from claws nor arrow.

"How . . . ?" My voice trails off. I can't quite credit my eyes.

"It happens sometimes. A waypek refuses to heed the voice of their animal soul, so it waits until the human part is weak or asleep and then takes over. Unfortunately, it didn't remove your clothes first. I watched the wolf rush out into the night, but I fell asleep before you returned. I've just awakened to find you quite naked."

I feel myself blush. I wonder how long he stood staring before covering me.

Part of me wishes the sight was not unpleasant for him.

But that twisted side of me I push away to deal with my other glaring defect.

I'm a damned gizotso.

Like Mikel.

Ayim takes a length of cotton from the leather satchel he wears strapped across his chest. He proceeds to demonstrate how to tie a loincloth.

"I would say you look like one of us now . . ." He laughs as I adjust the strange garment. "But it's clearly not true. You're almost as furry as your wolf form."

"Keep at your jesting," I say, giving him a gentle shove. "But you'll soon discover how much stamina a Basque farm boy can muster. Let's get moving. I'd like to meet my brother today if we can manage."

We move fast, sometimes at a flat-out run, each of us trying to outdo the other, laughing when we stumble or flag.

"You've seen my animal form," I say as we splash our way over a series of muddy puddles, "but I've never witnessed yours."

"Of course you have, Lope. When I first saved you."

I beetle my brow. "The . . . feathered lizard? That was real? That was *you*?"

"Yes and yes." He puffs up a little with pride. "One of the rarest of animal souls."

Without warning, there's a sharp whistle. The dirt at our feet craters inward slightly, and then comes the crack of musket fire.

We spin to face our enemy. El Mozo has found us!

Montejo is the only one mounted, astride a bedraggled mare, his armor besmeared with mud and vegetation. About a quarter of his company surrounds him on foot: twenty-five men with shredded quilted uniforms, most with just pikes instead of harquebuses.

"Lope Haritzmendi! You are a deserter. Surrender yourself for court-martial." Montejo points a glittering steel sword in my friend's direction. "Pablo de la Cruz! What a pleasant surprise. I've missed you, boy."

"My name," the boy at my side cries out proudly, "is Ayim Cher. Retreat with your men now before my friend and I kill you all."

His ultimatum elicits booming laughter. But as they cackle, the soldiers tighten their circle, getting closer, muskets raised.

"Shoot the Biscayne if necessary," el Mozo commands, "but bring me the Itza lad unharmed."

The guns swivel toward me.

"Ah, you stupid bastards," Ayim mutters. And with a shrug of his shoulders, he transforms.

How to explain the majesty of his animal self? Something like a caiman but also like a bird, with gorgeous feathers of orange, blue, green, and red. Long ones pend from the arms in an approximation of wings. But tipped with powerful claws.

Ayim cocks his head at me, opening powerful jaws in what seems a smile.

Then he hurls himself at the startled Spaniards, taking running steps before launching into a rushing glide. He snaps their weapons in two. Bites through arms and legs. Some manage to fire at him, but he twists and leaps, avoiding their lead balls.

A snarling comes from deep within me. A need to join him, to fight alongside him.

But I have no notion of how voluntarily to embrace my nature.

A net is thrown over Ayim. The remaining men pin him to the ground. One of el Mozo's captains advances on me, holds his pistol to my head, forcing me to my knees.

"Be still or your Hyacinth dies." I'm too shaken by the implication to wonder which of us he's addressing. Is it that easy to perceive between us the possibility of "Greek love," as the priest called it, trying to calm my parents when they saw . . . no . . . *I refuse to remember!*

But it is too late. The memories come like an avalanche.

First Mikel's voice, as we stand on the mountain.

"Save them? *They were going to kill you for what you are, Lope!*"

Then the village priest, assuring my parents that he would take me under his wing, set me on the righteous path, help me understand God's plan.

Finally that fateful day when Jordi Bajet kissed me beneath the apple tree.

And I kissed him back.

While my father looked on in horror.

Before his big hands dragged me home.

And beat me. Over and over.

While Mikel screamed for him to stop.

"Lope."

Startled out of a vortex of emotions, I look up at my companion. Eyes like liquid emeralds stare back at me. From his powerful mandible comes one more word. "Jelebnen."

In the end, I discover transformation is as simple as just saying yes.

Yes, I am a gizotso.

Yes, I am a waypek.

Yes, I release control to my animal soul.

Yes, I will protect this boy.

Yes.

It feels like a flower bursting from my heart. My human flesh falls away, dissolving as the beast within surges forward. Spinning, I slash at the captain's arm, severing it. Then I pounce upon the nearest man holding down the net. My jaws at his throat, I rip out his jugular with a shake of my head before rushing the next soldier.

Ayim shoves the net upward, slipping free.

"Fall back!" screams el Mozo to the last dozen of his men. "Retreat!"

A few poorly aimed shots are fired, but in moments, we stand alone amid the bloody, ruined corpses of our conquerors.

The furred beast and the feathered god stare at each other for a long moment, panting. Then we take the reins again as our animal souls recede.

Ayim, burnished brown skin as beautiful as his rainbow feathers, steps closer, an unspoken question visible in his gaze.

"Yes," I mutter, bending to kiss him.

Years of ingrained guilt make the next few hours difficult. I have surrendered myself to everything I was taught to abhor. But I am happier than I have ever been. At peace. The smile Ayim gives me when our arms brush makes every other worry fade.

By midmorning we reach a heavily forested area. In its heart, hung with vines and moss, gapes a large cave with a sloping floor. To one side lounges a tiger. On the other, a large spider monkey with a thick snake twined round its neck.

Ayim speaks in Itzat'an to the creatures, who I realize are shape-shifters like us. I make out the words *Lope Haritzmendi, itz'in* (younger brother), and *waypek.*

The monkey gestures at the cave as if giving us leave to enter.

We make our way down amid slanting sunlight and roots.

Ayim takes my hand. There's an almost electric charge, then a feeling of *rightness.* As though our palms have touched a thousand times before, become worn and supple like a favorite pair of boots.

He guides me through first a vast, vaulted chamber, illuminated by sunlight streaming through the entrance. At the entrance to the next, a massive stone head stares down at us with a knowing smile.

"That's Chin. Some say he was once an arux, elevated to godhood because of his devotion to the gods, his wisdom, and his boundless love for all creatures."

"An arux?" I ask.

"What's the Spanish word . . . duende. Little folk."

I raise an eyebrow. "In Navarra we tell children stories of iratxoak, magical dwarfs. But they aren't . . . *real*, are they?"

"They seldom walk the earth nowadays, but they *do* exist. Loltun was their home for a time, before they disappeared from the world as humanity encroached. Our lore tells us that wayob, shape-shifters, are descendants of children some aruxob once had with human lovers."

After what I have experienced in the last few days, I wouldn't discount it. In fact, I begin to muse aloud. "I wonder whether the same holds true for gizotsoak. Do we have some trace of iratxoak blood in our . . ."

My voice trails off as we enter the next chamber. Its ceiling lies some one hundred feet above us. Murals adorn the walls— people and animals and gods, engaged in rituals I can only guess at. By the flickering light of torches, I see the diminutive figure of Chin again and again.

Even in the hand of the older woman standing beside what seems to be an altar or a basin, brimming with water. She must be a priestess. She grips a scepter with the form of Chin.

Ayim translates as she addresses me.

"Come, drink from the lifeblood of the earth herself, water untainted even by nature. Only the worthy. Only wayob."

Ayim makes a cupping motion with his hands and prods me forward.

I dip my palms into the cold liquid and drink deep. The water not only quenches my thirst: it penetrates my soul, nourishing the wolf that lies almost quiescent within me.

"Your way is strong," says the priestess through Ayim. "Though you almost smothered that vital part of yourself, I see it has found its mate. The choice will now be hard. Do you abandon your purpose and move toward a different destiny, or do you abandon this joy?"

Hearing someone else give voice to my dilemma is bracing. Ayim pulls me away.

"Let's find your brother. Then you can listen to your heart."

We come to a narrow tunnel. Air blows in from holes on either side and then is funneled forward with a soft moan.

In the middle of the space, his hair twisting in the wind, is Mikel. He is tanned, wearing a loincloth and a cape woven from plant fiber.

"Lope," he says, his tone hopeful, "it's so good to see you. Whatever the reason, I'm glad you came."

I lift the makila, unsheathing the silver spike with a single, harsh motion. He flinches but doesn't step away.

"For months, I dreamed of slamming this point into your heart, brother. Not because you're a gizotso. Not because you made me one, too. But because I believed you were a coward. You let our parents die and then ran here."

Kneeling, I stab the spike into the ground. I stay there for a moment, head down, as tears well up within me and dribble onto the earth.

"But the coward was me. I refused to remember. Hid my true self deep. Blamed you for our parents' death to hide from my guilt and shame. You stopped him, didn't you? Father? And you went for the priest. I wasn't ready on the mountain that day, Mikel. I couldn't hear you. But now I do. And I hear my animal soul as well, the same snarling call that pulled you from the farm all those years ago."

Mikel drops to his knees and embraces me. "Thank you, little brother. Forgive me for not doing more."

My head buried in his shoulder, I mutter, "It was enough. It brought me here."

"Welcome home," he whispers.

Ayim takes my hand again, and the three of us walk into another massive space, with sunlight slanting through where the broken hills above have cracked completely open.

Four columns of glimmering stone dominate one corner of the chamber. Around them are gathered hundreds of men, women, and children, expectant looks on their faces. A group of older adults steps forward. One of them, wearing a skirt and cape and a profusion of jade jewelry that obscures their gender, addresses me in Spanish.

"I am Hunlol." Their voice is sweet but strong. "I speak for the wayob. You come at a difficult time. As your brother tells us once happened in your homeland, our towns are being conquered one by one by the Castilians. Our code forbids us from waging war. But we wayob have an option other than bending the knee. We can simply . . . leave. Our god prepared the way. Five hundred miles of caves and tunnels stretch from Loltun to Naj Tunich in the southern mountains. And at the heart of it awaits Sas Nohkah: the silver city the aruxob once abandoned, filled with everything we need to live freely for centuries, far from oppression."

I look from Hunlol to Ayim. My heart knows what it wants. What it needs.

"Can I . . . may I go with you? Be part of your community? Learn your ways?"

Hunlol gestures at the four columns. "These are the Cries of Chin. If you can hear all four and respond, then you are one of us and go where we go."

A man steps up to one column and strikes it with a stone hammer. It resonates with a loud, high-pitched sound. In its echoes I hear a word and grasp its meaning by instinct.

"K'uh!" I shout. "The Divine!"

A woman strikes another column. The sound is quieter, lower-pitched.

"Mak!" I answer. "The Human!"

Mikel approaches from behind. He nods at me before leveling his blow. The third column seems to make no sound, but my wolf ears perceive it.

"Way!" I hurry to repeat. "The Animal!"

To my surprise, Ayim strikes the fourth column. Its sound is indescribable. It fills my being like the sight of Ayim's smile.

"Yaamil," I gasp. "The Beloved."

The vast chamber slowly falls silent. For a moment, nausea twists my stomach. Where shall I go if I'm rejected?

Then Hunlol speaks, tears on their cheeks. "Welcome, Lope, twice-blessed. We take you in our arms, body, beast, and soul. We are your home."

"Thank you, thank you, thank you," I babble, weeping with joyful relief.

At last.

Home.

Our sodality makes its way through eight miles of tunnels, to what seems to be the last chamber: narrow, low-ceilinged, simple. At the far end is an ancient rock painting of Chin.

As Hunlol takes up position in front of the image, I whisper to Ayim, "Why twice-blessed? What did they mean?"

The boy pulls me close and kisses me. Though we are surrounded by hundreds of people, I feel no shame. Many stand holding hands with others of their own gender. No one appears to care.

"Chin is not just the god of shape-shifters. He protects love between two boys. Between two girls. And every other startling, beautiful iteration of sacred desire. To be a waypek and also the beloved of another boy? It means Chin has blessed you twice."

I pull him close, savoring the warmth of his flesh against mine.

"I . . . I love you, Ayim Cher."

He kisses the hollow of my shoulder.

"And I love you, Lope Haritzmendi. Now hush. Our future awaits just beyond this wall, if Hunlol can but concentrate enough to open the gate."

Our leader places their hands on either side of the painting.

Then they whisper a single word.

"Halk'abil."

Freedom.

MONSTER REFLECTION

When I was a boy, my favorite monsters were the duendes my uncles, aunts, and grandparents warned me about. They were elvish, gnomish creatures . . . the original dueños de la casa (owners of the house, hence the Spanish name). They lived under the floor or in the walls. As long as you left a little food out each night when you went to bed, they were content. But in the absence of that offering, they would start causing mischief: knocking over lamps, stealing socks, scratching at walls, groaning in spooky voices, etc. If the disrespect continued, they might even take the worst-behaved child of the family away. According to my grandmother, that was how they made more goblin-kind: transforming human kids into duendes. I thought that sounded wonderful. What a lovely job, scaring children and getting free food! So I behaved as badly as I could. But I was never taken, so now I have to content myself with being a little imp on my own.

THE FATAL SONG OF ATTRACTION

BY BRITTANY JOHNSON

Y ou'd think that because I live in the ocean, my eyes wouldn't burn from the salt as tears pour down my face. Yet here I am with bloodshot scleras and a stuffy nose for the third night in a row.

I shouldn't be able to cry anymore, but it's all I've done since I turned "of age." Tears, solitude, and confusion haunt my entire existence, and there's only so long I can hold out hope that things will change one day. As a young gup, I used to look into sea-glass mirrors, willing *someday* to be today, but whoever oversees our creation has decided to ignore my prayers, cursing me to be the worst possible thing a young siren can be—different.

Waves crash against pink sand twinkling beneath a full moon. I unclench my jaw and lower my shoulders in an attempt to relax. Usually, watching the tide roll in calms me, but tonight, it mocks me with its beautiful crests and dangerous troughs. The waves never once fail to abide by their nature, unlike me. This stretch of rocky, deserted beach is supposed to be my safe space away from my pod, where I don't have to worry about how I measure up to the other sirens who have had their "first time."

It should have happened by now. My parents prepped me with the most awkward of talks the moment my brain was developed enough to understand the birds and the stingrays. They told me about the weird things that will happen to me physically—how carnal the urge will be and how it will feel as if my entire body, from scalp to fin, is set aflame. My heartbeat will quicken, my mouth will water, and all my senses will heighten in a clear indication of my maturity. They said that very few feelings compare with the clarity that comes after it's over, and they warned me about the dangers of a one-track mind, how easily I could be consumed by thoughts of it. That one taste will make me nearly insatiable, but that I shouldn't be ashamed, because without that instinct, our species would cease to exist. It's a rite of passage that secures our place at the top of the food chain, but any sign of weakness could threaten our entire race.

That's why the elders watch me warily, because it *hasn't* happened to me yet.

I haven't transformed to kill my first human.

Right before a siren's first kill, our entire body morphs into something humans could never dream of—and that they should hope never to see. Our blunt nails turn into sharp talons that can shear flesh clean off the bone. Our normally bright white scleras turn black with bloodlust, eclipsing our eyes. We become horrifyingly unrecognizable, only to turn back into the beautiful and seemingly docile creatures that sailors sing sea chanteys about. We're dazzling nightmares, with songs sweeter than summer air, who lure even the brightest of people to their watery graves.

At least, we're supposed to be. I'm not, and that's what we can't figure out.

My parents questioned if my hormones were imbalanced, but after a few leech blood tests, our practitioners determined nothing was physically wrong. One of my older sisters says it's my mindset, while my younger sisters argue that I'm being "too picky." That phrase makes my stomach churn. I never know if I want to swim away to cry, like I did tonight, or curse them out. Everyone keeps blaming me, but why would I choose to delay this pivotal moment, something that comes so naturally to our kind?

No one chooses to feel this way—broken.

A deep sigh rushes out of me as I stare up at the moon. I like it here. It's quiet on the rocky outcropping, and I never have to worry about being discovered. The closest town is a few miles away on a separate island. I've never seen footprints along the shore or any other sign of human life here, and you can always tell when they've been around from their trail of destruction.

On my way here tonight, I saw one of them out on the water being too damn loud for no damn reason. Sometimes the downside of being an apex predator is my heightened senses, since they subjected me to his stench a mile away. When the fourth obscenity about some woman who chose not to lie with his oh-so-charming self left his lips, I swam away.

Filth, all of them. Just like what they leave in the sea and on the beaches.

A splash in the distance distracts me from my thoughts.

"Hello?"

Startled, I turn toward the voice to see a dark brown body bobbing in the water. A boy out this late and so far from the mainland? I shift my weight a little on the rock I'm perched on, making sure my feathery purple tail is obscured. It's too dark for him to recognize what I am from this distance. From the waist up, we appear human. Surreally gorgeous, but human, nonetheless. Our looks are key to luring sailors to their death, but I can't decide if it'll work for or against me right now. If he's drawn in by my beauty, he'll never leave.

I run my tongue over my teeth, willing them to sharpen and for those instincts to kick in. This is such an easy opportunity; a guppy could take this boy down. But a low growl rumbles out of my chest in frustration as my body refuses to change. While I could just pull him down and drown him, it wouldn't be the same. I need this change to happen.

He flinches, raising his hands quickly. "Hey, I'm sorry. I'm not here to hurt you."

"You should leave if you know what's good for you. It's not safe out here," I warn, hoping I'll be the reason he's in harm's way. I adjust myself away from him slightly, still hiding my long tail from his sight.

As I move, his eyes flick down quickly before meeting mine again. His eyebrows raise in recognition. He almost looks excited. Damn it. They can't know we exist. It puts all of us in danger. The fact that we are no more than a folktale that drunken seamen tell to nonbelievers keeps us safe and gives us an offensive edge. One slipup here could mean the end for sirens.

I want to transform, but that doesn't seem to be happening. If I drown him, I can bring the body back to my family for dinner. They'll know I didn't change, but it's a kill regardless. That should count for something.

It's decided. This boy has to die.

My intentions must be apparent in my body language because he jolts back.

"Stop! I'm not human, and I know you aren't, either. Look . . ."

As he leans back, something bright shines through the water before breaking the surface. A seven-foot tail rises up and flicks me with seawater.

Tension leaves my chest as I blow him a raspberry. I shouldn't be this disappointed, but maybe it's a blessing in disguise.

"Great. Now go away."

"Oh, I'm sorry," he says, shoulders drooping forward.

I give him a once-over and realize he must not be from around here. Sirens have anatomical variations from pod to pod depending on the location and environment of their home waters. Sometimes they're small differences, and other times they make us almost unrecognizable as sirens. My pod is known for having bright colorations, much like the fish in the area. Yellows, reds, oranges, and blues are the most common. Yet silver-to-black scales paint his bottom half. He must not get as much sun as we do. His fins are streamlined, long, and structured, which differ from our wide and fluttery ones. He's built to cut through rough currents, unlike the calm waters that I call home.

"You're from the north?" I ask, since it's much colder up there.

"I am. I didn't mean to sneak up on you. I thought you'd see me coming."

"If you're from up north, why are you down here?"

He casts his upturned brown eyes to something only he can see, which highlights his other features. There's still some fat on his face, so he can't be much older than me. His hair is braided back down his scalp, with sea kelp tying the long rows together. A jagged and discolored scar sits on his right shoulder. His skin is almost as dark as mine, and it's undeniable how gorgeous he is.

He flexes his hands a few times, shifting his focus to everything but me as he searches for an answer to my question. "I wanted to see what else was out there. Like, the kinds of sirens, I guess."

There's something he's not telling me, but as much as my natural curiosity wants me to keep prodding, I can't bring myself to do it. His expression is too familiar. It's full of rejection and loneliness, the same emotions I see on my own face when I peer into sea glass.

"Malia." My tone is softer than it was before.

"Huh?"

"My name. Malia." I slink off the rock and into the water up to my chest, getting a little closer to him. My hair, loose and kinky, floats around me. "What's yours?"

"Keyon." He bites his lip. "So you're from around here?" he asks with a crack in his voice.

I hide my smile.

"Yeah. My pod isn't too far away. I just come here to get away and think. By myself."

"I can leave if you want," he says, guilt taking over his features. "I'm sorry; I really didn't mean to bother you. It's been a minute since I've been around someone, and when I saw you, I just felt the need to say hello."

Keyon starts to retreat when something comes over me, and my hand shoots out to him.

"Wait . . . you don't have to go."

Keyon tries to hide his grin.

I want to roll my eyes, but I don't.

The silence is loud as we tread water. I've never interacted with someone outside my own community before. Do they hunt the same way? What's their social hierarchy? What else do we share?

"Is this as weird for you as it is for me?"

I snort.

"Yes. One thousand percent."

"Okay, good. I've been alone for so long that I feel like I completely forgot how to interact with other sirens. Humans are easy. I just avoid them. But I found a few other pods along my way that weren't too friendly. They assumed something was wrong with me because I was by myself. They never once considered that . . ."

He trails off.

"They never once considered what?"

He hesitates, emotions flashing across his face as he opens his full lips only to close them again.

Swimming nearer, I take his hand, and he freezes.

"You can trust me."

I can feel the heat off him, and it makes it hard to concentrate.

"They never once considered that maybe there was something wrong with everyone else," he admits.

"What do you mean?"

"Can I be honest with you?" he asks. My heart skips a beat, my eyes flittering over his form as he stares at me intently.

"Um, sure . . . ?"

He tightens his jaw and straightens his posture. "No, I mean it, Malia. This is important, and it's partially why I was exiled. If you reject me, it's fine. I get it. But it's been a while since I was able to tell someone and—"

"Keyon. Stop."

He shuts up.

"Tell me. I'm not going anywhere. I promise."

He stares at me for a long time before his features soften.

"I can't transform. I've never killed anybody before. I can't do it."

My mouth drops open, my breath catching in my throat. It's not just me? Does he know my secret? Maybe one of my family members put him up to this. It'd be just like my older sister to be that cruel.

But then I look at him, and I know that isn't the truth. He's stiff and scared, waiting to see how I react. This is real. There are two of us with the same curse in life. Can I finally talk to someone without having to explain what it's like for me to simply *exist*?

The corners of my lips curl upward, excitement running through me. As I'm about to tell him I get it, he closes his eyes tight, shaking his head. "I shouldn't have said anything. Damn it."

My smile drops. He misread my reaction.

"No, that's not what I—"

He releases my hand and dives into the water, not giving me time to explain.

Without thinking, I plunge into the sea, giving chase.

Using a telepathic link, I screech as loudly as I can for him to stop. I can't blame him for fleeing. I know the trauma associated with being different, but he doesn't know that.

Soon my muscles burn from the energy it's taking to catch up.

In a last-ditch effort, I confess my own secret through our link. "I can't do it, either!"

I stop, doing my best to calm my heart. A jet stream of bubbles dissipates, revealing that Keyon has halted ahead of me. "I can't transform," I continue. "I've never killed. I thought there was something wrong with me. Maybe there is, but at least it's not just me. Or maybe there's nothing wrong at all, but I get it." Feeling desperate, I paddle closer to him. "Just please stay." Now that I found him, I can't lose him. Not yet.

"Are you mocking me?" Keyon squints at me, but he doesn't budge.

"No. I swear I'm not. It's why I was on the beach. I tried hunting again tonight, and I embarrassed myself in front of everyone. During the frenzy, I just floated there like this." I wiggle my fingers in the water, emphasizing my blunt nails. "That's why I didn't try to kill you at first. I figured that I'd have to drown you if you were a human, which would have been annoying but—"

"You were going to *drown me*?" Shock colors his telepathic voice.

"Before I knew you were one of us."

"That's such a sad way to die."

His nose wrinkles, which is surprisingly cute, and the tension between us evaporates.

"Sadder than being eaten?"

He stares at me for a moment before we bust out laughing together. It feels like I have jellyfish in my stomach. I can't stop myself from beaming. This light bubbly feeling dances through my chest, and I've never felt this . . . *hopeful* before.

"This explains the bad mood," he says, and snickers.

"Yeah, and this explains why you're alone."

Maybe I shouldn't have said it. I meant it in the same light-hearted tone, but he sobers up, his fading smile tinged with melancholy.

"Yeah. I don't have to explain it to you. You get it. The one thing we prepare our whole lives for is the one thing we can't do. If we can't kill, we can't eat."

Flashbacks flit through my memory of weeks spent in agonizing hunger when I was younger and first started struggling to transform. No one minds taking care of you when you're a gup because you'll be able to fend for yourself when you mature. I felt guilty asking others to pull my weight, and they didn't take kindly to me living off their remains. My parents know about my situation, so they kill for me, but I can tell that's nearing an expiration date. "And we can't live off the scraps of everyone else forever."

He nods vigorously, snapping his fingers in agreement before growing solemn.

"My parents aren't bad, but they forced me to hunt so I could grow up. Be a real *killer*." His thoughts shift into a pseudo-macho tone that doesn't fit him, and I suppress a giggle. "I left because I couldn't keep living in the shadow of their shame. I've been surviving off discarded fish carcasses from wasteful poachers. I hate that they murder a fish and never have a use for all its parts, but it's those scraps that keep me alive, even if they don't satisfy me."

"You're pretty hot for someone who has been living off fish tails and shells."

My eyes widen as soon as the words leave my mouth.

"I mean you're buff," I correct quickly, cursing myself. "Muscled. You just don't look—"

"Like I struggle to survive?" A smile teases the corner of his lips. "No, I understand what you're trying to say. It's complicated. The more humans fish, the more they waste, which means there are more pickings for me to *dine* on." His tone drips sarcasm. "I hate that we need humans to survive. I thought that because I can't transform, I wouldn't need them. But I still do. Sometimes the pods get sloppy and leave bits of flesh on the carcasses. They're so busy engorging themselves on the juiciest parts that they don't notice me scavenging below. It's pathetic." His jaw is set, a vein throbbing at his temple.

"I get it. My pod is native to this region, but we weren't always this far west. We've been all over. Having such a weak link among us"—I motion to myself—"is a liability. So many fisherfolk out there keep getting closer to us. Sure, the rest of the pod can defend themselves, but me? I'm powerless in comparison."

"And the more of them there are, the more endangered we could become. Sure, we're predators, but our strength relies on numbers and we can only feed so much."

A school of sturgeons passes by as we digest the weight of our conversation. He's right, and it's terrifying.

"I've tried adjusting to this situation, you know? Accepting the fact that I'm different." His telepathic voice wavers, breaking the silence. "It doesn't have to be a bad thing." He seems as if he's trying to convince himself, rather than me.

I never got to the point where I considered accepting what is. Acceptance equals giving up, and that would mean I really am a failure to my species, my parents, and myself. That isn't an option.

"I'm scared." The thought has burdened me for a while now. I hesitate, afraid to speak my deepest fears into existence. "My parents love me, but what if this is it? I keep hoping that it'll happen someday. I'll wake up and my body will be different, and I'll feel all those feelings everyone tells me about. We have our role in the world. We kill, eat, breed, and die. That's all there is to our lives, and half of that is unavailable to us."

Once the words start pouring out, I can't stop them.

"And sometimes, Keyon? I've felt it starting, when I'm joining my family in a hunt. But it's never enough to do the damn thing. I get the urge, and it's so confusing. I know I can, but I can't, and I don't know why. I feel so—"

"—broken."

That one word encapsulates it all. We float silently for a bit. My arms are wrapped around my body, tightly keeping whatever remains of me in place.

"I get it, y'know. But I also feel different about it. I've never started to transform, like you, but my secret runs deeper than my ability. You know how you still feel that urge? I don't, Malia." He closes the distance between us, so he's near enough that I can touch him. Part of me wants to again, but I don't dare. "When I get hungry, I want to eat, but there's nothing within me that wants to kill innocent humans. Theoretically, I could attack the bad ones who ruin the coral reefs or poach fish they have no intention of eating, but I've never had a chance to go after them." He subconsciously rolls his scarred shoulder.

"How did that happen?"

He chews the inside of his lip, looking down at the scar.

"One of the bad ones." He flexes his hands a few times, sighing bubbles through his nose. "I was young and on my own. I wasn't supposed to be, but my pod was huge, and I often felt out of place and unnoticed, so I'd use the chance to explore. I saw a shadow on the surface and wanted to know what it was. When I got close, there was a little boy on the edge of a boat. He looked like me, and while I knew humans were food, he seemed so sweet."

His eyes haze over, lost in the memory.

"What happened?" I ask, though I'm afraid to know the answer. Gups are forbidden from interacting with humans because they can't defend themselves.

"It was a bigger boat, so the older ones didn't hear us for a while. We talked and laughed. I did some tricks for him, and he did this thing called a cartwheel where he ran and suspended his feet in the air for a second before landing on both of them. It was so cool. I was out too long, and I didn't want them to come looking for me and maybe eat this kid, so I had to leave. I found him again the next time they were out, and we played together again. It happened a few more times, until I went up to say hello to my friend one night. The vessel was a lot smaller this time, which I thought was weird, but humans are weird, so I brushed it off. My friend looked scared that night. I asked him what was wrong, and he told me to come closer. When I did, the older ones jumped out and grabbed me. I was slippery, but they still managed to slice me before I escaped. My friend helped them almost murder me."

My fingers twitch, wanting to reach out and hold him, but I refrain.

"Humans like them deserve the worst fate possible, Malia."

I start to respond, but a muted splash behind me steals our attention.

"What's that?" His head snaps toward the disruption.

"I don't know. Come on."

Curving my back, I swim in the direction of the commotion. Above us, a large shadow darkens the water as different types of rubbish steadily sink to the bottom. Metal cans and shards of glass. Thin, shiny plastic that a fish will surely mistake as food and the type with rings that I've rescued far too many turtles and dolphins from. Sure, dolphins are bullies, but no sea creature deserves to choke because of humans.

"I hate them," Keyon growls. "We kill to survive, but they kill because they don't care. There's no purpose for them. They're the true monsters."

"This is why I wish I could transform. People like this need to know what it's like to fear for their lives. I'd tip their boat, but that'd just pollute the water more."

"Well, you were willing to drown me." Keyon cuts his eyes to me, and I turn to face him. Is he suggesting what I think he is?

"Is he 'bad' enough for you to have no sympathy?"

Adrenaline starts coursing through my veins. All it takes is one devious look from him for me to swim up to the surface. I may not be able to transform, but that doesn't mean I still can't do some damage. I've watched my pod do this part a thousand times. I can do it and do it damn well.

As silently as possible, I break the ocean's surface.

At first, the human isn't recognizable, but the slurred, obnoxious crooning gives him away. It's the same sailor from earlier tonight, wreaking havoc everywhere he goes.

He stands next to a giant pile of garbage, muttering to himself. As I get a closer look, he seems even more pathetic. His dinghy is all rusted over and banged up on the sides. Barnacles and other sea life cling to the bottom of the boat, making their own little ecosystem.

I knew they didn't care about our environment. I guess they don't care about theirs, either.

"That prude broad . . ." He takes a swig from a bottle and shakes his head. "Says she didn't want me, but I know better. She wanted all of this." He thrusts his hips before taking another long drink. "All she had to do was enjoy it, but no. She makes me the bad guy when I just gave her a little affection." He huffs, shuffling through some garbage near his feet and throwing it overboard. Every word that comes out of his mouth makes my blood run hotter. His death can't come soon enough.

Raising myself up, I make my voice as melodic as possible. "I like your boat."

The man turns around so quickly he almost falls overboard. If he had, it would have taken the fun out of this for us.

I tilt my head to the side, peering up at him through my eyelashes.

His eyes widen, and his mouth drops.

"Are you one of those mermaids?" he stammers.

I flip my tail a little behind me for added effect. You could have heard his gasp from miles away.

"A mermaid? What's that?" I turn up the charm, batting my eyelashes and pouting my full brown-and-pink lips. His eyes watch my every movement, but his gaze lands on my lips.

Hook.

"You know, those beautiful creatures that bless you with money and riches and—"

"You think I'm beautiful? I'm blushing." I slink toward his boat. Humans are so small and fragile. One small slip and they're done for, and yet here he is, overconfident and overzealous, one rogue wave away from becoming orca food.

"Are you going to bless me?" he asks, and grabs his crotch. "I'd love to have a pretty young thing like you all to myself."

Pervert. If I didn't already want to kill him, that would have done it. I won the shitty human lottery with this one.

"Only if you do me a favor." I pause. "Listen to my song?"

He nods his head aggressively. "Anything for you. Anything."

Line.

Major and minor chords dance off my tongue. Instantly, he's in a trance, his mouth agape. Ever so slowly, I swim closer to him until his putrid breath fans my face. I reach up from the water to cup his cheeks, and he doesn't waste time in lowering his face down to mine for a kiss.

If I could transform, this is when it would happen.

I hesitate a millisecond. Nothing changes.

"What's taking so long?" he asks, making little smoochy sounds that turn my stomach. The final straw is when he lurches forward to steal the kiss instead. That's it.

Sinker.

I pull him underneath the surface, drowning any scream he might let out.

Keyon is right behind him.

The sailor struggles, thrashing about in the water, but he's no match for the two of us. We could hold him down here. He would be dead within moments, but that would be too kind.

"Not yet," I tell Keyon telepathically. He looks at me in confusion but doesn't argue.

As the man begins to lose consciousness, I bring him back to the surface, telling Keyon to follow me. I don't reduce my speed for the human, and it's clear his body can't handle the force of the waves against him. His pasty pale skin is red and raw. Good. This is only the beginning.

In a few moments, we reach the shallow water on the same stretch of beach as before.

"What are you doing?" Keyon asks out loud.

"Playing with our food the same way he toys with the lives of sea creatures."

Keyon nods once and moves to the other side of the now sputtering human, though he looks hesitant, unsure.

"Having second thoughts?" I ask him.

"He's hurting other creatures."

"And yet . . ." I trail off. If he can't do this, I won't judge him. I don't want to be like everyone else. "Don't do something that'll make it hard to sleep at night."

He looks at me over the man's head, with an expression equal parts grateful and shocked.

Eventually, though, his face settles.

"I'm good," he says finally, his words quiet yet firm.

While I would have let him change his mind, I'm happy he hasn't. Instead, he's helping me serve justice to this vile man. So many other sirens would have just killed him for food. They wouldn't have cared whether he was good or bad. But Keyon not only gets it, he gets *me*. He never questioned my anger. He listened to me. He's different, and I feel more connected to him than anyone else I've ever met.

While I'm deep in thought, the man glares up at us, eyes inflamed from salt water.

"You're monsters," he spits, his voice harsh from nearly drowning.

I stiffen, barely containing my rage. "Excuse me?"

"You're no sea angel." He coughs raggedly, then adds, "You're devils, dragging us to the fiery pits of Hell. Only Satan himself could conjure such evil creatures."

"We're demonic?" Keyon howls. "Do you not realize what your kind does? Our friends and family are poisoned at your hands, and you have the gall to say we're the monsters?"

Keyon picks him up by his hair, lifting him to his face.

"It's survival of the fittest," the man croaks. "You don't own the seas. You're beasts who prey on those brave enough to sail them. It's pathetic."

He spits in Keyon's face.

All at once, an uncharacteristic roar comes from my friend. Whatever hesitancy he had about killing is forgotten as he strikes him mercilessly. Although it's ruthless and vicious, there's something in Keyon's expression that belies that.

Something that looks an awful lot like pain.

I know very little about Keyon, but I know that he values all life. This heinous human is an example of everything he stands against. He's not being violent for selfish reasons, nor is it for survival or revenge. He's seeking justice for those who will never be able to find it.

That jellyfish feeling in my belly comes back tenfold, but something isn't right.

Something feels different.

My gums tingle. My hands tremble. Slowly, sharp claws extend from my fingertips as rows of serrated teeth emerge in my mouth. It doesn't hurt. It's uncomfortable, but not painful. My spine tenses up vertebra by vertebra; my thoughts race to make sense of the only possible explanation of what could be happening to me.

I'm finally transforming.

The world spins, overwhelming me. I shut my eyes to block out the onslaught of new sensations, only to peek through my lids to find that my vision has completely warped. Instead of vibrant colors, I see shapeless figures of gray and blue. One figure—no, a siren—is directly before me. It's Keyon, standing out as a bright blue blob. Disoriented, I squeeze my lids closed again. Everything feels too intense. Panic swells in my chest from the sensory overload, until the sweetest of aromas fills my nostrils.

My eyes snap open one more time, zeroing in on a bright red form in the sand below Keyon. The sailor's blood smells tantalizing. It wafts around me, calling to me like a lighthouse. My entire being is drawn to it. Everything shifts into overdrive. I can't stop myself. Giving in to the hunger, I let instinct engulf me and rip him limb from limb.

It's over in a flash—or so it feels. My mind is fuzzy. Did I black out?

"Malia? Malia!"

Hands are on my shoulders. Someone is shaking me. Keyon.

I let out a sharp gasp and look at him. He's not blue anymore. I can see and hear normally again.

"Are you okay?" he asks.

"Uh, yeah. I think so." What just happened to me? A glance downward answers that question. I'm covered in blood. It's everywhere, and the trail leads to the sailor. "I did that?" I couldn't have.

"You did. You were—" He shakes his head, unable to find the word. *"Magnificent."*

My cheeks grow hot.

"We need to move what's left of his body before the blood attracts other predators." I avoid his gaze, dragging the body with me. "I can't guarantee that I'll be able to do that again."

He hums in agreement.

When the remains are disposed of, Keyon and I dive down to the ocean floor and settle at the front of a coral garden. The sun has risen over the waves far above us, making the peach, gold, copper, and bronze tones in the reef shimmer in the early morning light. The coral doesn't look the way it did before all the humans' pollution, but it's still a sight to see.

It's Keyon who finally breaks the silence.

"So, what changed?" he asks.

"I've been trying to figure that out myself," I say, unsure. I've been around bloodied bodies before. What makes this time any different?

"Maybe it was the motive?" he says, leaning back on his forearms and exposing his well-muscled chest. "This jerk was ruining our home, so you felt extra protective?"

I need to stop ogling him before he notices. He's attractive; I've thought that all night. But there's something else about him. Something I can't put my finger on.

"Perhaps," I respond half-heartedly. "Who knows, really?"

I try to come off as aloof, so my big dopey goldfish eyes won't give away how I feel about him. He's passionate and cares for those around him. He's proof that there's so much more to sirenhood than just murdering and moving on. All of this became apparent during our "hunt," and it's still making my heart jump in my chest.

"Before you transformed, what was going through your mind?"

"You," I say quickly, before I lose my nerve. "I was thinking about you."

"Me? What about me?"

I hesitate. Do I tell him the truth? He's been nothing but honest with me all night. Will he leave if I tell him how I feel? I don't even know if I feel anything for certain. I just know that he was occupying every aspect of my brain tonight.

"I was thinking about you and me," I say, averting my gaze. "I've always felt misunderstood. Every day for years, I've been reminded of everything I'm not. But you challenged that. Within an hour of knowing each other, you somehow made me feel more seen and heard than anyone ever has."

"Do you mean that?" he asks softly.

I dip my chin and nod, looking everywhere but at him. After a few moments, he steals my full attention by gently cupping my cheeks and lowering his lips on mine.

I've never kissed someone before. We're taught to as a way of luring people in, but it's only a means to an end. Sirens ascribe nothing to it, but this is something else—it's pure and exhilarating, and it makes me hungry in ways I didn't know I could be.

We rest our heads against each other, panting in time and confused by what just happened.

"Maybe that was the key. You needed to feel something for it to work." His soft voice fills my head so sweetly.

"Is that possible?" I've never heard of a siren needing emotional intimacy to do what so many of us consider "natural."

"I guess so." He brushes a kiss on my forehead, but then his face shifts from relaxed to pensive.

"What's wrong?"

"Nothing to do with you. It's just that I really don't think killing is for me. I thought that maybe if the prey was evil, I'd be able to do it, but the whole thing still makes me feel slimy."

I wrap my arms around him, awkwardly at first, but after a moment, we both settle into the embrace.

"What will you do about food?"

"I don't know, but I'll figure it out." He leans into me. "Do you remember when you said half of our existence is transforming, killing, and then we die?"

I hum a yes that rumbles against his back.

"What if there's more to life we never thought of? No one knew that sirens like us existed, but we're different, so there must be others like us. Right?"

"I'm following . . ."

"That means they've found a way to survive. Emotional connection made you shift forms. We didn't know that was possible. Maybe there are other ways to survive—no, *thrive*—yet to be discovered. What else don't we know?"

I never thought of it like that.

"I don't like killing. It's not for me, even with what is a very real emotional connection. Do you think I'm broken?" He turns to me, his face serious.

"Not at all. You're the least broken siren I know."

"I feel the same way about you, so how much else is there for us to discover about the world and ourselves? There's nothing wrong with us. There never has been."

I repeat that last part to myself. There's nothing wrong with me. There never has been.

I'm not the problem. It's everyone else's expectations of me that is.

The sun is completely up now, but we have no reason to move. It's a new day, one where I don't have to be defined by what my body does or doesn't do. Sure, I may not be wired the same as everyone else, but that isn't a bad thing.

I'm different, but I'm *not* broken, and that's what matters.

MONSTER REFLECTION

When I was younger, I actually wasn't a huge fan of monsters, because I was a scaredy-cat. I resorted to happy little musicals about princesses who dared to dream impossible dreams. It wasn't until I was a little older that I fell in love with vampires, especially the melodramatic ones that we'd find on the hit TV show *The Originals*. Klaus Mikaelson was a vampire-werewolf hybrid that stole my heart very early on in *The Vampire Diaries*. He showed that even the scariest of monsters is still human on some level—looking for true unconditional love.

I believe love to be the most powerful entity in the world, and seeing it paired with a homicidal hybrid with severe daddy issues always left me with complicated mixed feelings. I was furious with him but couldn't help but empathize with him. He was a nuanced monster with a lot of heart and a high body count, and that's exactly what sealed the deal for me.

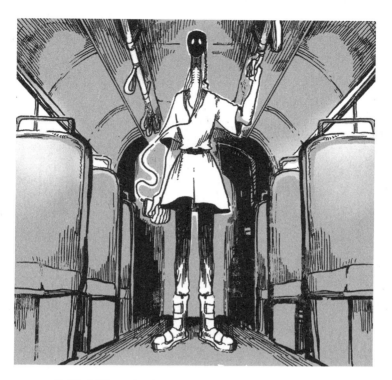

THE COLOR OF SKY
ON EARTH

BY ROB COSTELLO

oon wanted to know once why gay guys like house music so much, and so I told him it was on account of our hypothalamus. It was the most scientific-sounding reason I could come up with. It's this little gland in the brain, and some professor in Sweden did a study showing that it's supposedly bigger in gay dudes. So I told Hoon that's why we can't resist righteous house divas or throbbing beats, why we're so artistic and good at decorating, wear bright colors and expensive shoes, sip wine instead of beer, and prefer dick. Or whatever. It's all just stupid stereotypes anyway, right?

Except the liking dick part, obviously.

I mean, I don't even wear expensive shoes or decorate, so I guess I'm an outlier. But what else was I supposed to tell him? Hoon expects me to be the resident expert on all things queer, and he always needs to have reasons for everything. With Hoon, stuff can't ever *just be*, you know? I think it's because his dad was a scientist who believed in better living through chemistry. When Hoon was a kid, his dad would give him these little lessons about why grass was green or feet smelled or why drinking milk always made Hoon want to puke, and even though his dad is long gone now, I suppose he took those lessons to heart.

I'm not complaining, mind you. His need to understand why stuff is the way it is means that he excels at figuring out the rules of everything on Proteus. Like, why the sky is yellow there instead of blue, or why the Proteans have gills on their necks even though they breathe air through lungs like we do. He did serious time researching in the library and online to figure it all out. I don't even question him anymore when he tries to explain what the drag coefficient would be in an atmosphere of sulfur dioxide, or why the higher radiation levels in the binary Protean star system mean that the Proteans have thicker skin and more eyelids than humans do.

I just draw whatever he tells me to and leave it at that.

He's tenacious that way. Pure intellectual tenacity. It's hard to keep up with him sometimes, which is why I pulled that hypothalamus thing out of my ass. I had to say something, right? Even if it was kind of stupid. Actually, I do and say a lot of stupid things because of Hoon, but that's just the way it is when you're in love with your sort-of-straight best friend.

Don't judge me, okay?

"¿Qué hora es?"

I yank out my earbud and stare into the face of the weird old Latino dude who's just poked me in the shoulder from across the aisle. Since I wasn't planning to chat up random strangers on this bus, it takes a minute to recover from the rude interruption of JJ Royal's Masspool Mamma Edit of Miss Pepper MaShay's timeless classic "Does Your Mamma Know?" This guy's got a scraggly gray beard and smiling brown eyes. He's wearing a wool jacket and dusty chinos, despite it being hotter than the surface of Venus outside. He's also clutching a beat-up leather suitcase, so I figure he must be headed to Union Station like me.

I flash him the time on my phone and then slide over to the window seat, out of reach.

In response, he crinkles his eyes and says "Gracias," which I see rather than hear, because I've already plugged Pepper back into my ear.

People are so odd. I get this kind of crap all the time. Random strangers take it upon themselves to chat me up all friendly-like, asking me for the time, or directions, or help reading the Metro map, even when there are, like, twenty other people sitting around they could bother instead. Sometimes the really strange ones will gawp and grin at me as if they recognize me from way back. Usually it's the older men—and yes, I know how that sounds. Mom says it's because I have one of those faces people just naturally find "interesting," though what she really means is that I look marginally freakish. My skin's paler than skim milk. I've got gecko eyes that are spread too far apart. My abs are about as firm as a loaf of Wonder Bread, and my hair's already thinning and I'm only seventeen. And so, as frightening as I must sound, I guess I probably seem approachable to the weirdos of LA, who'd never in a million years dare to grin at or chat up anyone as hot as, for example, Hoon.

Anyway, this is why I can't wait until I can afford my own car. The endless parade of freaks and weirdos who take public transit in this city. Plus, it's just way too scorching to be riding the bus today. Even with the air-conditioning on full blast, I'm sweating like a drag queen's nuts in pantyhose. The lady on the news this morning said the air quality index would top 150. I wanted to go draw by the lake in Echo Park, but it's like molten lava even in the shade there, plus the sky's so thick with ozone and smog, it's turned the color of pus.

I might as well be on another planet.

Speaking of which . . .

I reach into my bag to grab my sketchbook so I can plan what I'm going to work on once I get to Union Station. I have a lot to do. Hoon wants a new set of drawings for the second-act chase scene in our graphic novel, and I need models for inspiration. He says I can't draw crowd scenes or action for shit. He says I still need to figure out how the Proteans move through space, how a Renegade like our main character, Gadriel, would actually look bursting through a crowded landing platform on the run from a troop of human invaders. He's given me pages of notes on the anatomy of the Proteans, on their unique musculature, how the lesser gravity of Proteus would expand their movements, make them quicker and more graceful than we are, yet physically weaker. How the planet's twin suns cast multiple shadows. How clouds of sulfur vapor coalesce at ground level like floating pools that the Proteans move through as easily as fish through water. He makes it all sound so exact and specific, yet his notes never give me enough useful detail to visualize what he actually wants to see on the page. He just keeps explaining things over and over, while I keep drawing, until finally, as if by osmosis, I get it right and he's satisfied. It's not an efficient process, but it's how we work together. Which is fine, I guess, because, let's face it, nobody else gives a damn about what I draw except Hoon. And besides, he's almost always right. He's got a good eye and knows what he wants to see.

The book is really coming along. We make a solid team.

I set my sketchbook on my lap so I can text him that I'm heading down to Union Station to observe the crowds, even though I know he won't answer me. Right now he's supposed to be on his way to Temecula with his mom to visit his Auntie Sook. His mom's letting him drive. It was the only way she could con him into going.

Of course, that's not the only reason he won't answer me. Last night we had this ridiculous fight while we discussed the arts and culture scene on Proteus. I kept insisting that the Proteans would totally be into dance music, but he got all serious like he always does whenever he talks about the Proteans and insisted, oh no, they wouldn't, because the atmosphere on Proteus isn't dense enough to carry sound waves like it does on Earth, and so they couldn't even hear our music, and anyway, if they could hear it, they would prefer free-form jazz or atonal classical, because their culture and religion are based on a philosophy of improbability and the incalculable randomness of existence, and so they wouldn't care for a repetitive beat at all.

He gets so weird about this stuff sometimes.

Still, I kept on pestering him, partly because I thought it would be really cool to draw a club scene or something, but mostly because I figured that if we're collaborating on this project, it's only fair I should get my way once in a while. But of course Hoon wouldn't budge—he never does—and so it wasn't long before he got so pissed off with me that he stormed downstairs to his mom's apartment.

He wouldn't even answer me this morning when I texted to apologize.

You're right: Proteans do not listen to EDM, okay?

I hit Send on my latest olive branch just as I feel someone tug on my shirtsleeve and turn to see the old dude grinning over my shoulder and pointing to the sketchbook in my lap.

OMG. Why can't this guy leave me the hell alone?

I don't say anything at first, but I guess my expression must be, like, *What the hell do you want?* because he points to my sketchbook again, pats his chest, and then plops back down into his own seat and reaches between his legs to unzip his leather suitcase. When he slides out a large cardboard portfolio, I start to get an idea of what he wants.

Like I'm supposed to care that he's an artist, too?

But okay, maybe I am a little curious, so I don't turn away or blow him off. Pepper is still kicking ass in my ears as he unwraps a little black string wound tightly around a black cardboard button that holds his portfolio together. He gingerly lifts the cover to reveal a sheaf of pages inside, and I slide back to the aisle seat to peer at the image on top of the stack.

It's a pastel of the Virgin Mary.

Duh. Of course it is.

Only, it's pretty good. He's set her floating above a soft, pearly cloud, dressed in a flowing robe of sky blue and a silver crown speckled with brightly colored dots that I suppose are meant to be jewels. She's very pale and lovely and gazes up at the upper left corner of the page, where a golden shaft of light shines down from just beyond the edge of the paper.

I guess that's supposed to be God?

The old dude looks at me for approval, and I nod and throw him a thumbs-up. It's not to my taste, but it's well done, and besides, who am I to dis another guy's art? He peels back the page with the Virgin Mary and flips through the remaining stack of pastels. There are more religious images, plus some sketches of kids playing, and a few landscapes of what looks like Griffith Park—only, oddly enough, as if seen from above, like he was circling in a helicopter when he did them. They're all brightly colored, competent, but not particularly exciting. I'm waiting for the sales pitch, but none comes. He just beams at me with pride, and I have no choice but to smile approvingly and thank him for sharing them with me when he's finished.

"Gracias, gracias," he mouths again, still not loudly enough for me to hear over Pepper breaking it down. Then he closes the portfolio and slips it back into the suitcase.

I'm hoping that'll be the end of it, but of course it isn't, because no sooner does he finish zipping up the suitcase than he starts gesturing toward my sketchbook like he wants me to hand it over to him for his inspection.

No way. No *effing* way.

I shake my head no, but he keeps on insisting, his graphite-stained fingers outstretched and all grabby, like he thinks I'm just being shy or fishing for compliments.

Fat chance.

Finally, I have to be a prick about it, right? So I shout "No!" really loudly and slide back over to the window, my hand clutching the sketchbook, trembling.

Even Hoon doesn't get to randomly flip through my sketchbook. He sees what I want him to see and nothing else. There are drawings of things for my eyes only in here. Private stuff, you know? Drawings that would freak Hoon out if he ever saw them, let alone some pushy old Catholic dude on a Metro bus. Drawings of Gadriel and the hot human boyfriend I wish Hoon would let me give him, even though he insists Proteans have incompatible sex organs and would never fall in love with a human, because love is nothing but a false emotional construct based on humanity's need for the social organization around which stable family units are built.

Sigh . . .

There are also a few drawings of, um, Hoon and me, too.

I mean, okay, it's like, sometimes I think Hoon purposefully forgets what it really means that I'm gay, even though he says he's cool with it and all, and I actually think he probably means that. Mostly, anyway. But still, he has all these rules and boundaries that he keeps in force between us, like how we can hug, sometimes, when something bad happens, like when my cat Truman got cancer or when Hoon's dad told him about the divorce. But we can't ever kiss, never, not even on the cheeks like French guys do. And though we've jerked each other off a few times, he had to keep his eyes closed for it, like he was pretending I was a girl or something, which made no sense at all with my dick in his hand. When I mentioned how weird that was, he explained how he'd read in this book that at our age, girls' hormones make them think and behave with their emotions, but boys' hormones make them think and behave with their bodies. He said that's why he lets me go down on him once in a while. It's just a body thing, right? A totally natural pent-up hormonal need, and it doesn't mean anything more than that.

Not to him, anyway.

I'm staring hard out the window now, willing this pushy old dude to leave me alone, although when the sunlight hits just right, I catch him still grinning at me in the reflection of the glass. Creeps like this one have no boundaries with me at all. Sometimes I think I should be flattered or something, like at least there are some guys in this city who can't keep their eyes off me, even if they are older than the woolly mammoths that got pulled out of the tar pits. Except that it isn't just old men, is it? Sometimes it's random girls and women that stare or smile or act as if we go way back. Actually, it's people of all races, shapes, sizes. It's been a pretty random assortment of humanity for as long as I can remember, except that the one thing they all have in common, I would say, is that they're usually as unattractive or strange-looking as me.

I notice this because in LA it requires effort *not* to be beautiful.

Take Hoon, for example. I don't think he's ever run a comb through his hair or washed his face, but he still gets out of bed each morning looking like a K-pop star in a *GQ* spread. Even Mom, as mom-like as she is, looks slamming when she fixes her hair and pulls herself together for work. I'm the outlier here, the sore thumb, the only guy I know who looks like he fell to Earth face-first from another planet, which makes me wonder sometimes, like when Hoon refuses to kiss me, if he wouldn't act a little less straight around me if I were a little better-looking.

Or maybe he's right, and it's just that hormone thing.

But why would his hormones care what I look like?

Sigh . . . This is my brain on Hoon.

Annoyingly, I'm yanked out of this particular rabbit hole when my gaze suddenly snags on the old Latino dude, now smirking at my reflection like he can read my thoughts. When I raise my eyebrows to challenge him, he just winks at me. What the hell? The whole point of being an artist is to be the one doing the looking (at Hoon, mostly). I can't stand being watched like some sad specimen. I'm about to jump up to find another seat when a passenger up front requests a stop and the bus heaves to the curb at the corner of Sunset and Innes. That's when I happen to glance outside and catch sight of this drop-dead gorgeous couple walking hand in hand into a Mexican bakery that Hoon and I like to go to all the time.

Okay, so maybe I've just got Hoon on the brain at the moment, but this couple looks an awful lot like him and this bitchy blond named Amber Sykes we know from Silver Lake.

But Hoon's on his way to Temecula with his mom, right? So I whip out my phone again to text him how weird it is that

I just saw this dude who looks exactly like him with this girl that could be Amber's supermodel twin sister going into our favorite bakery. I know he won't see the message until he gets to Auntie Sook's house, because he doesn't dare check his texts while driving with his mom in the car, but I don't want to forget to tell him about it later on, because it will make such a funny story, since he's actually the one who thinks Amber's a total stuck-up bitch.

Only we've barely even pulled back into traffic when he fires off a text at me that *Amber's not a bitch, asshole,* and it's like he's just yanked my stomach out of my belly and stomped all over it on the cold, sticky floor of the bus.

My first instinct is to pull the cord and jump the hell off this bus. But then I realize I'm frozen in place; I don't dare move, because if I did, I would end up storming into that bakery and making a total fool of myself in front of them, and then the whole world would end, and I would explode into a million tiny pieces and die, forever and ever, amen.

Finito.

My head suddenly feels like every last drop of blood inside it has rushed to my feet. I slump against the window and squeeze my eyes tight to keep them from watering.

Of course, that's precisely when the old dude decides to get up and cross the aisle to squeeze me by the shoulder, all concerned and fatherly-like.

"What the hell do you want?" I scream at him as a cold shudder passes through me.

He looks wounded for a minute as he stands tottering over me, but then he smiles again, like everything is A-okay, like he just wants to be artsy buddies or whatever. He hands me this little leather-bound book, which I take from him because I'm too stupefied to do anything else. Then he sinks back into his own seat, gesturing for me to leaf through his book as he gives me a big, yellow-stained grin.

That's when I realize we're being watched. My little outburst has drawn the attention of a couple of passengers in the front, plus the driver himself, who reminds me of Bilbo Baggins, with fat little hobbity fingers and wide hobbity eyes shooting us concerned glances in the mirror.

I feel like I should do or say something, but I'm still frozen in place. I can't believe I'm just sitting here. I can't believe Hoon lied to me about hanging out with Amber today. I mean, it's not like I'm his girlfriend. He doesn't need to sneak around behind my back. I should have gotten off this stupid bus and gone in there and confronted them. But that would have been a stupid thing to do. I would have looked stupid and felt stupid, and because I need to do something, anything, even something stupid, I drop the old dude's book onto the seat beside me and fire off another text to Hoon—*YOU'RE THE ASSHOLE!!!*—and then flick off my phone, damn it. I nearly fling it across the bus, but the old dude kind of clucks his tongue at me—literally, *cluck, cluck*—like he's scolding me, right? Like I've done something stupid, which, *duh*, I know I have, but it's none of his business anyway. So I flash him a nasty look, but he just keeps smiling at me, all angelic-like, because we're such good buddies now, and then he gestures at the book on the seat beside me and nods his head up and down, beaming.

I guess I'm too tired or sad to argue about it, and so I drop my phone into my lap and start flipping through his stupid book. At least it gives me something to do with my hands.

It's just a sketchbook, a seriously old one by the look of it, so tired and beat-up and raggedy I'm afraid the pages will fall out when I crack it open. It feels kind of warm in my hands, too, like he's kept it tucked in a pocket close to his heart, as if it were his most valuable possession, like a wallet or a passport. I don't know why, but the thought that this strange old dude I don't even know just handed me something so precious and personal makes me feel a little better, you know? Like there are other important things going on in the world besides Hoon and Amber and me. Inside the book, there are pages and pages of these charcoal and pencil portraits of random, everyday folks doing boring, routine things, like walking a dog, or sitting in the park, or shopping for groceries, or riding on a bus.

Only—and it takes me a minute of staring hard at a few of them to figure this out—they're not really people at all.

I mean, they're not, like, *human* people.

For example, there's this one drawing of a wrinkled old lady walking a little dog down the sidewalk, only her face has these wisps of whiskers darting out from the corners of her tiny nose, and I realize the hand holding the leash isn't a hand at all, but a finely manicured paw. Another is of this skinny guy in a wheel-chair at the beach, and he has this towel draped over his legs so you can't see them, but when you look closely, you can just make out the tip of a large fin poking out from the bottom of the towel where his feet should be. In another, this porky little kid scampers through a sandbox, and he's got a flat kind of piggish nose and a twisted little corkscrew of a tail poking out of the backside of his little OshKosh B'gosh overalls.

There are pages of these things . . . beings . . . *creatures*. . . . Shit, I don't even know what to call them, except that each one is kind of hideous and yet utterly amazing. It's like this old dude has revealed a whole community of monsters secretly living among us, only, with all their weirdness and strangeness, they're almost more beautiful than the *real* beautiful people of LA.

There's this one drawing of a sort-of-sexy homeless vampire who reminds me of the lead singer of a goth band picking through a trash bin behind a Baja Fresh. Another is a garden scene featuring a graceful feline socialite, whose long, sinewy tail is wrapped around the base of a honeysuckle bush. In another, a dude who could be Shrek's hunky brother sips a cappuccino in front of this trendy coffee shop in West Hollywood. There's a drawing of a buff motorcycle cop stopped at a traffic light with horns sticking out from under his helmet and a long, forked tail that looks like it's about to get caught beneath his rear tire. Toward the back of the book, there's even a rendering of our hobbity bus driver smiling warmly at his passengers, even though his big, furry feet can barely reach the pedals of the bus.

I burst out laughing when I see this one, and when I turn to the old dude to tell him how awesome I think his drawings are, he gives me a thumbs-up. For some reason this cracks me up even more, and I sit there laughing my ass off, with tears streaming down my cheeks, right? Because it's like I've completely forgotten about Hoon and Amber and have totally sunk into this awesomely weird moment.

But, of course, it doesn't last.

All of a sudden I flash on an image of Hoon and Amber sitting there in that bakery gazing into each other's sparkling eyes, while sharing a dulce de leche and laughing at me and how stupidly, pathetically gay I am.

Jesus . . . *Jesus Christ.*

I sigh and reach across the aisle to return the sketchbook to the old dude. "These are very cool," I say, handing him the book. "Bueno, bueno."

If I wasn't feeling so awful, I might've tried to muddle through a conversation with him about his work. I don't speak Spanish, but I know a few phrases, and anyway, we've been getting along pretty well with just grins and hand gestures so far.

But really, all I want to do is curl up in a little ball and wish the world away.

He takes the book from me, still grinning, and crinkles his eyes at me. Then he reaches into his jacket pocket and retrieves a slender lacquer pencil case, painted in these swirling swathes of red and gold and ivory. I slide back toward the window and lean my head against the glass. I feel numb all over as I watch him set the case in his lap, pop it open with one hand, and retrieve the nub of a well-worn pencil from inside. He jams the nub between his teeth, then snaps the case closed and tucks it back into his pocket. With his other hand he flips to one of the last empty pages in the book, and then grabs the nub and jabs it in my direction, pointing first at me and then at the empty page before him.

"¿Sí? Sí?" he says, and he looks so hopeful and eager, I don't have it in me to say no.

165

"Sure, go ahead." I sigh. "Sí. Whatever. Only turn me into something fierce like a werewolf, okay? I want to be sexy and badass for a change."

He flashes me a puzzled look, like he has no idea what the hell I'm talking about but finds me amusing anyway, which is fine, I guess. I'm glad to amuse somebody today.

I turn my face away to stare out the window again, trying to remember what it felt like when I got out of bed this morning and the sky was still right side up and gravity was still behaving according to the natural laws I've grown accustomed to over the past seventeen years on Earth. Back when I didn't feel like I was about to be sucked into the black hole swirling in the pit of my stomach at any given moment.

Okay, I admit it: I'm really good at being a drama queen.

Blame it on my hypothalamus.

Even over the roar of the bus engine and the useless earbuds still plugged into my ears, I can hear the old dude scratching away on his page. I try not to move too much because I don't want to mess him up, so I can't really turn to watch how he works. But by the sounds his pencil is making, he's going at it with some kind of religious fervor. Damn. On a moving bus, no less. Plus, he's got to be, like, seventy-five if he's a day. Sometimes it takes me a week to finish a drawing, but at this rate he'll be done before we reach Union Station.

After a few more stops to let passengers off, traffic slows to a crawl and we spend what feels like ten minutes parked on the overpass that crosses the 110. I stare out at the silver ribbon of the Harbor Freeway as gauzy ripples of heat rise up from its molten surface. The sunlight and smog are working overtime to flatten out all perspective. The high-rises downtown don't even look real from here. It's like somebody strung up a skyscraper backdrop to hide the secret face of LA. The smog is so thick the sky has gone almost as yellow as Proteus's. It's got to be over one hundred degrees outside, and I'm really starting to wish I never got on this damn bus. If I'd just gone to Echo Park to sweat my ass off by the stupid lake, I wouldn't have even seen Hoon and Amber go into that bakery.

I wonder how long they've been an item?

Maybe ignorance truly is bliss.

If Hoon were here right now, he would tell me there was some kind of reason this happened the way it did. That there's no such thing as coincidence. That some immutable law of probability could've predicted this through a complex mathematical calculation, and all I need to do is spend, like, the rest of my life researching the necessary equations to explain in agonizing detail why he finally broke my heart today.

But to hell with that shit.

Eventually, we start to inch forward again, which is great, right? Because this is a bus and theoretically it's supposed to be taking me someplace. And that's when it occurs to me that since we let off the last two passengers at Sunset and Marion, it's only been me, the driver, and the old dude onboard, and even for a downtown run on a Saturday afternoon, that's pretty sketchy.

Yet, no sooner do I have this thought than we edge past the intersection with Figueroa, where Sunset magically transforms into Cesar Chavez, voilà, and I see this dude standing on the curb waiting for us to pull over for him. There's a strong glare reflecting off the windshield of a car parked nearby, so I can't make out who this guy is, but I suddenly get a weird fluttering vibe that it's somebody I know, right? Like an unexpected little jolt of butterflies in my stomach. I start thinking these crazy, stupid thoughts, like maybe it's actually Hoon. Maybe that wasn't him and Amber going into the bakery after all, but just some random hotties who looked just like them. Maybe he did go to Temecula with his mom after all, but their car broke down on the way, and the tow truck driver brought them to this garage I know of that's a couple blocks down on Figueroa. Maybe when I texted him, he just said that stuff about Amber not being a bitch because he changed his mind about her and forgot to tell me, or because he was still pissed off about last night, and maybe now he's getting on a downtown bus—wait, why a *downtown* bus?

Um . . . maybe . . . yes!

Because he wants to catch up with me at Union Station! Because I texted him I was heading down there, right? And maybe that's why he's getting onto this downtown bus right now, and maybe that's why all of this had to happen in this exact, noncoincidental way.

It's the law of probability and whatnot. The solution to our equation.

Only just as I'm thinking this crazy, rambling torrent of bullshit, I happen to glance over at the old dude, who is leaning forward and still frantically working on his drawing of me, and I notice that he's taken off his jacket—maybe because he's hot, or maybe not, but whatever—and he's wearing this dingy short-sleeve dress shirt with these nasty yellow stains at the armpits that look like they're older than I am and these two very enormous, white gossamer wings sticking out the back where his shoulder blades should be. They're spread out behind him, flexing, ever so gently flexing, like they've fallen asleep on him and he needs to stretch them out to get the blood flowing again, and that's when I remember that I still have my earbuds plugged into my ears, and I should probably turn my phone back on, because Hoon may be trying to text me right this very second. Not this impostor Hoon or whoever is climbing up the steps of the bus, but the real Hoon, who's just finishing up his dulce de leche with Amber and is starting to feel guilty about laughing at me like that, and so I reach down and turn the phone back on and wait for it to ding.

Of course, it doesn't ding.

But that's when I notice that it's Gadriel who's gotten on the bus.

My Gadriel.

Our Gadriel.

Well, actually, Hoon's Gadriel, really, since I don't even know for sure what he looks like yet. Not completely, because I haven't fully deciphered Hoon's instructions well enough to correctly draw a Protean—not according to him, anyway. But it's got to be Gadriel, right? I mean, he's wearing the sweet little red-and-gold-and-ivory tunic I designed for the Renegades to wear. He's tall and skinnier than a circuit boy, with skin like an avocado and enormous glistening black eyes with four eyelids each that meet in the middle when he blinks, plus a little pad at the end of each of his eight spaghettilike fingers and this fierce braid of silver hair dangling down in a rat tail from the left side of his head.

As soon as he sees me, he gives me a big, toothless Protean grin, like he's delighted to run into me on a Metro bus—what a surprise!—and I return the smile, because, *duh*, it's Gadriel, and even though we've never actually met, I do sort of know him.

He comes gliding down the aisle in that expansive, graceful way that Hoon says the Proteans walk, and I pat the seat beside me in welcome. I start to say "Hey," but then I remember that the Proteans can't properly hear in our atmosphere and can't even speak, because they have no vocal cords, and so I just kind of smile a lame greeting, and he smiles one back at me and sits down, and then the old dude with the enormous wings smiles at him, too, like they go way back, and I think how funny it is that the three of us are here, and while we all kind of know one another, not one of us can actually talk to the others. I mean, even for public transport in LA, this is a pretty strange encounter, right? When I tell Hoon about it, I wonder what he'll say to try to explain it away. Maybe he'll insist I had a stroke or experienced some kind of mental break brought on by the shock of catching him with Amber. Maybe he'll say I inhaled too much bus exhaust and all of this is some sort of carbon monoxide–induced hallucination. Maybe he'll even accuse me of making the whole thing up. If nothing else, I *know* he'll be pissed I got to meet Gadriel first, though I bet he'll come up with some rational-sounding excuse for that, too.

Poor Hoon: he can't ever let things *just be*, you know?

It's a good thing I can.

I guess that's why we're still best friends.

Though the hobbity bus driver keeps grinning at the three of us in the mirror like we're his long-lost cousins from the Shire, he somehow manages to swerve the bus back into the traffic on Cesar Chavez without running over any nuns or puppies. We cruise in silence for a while, and I lose track of which blocks we're crossing, although I can smell the delicious aroma of Chinatown wafting in through the air-conditioning, so I know we can't be too far from Union Station.

After a while, the old dude pops the pencil nub back between his teeth and sets the sketchbook on the seat beside him. Then he slowly rises to his feet, gripping the seat back in front of him to steady himself against the swaying of the bus. He flaps his luminous wings back and forth a few times, brushing their tips against the ceiling of the bus and creating a small vortex of wind that flutters the gauzy red-and-gold poofs of fabric at the shoulders of Gadriel's tunic. You can see that it makes the old dude feel really good to stretch his wings like this, and I figure since he's probably getting on a crowded train soon this may be his last opportunity to do so for a while.

Go for it, man.

After a moment of doing this, he stuffs the pencil nub into his pants pocket and bends down, picks up the little book, and passes it to Gadriel to show off the drawing he's just completed of me.

I can tell that Gadriel approves of the drawing because he blinks his eight eyelids five times in a row, in that way Hoon says the Proteans do to show that they're pleased with something. Only, when he tries to pass the book to me so that I can see for myself what the old dude has drawn, I suddenly realize that

I don't want to see myself the way this nosy old angel sees me. Maybe I like not knowing yet what kind of monster I secretly am.

Maybe the artist in me wants to figure that out for myself.

I push Gadriel's hand away as politely as I can, and he blinks his eight eyelids three times in a row in that way Hoon says the Proteans do to show that they agree that you've made the absolute right decision. Then he passes the book back to the old dude, who just smiles at me again with his same old warm and fuzzy smile, only this time I think I can detect just a trace of irritation spark across his eyes.

And that's when I notice the little phone thingy in Gadriel's hand.

It's all green, like the color of his skin, and attached by a slender white wire that trails up to these two white pads that are Velcroed or something over the gill slits in his throat—which Hoon once explained to me are not gills at all, but the Protean version of ears. And so I nudge him in the arm and nod at the phone thingy, right, because *I've just got to know*, and he must truly be telepathic like Hoon says the Proteans are, because he doesn't miss a beat and lifts the phone thingy to where I can see the album cover of Ravisha Mann's *MANNeater DJ Uri Firebrand Remix EP* glowing up at me on the screen, and I laugh to myself and wonder if Hoon realizes that some Proteans have bigger hypothalamuses, too.

So I flip my own phone to him to show off the album covers of a few of my own favorite selections, right? Because I feel like we've made this deep connection already. And that's when my phone beeps at me, and I look to see that Hoon has finally texted me back:

*Temecula canceled. Auntie Sook 8 bad pork. Me and Amber
bringing you home galletas.*

No worries: No Kissing :-o

Sorry for being a dick last night.

My heart skips a beat, and suddenly I feel like a lemon that
somebody has squeezed out all the juice from. I remember how
Hoon says that Proteans don't feel love, because love is nothing but a false emotional construct based on humanity's need
for the social organization around which stable family units are
built. Or some shit.

But I think he's probably wrong about that one, too.

MONSTER REFLECTION

Although my parents tried to raise me Catholic, when I was a teenager I couldn't make myself believe in God. I did my best, however,
to cultivate faith in the existence of visitors from other worlds. You
could say I *wanted* to believe, and it was popular to do so back
then. We're talking the 1980s, when aliens were everywhere. Spiel-
berg movies. Daytime talk shows. Best-selling memoirs. Abduction
stories were all the rage. I remember attending a UFO seminar at
a Ramada Inn with my Aunt Lucille and hearing true-life accounts
from abductees. They described being taken in the night by small,
gray beings with enormous black eyes and the ability to project
their thoughts telepathically. While I found these stories innately
terrifying (and a little preposterous), they also filled me with wonder.
They reminded me of the biblical tales of angelic visitations the nuns
had taught us. When you got right down to it, there wasn't much
difference between getting taken by an alien and being touched by
an angel, was there? Both demanded a level of faith beyond proof
or rationality. I longed for that kind of faith, though I never achieved

it. Still, I would lie awake at night and imagine what it would feel like to be chosen by godlike creatures who traveled millions of light-years to commune with the human race. Why hadn't they chosen me? Would I ever truly believe?

Nowadays, I do believe in aliens—the plausible kind that exobiologists theorize may thrive in our own solar system, beneath the frozen oceans of moons like Enceladus and Europa. I still don't believe in God, nor do I want to. Instead, I need only to step outside on a clear night and behold the infinite wonder of the universe swirling above me to know that we are not alone.

BOYS WHO RUN
WITH THE BOARS

BY SAM J. MILLER

The autumn I turned sixteen, Mom's adjunct pod got assigned to some reclamation shithole south of Node Nine—a place the people who lived there insisted on calling "New Jersey"—and the first day she went to work she gave me a gun.

It came with a whole long speech about how bad guns were, how easy it would be to hurt or kill myself or others, how Back In The Day she'd lobbied and protested against guns but Things

Are Different Now. She set me up with a whole lot of videos to watch, on how to put a gun together and use one without dying, and said when she got home she'd test me and if I passed she'd give me the bullets.

I watched the videos during math class, on my fifth screen, the shittiest of all my shitty hand-me-down devices, acing both the virtual-school pop quiz and the *TEST YOUR RECALL* survey that popped up at the end of the playlist. At the same time. While also grinding XP in *Gaijin Ninja* for a party out of Fujian. While *also* chatting with the kinda cute boy we'd met in the boxcar on our journey east away from burning Texas, even though—or because—I knew I'd never see him again. WHILE ALSO crouched down in the dirty bathtub avoiding the windows just in case the cannibals Mom was convinced were prowling these sunken trailer parks came through.

But, yeah. Passed Mom's test. Got the bullets. Scoffed at the thought of ever using them.

And then, at night—our third in the new home—I heard the pack. Sounding like a small army moving through the forest, calling out to one another in the dark. Grunts and whines and weird *ukh! ukh!* sounds.

And laughter. Deep, throaty, human-adjacent laughter. A terrifying exhilarating noise, like a party you're not invited to, one that you know will be dangerous and want to go to anyway. Some primal, ancient part of me recognized the sound, knew it to be boars. Lock eyes with a pig, and you'll know in your heart how close they are to us.

So in the morning, still damp from a prickly kind of fear sweat, I did my research. Read the articles. Saw the clips. Turns out wild boars have been breeding like crazy in the reclamation zones, the flooded towns and burned-out forests and radioactive swamps. Living in abandoned houses; losing their natural fear of humans. And there's a whole fight, between the people who point to the environmental benefit they bring and the ones who point out how destructive they are, what with their tendency to destroy the burrows of ground-nesting species, ruin crops, eat baby trees, damage water quality, and on and on, a whole long list of bad behavior capped off by their aggression toward humans.

Gnarly little fuckers. I was frightened. And I was fascinated. So when Mom went to work, I put the bullets into the gun and went out for a walk.

Our trailer park was almost entirely empty, since down the mountain was a whole suburb of big, nice houses abandoned when the highway flooded and suddenly no one could get in or out except by boat. That's where the squatters mostly went, though there's a gregarious old lady in the trailer across from ours who never left, and a couple drug cookers who are polite and keep to themselves.

And Mom and her pod. Scrappy, hungry grad students still clinging to the vanished prestige of the academy, unaware they were pledging their lives to poverty and exploitation.

I pulled up a handful of Japanese knotweed and chewed on a sour stem, even though Mom says nothing foraged out this way is safe. I think she's just got a grudge against knotweed.

Mom's obsession is invasives. She's a biologist, dedicated her life to studying the impact of humanity's devastating stewardship of the earth. The way new creatures move in and drive out the old. She dreamed of molding young minds, arming future eco-warriors with the knowledge they needed to fight to save the planet, but that ship has fully sailed and we're well and truly screwed. Anyway, the only university gigs are corporate-sponsored field studies to see what shreds of profit can be squeezed from blighted lands left unlivable by the consequences of our actions.

She says humans are the ultimate invasive species. How just like the boars can't help wiping out rodent species wherever they go, we can't help burning the whole planet to the ground. We're existentially fucked, and extinction can't come soon enough. Her monologues were always running in the back of my brain, but as I walked through the woods in search of wild boars, I found myself seeing the forest for what it was. Damaged but alive. Dying, as October leaked into November and leaves fell and green browned, but capable of rebirth.

And, apparently, packed with wild, thriving, monster boars.

"Hey," said a gruff, low voice, startling a yelp out of me.

"Sorry," he said, not looking sorry at all. A boy, my age but somehow bigger, not in size but in scope, in exuberance, in confidence and charisma. Grinning, stepping silently closer like he might have been tailing me for who knows how long. Dressed in a worn old T-shirt and frayed jeans.

"Aren't you cold?" I asked.

"Hot-blooded," he said. "What are you doing out here? Don't you know these woods aren't safe?"

"My mom and me just moved into the trailer park over—" I gestured in one direction, but suddenly I wasn't sure which way I'd come from. "There."

"And you're lost," he chuckled.

"I wanted to see if I could see some wild boars. I heard them last night. There's like a whole pack out in these woods, I think."

"Drove," he said, smiling. "Not pack. A group of boars is called a drove. You're not scared? They're pretty badass, wild boars."

It didn't feel like the right moment to pull out my gun, brag about how I could take care of myself. Just because I wanted desperately to make out with this guy didn't mean he wasn't a threat. The cute bait the cannibals used to lure in unsuspecting prey. "I'm scared, but I'm curious," was the best I could do, deflecting and flirting at the same time. Doing both badly.

Understand: I'm not an amateur. I knew what I was. I'd been with boys before. The newness here wasn't lust. It was something bigger, scarier, sharper-edged, and more likely to slice me up.

My life was as close to conventional as anyone's could be, in the Sunken World. I'd grown up in a nice apartment building; my mom was a professor (even if professor-ing wasn't what it once had been). At night we still sat around and watched shows together. This guy's whole way of being was wild and alien to me, I could tell that right away. And I was shocked to see how badly I wanted it.

"I'm Wreck," he said.

"Darren," I said, hating its polished banality. Why couldn't my name be something rad and rough like Wreck or Ruin or Rott? "You live out here?"

He shrugged. "We come and go."

I knew there were people like that. Rootless; moving from abandoned town to abandoned town, foraging and gleaning what they could from the land, forming new communities, swapping seeds, sharing apple-tree grafts and fungal spawn and perma-culture strategies, creating whole intricate infrastructures of food production seamlessly integrated into the devastated landscape. Mom wanted to study them, but since no one saw potential corporate profits, there'd never be a university project.

"You wanna see some boars up close, Darren?"

I nodded. Swallowed hard.

"Come back tonight," he said. "I'll show you something."

"What time?" I said, heart hammering so hard all that came out was a whisper.

Wreck laughed, held up both wrists so I could see he had no watch. Turned out his empty pockets. A boy unburdened by time. By things. Screens. Schedules. Not psychically chained to five devices streaming school and work and friends and stress and an unending flood of nightmare news from around the globe. "Whenever you get here, I'll know it. And I'll find you. I have a very good nose."

He tapped its adorable snub tip to show me. I moved to kiss him, and he laughed. Wagged a finger. "See you later, Darren." He pointed. "Go that way."

School and dinner and shows with Mom took forever that night. My mind was elsewhere, prowling the woods with boars and boys and other fearless beasts.

Mom talked about work, her pod, the things they'd found in the field that day. Dying oak trees with no young ones coming up, their acorns all eaten before they could grow.

I was sad about the trees; I truly was. Oaks are awesome. All trees are. And yeah, the land was doomed and so were we. Evidence of it was everywhere. It'd never occurred to me my mom might be wrong. But for the first time I thought: invasives might be bad, but they're also alive. They have as much right to be as anything else. The boar that ate those acorns wasn't better or worse than the tree that made them. I didn't say it out loud. It'd spark a conversation I wasn't ready for. One we maybe couldn't come back from.

But that night, long after she'd fallen asleep with her aging laptop blaring ancient cop shows, I got dressed again and silently left the trailer park.

And didn't take my gun.

It was dumb, I know. I wasn't making good decisions.

Wreck had done something. Proximity to him had destabilized me; his pheromones dizzied me in a delicious kind of way. Like they'd turned me up all the way, set my senses blazing. My nose pulled me through the blighted night forest with a clarity I'd totally lacked when I'd made the same trip mere hours ago.

I told myself it was just the night, the electric feel of the cold air and the adrenaline surge of the darkness. I said it, but I didn't believe it.

My nose took me right to the spot where I'd met Wreck. His T-shirt hung on a branch, undulating enticingly in the fall breeze. I grabbed hold of a handful, marveled at its softness. Its warmth, like he'd just taken it off. I buried my nose in it, sucked up all the information contained in his scent. The raw boy smell of him, bad in a good way.

My head jerked to the side, compelled by a sense impression I couldn't pinpoint. Turning my attention to where a boar eyed me from between two trees. Big, broad. Sturdy. Strong. Smiling, sort of. Exuding exuberance; confidence; charisma. Tusks.

"Hey," I said, because what else do you say to a creature standing six feet away who's capable of killing you?

It took three steps back, hiding itself behind a tree.

And then it was looking at me from the other side of the tree, except it wasn't a boar anymore.

"Hey yourself," Wreck said. Standing there, naked.

Cold as the night was, I felt warmth wash over me. My clothes were suddenly heavy, excessive.

"What'd you do to me?" I whispered.

"What do you *want* me to do to you?"

His smell was intoxicating, overwhelming. What a complicated story it told, in images that flashed through my head like a slideshow. Sun on his bare back; hunters with guns stomping through the forest after him; sleeping in empty elementary schools, the whole ragged drove of boars nestled together for warmth in winter.

My voice was husky, tusked. Porcine. "Whatever you want."

One strong hand grabbed me by the back of the head, pulled me in for a kiss. His hunger was bottomless. I could see the shape of it, sip it from his lips. Matching my own. A thirst for things, yes, but for life as well: the taste of the wind in the trees, the sight of bare branches black against blue sky. The world was still so full of beauty. Even if much of it was ugly.

Wreck's arms grabbed hold of my shoulders, pushed me up against a tree. His mouth moved to my neck, gnawed probingly at my ear.

They weren't werewolves. Wreck wouldn't need to bite me. All I had to do was want it.

My mom's life was dedicated to mourning what was, what we'd destroyed. Most people's were. Which was understandable. Humanity *was* existentially fucked. We couldn't help being monsters. But I opened my arms and I let Wreck in because every one of us gets to choose what kind of monster we become.

MONSTER REFLECTION

My only friends were monsters when I was a kid. The ones in books and the ones in movies. My bullied self connected with their out-cast status, the inexplicable anger their mere existence provoked in people. I had many loves—Frankenstein's Monster, the Martians in *The War of the Worlds*, the priest-werewolf in *Silver Bullet*—but none grabbed hold of my heart the way King Kong did. It's not just that he fought dinosaurs and New York City subway cars: the power of cinema, of special effects, made him feel alive in a way no one else in the movie was. Surrounded by mediocre actors reciting a mediocre script, Kong is the only human character. I ached to break free and go on a destructive rampage like he does. My seven-year-old heart broke when I first watched him fall; my heart is still breaking.

THE HOUSE OF NEEDS AND WANTS

BY KALYNN BAYRON

My caseworker, Jasmine, is standing outside the house on Ridgemont Lane when I walk up.

"I could have picked you up from school," she says.

"I wanted to walk." I grip my duffel bag, and I'm reminded of how light it is even though it holds everything I own, which isn't much.

Jasmine eyes me carefully. "Halle, I'm here if you need to talk."

Jasmine is nice. She's been there at the last three transitions, but she says the same thing every time. I just nod and smile.

I realize that even though I've heard all kinds of things about the Ridgemont Lane house, I've never actually stood in front of it. I'd passed it by a dozen times and never really bothered to give it more than a passing glance.

It's a three-story Queen Anne–style house that looks like something out of a fairy tale turned upside down. It's painted a dark gray color, and the trim is white. It has a turret. The front door and ornately decorated portico look like a giant gaping mouth. The windows remind me of empty eye sockets. No wonder everybody thinks the place is haunted.

There are a million stories about why it's supposedly infested with ghosts, the most popular being that the souls of children who died in the house still reside there. I don't like those rumors, because it's a known fact that the house served as everything from a halfway house to a group home over the last twenty years, mostly housing people just like me. So, no. I don't think rumors about the place are something to laugh at.

I follow Jasmine up the front steps, and she rings the bell. There's a flurry of footsteps from inside, and a moment later, the door creaks open. A small girl stands in the crack. She has a head full of braids with little colorful beads decorating the ends. She's wearing a frilly pink tutu and pink ballet slippers.

"Hi!" she says enthusiastically. "I'm Ruby and I—"

"Ruby," a gentle voice says. The door opens wider, and standing there is a tall woman with a tangle of neatly twisted locs piled in a bun on top of her head. A pair of black cat-eye glasses frame her face as she gathers up the edges of her long black cardigan. She doesn't look older than forty. "Excuse Ruby. She's been anxiously expecting you." She smiles warmly at me.

I smile back. Play my role.

"Come on in," she says. "I'm Vee."

Jasmine goes inside, and I follow her. The house is warm and smells good, but it's decorated like some kind of forest witch lives here. The walls are dark green and accented with shelves full of brass figurines. A fire crackles in a real fireplace in the front room. Ruby watches me as I sit down in an overstuffed chair.

"I'm really glad you're here," Vee says, sitting down across from me.

I smile . . . again.

"We've been through all the paperwork," Jasmine says, nodding to Vee. "Everything is good to go. Any questions for me?"

Vee shakes her head, then turns to me. "What about you, Halle? Do you have any questions about this process?"

I almost laugh out loud. "I'm probably more of an expert on this 'process' than anyone should be."

"Halle—" Jasmine begins, but Vee holds up her hand in a plea for patience.

"Whatever you're feeling right now—anger, frustration, sadness—it all matters," says Vee. "It's all valid."

I meet her gaze, and she looks sincere, which throws me off a little.

"This is your twelfth home in the past fourteen years," Vee says.

"I know. That's what happens when your parents . . ." I grip my hands together in front of me as the words trail off. *That's what happens when your parents die and nobody else even pretends to give a shit about you.* I want to scream.

"The system is broken," Jasmine says.

"The people are broken, too," I say. "The last two homes cut me loose because they found out I was dating another girl."

"Exactly!" Ruby says. She sounds way too grown for her little frame. She pushes her hand down on her hip. "The last place I was at didn't use the right adjectives—"

"Pronouns," Vee gently corrects.

"Right," Ruby says, unfazed. "Pronouns. And they wouldn't let me wear my dresses, and they wouldn't let me have my hair long. And you know what?"

I look Ruby over and then make direct eye contact with her. She grins. "Now I'm here, and I don't have to worry about people being ugly and wrong." She does a little spin with her arms high over her head.

"Can I have a word?" Jasmine says to Vee.

Vee and Jasmine disappear into the hallway, and Ruby plops down onto the arm of the chair. I study her. She is grinning from ear to ear. The faint scent of bubble gum wafts off her.

"You don't ever have to leave if you don't want to," she says. "Vee will take care of you."

"How old are you?"

"Eight and a half," she says.

I've been in homes with younger kids before. It's not my favorite thing in the world, but Ruby seems pretty laid back for an eight-year-old.

"Do people tell you this house is haunted?" Ruby asks the question like she's asking about the weather.

"That's the rumor. But you live here, so you tell me. Is it haunted?"

Ruby narrows her eyes. She opens her mouth to say something, and that unsettling feeling courses through me again. She's about to speak when Vee and Jasmine reenter the room.

"Will you be all right?" Jasmine asks.

"Yeah," I say, not knowing if it's the truth.

"You know where to find me if you need me," she says.

She gives me a hug, then leaves.

"Ruby," says Vee. "How about you show Halle to her room? Give her a little tour on the way up."

Ruby jumps up, grabs my hand, and pulls me out of the chair and toward the wide staircase.

"I'm here if you have questions," Vee says as she drifts toward the kitchen. "But I find it best not to hover. Not right at first."

Usually all anybody wants to do is hover. Vee's hands-off approach is a welcome relief. As Ruby leads me up the staircase, I take in the art on the staircase wall—framed children's paintings and black-and-white photos of forests, small oddly shaped mirrors, and a few pictures of Ruby at what looks like a ballet recital.

"So you have a girlfriend?" Ruby asks. "That's what you said downstairs."

"Ex-girlfriend."

"Ex is good. Kissing is gross, and I hate it."

"That's fair, I guess."

Ruby smiles again, and as shitty as I'm feeling, I can't deny how infectious her little aura of joy is. I smile back at her, and she puffs out her chest like she's won a prize.

At the second-floor landing, the hall snakes off to the left and right. From the corner of my eye, I see a shadowy figure move from the bottom of the stairs toward the kitchen. I stare down from the landing. On second glance, there's nothing there.

"The house has three floors and a basement," Ruby says. "The basement has mice, and it smells like armpits, so don't go down there unless you're doing laundry. All the bedrooms are on the second floor. Third floor is just old boxes, furniture, and probably more mice. Oh! Wait till you see your room!"

"I get my *own* room? I'm not sharing with anyone?"

I grip my bag.

Don't get comfortable. It won't last.

Things never work out the way I dream they will, so it's better not to dream. Ruby leads me down the narrow hallway to the right of the stairs.

"Here it is!" she says as she pushes the door open.

It's a real bedroom, not some leftover closet space. It has two big windows that overlook the side yard. A maple tree stands just outside, swaying gently as the afternoon sunlight slants through the glass. There's a bed with a set of clean sheets folded on top and a closet. Other than that, the room is bare but clean and apparently . . . mine.

"It gets better," Ruby says.

"What's that mean?" I ask.

"You'll see." She turns and skips away, her frilly pink skirt swishing around her legs.

The bubble-gum smell that clung to Ruby still lingers in the air. I breathe deep, trying to steady my nerves. Ruby is sweet. Vee seems nice, but this isn't a permanent stop. I don't even let myself pretend it could be. Painful memories push their way to the front of my mind—Jerry the mechanic bagging up my clothes and tossing them in the back of Jasmine's car as I sit silently in the passenger seat with a bruise on my face. Maddie rummaging through my notebooks and other personal belongings trying to find "evidence" that I was still seeing my girlfriend against her wishes. Tom and his wife, Karen, taking one look at me and deciding I wasn't the "right" type of girl for their family. I grab my bag and pull out my sketchbook, flipping to a blank page and roughly sketching the house. I draw the front door the way I saw it, like a giant gaping mouth ready to swallow me whole and spit my bones out after.

Hours pass as I lose myself in the sketch. Now the front door is not only a mouth, but a monstrous gateway bearing sharp, wrought iron teeth. The windows are glowing red. My artwork has a habit of showing me things, and it makes me wonder if this is what the house feels like to me. I close my sketchbook and toss it onto the bed. I get up, stretch, try to put my mind elsewhere.

Ruby's voice floats down the hallway, and I catch a few notes as they drift into my open door. She's singing. The cadence is cheery, but I can't make out the words. I go to my bedroom door and stick my head out. I don't see anyone in the long, shadowy hall, but I do feel a chill run straight up my back. I almost close the door, but Ruby's voice sounds again. This time, I hear my name.

I step into the hall and make my way toward what I assume is Ruby's room. It's clear at the other end of the hall, and her door is painted pink. As her voice drifts out, I knock.

"Come in."

I push the door open and am immediately accosted with that bubble-gum scent. Her room is pink—the walls, the carpet, the furniture, bedding, curtains—everything. She's twirling around in front of a large mirror. The lights in the ceiling cast a gauzy pink glow throughout the room. It looks like a little spotlight is on Ruby no matter where she stands, but it's hard to tell where the light is with all the pink tulle draped from the ceiling in big swoops.

"Wow," I say.

"It's the best thing ever, right?" She pulls me in and shoves me into a fluffy pink beanbag chair. "Pink is my favorite color."

"No shit."

Ruby's eyes grow wide.

"Sorry," I say quickly.

Ruby narrows her eyes at me, and a mischievous little smirk spreads across her face. She cups her hands around her mouth and whispers, "Sometimes I say *shit*, too. Don't tell Vee, okay?"

I can't help but laugh. Ruby giggles and continues to twirl around.

"I love it so much!" she squeals. She stops spinning and looks at me. "Were you just walking around in the dark?" She looks concerned.

"I heard you singing. I thought I heard my name."

"I like to put people's names in songs. Don't worry. It's nothing bad. I was just saying how your name is Halle, and you kinda look like the girl who plays the Little Mermaid, and her name's Halle, too!"

"I mean, I'll take that as a compliment."

I find that every detail imaginable has been put into Ruby's room. From the crown molding to the thick pink drapery, it's clear that Vee cares enough about Ruby to make sure her room is fit for a girl who loves all things pink and bubbly.

"You like the smell of bubble gum?" I ask. "Is it like a perfume or something?"

The corner of Ruby's mouth twitches. She nods. "Wanna meet Taye?" she suddenly asks, changing the subject abruptly.

"Who's Taye?"

"He lives here, too."

"Oh," I say. "Are they little like you?"

Ruby's face scrunches up. "No. And I'm not little."

"If you say so."

She grabs my hand, and I get up slowly. Ruby pulls me out into the hall. The room immediately across from hers has a door painted the color of the night sky. Ruby knocks twice.

"Yes?" someone calls.

"It's me," Ruby says. "And Halle."

Ruby pushes the door open. The room is dimly lit, and there is someone sitting on the end of a twin-size bed. I take a step in, and the lights dim even further. I catch only a glimpse of the person's face—deep brown eyes and a wide, expressionless mouth—before the light shifts and their face is completely shrouded in shadow. I glance up to see if maybe a bulb blew out.

"Taye, this is Halle," Ruby says. "She's nice and I like her, so be nice, okay?"

"Why would I not be nice?" Taye asks.

I lean a little closer, trying to get a better look at Taye, but the shadows in this room are weird. They're too deep, too dark. "Is there something wrong with the lights in here?" I ask.

Ruby covers her mouth and giggles. "Taye likes the dark. He's weird like that."

"Not weird," a voice says from the doorway.

Vee's standing there with her arms folded.

"Nobody here is weird," she says. She gives Ruby a little nod, and Ruby skips out of the room and across the hall. Vee smiles warmly at me. "Halle, would it be all right if I talked to you for a minute in the kitchen?"

It's time for "the talk." It's usually just rules—curfew, what I can and can't do, and probably something about how I should be grateful. As I follow Vee to the kitchen, I prepare myself to smile and nod politely at whatever she has to say because that's the best way to keep the peace.

The kitchen is old-fashioned, with a clunky cast-iron stove and wide countertops, a deep farmhouse sink, and lots of matching jars with labels that say *sugar, salt,* and *flour.* A small table and four chairs sit in the middle of the room, and Vee motions for me to have a seat. I do, and she goes to a cabinet and pulls it open. Inside are several small canisters labeled *cocoa mix.*

"Hot chocolate?" Vee asks.

I shake my head. "No, thank you. How about tea?"

Vee smiles. "What kind?"

"Chamomile."

Vee closes the cabinet, and there is a shuffling noise. I look around, wondering if maybe the mice Ruby mentioned aren't confined to the basement. When I glance back up, Vee is opening the same cabinet door, which is now filled with yellow boxes labeled *chamomile tea.*

I blink a few times. I could have sworn . . .

Vee sets a mug down in front of me, drops two tea bags into it, and fills it to the brim with water already piping hot from the electric kettle. As the steam billows up, Vee sits across from me.

"I know I said I'd give you some space," she begins. "But Ruby has taken a liking to you, so I thought I'd level with you about how things are around here."

Here it comes. I wrap my hands around the steaming mug, gripping it until my palms burn.

"I know we don't know each other," Vee says. "But I need to let you know that I want you safe. I want you happy. And the thing is, I know it doesn't always end up like that."

I'm struck quiet. Usually, these conversations are all about house rules, and they're almost always wrapped in a fake sense of optimism.

"Ruby has been with me for three years," Vee says. "She's bubbly, smart as anyone you've ever met. But she's triggered by the smell of cigarettes and beer because of the situation she was in previously. She's also deathly afraid of the dark. Taye has been here two years. He's sixteen. He's struggled with letting his guard down because he was bullied terribly by his previous caregivers." Vee sighs. "And me, I've had my struggles, but now my only goal is to keep kids just like you happy and safe."

I huff. I don't mean to, but I've heard it before.

"You don't believe me." Vee says it like a statement of fact, not a question.

"I can't," I say.

"So you don't get hurt when things don't work out."

Her eyes are still kind. I take a swig of the tea. Its flowery scent fills my nose, and the liquid almost burns the inside of my throat.

"It's better that way," I say.

"Is it?" Vee asks quietly.

"This is just a place to stay. It's not home. Maybe for Ruby and Taye it is. I think it's nice you put their rooms together like that. Maybe they feel at home, but I don't." My throat is tight, and I clench my teeth to bite back the tears.

"What do you need, Halle?" Vee asks. "What can I do for you that will make this easier?"

I push the chair back and stand up. "Nothing." I angrily wipe at my face. "Is it okay if I go draw?"

"You like to draw?" Something flashes in her dark eyes.

I nod.

"Of course," she says. "You never have to ask my permission for that."

"Thanks."

I trudge up the stairs feeling like I'm carrying the weight of the world on my back.

At the second-floor landing, I pause. The hall is darkened aside from a soft pink glow emanating from under Ruby's door. I suddenly feel as if I am not alone. I spin around, expecting to find someone standing there, but there is no one. The shadows are deep, and now that the sun has set there isn't as much light as there was earlier. I quickly move down the hall toward my room, and by the time I get there, my heart is beating against my ribs like a drum. I slip inside and gently close the door, but it doesn't do anything to stop the strange feeling I had in the hallway. Even in the confines of my room I feel like I'm being watched.

I sit down on the bed and reach for my sketchbook only to find it gone. I run my hands over the covers; I crouch and check under the bed again. My hands begin to tremble. There are so many drawings in there, and not many of them are things I want anyone else to see. I check my bag, even though I don't remember sticking it in there before I went down the hall to see about Ruby. I search every inch of the room and come up with nothing. It's gone.

I try to think who the more likely culprit is. Ruby is bubbly and bright, and I know all too well that those things can be a mask for something else. Taye is quiet, and that's all I know about him. Then there's Vee. Is she one of those people who feels like if I'm in her house then everything that's mine is actually hers? I think about going downstairs and confronting her but stop myself. This is literally day one.

A noise suddenly draws my attention—a long, low groan, like someone is dragging a heavy piece of furniture across the floor in the room next door. The noise sounds again, and this time it's coming from somewhere behind the wall in my room. Old pipes maybe? This house has baseboard heat, and that always creates a cacophony of annoying knocks and bangs.

The sounds stop.

I stand still. The hair on the back of my neck stands up.

There's a low rumble, and then, from the darkened corner of the room, there is a shift in the shadows. I freeze. I feel like I'm stuck to the ground. I will myself forward and leap into the bed, pulling the covers up over my head. I try to hear over the rush of blood in my ears, but it's too loud. I take a deep breath and slowly lower the blanket. In the corner, there's nothing except the small honeycomb-shaped shelf built directly into the wall.

I didn't notice it before.

I usually measure my time at school in unbearably long minutes, but not today. I'm not eager to go back to Vee's. The feeling in the house is way beyond new-place-to-stay jitters. Images of the house's front door hanging open like a mouth stay in my head until school is done and I'm standing in front of it again.

Today, in the gloomy afternoon, the house is even more disconcerting. I reach for my bag to grab my sketchbook, but then I remember it isn't there and I get mad all over again.

I sigh and glance up at the windows in my room. Something moves behind the curtains. I can't recall there even being curtains on the window the day before, but now somebody is moving around in there. Maybe it's Vee or Ruby or Taye and they're in my stuff again.

I rush up the front steps, and the front door pops open before I can grab the handle. I expect Vee to be standing on the other side, but there's no one there. I push the door closed behind me, and I slow my pace as I climb the stairs. I want to catch the thief in the act. When I get to my door, I throw it open and step inside.

"What are you—"

I stop.

There is no one in my room. There is, however, a desk, and sitting on top of it is my sketchbook.

I step toward the desk. It isn't some rickety thing made from particleboard and plastic. It's an intricately carved desk built directly into the wall and wide enough to set an entire canvas on with room to spare. There isn't a chair, but I can tell that if I were to sit at it, it would be the perfect height for drawing. I snatch my sketchbook up and flip through it. Everything is as it should be. I run my hand over the desk, and in spite of my confusion, I smile. It's the kind of space I've always dreamed about having.

I glance at the window and see that curtains, in my favorite shade of evergreen, are newly hung and blocking out most of the afternoon light. I turn toward the hall when something catches my eye. In the corner, where I thought I heard noises the night before, there is something sitting in the tiny alcoves of the honeycomb-shaped shelf. A set of figurines—one butterfly, one doe, one bird. Their paint is chipped and fading because I've had them for so long. My kindergarten teacher, Miss Annie, gave them to me so that I could have something that belonged only to me. They were, last time I checked, wrapped in paper and secured in an envelope at the bottom of my bag. Now they're sitting in the little cubbies like they've always belonged there.

Downstairs there is suddenly a rumble of footsteps and voices as the front door creaks open.

"We forgot the Rice Krispies Treats!" Ruby wails.

"Can't we just—" Taye begins.

"No," Vee says. "We'll go back to the store later and get some."

I toss my bag on the bed and go downstairs. Vee and Ruby are putting groceries in the fridge.

"Hey," I say.

Vee turns and shoots me a big smile. Ruby drops a bag of cereal onto the table and bum-rushes me, wrapping her arms around my waist.

"I've been waiting for you to get home!" she says. "I lost a tooth!" She grins and sticks her tongue through the little gap on the side of her mouth.

"So the tooth fairy is going to pay you a visit?"

Ruby laughs. "The tooth fairy isn't real, silly. But Vee is going to give me five dollars." She goes back to the counter and picks up a box of Rice Krispies Treats, shoving them into the very back of an open cabinet.

"So you didn't forget them after all," I say.

Ruby's mouth flattens into a straight line.

"I'm not trying to spy on you or anything," I say. "I just heard you say you forgot them."

Vee clears her throat, and Ruby skips out of the room with a Rice Krispies Treat poorly hidden behind her back.

I clasp my hands together in front of me as I face Vee. "I wanted to say thanks for the desk and the curtains."

Vee faces me with a gentle smile. "Oh, you don't have to thank me."

"I'm a little confused as to how you did it while I was at school. I didn't see any dust or anything. Somebody had to have cut into the wall to make it, right?"

Vee lowers herself into a chair at the table. "It didn't require any cutting."

"How? It's built right into the wall."

Vee nods. "It is."

I sit down at the table across from her just as Taye reenters the room holding a bag of groceries. The lights in the kitchen dim, casting a shadow across his face. I glance up at the light fixtures in the ceiling.

"I'm not trying to be difficult," I begin. "But my notebook was moved. And some stuff I had in my bag is now on that little shelf in the corner."

Vee's brow pushes up. "Oh?"

I gather the courage to say how I feel. It's always a little risky. Most people, especially adults, don't like to listen. "I just—I don't really like it when my stuff gets moved around. I don't have a lot of things that belong to me, and I'm just . . . protective."

Vee nods. "Of course. I'm so sorry. I'll see that it doesn't happen again without your permission." She taps her foot on the hardwood floor three times and then smiles.

I stand and push my chair back. "That reminds me, can I use one of these chairs? I love the desk. I just need something to sit on."

"Of course," Vee says. "Take one of these for now, but what kind of chair do you need? I can keep an eye out for something that might work better."

I think for a moment. "Something with good back support. Something I can adjust the height of. Other than that, I'm not picky."

Vee nods. "Taye, would you help Halle take the chair up to her room?"

Taye, who is stacking cans inside the kitchen cabinet, immediately comes over and lifts one side of the chair. I grab the back, and we haul it toward the stairs. As soon as we start our ascent, the lights over the staircase dim.

"What's up with the lights?" I ask. "Is something wrong with the electricity?"

Taye smiles and looks down at the floor. "It's always like that."

"Right."

Taye grips the edge of the chair, and I notice that his nails are a brilliant shade of green.

"It's called Super Sonic Evergreen," Taye says, following my gaze. "I've had it on for a few weeks now. I'm gonna go with fire-engine red next time."

"Weeks?" I ask. "How do you get it to last so long? My shit is always chipping."

"It's a gel manicure. Lasts longer than the regular stuff. My boyfriend put me onto it. Maybe you wanna come get a manicure with me next time I go?"

I glance at Taye, and his face is still shrouded in shadows that seem to extend themselves well beyond their reach.

"Maybe," I say. It sounds great actually, but a familiar hesitancy builds in my chest.

We lug the chair the rest of the way down the hall and pull it into my room only to find that there is already a chair behind my new desk.

"Umm," I say, confused. "This wasn't here a minute ago."

The chair has a high back and is padded on the seat. There's a lever underneath for adjusting the height.

I look to Taye for some explanation, but he keeps his gaze on the floor. I quickly and quietly close my door, standing with my back to it.

"Listen," I say softly, making sure none of the fear and confusion I feel bleeds into my words. "What is going on in this house? You can tell me."

Taye shrugs. "I don't know what you mean."

"Yes, you do," I say a little more forcefully. "The lights and the noises. I thought somebody was moving furniture around last night. And somebody *is* moving my stuff around. And in the kitchen—" I stop myself before I tell him about what I saw with the tea and the Rice Krispies Treats.

Taye glances around the room. "I don't—I don't think I should say anything."

"Why?" I ask. "There's nothing you can say that I haven't heard. You know how many places I've been? The secrets people keep . . ." I trail off as a knot grows in my throat. "I need to know."

Taye raises his head and meets my gaze. "What do you really want, Halle?" He shakes his head. "I'm saying it wrong. I mean, what do you need? What do you need to be happy?"

It's not a joke, but I laugh anyway. "Are you serious right now?"

"I know what it sounds like, but here . . . in this house . . . you really have to think about that." He shoves his hands deep into his pockets. "It's hard to be really honest about what you need sometimes."

I sit back in the chair that seemingly appeared out of nowhere. It fits my body perfectly.

"What I really want is to feel like this is the place for me," I say. "I need to feel like I belong somewhere, like I'm not just blowing in the wind. I need a place to land."

"I get that," Taye says. "I didn't have that before I got here."

I look down at the desk.

"I'm gonna give you some space," Taye says. "Just think about what I said. I'm sure Vee will fill you in when it's time."

"Time for what?" I ask.

Taye continues into the hall without another word.

I change into a pair of sweats and pull back the blanket on my bed. The sheets have been changed. This morning when I left the bed a rumpled mess, the matching fitted and flat sheets were a generic beige. Now they're a black-and-white polka-dot pattern with some of the clusters of dots accented by a purple triangle. Something stirs in the furthest part of my memory. I grasp at the thought, but it slips away. I crawl under the covers and put my cheek on the pillow. I run my finger over the polka-dot pattern. It's familiar, but I can't place it. I close my eyes and try to remember.

I can almost see the pattern in my mind. It's wrapped around me like a blanket, and someone is there, someone whose face isn't clear to me, though I feel happy. And then the memory is made clear, and it's the house I lived in when I was little, the place I was before everything went sideways. I was in my room, and the polka-dot blanket was tucked in around me. It was mine, and it was with me when everything was right.

I sit bolt upright. The sky outside my window is dark, and my eyes are bleary from sleep. Disoriented, I swing my feet over the edge of my bed and run my hand over the sheets. What are the odds that I would come to a house that has a sheet set with the exact same pattern that was on my bed when I was a kid? The same pattern that was wrapped around me the last time I felt truly safe.

A murmur of voices echoes from somewhere down the hall. I get up and go into the hallway as quietly as I can. I peer over the railing as Ruby emerges from the living room. The lights in the hall flicker on. As she progresses toward the kitchen, the lights keep her bathed in a soft glow. They don't leave her in shadow for a single second.

I sneak down the stairs and into the lower hall, pressing myself against the wall as I peer into the kitchen. Ruby opens the refrigerator door, and her shoulders slump. Inside is a glass bowl filled with freshly peeled orange slices.

"Apple juice should work," Ruby says. "I'm sick of orange slices."

She shuts the door, waits a moment, and then opens it again. Sitting there on the shelf is a single glass of amber liquid. Ruby chugs it and then sets the glass on the counter.

"Halle."

I jump so hard I knock my knee on the doorframe. Ruby spins around and grins at me before skipping off. The lights follow her as she goes, and I turn to find Vee standing in the doorway to the living room.

"Can I talk to you for a minute?" Vee asks.

"Yeah. I—did you see that?" I stammer as my mind races. "There were oranges in there and then—and then—well, then there was something else."

Vee glances at the fridge, then at Ruby as she disappears at the second-floor landing. "Let's have a chat, shall we?"

I join Vee in the front room as a strange feeling takes hold of me. When I settle into an overstuffed chair by the fireplace, I realize that the tingle at the base of my neck is the unmistakable sensation of being watched. Not by Vee or Ruby or even Taye. It is someone—something—else.

"Do you know why I'm down here right now?" Vee asks as she sits opposite me.

I shake my head.

"I was thinking of having a cup of tea by the fire all day," she says. "It's a comfort to me. Makes me feel like I can relax."

"Okay?" I say, confused. "Listen, Vee, I'm not trying to sound ungrateful—"

Vee holds up her hand. "I don't think you're ungrateful at all. It was the same way for me, you know."

I stare into her face, and there is nothing like pity, only kindness.

"What was?" I ask.

"In and out of different homes." She takes a deep breath. "I learned how to put on a friendly smile and make people believe it. You know all about that; I can tell."

I say nothing. I'm afraid that if I speak, I'll scream.

"It wasn't until I came here that things changed."

"What do you mean *here*?" I ask.

Vee smiles. "This place was a group home run by a woman named Kate Sheffield. She took me in after thirteen homes, when everyone else had given up and decided to let me age out and figure it out on my own. I was sixteen. Just like you. I was a queer kid with nobody to tell me I was going to be okay." Vee glances around the room, then back to me. "This place is different for a few reasons. Have you noticed any of them yet?"

Vee takes a steaming cup of tea from the little table next to her chair.

Was it there this whole time?

"I saw—something," I say. "When Ruby opened the refrigerator—"

"Sometimes her blood sugar gets a little low. It's nondiabetic-related hypoglycemia. She usually just needs some fruit or juice to get her back on track. This place helps her by making sure she has what she needs."

I grip the arms of the chair. "What do you mean?"

Vee sips her tea, then sets it back on the table. "When I came here, I was sixteen and I had one outlet . . . music. I taught myself to play bass and got my hands on a really terrible one. I fixed it up, and it was the only thing I brought with me here. I thought Kate would tell me to put it up and not play it, but when I arrived, she showed me a soundproof room where I could play to my heart's content without bothering anyone."

"I didn't see a studio up there."

"It's gone now," Vee says. "I don't need it anymore."

"So you converted it to a bedroom or something?"

"No. It disappeared when I didn't need it. *That* is the nature of this place. That's what I'm trying to tell you." Vee leans forward. "The juice in the fridge is there because Ruby needs it. The bubble-gum scent that follows her everywhere she goes is because she is terribly triggered by other smells. Taye is almost always cloaked in shadow because he's shy. He's been bullied and prefers to stay hidden sometimes. Ruby hates the dark, and so the lights are on around her. I love Earl Grey tea." She picks up her cup, which is now full to the brim. "And you, Halle, needed a place to draw."

The house groans behind its walls. I'm on my feet, my heart racing wildly. "I—I don't understand! I thought this place was haunted or something!"

Vee stifles a laugh. "Ghosts? Halle, sweetie. There are no ghosts here."

"Okay, so not ghosts but . . . what—what is this?" I grip the edge of the chair and realize that it has changed right before my eyes. The fabric is now the same black-and-white polka-dot pattern that was on my bed.

Vee eyes the fabric. "What is this from?" She runs her hand over the fabric.

"It doesn't make sense," I say as I stumble back.

Vee stands up and slowly approaches me. "This house is not just a house. It is a living, breathing thing. I can try to explain if you'll let me."

I stay as still as a statue.

"For a long time the people who took turns living here didn't understand it," she says. "They would find new tables and chairs, new rooms that weren't there before. It scared them. So it sat unoccupied for years. That's probably how the rumors started of it being haunted."

I suddenly feel like I need to sit down, and as the thought enters my mind, the chair slides across the floor and positions itself behind me. I sit, but only because my legs have turned to jelly.

"It wasn't until Kate bought the place that someone paid attention to what was really going on. The house gave Kate everything she needed after her wife passed away. It cared for her."

"That doesn't make sense," I say again, unable to find a better way to express my disbelief.

"It doesn't have to make sense, Halle. I stopped questioning it a long time ago. I don't know how it came to be or why. I only know that the house is trying to give you what you need. Is that pattern familiar to you?" she asks, looking at the chair. "Is a happy memory associated with it?"

All I can do is nod.

Vee gently squeezes my hand. "It's a reminder that while your life has not been easy, there are things that have been soft when everything else was a sharp edge."

Tears are flowing out of me before I have time to stop them. Vee is there, wrapping her arms around me.

"This is a special place, Halle," Vee says. "It provides for those of us who are most vulnerable. If you allow it, it will provide you whatever you need to make you feel safe." She takes my face in her hands. "You deserve so much."

Something inside me breaks open. I rest my head on Vee's shoulder, and she hugs me.

"Can I ask you something?" I say through the tears.

"Anything," Vee says.

"Why didn't you tell me this straight out of the gate?"

Vee smiles. "This is a big enough transition without also having to explain that now you technically live inside the belly of a sentient, but very protective, house."

All I can do is laugh. "You know what? You're absolutely right. You don't lead with something like that."

I hug Vee, and she hugs me back, and the house feels like it's smiling.

The house isn't haunted, despite the rumors. It is full of kids like me, queer kids, who need more than we've ever been given. The house is a shelter, a protector. When I first came here, I saw its entryway as a gaping mouth ready to devour me. Now I know that mouth is there to bare its teeth to the outside world while keeping me safe inside.

The new kid is eight, and he's wearing a Wonder Woman T-shirt and clutching a Wonder Woman action figure. I give him a little wave as he steps into the foyer. His wide eyes tell me he's looking for a safe place. I want to run up to him and share the good news—that this can be that place for him. But I hold back, letting Vee do her responsible-caregiver thing. She's really perfect at that.

"I'm so glad you're here, Isiah," she says.

My heart swells. I hope Isiah can tell that she means it.

"Is this place haunted?" asks the brown-eyed boy. "That's what people in my class say."

Vee crouches in front of him. Isiah looks at her from under his brow.

"I've lived here since I was a kid, and I've never, ever seen a ghost."

"Promise?" Isiah asks.

Vee nods. "What can I do for you, Isiah? Is there anything I can do to make this easier for you?"

Isiah chews his bottom lip. "Do you have *Wonder Woman*? The movie? I like her a lot."

There's a rumbling from behind the wall. Vee doesn't even glance in the direction of the sound. "I like her, too. I can put it on for you, but how about we check out your room first? Halle? Would you show Isiah upstairs?"

I nod and lead Isiah up the stairs. Halfway to the top he slips his warm, clammy hand into mine. There's another rumble from down the hall, and Isiah squeezes my hand.

"The house is just saying hello," I say.

He looks a little confused. "It's dark down that hall."

"Are you afraid of the dark?"

The lights above me begin to flicker on.

"Not really," Isiah says.

They sputter back out as I push open the newly formed door to his bedroom. As Isiah gets a look inside, all thoughts of strange noises and dark hallways leave him. He's standing with his mouth hanging open as he takes in the red walls accented by blue and yellow stripes, the movie posters that show Wonder Woman posing triumphantly, her golden lasso hanging off her hip, the Wonder Woman bedsheets and matching curtains.

"Is—is this for me?"

I rest my hand on his shoulder. "All for you."

"How did you know I liked Wonder Woman?"

"Call it a hunch."

Isiah bounds into the room and rolls on the bed, runs his hands over the painted walls, spins in a circle in the center of the room.

The doors fronting a small wardrobe pop open, and hanging inside are several different Wonder Woman costumes. Isiah pauses. His eyes dart between me and the wardrobe.

"Just promise me that when you dress up you won't use the lasso of truth on me," I say.

Ruby appears in the doorway, and almost as soon as she and Isiah make eye contact, they dismiss me.

As I leave, their laughter echoes down the hall.

I go to my own room and sit at my desk. My sketchbook sits open to the self-portrait I started a few months ago. It's unfinished, and I think about what it will look like when I'm done with it. There's a rumble in the wall, and suddenly a small, round mirror materializes from the wall. I look at my own reflection and smile.

MONSTER REFLECTION

I grew up with haunted-house stories. Tales of houses that are somehow cursed by the events that transpired within their walls have always been fascinating to me. As I was preparing to write for this anthology, I thought a lot about this specific horror trope and how I could rework it in a way that felt new and fresh, and I realized that I didn't need ghosts to do it. So often it isn't the structure that is "haunted"; it is the people. From *Poltergeist* to *The Amityville*

Horror to *The Conjuring, The Haunting of Hill House,* and *Beloved,* haunted-house stories are the stories of the people within.

Home isn't just a place to stay. Home should be a place to feel safe and where you can be surrounded by people who love and respect you. But we don't always get to have that. We are often forced to make do with what we have simply to survive. Living in a constant state of uncertainty, especially for children, is incredibly destabilizing, so much so that when something comes along that is good, that is right, we may not be able to recognize it, because we are fearful. Being vulnerable is incredibly scary sometimes. But having our needs met, having our passions nurtured, having our health and well-being prioritized is cathartic. We all deserve a soft place to land.

A SERPENT
AND A WISH

BY SHAE CARYS

N o one ventured close to the dark forest just beyond the village, but Nathaira found herself walking toward it with a stern determination. The black-and-gold serpent winding about her hand was agitated, having almost been cut in half by a panicked farmer. Though Nathaira had argued that the creature helped keep the rats who ate the farmer's grain at bay, he had not cared. Serpents, he claimed, were evil. God said it. The first evil was the serpent in the garden.

So Nathaira had scooped up the poor creature and rolled her eyes, walking toward the forest. These were the same people who called her cursed and bad luck, simply for the birthmark upon her face. Such small minds. They did not know any better.

The dead branches had not been cleared since last autumn, creating a gateway of spindly fingers, crisscrossing high enough to make an entrance to the forest. Clearly, the villagers had left this path to overgrow. They were forever superstitious. It reminded her of that game children played, cat's cradle, where they strung wool string between their fingers and tried to make patterns but just ended up with tangles. It was dark thanks to the cover of trees, and she shivered.

"You won't be safe unless I put you in there, will you, little friend?" she asked the serpent, lifting it in her palm, where it bent over her knuckles and hovered in the air, its tail curled around her hand for leverage. It tasted the air, calmer now, and she sighed. "Into the forest we go." She stepped across the threshold, dry leaves and branches crackling beneath her feet.

Once inside, she was surprised at the shafts of sunlight that pierced the canopy, guiding her into the woods proper. She followed the light, dazzled by its beauty. The serpent wove around her fingers, her arm, as if eager to finally be in its home. Once she was certain she'd traveled far enough into the forest, she paused. Closing her eyes, she listened.

It was beautiful.

Birds. Their songs and wingbeats between the high branches. The scrabbling of tiny paws. Chittering in foreign animal tongues. The soft creaks of the stalwart trees as they swayed in the slight wind, the rustling of their leaves. No voices. No yelling, no crying.

Just peace.

For as much as she had always been surrounded by the people of the village, she'd always been alone. Opening her eyes and kneeling, she lowered the serpent to the brown and red leaves covering the ground, letting it slither from her hand and onto the forest floor. "Now go, friend. It is not your fault people are superstitious and frightened of what they do not understand. Take care not to return to the village, though, even if the rats in Farmer Gaul's cellar are fat and juicy." She chuckled, watching the snake slither away across the dirt with a certain satisfaction.

"How kind of you," a voice called from behind, and Nathaira turned to see an elderly woman. Her garment was woven from vines and leaves, her fingers dirt-stained, one hand holding a staff made of a long, gnarled tree branch with a cascade of flowers, dried seeds, and moss hanging from the tip. Her white hair was pulled up into a messy bun, and her green eyes shone with a youth that surprised Nathaira. Everything about the woman surprised her. "Apologies if I've startled you. I was beginning to think the people had forgotten the forest."

"No. They're just afraid of it. . . ." Nathaira hesitated. "Are you a witch?"

The old woman's laughter was like crackling leaves. "No, child. Not a witch. Though I miss them, the herb women, the worshippers, the ones respectful of the seasons of the trees." She lowered herself to a fallen log, using her walking stick for aid.

"I apologize if the snake was yours." Nathaira frowned.

The woman laughed. "Oh, he's no pet. But he does belong here. He'll be happy enough hunting some mice."

The girl was confused but almost certain she had run into somebody's grandmother who had become lost in the woods. She slipped her hands into the pockets of her apron and tented them out, a nervous gesture she'd had since she was a child. "Do you live in the village? Is there someone who might be looking for you?"

Another laugh, one that made her rattle her stick, the leaves and flowers shaking. "Oh no, no, no! You think me some daft old woman who's wandered away from her home?"

Bemused, because she'd been rightly caught out, Nathaira shrugged. "Might've. If you're not, who are you?"

"Ah, but it's you who's wandered into my forest, child. It should be me asking you."

"Your forest? I wasn't aware that any but the lord owned this land."

"Lords. What a curious notion you mortals have, that metal and stones mined from the earth can make one man better than any other. Tell me—can you eat gold? Can a ruby stave off starvation?"

"Of course it can, if a man trades for it." Nathaira thought with logic. It only made sense to her you could trade something like that.

"But what if there is no one to trade with, and a man is alone?"

"Then . . . no, I suppose a ruby isn't a meal. At least not one that will sit well."

"Ah. See. It is the scarcity that gives it value, not its actual use. It is terrible that people do not feel the same about their own kind." The woman gestured to Nathaira's face, and the girl flushed, turning away the half with the vivid purple mark. "All for a bit of marking on your face? Which is perfectly natural."

"So is red hair, but they say they're witches, too." Nathaira didn't like that, but it didn't matter.

"Well, you asked if I was a witch? Does that idea frighten you?"

"No. I'm not afraid of witches. A witch has never spat on me or called me cursed, thrown stones at me, or accused me of killing my mother and father."

"I am sorry, girl." The old woman clucked her tongue and rattled her stick again. "You showed a kind heart, so I will grant you one wish. There will be a cost, depending upon what you wish, but it will be fair and just."

"A wish?" Nathaira laughed. "What could you give me, grandmother-not-a-witch? Are you a vessel of God, then, granting His miracles?"

"Ah. You still think me one of your own kind. Tsk. No, I thanked you for bringing me the serpent because he is a part of me, as is everything in this forest. The loam, the trees, the insects that buzz, the leaves that fall, the birds that sing and sing . . . I am not God, but I am not of man."

Nathaira's eyes widened. "How do I know you're not Beelzebub himself?"

"Because you don't believe in him, my darling. Man is his own devil and his own god. He became such when he stopped believing in anything but himself."

"That's heresy," Nathaira said, her voice shaking.

"It's true," the elder snapped, fixing her a sharp look.

"I . . . You said that there was a cost. What is the cost?"

"Ah, smart child. You listen well, unlike many of your brethren." The woman opened her hands, and Nathaira saw the serpent from earlier winding about her wrist to coil into her outstretched palm.

"You see, a little while ago, the forest had a protector. A fearsome, beautiful creature who would never tire, hunger, or grow old. Despite having the birdsongs, animals, and trees, they were lonely. There was no other like them. They had seen humanity and wanted to walk amongst them. I let them go. If I hadn't, their heart would have withered and died from want, and the forest has been without a protector since. You will become that protector."

"What does that mean?"

"It means, you will change to be what the forest needs. But it will happen only when you are ready to leave your mortal life."

Nathaira had never had to make a choice like this. She hadn't been given a choice when the monastery took her in. How often did a wish such as this fall into one's lap? Was it too good to be true?

"What if I'm never ready?" Nathaira raised her eyes to meet the old woman's gaze, still that vivid green, even in the dark.

"I would never have chosen you if you weren't, if you couldn't be. And you never would have saved him." She gave a little bob of her hand, the one holding the serpent, who sat curled in her palm, tasting the air.

That warmed Nathaira, but she was still uncertain. A wish for a duty. There were so many things she could think of, so many possibilities, but all she could really think of was one thing. The past couldn't be changed. Only the future could.

"If I'm not ready to make my wish yet, what can I do?"

"If a seed is not ready to sprout, one cannot force it. But there are plenty of things for mortal man to wish for. Metals from the earth. Stones and gems. A house made of wood or stone, perhaps?"

"No, none of that," Nathaira said. "The church would probably take it. As a tithe or some such."

"How about a handsome lord for a husband, then?"

She shrugged. "I've never really had much use for men."

"Very well. I will give you until next the moon sits in the sky. Return here, and tell me what it is you desire. If you do not . . ."

Nathaira nodded, understanding the implication. It was not often that one was offered their heart's desire by a forest, simply for saving a snake.

Nathaira returned to the village, carrying a pile of thick sticks she'd collected as an excuse for her absence. Firewood was always a good excuse, and she'd waited until she was out of the forest proper to collect them. It just seemed polite. As she walked along the row of homes and shops, she spotted the golden head of Lindie, her heart skipping for the second time that day.

"Lindie! Wait!"

The girl stopped, her smile widening as she saw Nathaira with her arms full of wood. "Ah, you've saved me a task today, bless you. I was supposed to do that, and here you've gone and done it for me."

"I had to escort a tiny visitor to the forest, and there was wood to spare along my way. All fallen branches from the storm a few nights ago." She shrugged, trying to play off her giddiness at the fact that Lindie was pleased with her. The two, both orphans, had been taken in by the church a few years back. Lindie was sent from a neighboring town with no monastery, bearing a letter with a plea to take her in. Nathaira had grown up here, after her parents had succumbed to a winter sickness that folks had cruelly whispered was Nathaira's own doing. Thankfully, Lindie was one of the few who had never treated her with such superstition.

"A tiny visitor. Did it have scales?" Lindie asked, leaning in to whisper conspiratorially.

"How did you know?" Nathaira grinned.

"I heard Planc shouting about it earlier. For the life of me I'll never understand how a journeyman farmer is afraid of snakes, of all things."

Nathaira laughed. "We women deal with much more frightening things than snakes on a daily basis, do we not?"

"Oh, you mean like leering boys and our monthly curses?" Lindie said, a gentle smirk on her lips.

"Precisely!"

Brother Florence, the monk in charge of the orphans and foundlings at the monastery, called to them and gestured toward the fence.

"Ah. Duty calls." Nathaira handed the wood to Lindie, happy to let her friend take the credit for collecting it. Her own chores awaited, and with a farewell nod, she went about them.

Nathaira daydreamed all morning and afternoon of her wish. What would she ask for? What could she? She could wish anything. To fly. To be immortal. All the wealth she would ever need. To have her parents back. As she worked in the churchyard, cleaning the stones of the fence, she thought on it. The wishes became more and more absurd in her mind until she was certain she'd drive herself mad.

"Nathaira! Come get yourself some dinner," Brother Florence called kindly to her, his portly cheeks ruddy from the sun that was beginning to set. "You've been cleaning that same stone for half an hour past."

She nodded and dropped her cloth into the pail, which she picked up and carried with her into the monastery. After cleaning up, followed by a few bites of the usual modest stew the monks made for dinner, she walked to her bedroom and heard a soft sound coming from inside.

It was weeping.

Lindie.

Nathaira stopped outside the door, her heart aching.

"—miss home. I miss you. You were right, Mother. I don't belong here," Lindie said, sniffling behind the door of their shared bedroom.

Nathaira paused. Lindie had never mentioned her mother before. The woman still lived? Perhaps she spoke to her spirit, as Nathaira did sometimes. She immediately felt guilty for eavesdropping and gently rapped her knuckles on the door, then opened it. "Lindie? Is everything all right?"

"Oh, yes." The other girl raised her sleeve to dab at her eyes. "It's been such a long day, hasn't it? I've never quite adjusted well to the sun disappearing earlier and earlier."

Nathaira smiled softly, taking a seat on the edge of Lindie's bed beside her friend. "Well, the good thing is that they can't work us any longer than the sun is out, so . . ."

Lindie laughed. "That is exceedingly true."

Nathaira gently nudged her friend, and Lindie rested her head against her shoulder.

Nathaira stared at the small tapestry that hung on the wall across from them, old and threadbare. What kind of life was this? A ward of the church? She knew what was expected of both of them—they would enter into service at a cloister of their own. What choice was that?

She turned her eyes to Lindie, then smiled. "I've a need to fetch something, but I will be back soon. Tomorrow is the festival, remember? At least there is that to look forward to?"

Lindie nodded. The harvest festival was one of the last remaining vestiges of the pagan traditions they still had in the village, no matter how the brothers wished to drive them away.

Old superstitions stuck, for better or worse.

Nathaira had to sneak out, slipping past the dormitories of the servants and the few novices that called the monastery their home. The creaky wood door was silent for her tonight, and she murmured a prayer of thanks to it as she slipped out into the dark monastery yard. Her eyes scanned the starless sky. The moon must have been blocked by clouds, for she could not see where it sat. There was a way around the back of the village that was rare for others to use. Nathaira took it often, when she didn't want to field the crosses and gestures of the other villagers when they looked upon her face. She made her way around toward the entrance of the forest, then heard a voice call out.

"Nathaira? Is that you, girl?" It was Farmer Gaul's voice, slurred. He must have been drinking. No one came this close to the forest at night. No one but her, apparently. "You going to your master?"

Damn. Nathaira stopped and looked back, frowning. "Farmer Gaul."

"That's why you took that snake! Saving your master's other servants! I knew you was from the Devil!" He waggled the torch at her before swinging it wildly in the air. Nathaira raised her hands, backing up toward the mouth of the forest. The moon would be high in no time, though she couldn't see it to tell just where. She couldn't waste her time with this. Too much was at stake.

"No, I rescued the snake because your boy was about to cleave it in half with a shovel! No creature deserves that."

"It was lying in wait to kill me. Just like you with your mam and pap!"

Nathaira flinched, her eyes suddenly burning, the pit in her stomach gnawing back to life. It was what they all believed, wasn't it? That she'd been responsible. "You know nothing, Farmer. Stick to your plows and plants." She spat.

"You go in there, girl, and I'll be sure to tell them all you're consorting with the Devil! They'll rightly put you out."

"Perhaps they should have left me in the forest, like you would have. You *good* people who whisper and sneer. Now leave me be, you drunken sot." Nathaira knew he'd never go in after her, so she stepped toward the threshold to the darkness, the moonlit gnarls and briars. The forest may have been dark, but at least she thought she knew what lay in its heart.

Farmer Gaul's voice swelled. "Brothers! Good brothers, your ward is sneaking away to consort with a demon!"

Nathaira froze. What if . . . what if he was right? What if this was some devil attempting to trick her? What Farmer Gaul was shouting, though . . . she could be pilloried for this. Or worse.

A torch flared to life from the back of the monastery, and Nathaira darted toward the brush at the mouth of the woods, trying to see who had awoken. If it was Brother Alms or Brother David, she was in dire trouble. They were the most eager of the brethren to seek out heresy and burn it at the root. And she had been heretical, hadn't she? Consorting with . . . whatever that elderly woman had been. She might have said she wasn't a witch, but the church had long established that witches employed trickery.

When she saw the red face of Brother Florence once again, she felt relief. The monk trundled out from the back of the monastery toward them.

"Farmer Gaul, what have we told you about shouting while you're in the drink—" He was kind about it, but there was a consternation to his portly face. No doubt he had been pulled away from his manuscripts. When he saw Nathaira, surprise registered on his face. "Now, Nathaira. You know better than to be out in the darkness of night. It is not safe and is quite forbidden."

"I'm sorry, Brother Florence. I was ... I—"

"I dared her," came Lindie's clear voice from the door of the monastery, the girl standing there in her nightdress, rue in her face. "I told her that only a coward would not enter the forest at night, and ... it was wrong. I should not have done that."

"Ah. Children and their foolish pride. Come, come. Back to your beds." He waved in a circle, gesturing toward the door.

"Yes, Brother." Nathaira nodded, though she felt her opportunity slipping away behind her. The old woman had told her that she must return by moonrise, else her wish would be all for naught. Perhaps it was better this way. Her immortal soul would not be at risk. A wish, though ... What else could be worth the risk? Her eyes trailed to Lindie, who shook her head gently, as if she knew the temptation that plagued Nathaira. Her friend had already risked trouble to save her. The brothers were kind but would tolerate disobedience only to a point, and as much as she treasured the other girl, she didn't want to leave both of them without a home. Nathaira entered the monastery with Lindie and the monk followed, shutting the heavy wooden door behind.

"Why were you outside? At night? This village has no shortage of troublemakers—"

"Lindie, I know. It was a fool's notion," Nathaira said, following her friend into their shared quarters. She didn't know how to explain it to Lindie without sounding mad, so she remained quiet, unlacing her bodice and changing into her nightclothes.

"You should have known better." Lindie gestured her brush at her, scolding.

"What if . . . what if there was something in the forest, something worth risking going out at night for?"

Lindie turned, pausing with the brush in her hair, staring at her a moment. Some unknowable thought crossed her face, and she frowned. "What could be in the forest worth your life?"

"I'm afraid now I'll never know." Nathaira dropped to the edge of her bed, glancing at the door. Despair filled her heart.

One wish. She hadn't even known what to wish for, truly, and it had slipped from her hands.

The belfry rang loud that morning at sunrise. Villagers approached the monastery with their covered loaves, made from the first fruits of the harvest. The scent of baked bread filled the air as Nathaira dressed. While the sounds of celebration would fill the streets and the other villagers would rejoice, she would stay to the side, as she always had. She'd never truly loved festival days. The superstitions that hung around her meant that most traditions were not meant for her. The excuse that she was an orphan was mostly used. She had no family to engage with, nor any true friends save Lindie. Even Lindie's excitement could not drive away the feeling that she'd truly missed out on something. Something old. Something special. Something she'd been looking for her entire life.

Lindie had already gone, but on her cot was a crown made of the last flowers of the fall, clearly meant for Nathaira. She lifted it, studying the intricate weaving, the colors of the dried flowers, vivid and varied. She'd never seen anything as beautifully made. If any other hands had made it, she would have refused it, but . . . for Lindie, she would wear it. She placed it delicately on her head and left their room, winding through the dormitories, past the kitchens and the refectory, past the calefactory where they could warm in the winter. When she finally made it outside, she saw the sun, heard the cheers and voices of the people, and was filled with dread.

"Blessings!" Lindie lit up when she saw the crown on Nathaira's head. "You found it." She embraced Nathaira and kissed her cheek. "It's nice to not have to scrub floors or clean the privy for a day, isn't it?"

Blushing slightly, since the kiss to her cheek had felt rather nice, Nathaira raised an eyebrow and scoffed to cover her flush. "I'd rather scrub the privy if it meant not having to deal with people."

"You can't mean that." Lindie glanced toward the square, where the main festivities had been prepared. "We've a little time before it's our turn to serve. Shall we dance?" Lindie extended her hand, and Nathaira shook her head.

"And give them reason to throw stones at you because you're with me? No. You go and dance. I'll stay here."

"But—"

Nathaira glanced at the food carts. "I haven't eaten. I'll find some food and meet you in a little while."

Lindie could hardly argue with her friend's need for food. She nodded and ran off to the cluster of dancing youths, swiftly finding a partner. Nathaira lingered and watched her friend. She never had any trouble fitting in, but . . . what Lindie had wept about struck her. Perhaps that was why she liked festival days. It wasn't hard to lose oneself in the festivities, to become a part of everything . . . well, at least if you looked normal. As Nathaira walked toward the cluster of booths, she heard a commotion. Shouting. *Roaring.*

She pivoted, and her steps picked up pace toward the sounds as others ran away. When she came upon the group near the edge of the forest, she saw a young black bear, no doubt called by the smells of the cooking meat and baking bread. Young though it was, it was still large, and the cluster of boys around it jeered as they tried to hit it with their axes and pitchforks. The bear swiped its paw at the group that laughingly circled it. The people of the village were gathering, watching the fray.

"Stop! Stop it!" Nathaira pushed a few bodies away and approached the group, heart beating fast. The bear rounded on her, stood on its hind legs, and laid back its ears. "Shh, shh, it's all right. Just go back home. . . ."

"Move, you stupid girl!" Farmer Gaul's voice cut through the shouting, and she turned. He held a pitchfork aloft, preparing to stab the bear. There was a shout, and Nathaira caught a quick movement from the corner of her eye.

"No, please!" Lindie dashed in front of the creature, and the pitchfork hurtled toward her instead.

"Lindie!" Without a second thought, Nathaira darted forward, her arms outstretched and her body now blocking Lindie and the bear. At the moment she felt the pitchfork pierce her skin, she thought only of her friend, and she knew her wish.

I would have wished for Lindie to live a happy life.

The world stopped. It was silent, except for the sound of the wind. The rustling of the trees. The stabbing pain of the pitchfork disappeared. When Nathaira finally heard footsteps, she looked up to see Lindie standing next to the old woman from the forest.

Nathaira slowly pushed herself up, running her hand over her chest. There was no blood. The bear was gone, the young men, the village. There was no commotion around her, no people. She heard only the beating heart of the forest, the birds, and the leaves. They were in the forest, and Lindie looked at her in awe, smiling.

"Oh, Mother. Thank you."

A black snake with a gold crown slithered across Nathaira's cheek, and its tongue flicked out, kissing her nose, and she recognized it as the serpent she had rescued earlier. Nathaira reached up, feeling her own hair, only it wasn't hair. She felt the vines, the smooth, soft bodies of the winding serpents. The bear? Had this been a test? She laughed in disbelief, delight. "What . . . what happened?"

"A test," the old woman said. "Simply a test. You earned your wish." She shook her stick again.

"But . . . you said when the moon was high. I missed it. I missed my chance."

"The moon?" Lindie looked confused, then laughed softly. "There was no moon last night. Mother does like her riddles. She let me leave to find my heart's content, only I thought I would be less lonely with them. The humans. But they weren't like me, and they just made me feel more alone. All of them but you."

"I only wished for you to be happy," Nathaira said, her voice soft.

"And I only wanted not to be alone."

Lindie extended her hand toward Nathaira, who took it and glanced around the forest, which seemed no longer so dark and dangerous. A golden shimmer flickered in the air, and Lindie changed. Instead of her long golden hair, she wore a crown of vines, inside which a nest of serpents slowly wound. Her eyes were a shifting amber and green, the same colors as the forest. She was still beautiful, but otherworldly. Her friend looked down at her with surprise, then recognition, and . . . hope?

"Can we dance now?" Lindie asked with a soft laugh.

"Oh, yes. We shall dance."

MONSTER REFLECTION

The creature I chose was the gorgon. I remember being a child and watching the old classic *Clash of the Titans* on television with my father. I was never frightened by Medusa but rather fascinated with her instead. I didn't understand why she deserved to get her head cut off. Was it just because she was fearsome? When I started to read Greek mythology, I realized that most of the humanoid monsters had tragic stories or were simply misunderstood. I didn't want to make a Medusa story straight-out, so I built into the story what I felt Medusa truly stood for—loneliness. Through no fault of her own was she outcast. She was a beautiful woman once who became a gorgon, and I wanted to play with both sides of that. I know, I know. Another origin story. At least this one has a happy ending!

THE GIRL WITH THIRTEEN SHADOWS

BY MERC FENN WOLFMOOR

I can fix you."

That's the first thing the doctor says. Not even a hello. Behind the disposable mask, you can't tell if he's smiling. His eyes are sharp blue like a new highlighter.

"That's what we all want," your dad says, squeezing your hand.

You nod, keeping your shadows carefully aligned so it looks like only one under the fluorescent lights. You already tried to be normal. You tried so hard, and it just didn't work, and you're scared you're broken forever.

The doctor waves you toward the examination table. The room smells like disinfectant, and the paper cover crinkles under your thighs as you take a seat. You bite the inside of your cheek, your stomach in little knots. You're nineteen, and this is the first time you've been to a doctor since you were small and got your booster shots. You have no idea what to expect.

All you know is that the neatly groomed man with intense eyes is a professional, the only one of his kind. You're lucky he had room in his schedule to treat you. But most important, he's going to fix you.

"First of all," the doctor says, "tell me what kind of monster you are."

The shadows multiplied when you were six years old. They shimmied out at different angles, little-girl shapes like a reverse prism: darkness instead of rainbows.

You counted ten, but that was a trick of the light; there were only five total. Five shadows were exciting! One of them was normal and stayed in place when it was bright. The other four could make cool shapes and move by themselves when you let them. You didn't think any of your friends had that many.

When you showed off your shadows to your dad, all the color vanished from his face, like actors in those black-and-white vampire movies.

"Mel," he said, kneeling in front of you, his hands shaking as he held your shoulders. "You can't ever show other people this, okay?"

"But why not? I'm so cool!"

You made your shadows spin and dance around you, grinning because your body didn't move.

Your dad flinched, and suddenly you got scared. You'd never seen your dad shaken up before.

"What's wrong, Daddy?"

"Honey, there are going to be people who don't understand you because you're different. Sometimes people get frightened, and they try to hurt the things that scare them. I don't want you to get hurt, okay? So you need to promise me you'll never show off your shadows to anyone. Promise me, Melanie."

"Okay, Daddy. I won't."

But one of your shadows crossed its fingers behind your back for you, so you didn't *really* swear.

Your dad laughs nervously at the doctor's question. "You get a lot of supernatural patients?"

The doctor ushers your dad to the door. "Would you give Melanie and me a moment to discuss her symptoms?"

Your dad opens his mouth to protest. You shake your head. You want him to stay so badly, but you need the doctor to fix you. Besides, you're not a minor, so you don't technically need a parent present for this.

"I'm fine." You and your dad both know you're not.

Once your dad is waiting outside in the lobby again, the doctor logs into his computer.

"When you filled out the questionnaire," he says, "you listed several causes of concern, namely your lack of libido for a healthy young woman your age, and the excessive shadows."

Your cheeks flush, and you dig your fingernails into your jeans. Your shadows ache, the edges shifting, the anchor points along your spine chafing. Like sitting in one position for too long, the shadows want to move and flex—but you keep them pinned. You want to itch, except you've already got sores on your back from scratching too much.

"I don't know what's wrong with me," you blurt out.

The doctor nods. "Show me."

"What?"

"You're in a safe place here, Melanie. I specialize in helping people with monstrous handicaps overcome their . . . unique impediments. I can fix you. But only if you cooperate and show me."

You squeeze your eyes shut against the tears, then let the shadows unfurl. They dance and whisper, four shades of you swaying on the plain white walls of the examination room, while your static—*normal*—shadow remains the same.

"Incredible," the doctor says.

"I don't want to be a monster," you whisper.

"Don't worry, Melanie," the doctor says. "I can take away your shadows and give you back your life. I've little doubt these are the root of your other problem, too."

You don't ask how much it will cost. Anything is worth it to be normal.

Your dad loves romantic comedies. You've tried to enjoy romance, too, because you're a teenage girl and you ought to be crazy for boys—or girls, or both—and yearning to go on dates or anticipating your first kiss.

The thing is, you just . . . don't think about those things. Or maybe you think about *not* thinking about them. It's confusing. Kissing sounds kind of gross. Sex is a whole other topic you don't even want to imagine. The idea of someone's hands or dick or lips touching you makes you cringe.

For a while, that was fine. You turned thirteen and never had a boyfriend/girlfriend like most of your peer group. You hit puberty at fourteen and braced for the raging hormones. You got them, too, but mostly the sucky kind with period cramps and mood swings.

You still didn't have any desire to kiss a boy (or a girl) at fifteen. You had to start faking a long-distance online relationship so your friends would stop trying to hook you up and you could avoid that specific brand of bullying. You lived in a fairly liberal college town, and your dad was queer, proud, and open-minded. So it wasn't like you were trapped in a puritanical small-town horror show, suffocated with rigid social norms and gender expectations.

Hell, your dad was even chill about you waiting until you were older to start dating.

Your dad is trans and a single parent, and you love him, but he doesn't get it. He's normal, not a monster. He's had some good long-term boyfriends, men you like to hang out with, but

235

he hasn't been willing to commit to anyone since your bio father died when you were little.

So, as much as you love your dad, he can't help you. He's tried: he lays on the dad jokes, falls down research rabbit holes, and wastes so much toner printing off reams of forum discussions and articles and blog posts instead of, like, just linking you to the sources.

When you were ten, he started telling you about other monsters in the world. His sister had been a monster girl. The aunt you never knew. She disappeared when your dad was a teenager. He still does online searches for her name once a year. Nothing ever comes up.

"Can I meet them?" you asked once. "The other monsters?"

"No, sweetie," your dad said with that awkward, forced smile he wore when he was trying not to be sad. "It's safer if we don't talk about it. Just focus on school and living your life, okay?"

And you *tried*; you really did. The problem was everyone around you was dating, talking about romantic partners, or ranking boys on how hot they were. Your peers were mimicking the latest fashion icons in magazines and social media. You felt like an extra shadow on everyone else's happiness: wrong and unsettling.

"You'll meet someone perfect for you," your dad would promise, over and over, eternally optimistic.

You made yourself read romance books and watched romcoms with your dad, and you even sneaked a peek at his gay porn collection once. It didn't do much beyond making you horribly embarrassed about possibly being caught.

You were just a late bloomer, you told yourself. You were shy, and besides, once you had to worry about controlling your shadows, it made dating seem like a real hassle.

By this point, though, your dad is worried. You've never been on a date. You've never wanted to kiss someone. It's not just the shadows that make you a monster. There's something broken inside you, too.

That's the only explanation. You need someone to fix you because you're scared that once people find out how wrong you are inside, you'll always be alone.

You catch your dad staring at a crisply printed letter in the kitchen. He doesn't notice you, wrapped in shadow like you are when at home since it makes you feel safe, so you peer over his shoulder.

It's a bill for your doctor's visit. A co-pay of a hundred dollars. Honestly, given he's a specialist, that seems low. But then you scan down to a section labeled *cost for full treatment*, and your mouth sags open in horror.

"Holy shit," you say before you can stop yourself. Twenty thousand dollars? It's not like you have cancer or need emergency surgery—

Your dad jumps and looks at you. He forces a smile. "It'll be fine, Melanie. If it helps you, I'll figure out how we can afford it. I could talk to your grandma. . . ."

You shake your head, tears clouding your eyes. You know how much your dad hates to ask his mom for anything, given the shit she put him through as a kid. Even if she *would* chip in for legit medical bills, you can't let your dad get hurt again.

High school was the worst, not just the bullies or the systematic grind designed to wear you down into passive acceptance of authority. You struggled so hard to keep the shadows contained. It was somehow easier when you were younger, when you wrapped yourself in darkness and could sneak around undetected. You *tried* to be normal, you honestly did, but it was a losing battle. Poor grades because you couldn't focus . . . too many absences because the thought of the brutal lighting gave you panic attacks . . . and the constant strain of just existing with your shadows led to more than one breakdown. So you dropped out.

You know how much it hurt your dad, but what else could you do? There was no room for a monster like you.

Your dad tried to hide his feelings and told you he understood, but you know it's a lie.

You figure you can get a GED or fudge your résumé when looking for a job. The trouble is, you can't work a normal job to help with bills, when everything in-person involves light sources that force you to concentrate to keep your shadows hidden. It's like school all over again. You just can't.

You want to study for college via remote programs (you figure accounting is a good choice, even if it's boring, because at least you could do that at home and not in an office). Your dad's job is always precarious as an elementary math teacher, what with budget cuts and the ever-restrictive state rules on who gets to be a person in the first place.

So no, you can't afford medical bills like this.

"We'll figure it out, sweetie," your dad says, hugging you.

You keep your shadows reeled in tight when you hug him back.

The hospital is an old building, crouched on a windswept hill. It's Gothic and intimidating, and it reminds you of horror-movie castles. All it needs is lightning cracking open painted sky backgrounds in chiaroscuro. It's a private institution, established by a family whose bloodline founded the town.

Your dad is stuck in meetings today, so you bike over to the hospital for a follow-up appointment.

"The doctor is expecting you," says the receptionist at the front desk. She doesn't smile.

"You won't have a life worth living if you remain like this," the doctor says. He's spent the first five minutes explaining that he ran tests on your blood draw from last time. "Likely the corrosion of these extra shadows will shorten your life span by decades. I would make an educated guess that without correction, you would have less than six months to live. . . ."

Your heartbeat gathers like a hurricane, turning into a roar in your ears. You'll die? But the shadows don't hurt you. They never have, unless you keep them repressed for too long. Then they itch uncontrollably.

When you were a girl, you used them like a sunshade when you played in the park, and at sleepovers, you made the best shadow puppets, better than anyone else.

Then the other girls stopped inviting you over, and your dad took you to the park less and less. He had awkward, half-whispered conversations with you in the bathroom about how you were going to hit puberty at some point, and your body would change, and these *other* changes—these shadows—were too scary for normal people to handle.

It broke your heart into little puzzle pieces. Your dad was almost in tears as he explained things like menstruation and hormones and the way men would see you, a girl, as prey.

"You're not," he said, wiping his nose. "You're not prey."

"Because I'm a monster?"

His eyes widened. "No! Sweetie, no, you're . . . you're just different."

But that was a thing you learned young: different was bad. And only monsters had too many shadows.

The doctor is still talking to you, listing statistics and case studies; you missed all the specifics. You blink hard, trying to focus on him under his halo of light.

You clench your hands in your lap. "You said you can fix me?"

"Yes." He's taken off his mask for the first time, and you notice a faint dent along his lower jaw as if it'd been broken once and didn't heal quite right. "But we need to get started right away."

"I can't. I mean, my dad and I can't afford it," you say, surprised at how steady your voice is. Hollow, distant. You feel like you are at the bottom of a well, a drowning girl trying to shout past the murky water filling your lungs.

The doctor nods. "I understand. My expertise is a costly investment. But I think we could work something out. If you'd agree to work here at the hospital part-time, say as the receptionist, I could significantly reduce the costs of your treatment."

But he already has a receptionist? Or does he need a replacement? It doesn't matter; this is an offer you can't turn down.

"Okay," you blurt out, because if you think too hard, you'll chicken out and run away and then you'll *die*.

The doctor beams at you, his eyes that same highlighter blue. "Well, Melanie, let's get started, shall we?"

You and your dad have your first major fight when you get home and tell him the news. He thinks you're being taken advantage of, even though you signed the W-4 and the I-9 and the NDAs one of the staff handed you. It's legal, you're nineteen and entitled to work, and the hospital is only a forty-minute bike ride from home.

"This isn't ethical!" your dad shouts.

"I'm going to die!" you scream back, and your shadows flare out, four sharp-edged wings that quiver and hum.

Your dad's eyes widen. "What?"

You tell him the rest of it—maybe you should have started with that fact, but it's too late now; the fight is already written into the fabric of your lives like indelible ink. You show him the report the doctor gave you, which outlines how the shadows are absorbing your bone marrow like cancerous growths.

"I'm going to work tomorrow," you say, ending the discussion. Your shadows flutter back into your skin. Funny how they always feel like a beloved sweatshirt or a cozy blanket and never like the bone-chewing disease they are.

Your dad looks so tired. Worried. Defeated.

"Okay, Mel," he says. "Let me drive you, all right?"

"Think of it as getting your wisdom teeth pulled," the doctor says, but since you've never had that surgery, you don't have a point of comparison, other than it will hurt.

Even with the anesthetic, it hurts, it hurts, it *hurts*—

You aren't sure when you passed out, but once you come to your senses, groggy and confused, you're down to four shadows. There's only an aching hole in your awareness where the fifth had been.

You start crying and don't know why.

The receptionist job is pretty easy. Strangely, the hospital doesn't get a lot of patients. Maybe because it's so exclusive? Barb, the other receptionist, has made no mention of retiring or looking for a new job. You're still not certain why *this* specific position is what you were hired for.

Most of the patients who check in don't have any obvious . . . monstrous qualities. Not that there *are* many visitors to begin with.

You're intrigued by one boy, perhaps around your age, who comes in with a middle-aged woman on your second training shift. Barb sends you to get more printer paper, so you don't even get to meet the patient. He wears a big trench coat and a wide-brimmed hat pulled low over his face. His features are shadowed, unreadable.

He comes in a second time, without the woman—a parent?—but it's just as you're getting off and Barb is taking over the desk. She waves you aside before you can say hi to the boy.

You start online courses for your accounting degree, and the receptionist job gives you time to study.

The doctor says he needs to "pull" one shadow at a time over the course of several months, though when you ask why, he's evasive and says it's to keep your body from suffering from a massive shock.

You don't feel any better after the second monster shadow is pulled. It's hard to focus. You suspect you've lost weight, which gets you compliments from some of the staff but secretly makes you sick to your stomach. You feel like you're wasting away. No one seems to find it problematic.

You're too nervous to ask the doctor about your other issue. The whole "not attracted to people or interested in sex" thing. The broken piece of you.

The shadows are more malignant, of course. It makes sense to triage those first.

Yet you can't shake the desperate undertone in your thoughts. What if he can only excise your shadows? That's all that he focuses on. What if he can't fix the rest of you?

After the third shadow is removed, you call in sick because you're in too much pain. The doctor sends a car to pick you up, explaining that there is a complimentary room for you at the hospital, like a boutique hotel, where you can stay and work under medical supervision. Your dad isn't home yet, so you don't have much of a choice. You agree.

You never had nightmares growing up. The four monstrous shadows ate all your bad dreams. Now, after surgery, you can barely sleep. The nightmares are awful: constant scenes of being picked apart by scalpels and needles, and all you can see are the doctor's cold blue eyes. He never helps you in your dreams.

You have only one monstrous piece left.

You miss your shadows, but if this is the price of normal, what else can you do?

With three of your shadows excised, you are desperate to test how far your cure has progressed.

You see the boy in the trench coat enter the front doors and shuffle into the waiting room. Barb pays him no heed. You clench your hands inside your pockets. You desperately want to know if the other patients here are improving.

He has his back to you as he shrugs out of his coat and hat. You put a hand over your mouth.

His head is covered with wavy black hair . . . and a pair of sharp wolflike ears poke through his curls. His arms are covered in soft, dark fur. When he turns to sit, you see his face. His eyes are big and liquid brown, like the saddest puppy's in the world. The rest of his face is covered in patchy fur, which spreads down his neck.

He jumps like he's seen a ghost. A high-pitched yip escapes him. "Ah, shit!"

"I'm sorry!" You hold up your hands, palms out, and back into the wall. "I didn't mean to sneak up on you."

He snatches his hat and holds it in front of him like a shield. "Who are you?"

"I work here," you explain, your cheeks burning. "Part-time. I'm also a patient."

Slowly, the boy relaxes and twists his hat between his hands. Each fingertip has a blunted little claw in place of a regular fingernail. He wears a blue T-shirt with the Superman logo on it and jeans with frayed knees. Fur peeks out from the patches. "That makes sense. I hardly ever see anyone else here. . . ."

Your heartbeat drums along at its own tempo, though you focus on breathing evenly, in and out, in and out. You hadn't expected to see someone else so clearly different. "I'm Melanie."

The wolf-eared boy sinks down onto the edge of a chair. He smiles. His teeth are yellowed and sharp.

"I'm Ramsey." He tosses his hat aside and digs into his coat pocket, pulling out a thick stack of trading cards. "Do you like Pokémon? Do you want to play?"

You glance over your shoulder, but Barb is absorbed in one of her paperback romance novels and ignores you.

"Sure."

You settle cross-legged on the carpet near him. Ramsey excitedly explains the rules of the Pokémon cards, though you only half pay attention. You want to ask how he found this place, how the doctor's treatments are going, what he'll do when he's normal. You bite the inside of your cheek, reeling your remaining shadow tight under your skin.

You shouldn't pry, and you don't want to come across as rude to a guy you just met.

His ears are velvety and pointed, and they look so soft. You wonder if he likes them. Or if he's getting rid of his wolf ears like he wants to be rid of his fur and his claws.

". . . and like, Mom says that her great-uncle had hypertrichosis, but it's not just werewolf syndrome." Ramsey blinks, as if startled from his own babbling. "What I have, I mean."

You struggle to follow along. He was explaining the game's mechanics, and then he switched almost midsentence to why he was in the clinic. He lowers his voice, his eyes wide and dark and a little scared.

"I'm actually a monster."

"Me too," you whisper back.

Ramsey gasps. "You *are*?"

You flinch away, unsure if it's wonderment or horror in his expression.

"But not much longer," you hurry on. "Are your procedures almost finished, too?"

"Oh . . ." All the cards are laminated so his nails don't leave scratches. "I'm not sure. We keep hitting . . . complications, but—"

"Mr. Lawrence," Barb calls from the front desk. "The doctor will see you now."

Ramsey's ears flatten against his curly hair. His shoulders hunch as he gathers up his cards, shoving them back into his coat pocket. You realize you're still holding a Pikachu card and offer it back to him.

Ramsey smiles with closed lips. "You can keep it. Maybe we can play a match next time."

You watch him go, your stomach knotting into pretzels.

When you were twelve, you began Googling phrases like *why don't I feel attracted to anyone* and *zero sex drive* and variations. You'd gotten a lot of ads for Viagra and sites offering online therapy for depression, but once you weeded out the obvious dead ends, you eventually came across a Medium post titled "How I Discovered I Was Ace."

I began wondering if something was wrong with me after I broke up with my boyfriend because I didn't enjoy having sex nearly as much as he did. In fact, I didn't like it at all—and I didn't like him the way he seemed to like me. Not, you know, as a person. It was more like, he was fine, but I didn't desire him the way he desired me.

At first, I thought I was broken or just a freak. But then my best friend asked me, "Do you think you might be asexual instead?"

A shiver crept through your shadow as you read on.

There is a wide spectrum of ace-ness! Gray ace and demi-ace, for example, and some ace people do like having sex or do it to please their partner(s). It's not a rigid binary of does/does not like X. But what really clicked for me was learning that not having sexual or romantic attractions to other people didn't make me a freak. Like, not everyone is straight or cis, right? So why would everyone be allosexual (that is, experiencing sexual attraction to other people regularly)?

You wondered, Could this be it? Was this the answer? It took you a week to work up the courage to print the essay and show it to your dad. *I know it can be scary and confusing, but questioning is a valid part of every journey, regardless of where you ultimately end up.*

After he read it, your dad looked at you with an expression you couldn't quite define. Worry?

"Do you think I'm ace?" you asked him, terrified he'd laugh at the idea.

He rubbed the back of his neck. "Oh, it's totally possible, sweetheart." He smiled. "I'm glad you're questioning things. That's great!"

You could feel the *but* coming and braced yourself. Your eyes stung with tears you desperately didn't want escaping.

"I'm so glad you trust me enough to talk to me about this stuff, too."

Dad held his arms out, and you flopped into a reassuring hug. Your heartbeat didn't slow.

"Just give it time, okay?" he went on, rubbing your back with one hand. "You're only twelve. People change as they grow up."

You nodded, sniffling, and hoped he was right.

Except he wasn't.

Your thirteenth birthday rolled around. Fourteen, fifteen, sixteen . . . you kept expecting to wake up one day and find yourself horny for boys, or wanting to kiss girls, or some combination of lust for both. Like a switch biology hadn't gotten around to flipping on.

Was the switch broken, or were you asexual? You didn't want this. You wanted to be normal. Like your dad.

You didn't bring up the subject with him again.

When you Googled things, later, it was about how to stop being a monster.

A week later, you spot Ramsey in the waiting room again. Relief spirals through you. You'd worried you'd missed him, that he'd been discharged without saying goodbye. You've tried to find innocuous ways to meet other patients, but it's been fruitless. Either no one lingers in the waiting room when you're off duty or they don't want to talk to you at the front desk.

Some have transitioned to in-patient care, according to the records. You don't see any of these people.

Ramsey gives a tiny wave. You check your phone. You have a few minutes before you're supposed to clock in.

Ramsey looks tired. Patches of fur on his neck are missing, showing irritated skin underneath, and his hair is limp and thin. He sits listlessly on a chair.

You perch beside him and show him the Pokémon card he gave you. "I read up on how to play online."

Ramsey turns his head, his eyelids drooping. His gaze keeps wobbling, drifting past you and then back to your face. "You did?"

"When my treatment is over, I'll buy my own deck."

His breath comes in slow, rattling wheezes. "Cool."

"Are you okay?"

He forces a smile. His lips are chapped. "Yeah, just the . . . treatments . . . are kinda rough."

A sudden flare of jealousy zips through you. Ramsey must be almost finished. He'll be cured soon. When he is, will he even want to play cards with you if you're still partially a monster?

You glance around the empty waiting room. "Do you come by yourself?"

His chin droops; then his head snaps up in a startled response. "What? Oh, sorry, Melanie. I'm just . . . tired."

The momentary envy fades to worry. He dresses in an oversize hoodie and baggy jeans. His hands are thinner than before, the fur patchy and scabbed with dandruff. You're reminded of pictures of kids with leukemia. The frailness, the easily bruised skin made papery from chemo.

"Where's your mom?"

Ramsey's shoulders hunch, and he curls in on himself. "She doesn't want me to come back until I'm better."

You hide a wince. "I'm sorry."

Your dad would never turn you away, yet you've been avoiding him.

"It's okay," Ramsey says, rubbing his eyes. "Doc says I'm almost there. . . ."

"Do you have anyone else?" you press. "A girlfriend? Boyfriend?"

Any friends? You keep that last part to yourself.

Ramsey's ears twitch. Then he laughs. It's a weak, crackling sound, but genuine. "Do I look like the kind of guy girls wanna kiss?"

Your heartbeat skitters. Is this an opportunity? A challenge?

You've been thinking about Ramsey. You kept the trading card under your pillow, willing yourself to dream about the wolf-eared boy. He's cute, even with the fur—or maybe because of it. It's hard to tell.

You've got to prove to yourself the treatments are working. With three shadows gone, you should be feeling *something* for a boy. Or another girl. Maybe not love, but a crush—how hard can it be?

The doctor is fixing you. Once the shadows can't mute your desires, you'll fall in love. You're positive. You just have to fucking *try harder.*

You brace yourself, then lean in and kiss Ramsey on the lips. His skin is dry. He tastes like breath mints.

His eyes pop open wide, and he jerks his head back.

"Shit, sorry!" You scrabble over the chair arm, your face burning with embarrassment. "I'm sorry, I—"

He stares dumbfounded at you. "You kissed me?"

You uncurl your remaining monster shadow before you can think straight and wrap yourself in the darkness. God, what is *wrong* with you! This was a mistake; you've probably made him cringe—

"Whoa," Ramsey says. "Are those . . . your powers?"

You want to melt into the floor, sink through the foundations, and keep going until you burn up in the earth's core.

"That is so cool."

Startled, you peek through your shadow. Ramsey looks at you in wonder.

"You're not, um, mad?" You kick yourself mentally. Well, of course he's gaping at your monstrosity, like that will make him forget you kissed him without asking.

Your dad would be so disappointed in you. He taught you better than that.

"What?" Ramsey rubs the back of his hand across his mouth. "Oh! Um, sorry if I freaked out. I just . . ." He ducks his head. "I wasn't expecting that."

"I should've asked," you stammer.

He blinks several times, gazing at you through his lashes. "I was, um, it was a joke? About girls wanting to kiss me. 'Cause, like, I'm ace?"

Your mouth falls open in shock. "You are?"

Your thoughts whirl. How is he so bold? Admitting that to an almost stranger?

Ramsey pulls his knees to his chest. "I didn't mean to hurt your feelings. . . ."

"You didn't," you reply. "I just . . . I mean, I'm . . ."

His eyes brighten. "Wait, are you ace, too?"

Before you can answer, one of the orderlies steps in and motions for Ramsey. He shuffles after the man.

"Maybe?" you whisper to the empty room.

And what's scarier is that you almost feel okay saying that aloud.

You stop answering your dad's texts, though. He leaves worried voice mails. He even tries to visit you, but without an appointment, the security at the front gates won't let him in.

You're supposed to be getting better by now. There's only one bad shadow left.

Your dad is trying to protect you, and you know this, but it's too much pressure. You're not better. You don't want to disappoint him this badly.

You're failing your classes. Most of your concentration goes to *not* thinking about your missing shadows. Even your normal shadow looks . . . drained. Like it's fading, even when you stand in bright light. Why do you feel so awful, so piecemeal and thin, like tissue paper stretched over a cardboard box?

You'll have to drop out of online college if you can't fix your grades, and it's so pathetic you almost rage-quit instead. It's been a while since you've felt something sharp and real, like being mad at the world. Once you were happy, weren't you? You wish you could remember what that was like. Everything is gray and numb now.

Just two more weeks, you tell yourself. Two weeks until the last surgery and the monster shadows will all be gone.

On the day of your final appointment, the doctor pages you at the receptionist's desk and tells you that he must postpone your treatment.

"A very sick girl needs my full attention," he says, and the bottom falls out of your stomach. You're grateful the lobby is empty because you're almost in tears.

"When can we reschedule?" you ask.

"I don't know yet," the doctor snaps, and that sudden flare of impatience startles you. He's never been rude before. "Just focus on your job, and I'll let you know when we can finish your treatment."

He hangs up.

You stare at the phone, your hand shaking, then slam it back into its cradle. Your lone shadow flutters. For a moment, you're so mad you could scream—you're fucking *dying*, and he told you he could save you! You maintain your composure, though. Getting angry—or rather, letting it show—agitates your monster shadow. You force yourself to take several deep breaths, locking your jaw against the urge to yell.

"The trick is to work out your feelings where no one can see," your dad explained. "I know it sucks, but you'll get used to it."

Why should you, though? Because it makes other people— nonmonster people—uncomfortable if you *do* get angry?

The doctor says he's the only specialist in his field, but you're beginning to call bullshit.

"Hi, Dad, sorry I haven't called you back."

"Oh, thank God, sweetie, I was so worried! Are you okay?"

"I will be." You swallow the lump in your throat. You want to apologize, and also you're scared that after his initial relief, your dad will be angry. "I'm going to get a new job."

His voice cracks when he laughs. "That's a great idea. I love you."

"Love you too, Dad."

You're drafting your two-week notice, even though in truth you plan to just walk off the job after your last shift. If there are medical bills, well, you've begun to have doubts about the legitimacy of this hospital. You've carefully—secretly—saved screenshots of patient intake forms you've been told to file, and the emails the doctor sends. He doesn't suspect anything. Why would he? He's the most important man in the world, and you're just a sick girl who needs his help.

You hesitate before you print off your notice. You still have one monstrous shadow. Wouldn't it be smarter to wait until your last session before you quit?

The darker, needling worry that the doctor will not let you leave so easily has been growing in the back of your mind for days. You're trying to find proof that the outpatients have been okay. You see people admitted, not discharged. Sure, you're only the receptionist. Obviously, things happen outside your shifts.

You decide to ask Barb, who comes in only one day a week now.

"You can't quit," Barb says. Her voice is a rasp. She used to have such a rich, booming laugh when you first started. Now she scarcely whispers. "You'd be better off running."

You stiffen. Barb stares into the middle distance.

"Is this a joke?" You try to smile, even though it takes a lot out of you. You've been so tired lately, even if you can't sleep.

"We don't leave this place," Barb says.

You're going to prove Barb wrong, so you gather your clothes and laptop into a backpack after you clock out and head to the employee entrance. The door is locked. Your heartbeat quickens. You swipe your badge. Nothing happens.

What the hell?

You pull out your phone. Zero signal.

Panic whistles through your head. This is wrong. You were *just* talking to your dad not an hour ago.

You jam your thumb against the intercom button.

"Yes?" Barb asks.

"I need to leave," you say as calmly as you can.

"Sorry, honey," Barb replies. "Doctor's orders are for you to stay."

This can't be happening. You hurry back to your room and turn on your laptop. The Wi-Fi code isn't working.

"You signed an NDA," comes the doctor's voice from your ceiling.

You jump, horrified, and realize there is a well-camouflaged speaker over the door.

You feel so stupid—of course he would secure his interests. Has he been spying on you since you "moved in" here? You don't know how to reach out for help if he's blocking your cell reception and has knocked you offline. And the doors are locked.

"Don't worry so much, Melanie," the doctor says, an edge of contempt in his voice. "I'm here to help you, remember? But you're acting irrationally. You're not better yet. Once I've fixed you, we can discuss your future."

"I want to go home."

"Of course. And you will, soon."

You clench your hands, suddenly dizzy. Can you believe him?

"When can we complete my surgery?" you ask, forced to sit down on the edge of your bed before your knees buckle.

"As soon as I've finished with dear Phoebe here," the doctor says.

You numbly take over from Barb after a sleepless, exhausting day. You usually work the evening shifts anyway.

You check your cell phone, but still no signal. You wish you'd gotten Ramsey's number. You haven't seen him—either leaving or arriving. Is he here, trapped like you are?

Even if you could find the emergency release for the doors, you don't think you'd be able to run fast enough to get out before you're caught by security. And without all your monster shadows, you can't hide in the darkness and walk unseen past human eyes and electronic sensors.

Your only chance is to wait, hold on for a little bit longer.

"I'm receiving a visitor soon," the doctor tells you, and you hate the dull press of the plastic phone against your ear. "Show her up."

A fierce-eyed woman stalks through the lobby. Dark hair frames her shoulders, and she moves with the grace and intent of a lioness hunting on the savanna.

"The doctor is waiting upstairs," you say, smiling as expected, your thoughts racing. Could you slip her a note? You didn't prepare. You should have written your dad's name and number on a slip of paper, or scribbled *SOS* on your palm with permanent marker to show her. There's no time now. The doctor is waiting. "Come on; I'll show you up."

You'll escort her up to his office near the surgery wing. As soon as you get the opportunity, you'll ask her for help. It's probably your only chance before the doctor catches on.

You eavesdrop at the closed office door and learn the fierce-eyed woman's name is Zaria, that she and the doctor used to date, that it ended badly. She's a monster, like her sister, Phoebe. He demands she see reason. She just wants her sister back. He refuses. You listen with growing anger as he monologues about his own greatness and how he'll "fix" Zaria, too. How he'll *fix* all the monsters in his care.

Your hands shake.

"No one is leaving my hospital."

The possessiveness in his voice infuriates you as much as it shocks you. Why didn't you see it before? The scorn he feels for all his patients. They aren't people to him, just experiments. Like you. He doesn't want to cure you. He wants to unmake you because you're a monster.

This must end.

You shove open the door, too furious to care that you're intruding.

One wall of the office has a window showing an operating room, and now a girl with bandaged hands, Phoebe, is standing next to the fierce-eyed Zaria in the office. They face the doctor as if this is a showdown in a classic western movie.

"You don't belong out there," the doctor spits at Phoebe. "Freaks shouldn't be seen."

"You told me I'd die," you whisper, unable to keep quiet any longer.

"I meant you wouldn't have a life worth living!" He whirls on you, one arm raised. He has a hypodermic in one hand, and his face is stretched in disgust. "And it's true!"

You flinch back a step.

"No, it's not," says Phoebe. "There's nothing wrong with us."

Her words smack you like a tidal wave.

There's nothing wrong with us.

It's simultaneously the last thing you ever expected to hear, and the words you need so desperately to believe. She says it with such conviction, you immediately believe her.

There is nothing wrong with you, is there? Nothing about you is wrong. Your shadows were never linked to your sexuality. If they were, you'd feel different by now. No, you're simply a monster girl who happens to have zero sex drive and no sexual attraction to other people. Like Ramsey. *Ace.*

"I liked my shadows," you say quietly. It's a truth you haven't dared to say aloud since you were little. Your shadows were— are—part of your whole. So what if the world doesn't see you as normal? You're different. You're a monster girl, an ace girl, and there is nothing fucking wrong with that.

Your skin aches. Your shoulder blades itch. You remember the comforting weight of your shadows wrapped about you, the way they ate your nightmares so you slept in peace, how you could make the best shadow puppets ever.

If you had your shadows, you're certain you could have gotten out of here. Ironic, maybe, but true. If the doctor had excised the last shadow . . . would that have killed you? Did he ever care?

"You hurt all of us," you say, the truth shattering the last of your fear.

You're so *angry*. You think of Ramsey in his trench coat and hat, clothing to hide his wolfish features; of yourself, frightened and pressured to fit into a world with no space for you and your shadows.

Too bad, world. You will make space.

Your skin shivers, darkening beneath the surface, and your shadows ripple free. One. Two. Three. Four. All monstrous. All beautiful.

Phoebe sees you and flexes her hands. She tears at the bandages, and long, heavy claws begin to regrow from her fingers.

"Our mama was right," she says. "When we're happy, we don't hide. We don't hide when we're angry, either."

Sweat drips down the doctor's temples. "That's impossible. I cut them off—I fixed you!"

"You hurt me," Phoebe says.

"You hurt all of us," you growl.

And then the rest of your shadows bloom.

You have always had more shadows, and now they unfurl, spreading wide, dark, and powerful.

Thirteen is a perfect number.

Phoebe closes in on the doctor. Zaria unfolds massive, glorious wings as horns emerge from her skull, long and sharp like polished ebony. She gives you a knowing look, one of camaraderie and understanding.

Your shadows still hurt, raw and skittish, the wounds the doctor made in your body not yet healed. The doctor didn't fix you, and the shadows were never going to kill you. He wanted only to control you, to erase you, to make you fit his version of reality. Maybe it's time the doctor had a taste of his own medicine.

"Melanie!"

It's Ramsey. He shuffles down the hallway, his dark eyes enormous. Dozens of other patients appear behind him from different parts of the hospital.

You had no idea there were so many.

"Are you okay?" you ask Ramsey, catching his hands with yours, and your shadows'.

He stares in wonder at the darkness that gently strokes the fur of his wrists. "I think so," he says. "I heard everything—my ears are pretty sharp."

Your shoulders relax. "I'm glad."

He bobs his head. "Me too. Your powers are really cool."

"So are yours."

He grins. "Oh, and I heard you. In the waiting room. When you said 'maybe.'"

"You did?"

He nods again. "It's okay if you're not sure, you know?"

You give his hands a reassuring squeeze. "I know. And I'm sure now."

"That's awesome!"

It's over—the doctor is gone. Zaria and Phoebe invite you and the others to come stay with them in their home, but all you can think about is seeing your dad again.

Ramsey hesitates, though. "My mom isn't going to want me back. . . ." His ears flatten, and his voice quavers.

You loop your arm through his. One of your shadows pats his shoulder, and another fishes the Pokémon card from your pocket to give to him. "My dad would love to meet you. You'd be welcome to stay with us. We can teach him how to play this game together."

Ramsey's eyes widen, a smile spreading across his face. "Really?"

"Of course."

You turn to Phoebe. "Can we visit?"

The monster girl shows off her teeth in a happy smile. "Yes! Anytime you like."

Ramsey lets out a yip of delight. He turns and hugs you. You hug him back, surprised but pleased that his fur is already regrowing thick and healthy, along with his curly hair.

Your heart patters faster, and this time it's with excitement. With happiness.

You have a new friend, someone who's also ace. You can't wait to get to know Ramsey better.

Your dad will be waiting. You have a lot to tell him, and you look forward to the years ahead in a way you never have before. The future is one filled with other monsters, ready to welcome you as one of them. Together, you aren't alone.

You're fine just the way you are.

MONSTER REFLECTION

I saw the classic 1931 version of *Frankenstein* probably far too young, and it made an impression on tiny Merc. I loved it, I was scared that I loved it, and I wanted more. (It's the scene with the flower petals that got me.) I would sneak out of bed once my parents were asleep and watch the late-night horror movie channel on TV. I've been fascinated with monsters, particularly iterations of the Creature or human-made beings (including robots) ever since.

BONNE NUIT

BY CLAIRE KANN

No one knew how or when the Gargoyle of Farnsworth High School came to be.

One unremarkable day many years ago, a pair of students looked up at the roof. "Has that always been there?" the first asked.

"I think so?" answered the second.

Empty one day. A gargoyle the next.

Tonight, three different students stood in the same spot, staring at the same creature.

"It's not even our mascot," he said.

"It's still a part of the school," they said. "We can't just take it."

"We can and we will. Why else would you come all the way here?" he asked.

They'd wondered the same exact thing as they waited for their parents to go to bed, got changed, sneaked out their bedroom window, and walked to school. They chanted *go home go home go home* with each step but couldn't force themself to turn around. For better or for worse, they wanted to be there.

They glanced at the roof and shrugged. Currently, the gargoyle resided on the street-facing north corner of the main school entrance.

Everyone assumed the faculty moved the gargoyle—a statement art piece representing academic vigilance. Pervasive rumor had it that staff were given a rotating schedule. When it was their turn, they carried the gargoyle to a new spot as if it had decided to take a stroll along the ledge and forgot to return to its initial position.

"We're losing moonlight," she said, laughing. "Come on, let's do this thing."

He began leading the way toward the back, and when they hesitated for the briefest moment, she looped an arm through theirs to urge them forward. "Stop being so serious," she whispered. "It's supposed to be fun."

"I know," they whispered back. "It just doesn't *feel* fun. I think this might be a bad idea."

"Well, if it is, at least we'll be together." She grinned.

"I *guess* that's a good thing." They playfully rolled their eyes and laughed. They'd willingly follow that smile into the dark any day.

He'd paid a janitor to leave the service-access door propped open. Inside, a steep set of metal stairs provided direct access to the roof. He went first, and they concentrated on the back of his jacket to keep from looking down. It was emblazoned with the school's actual mascot—the Farnsworth Owls. He'd earned it from dedicating countless hours to football and the money his parents paid to keep him in the sport. At the top, he held the door open for his two childhood best friends, all grown up.

Correction: his childhood friend and new girlfriend.

Doubt poked at their common sense again. They had to take a deep, calming breath because they were *really* about to do this. "Maybe we should come up with something else for a prank. I just don't think vandalism is what we should go with here."

Plan A involved carrying the gargoyle from the roof and down the stairs to the industrial pushcart. From there, it'd be hidden in a shed in the woods behind the school.

Plan B involved pushing the gargoyle off the ledge, sweeping up the broken pieces, and burying everything in the woods behind the school.

"It's not vandalism unless we have to break it," he said.

"It'll be *fine*," she said, gesturing to her overstuffed hiking backpack. "I brought enough supplies for either option."

He came up with the idea and immediately put her in charge of supplies. She came in clutch as always, bringing a thick roll-able mat, rope, gloves, garbage bags, hand shovels, hand brooms and dustpans, flashlights, and snacks. Being prepared was a way of life for her.

"In a way, it's super altruistic for us to do this," she continued. "Now some poor teacher won't have to deal with moving it every morning."

"Altruism is like volunteering at an animal shelter and walking dogs," they said.

"Well, we are technically taking it for a walk," she said. "And it does look like an animal."

"It's also ugly. After this, no one will be forced to look at it anymore," he said.

"It's not ugly. It's art, which doesn't have to be pretty. You're supposed to concentrate on how it makes you feel," they said.

"I never said it wasn't art." He sneered. "I said it was *ugly*. It makes me feel like I want to bleach my eyes."

"That's harsh." She laughed. "I don't feel anything when I look at it. It's just sort of . . . there."

"You guys are just mean," they said. "I've always thought of it as a guardian watching over everything." Because the gargoyle had strangely always made them feel safe looking at it. They couldn't put a finger on why, but the feeling was unmistakable—as comforting as a hug to share body heat on a cold winter night.

"That's angels, not gargoyles," he said.

They silently huffed in exasperation. Of course, he *had* to disagree with them. It was all he seemed to do lately, when he bothered to talk to them at all.

"Real angels are supposed to look like monsters," she said. "If you saw one, you wouldn't like them, either. That's why the first thing they literally have to tell humans is 'Be not afraid' because they know we will be."

"That's a meme," he said. "You don't even go to church."

"Well, if I did, I'd do more than snore in the pews. Don't act like you don't fall asleep every time you go," she teased. He grabbed her waist and kissed the corner of her mouth as she giggled.

They quickly turned away. "Maybe humans are just shallow," they whispered, touching the gargoyle's wing with an index finger. Then, their whole hand—pushing and squeezing the curiously pliable texture. "Hey, this doesn't look or feel like stone to me?"

"Doesn't mean it's not." She snorted as she walked toward them. "Have you seen what artists do with a block of marble? My mom has a framed picture of a sculpture that looks like a woman looking through a transparent curtain."

"No, that's not what I mean. Feel it," they said.

She pursed her lips, stopping short of frowning because she touched it. "*Whoa.* It's . . . squishy. And kind of leathery. I wonder what it's made of."

"That must explain how teachers can carry it. It only looks like stone," they said.

"It doesn't matter." He finished preparing the rope and laid the mat directly below the gargoyle. "Someone take this end."

All three worked together, winding the rope behind the gargoyle's legs, midsection, shoulder, and neck, then got in position to begin pulling.

"On three," he ordered.

Nothing happened.

"Again, on three."

Still nothing.

"One more time. Ready, pull!"

But the gargoyle would not be moved.

"I thought it wasn't supposed to be heavy." She shook out her arms.

"Maybe we need more leverage," he said. "You, go stand on the ledge and push it."

They balked, blinking in surprise. "Why me?"

"You're closest," he said.

They *were* closer, but he *knew* they were terrified of heights. Vertigo sent them spinning every time they even looked down from the second story of their house. Calculated cruelty like that really drove it home that he didn't care about them anymore.

If he had his way, he would've done a senior prank with his football teammates, but they'd left him out. So, of course, he came running to them for help to pull off a bigger, better prank. And, of course, they'd said yes because . . .

Because they didn't know how to let him go. Even after months of being ignored, thinly veiled contempt, and back-handed insults, they still said yes. And now they were on the school roof, about to commit a probable crime with someone who didn't even like them.

Hurt and confusion ached in their chest. They looked to her for help, but all she did was smile. "Out, not down. You can do it. Out, not down."

"Out, not down," they repeated with a nod. "Out, not down."

The ledge was thick, wide enough for them to sit, kneel, and stand comfortably. Gripping the gargoyle's shoulders and frowning at the unfamiliar texture, they said, "Ready."

"On three," he ordered again.

Looking down would've been a mistake.

They kept their gaze level with the horizon. The tall football-field lights and forest treetops blurred in the background as the gargoyle dominated their field of vision.

That was also a mistake.

Standing on the ledge put them eye to eye with the gargoyle, whose eyes opened at the exact moment they pushed. Dawning horror struck like lightning as the black pupil expanded and contracted into a slit, zeroing in on them. They jolted in surprise, wheeling backward as they gasped, and then, just like that, they were falling.

Falling

Falling

Falling

Falling so fast, the wind caressed them as if to say, *We cannot hold you; we are sorry,* with only enough time for them to think, *Please don't let it hurt,* with their future disappearing behind their hands as they covered their face.

A snap like a whip. A roar like a lion.

Instant pain like a vice wrapped around their body. It crushed their torso and legs, and thoughts of prolonged agony rapidly outpaced the fear of dying. Their life didn't flash before their eyes because their future took its place. Visions of watching their dad collapse and hearing their mom scream and their little sister sob—there were worse things to experience in their life than it all ending too soon.

But somehow, beyond the hurt, they still felt the cold wind careening past and a strange weightlessness as if they were floating. Something both soft and hard pressed against their side, their shoulder digging into it.

When they finally touched the ground, it was mushy, damp earth instead of hard, prickly grass. Dead leaves crackled beneath them as they rolled over, and their hands shook so badly they could barely see through their fingers as they spread them.

The gargoyle crouched a few feet away, ever in repose. Horns and fangs and claws. Giant yellow eyes beneath slanting thick brow bridges watched them closely. Its skin had a faint bioluminescent glow, the same color as its eyes, delicately outlining precisely how massive it was against the dark.

"I'm not dead?" Their voice sounded tinier than it ever had. They didn't scream on the way down, but their throat felt as if they had. "You're alive?"

The gargoyle blinked. "What a keen sense of observation you have." Its voice was deeper than any they'd ever heard before, resonating with enough power to send vibrations through the ground.

"You can talk?"

"The school teaches language, does it not? I have spent all my days learning there, as you do."

Fear, anger, and shame swirled inside them, creating a heady mix of defiance. "If you're alive and you can talk, why did you let us put the rope on you?"

"I have been adorned in decoration by students before. I hate it, but it is harmless. I did not realize your intentions until you three began to pull."

They stared at the gargoyle in disbelief. Not because it wasn't a statue after all, but because they nearly hurt it with a stupid prank. They *knew* it was a terrible idea, and they shouldn't have said yes, and they shouldn't have ignored their instincts, and they shouldn't have been on the roof, and they almost *died*, and and and—

"Why did you save me?" they whispered, bottom lip and chin trembling, face burning the way it did right before they were about to start crying.

"You are a student in the place I call home and were, therefore, under my protection."

"Were?"

"It has since been revoked."

They scrambled to their feet as adrenaline spiked and fight-or-flight kicked in, swiftly displacing every other thought. Around them, the woods were dense but instantly recognizable, stretching for several miles between the football field and a shopping center. "Why are we in the forest?"

"Because my instincts command me to protect, but not at the expense of myself."

They frowned, confused by its answer. Did that mean it wanted revenge? Darkness obscured almost everything, hiding the landmarks that would tell them which way to run—the school had added signs and markers as a safety measure—but the gargoyle was the only light in the woods.

It must have brought them there on purpose to take its time. They survived the fall only to be eaten in the woods, bones and all, probably. No one would ever know what happened to them. Had their friends even called them to see if they were still alive? They guessed the answer, and sorrow punched them in the chest. Their broken heart somehow still hammered and thundered in their ears as they stepped back. Alone and on their own. "I'm sorry. We shouldn't have done that to you."

"Oh?" The gargoyle tilted its great horned head. "Are you certain?"

"*Yes.*" They nodded.

"I am not convinced."

"So, what? You saved me just to kill me?"

"I have seen your heart. Were it possible, you would have participated in my destruction. Is it not fair that I repay such kindness?"

"But we didn't."

"And so, I will not. However, we have not yet reached the apology portion of our night." Its eyes began to glow deeper yellow like old headlights suddenly appearing on a darkened road. A sound reminiscent of falling rocks clicked and crashed in its throat. "The world is much more intricate and far grander than you realize. Come along, child."

"Where are we going?"

The gargoyle walked on all fours, with the top of its wing-clad back reaching past their waist. "Back to the school building. I will escort you."

"We're not flying?"

"I was not aware you possessed the ability to do so."

"I mean, you brought us here—"

"And you are free to stay." The gargoyle continued moving forward at a steady pace, leaving them behind.

They hesitated for only a second more before running to catch up. The forest was nearly solid black but mottled with thin, dark gray trees. If it weren't for the light the gargoyle generated, they wouldn't even be able to see their hands in front of their face.

"Are you going to eat me?" they asked.

"I do not eat humans."

They stood as close to it as their nerves could take. "So do you have a name?"

"I do not."

"What should I call you?"

"Whatever you'd like," Gargoyle said. Its body felt warmer than it had on the roof. It exuded heat as if it were a radiator.

"Does the school know you're not really a statue?"

"I suspect knowledge of my existence is handed down through positions of power—a warning to leave me be. Removal will be a waste of resources. I will always return."

The gargoyle had been there when they began school four years ago and when their parents met twenty-five years before that, and when their grandmother graduated as valedictorian eighteen years prior to that.

"Why our school? Is there something special about it?"

"A place need not be special to be worthy of protection. I spent my birthnight with my creator before being cast away, and by the dawn, I'd found my home."

Gargoyle paused suddenly, standing on its hind legs, several heads taller than them.

A strange hissing sound slithered through the air, making all the hairs on their neck stand up. "What is that? What's making that noise?" Anxiety, familiar and intense, began constricting in their chest. It reminded them of first days of school and gym and sitting alone in the cafeteria and wearing the wrong clothes and being called on in class—so concentrated like that, it felt silly. But something about it deeply upset them. As if it were only the tip of a very massive iceberg.

Gargoyle grunted once and fell back onto all fours. "Keep moving."

"Is something out there? I can't really see, but I think I feel something."

"It is still there. In the woods and in you."

They stood closer to the gargoyle, suddenly afraid of being separated. "What is it?"

"A consequence."

"Of what?"

"Of humanity's collective existence," Gargoyle said. "It is a corpus of eyes and teeth. Born from human hearts, bones, and minds, the indelible experiences that shape your existence."

They thought about its answer and the inexplicable anxious feelings weighing their heart down. "I'm guessing that doesn't include good experiences."

"It does not," Gargoyle confirmed. "It is an intense, pervasive, mass hysteria that influences humans to behave irrationally when left unchecked. It overwhelms as quickly as it devours. It will make you wilt in ways, agree to acts you normally wouldn't. Before I arrived, all its records roamed freely, wreaking havoc and sowing discord. Now I keep the larger ones regulated here, as it's not possible to destroy all the forms suffering can take. Some are older, heartier than others."

"So these things are just . . . everywhere?"

"Yes. Teenagers have the highest creation probability, and schools contain thousands of teenagers at a time. I will leave the math to you." Gargoyle turned its glowing gaze to them as if that were a joke. "Most have not learned the tools necessary to combat this suffering on their own."

"If that's true, then you're not *really* protecting the school. It's us."

"They are inextricably linked. I protect the grounds to give students more time. I protect students to keep my home safe. Although I am not always successful, I am proud of what I have managed to do in my lifetime thus far. Becoming a guardian is a choice, and I accepted this particular fight."

They narrowed their eyes in suspicion. "You brought me here to show me the corpus, didn't you?"

"Yes, and it can hear you. It is deeply interested in what you have to offer."

"But . . . *why*?"

Gargoyle stood up again—exhaling through its nose, steam misting into the night. The muscles in its arms tensed and rippled as claws extended from its three fingers and thumb. A low, clicking growl started deep in its chest, echoing through the still night air.

They swallowed hard, taking an unconscious step back.

That *thing* rattled every nerve under their skin. Insistent hissing snaked its way straight into their head, coiling between their ears. It tricked their instincts into choosing to freeze them with fear.

Sensations and images flooded into their mind as shimmering white tendrils of smoke coiled up their arms, around their shoulders, into their mouth and nose, and eyes and ears. A void swallowing everything.

And then it stopped. They held their hands out in front of them, turning them over and making fists. Nothing.

Another grunt and Gargoyle relaxed, back on all fours again. "Keep moving."

They held a hand against their heaving chest and took deep gulping breaths but managed to keep pace with Gargoyle.

What the absolute hell . . .

What was happening? Why was this happening? Gargoyle might not have wanted to eat them, but that *thing* absolutely wanted to.

"Why did you bring me here?" they whispered.

"Because you are lost. I will show you."

The only reason why they were *lost* was because it brought them there. Before that . . . they would've gone *splat*. A nervous giggle erupted out of them before they gasped into a near-sob. They almost died. They were on that roof with their friends *and* almost died. *Friends* who still hadn't called or messaged. Their phone wasn't on silent—they would've heard it.

"You've been around a long time, huh?" they asked to distract themself. "You're probably full of good advice since you've seen so much."

"Are you in need?"

"I don't know. Maybe." They laughed again, feeling uncomfortable. "Online, everyone says stuff like 'Go to therapy; it's amazing,' but I can't afford that. I try to talk to my parents, but they're busy with their own stuff, so I get it. My sister is only six, and my friends are . . . well, you saw them. I've known them since I was five, but it doesn't feel like that anymore. They're different, but I'm different, too. It's all of us."

"Is there something specific you would like to ask?"

"No. Not really. I just . . . I just wanted to talk," they said, worrying at their hands. "Do you ever get tired of being by yourself all the time?"

"I have no counterpart. Shaped one by one. Forged complete onto ourselves."

"You don't ever feel lonely?"

"Hmm." Gargoyle raised its gaze to the treetops. The branches, both spindly and thick, were dense with leaves and blocked out the moon. "My answer depends on your definition of lonely. I do not crave a mating-based companionship. Having a partner, another of my kind, by my side is of little interest to me. If I were given a choice, I believe I would happily welcome a community that embraced me. Speaking to students tends to be unexpectedly fulfilling."

They frowned. Gargoyle talked to other students? They'd never heard a single story or rumor about that. "What do you like about it? Talking to students, I mean."

"Human minds work differently from a gargoyle's. I enjoy finding elements of commonality we share, listening to their odd perspectives, and watching the expressions they are capable of making with their faces. However, with students such as your friends, I find the likelihood of my acceptance to be on the low end these days."

"But it's not impossible."

"Which one should I approach first? The one who referred to me as ugly, perhaps?"

"You're not ugly."

"That is irrelevant. I am a gargoyle. I appear as intended."

The hissing started again. This time, they felt it directly behind them, as if it were attached to their shoes and being dragged through the foliage.

"Do not look," Gargoyle warned, not breaking its steady stride. "You are fine."

The tension in their neck from resisting ached like a yearning born from separation. "But—"

"It has latched on to you. It wishes to feed on the emotions you currently carry in your heart."

"What should I do? It hurts."

"Speak your truth. I suspect something has prompted your current predicament."

They bit their lip, gaze downcast to keep from turning around. Their white shoes reflected the gargoyle's light, bright enough to follow in the dark. "I didn't want to do the prank."

"If your next words are *They made me,* spare yourself the trouble now."

"My friends didn't make me, but if I didn't help, it would've made things worse between us. I know you probably don't care about this, but the three of us have been friends forever. It's always been the three of us."

"You are correct. I do not care, because I already know this part. Do not think I do not know who you or your friends are. I know the names and faces of all my charges. I have never forgotten a single one."

They couldn't imagine wrapping their mind around that and didn't even try. "Right. So. Well, one day, Alexis asked me for . . . something I didn't want to do, and I said no. He said it was fine, but a week later, Taylor told me he asked *her* out, and she wanted to say yes. It's been really strained and weird ever since. The two of them hang out without me, and I don't have other friends." They had to stop to take a breath before they got upset again. "When he asked for our help with the prank, I said yes because I thought it'd be like the first step to going back to how it was before. I didn't want to kidnap or murder you. It wasn't my idea."

"I am indestructible."

Ah, that was nice to know. They felt a little bit better. "I said yes because I wanted my friends back. I'm not stupid. I know he was only using me because he knew I was desperate. I feel like I've always needed them more than they wanted me."

Gargoyle grunted in response.

The tethers around their shoes swelled, inching past their ankles and up their calves. Gargoyle suddenly snapped in their direction, biting at the air with a resounding growl. They stumbled as if they'd been tripped, but Gargoyle angled its body in one fluid motion—instead of falling face-first, they crashed into its side.

"Stand up," Gargoyle ordered. "You are fine."

They righted themself, feeling unburdened again. "Thanks."

Gargoyle grunted in response and began walking again. "Do you have more to say?"

"If I do, will that thing come back?"

"It will find you either way. You can lie to yourself, but it already knows how to bring the burdens deep in your heart to the surface. It aims to expose, exploit, and deceive—better to speak your mind while I am by your side. I will not let it devour you," Gargoyle promised. "We are close."

The trees had become sparse without them realizing it. Darkness had a hard stop at the parking lot filled with security floodlights.

They nodded. "I guess I just get lonely sometimes. But I don't think it's the same kind of lonely as other people." They kept looking down because if they looked up and into the light, they'd lose their nerve. "There's all this pressure to pick someone. This person likes that person. Why can't you give them a chance, *blah*. I don't want that. I'm not interested in any of the stuff that comes with that. I want . . . friends. A lot of them. Good, funny, understanding friends who care about me and have time for me. Who won't ditch me when they finally pick someone."

"You believe this to be improbable?"

"It's just hard. Like really, really hard." They didn't know how else to express their misery. "If I went back in time, knowing what I know now, I think I might still say yes to the prank because I still want my friends back. We would get to the school, and I'd try to talk them out of it. But it wouldn't work, because Alexis hates me even though he pretends like he doesn't. He wouldn't listen to me, but Taylor might. She still wants me around, but Alexis is more important. We used to be equal. No one had favorites."

"If that is how you feel, why did you apologize? Your imagined scenario would most likely end with me being ensnared once again."

Explaining didn't excuse their behavior. Their parents taught them that. Nothing about what they said even suggested they were sorry. *Were* they sorry? They'd said it reflexively—a habit of apologizing for everything under the sun for no reason. As if their very existence required a blanket apology at all times. Their mom hated when they did it. But they'd done it for so long that they didn't know how to stop.

"I don't know. And I'm sorry that I don't know, which only makes things worse."

Gargoyle grunted in response again. "The school is close."

It led them around the football field, across the front lawn, and back to the corner where they would've hit the ground. They looked up to the roof, immediately feeling light-headed. There was no way they would've survived a fall from that high.

As expected, their friends were nowhere in sight. With a heaving sigh, they finally allowed themself to check their phone. It had been burning a hole in their pocket the entire walk.

No missed calls. No texts.

Alexis and Taylor had abandoned them to their fate.

Gargoyle sat in its crouched position. Eye to eye. "What do you have to say for yourself, child?"

Earlier, Gargoyle had said it didn't believe their apology and that it wasn't time yet. They took a deep breath. "I think

I apologized because it would've always been this way. I might not have consciously known it, but deep down, I think I did. I just wanted my friends back. That's not an excuse. What we did was wrong. My dad says that forgiveness isn't for you. It's for the other person. Saying sorry in hopes of making yourself feel better defeats the purpose. It's selfish. I didn't mean it earlier."

"And now?"

"I still wouldn't," they said. "But I am grateful. Thank you for saving me. If you give me a chance, I'd like to repay your kindness."

"What is it that you believe you can do for me?" Gargoyle considered them for a moment, chest rumbling at a steady pace and volume, which they realized was laughter. It didn't feel malicious or mocking. More like it was genuinely amused. "You presume that I would want anything you have to offer."

"Uhh, I wouldn't go that far." They held up their hands.

Gargoyle said, "Then please continue."

They nodded. "Not being presumptuous, but I did realize something. I helped my friends almost do something terrible because I was afraid of being alone. That's not friendship or even loyalty. I want to find the people who will embrace me, like you said. And I want to help you find yours, too. That's how communities start, isn't it? An agreement to coexist and help each other?"

Gargoyle stood to its full height and pointed one hooked talon directly at them. "I have judged the depths of your gratitude and find them acceptable."

"Oh, okay?" That claw was bigger and sharper than any knife they'd ever seen.

"I also find the terms of your agreement acceptable. I look forward to seeing how you will proceed, given that you are graduating at summer's start. Be aware: I have only delayed your inevitable end. Prove you are worthy of the extra time. Live a good, full life, and I will see you soon."

"I'll do my best." They laughed nervously, shaking a little. "Please stop pointing at me."

"Give your accomplices my regards. I will also see them soon." Gargoyle smiled, baring its mouth full of sharp teeth, eyes glowing dense and yellow in amusement. Its wings snapped open with a crack, and it shot off into the air like a rocket. It circled overhead twice before flying off into the night, calling out, "Bonne nuit, Riley."

"Bonne nuit," they whispered, waving. "And thank you. For everything."

MONSTER REFLECTION

Looking back, I don't think there was one monster I loved more than the rest. If I made a top-ten list, you'd find Slimer and the demon gargoyle dogs, Gremlins, Xenomorphs, Graboids, and the like. I watched more spooky horror movies than any child probably should have been allowed—shout-out to my parents for letting me manage my anxiety in one of the few ways that felt safe but were admittedly age inappropriate. In their defense, I rarely had nightmares about any of it.

SONS OF GOD AND DAUGHTERS OF HUMANS

BY H.E. EDGMON

When human beings began to increase in number on the earth and daughters were born to them, the sons of God saw that the daughters of humans were beautiful, and they married any of them they chose. Then the Lord said, "My Spirit will not contend with humans forever, for they are mortal; their days will be a hundred and twenty years."

The Nephilim were on the earth in those days—and also afterward—when the sons of God went to the daughters of humans and had children by them. They were the heroes of old, men of renown.

The Lord saw how great the wickedness of the human race had become on the earth, and that every inclination of the thoughts of the human heart was only evil all the time. The Lord regretted that he had made human beings on the earth, and his heart was deeply troubled. So the Lord said, "I will wipe from the face of the earth the human race I have created—and with them the animals, the birds and the creatures that move along the ground—for I regret that I have made them." But Noah found favor in the eyes of the Lord.

This is the account of Noah and his family.

NEW INTERNATIONAL VERSION BIBLE, GENESIS 6:1–9

The long-dead streets of Brooklyn are sunlit and quiet, nescient of the hurricane looming hours offshore, and still Ana abandons them for the frantic and suffocating tunnels beneath.

It was only four days ago that the people in the underground city learned of the storm growing stronger and more vicious as it moved toward them through the Atlantic. Means of predicting things like the weather have become increasingly impossible to come by—and even when successful, word travels slowly in the days of reckoning. With more time, the city might've been able to prepare. With less than a week, all they can do is evacuate, run back to the surface, and hope they find somewhere that will take them in.

Or hunker down here and wait to drown.

Most who will leave have already gone. Ana themself has just returned from shepherding the elderly in their community able to travel across the Hudson, to a still-standing safe haven that would accept only those who were soon for death anyway. Other city leaders have led similar trips for other vulnerable groups among them.

But now they're out of time. As Ana makes their way through the endless, dark tunnel of the city, surrounded on all sides by the frenetic energy of stragglers, the whispers and shouts and cries of rage and grief, they are *too* aware that the most vulnerable are still here. Those for whom leaving is simply not an option will be forced to wait out the end of the world, trapped in the crypt of the former subway system. The most vulnerable and the most stubborn—like their boyfriend, Noah.

Their *human* boyfriend, Noah.

That such a thing could exist in their life is befuddling to Ana, despite having lived through the events leading up to it themself. That their life could look *anything* like it does now is possible only through enormous amounts of both senselessness and sacrilege.

And there will come a reckoning day of their own, when they are finally called before the Father to answer for their crimes against His throne. Were they to repent now and turn their back on the blasphemous life they've created on Earth, He might show them mercy.

But for all their bitching and moaning about Judgment Day drawing nigh, Ana is unrepentant.

Both about pissing on the Father's plan and about their own newly formed plan to drag Noah out of here before the storm hits, even if that means literally. They've done their duty to the others, sacrificing their time and energy for the collective good long before this trip to Jersey. Now their only duty is to themself and the boy they love.

This city was built by Noah's people. But there is another, on Rikers Island, built by those like Ana themself. If any stronghold will survive the night, it will be the one guarded by angels.

Noah's not going to be happy about it. He's committed himself to staying underground. When their group first realized the storm was coming, that it would hit in only days, it became obvious that not everyone among them could be saved. Those whose disabilities made quick travel impossible, or who were too old or young to easily survive elsewhere, or who simply had nowhere else to go—they would be trapped. And with that realization, some of their number fled, refusing to drown alongside the *weakest links* in their community. Noah wished them all exactly what he believed they deserved for their cowardice.

Say nothing of the fact that he loathes the angels with the same fervor he loves his people—only Ana is the exception, balanced on the razor's edge between either side. He would rather die with those he was loyal to than survive with the same monsters who've condemned him. And it isn't even that Ana disagrees with the principle. Were it only about *their* life, they would stay in the tunnels, too. But the two of them can argue all of that through in the morning, when Noah's still breathing.

Ana sucks in a breath when their tent comes into sight. Though, *tent* is not the correct word—the makeshift home is a series of old quilts patched together and strung up over metal poles to make a warm, soft-edged hiding spot. Normally, the sight might make Ana's heart flutter for different reasons. This little den, queer and unassuming, has become the pulse point of their life here. Even now, they want nothing more than to burrow inside it and drag Noah down into a pile of blankets along with them, to disappear and pretend and refuse to let the storm touch them in all their cozy togetherness.

Fantasies won't keep Noah alive, though. So they push forward.

For the briefest moment, as their hand curls around one blanket to peel it away and step inside, they entertain the idea that perhaps Noah isn't here. Perhaps he's off checking in on the animals—a veritable underground farm, grown larger and larger since the city's inception—or the garden—kept alive by solar-powered lamps all this time. Or perhaps Noah is off with the other leaders. Ana caught sight of several on their way through the tunnel, soldering closed manholes and clearing the way for any drainage pipes, trying to safeguard the city from drowning in its final hours.

But no. When Ana steps inside, they find Noah already waiting for them.

At first, he's turned away, just a mop of curly hair and a snug hoodie to indicate his identity, both of them the same shade of pitch black.

"Baby," Ana begins, easing their way into what's sure to be a terrible conversation.

Noah turns around, and Ana's blood chills. His eyes are bloodshot and swollen, cheeks wet with fresh tear tracks. In one shaking hand, he clutches something curled in his fist. "I'm sorry."

When their bones can move through the frost of creeping fear, Ana steps forward and curls their own hands around

Noah's. He whimpers as they pry his fingers open to reveal what's hidden in his grip.

A rare pregnancy test, taken from the city's limited (and unreplenishable) stock.

A positive.

Theoretically, Ana—or the spirit currently *known* as Ana—is without age. They were not born. If they were created, it was so long ago that time did not yet exist, so there is no gauge by which to measure when such a creation took place. They have always been. For as long as existence *itself* has existed, there has been Ana.

Practically, it doesn't actually work that way. Wherever they were before they were here, floating in limbo or reveling in the light of the Father's kingdom, there was no concept of age. They certainly don't *feel* ageless. They *feel* eighteen, four years older than they felt when they formed their own pubescent human body, just as the days of reckoning on Earth began.

They have never—and suspect they *will* never—understand why they were chosen for Father's mission. If they were to wager a guess, it seems a safe assumption that He regrets it now, since they haven't done fuck all they were sent to do.

Of course, Father has His reasons. And in any case, it's not like they were the *only* one chosen. There is an army of angels walking the postapocalyptic streets of this world, spread to the four corners to usher in the days of Revelation. Like Ana, they hide in their human masquerades, wolves puppeting the bodies of sheep. It seems a fair assumption that most of them, unlike Ana, have stuck to their task, guiding humanity to its ruin.

Most of them. Ana is not so special as to be the only one who has fallen from the path. In fact, there is another of their kind in this very tunnel, at this very moment.

Gabriel. He was once one of their Father's most beloved children; Ana still does not understand how he came to fall. And the disgraced archangel has no answers for them, refusing to offer insight or guidance on the rare occasion Ana has dared to seek it. In any case, his presence in the tunnels only makes them more eager to leave—if this storm is truly their Father's wrath unleashed, surely He will target those who have betrayed Him most fiercely. Gabriel must be near the top of that list.

Antithetically, there are humans who will be saved—rare mortal souls who have earned His favor. But most humans are not so consecrated. *Most* humans are heathens, perfectly corrupt by nature of their own flawed design. And pitiful, impuissant Ana adores them.

That is *why* they fell, after all. Fourteen-year-old and ageless Ana, the homeless sword of God alone in Brooklyn during the unfolding of Armageddon, was offered no guidance—and certainly no affection—from other *angels*. It was humans who found them. Humans—overwhelmingly Black and brown, queer and trans, disabled, and poor—took Ana in. They offered them food and shelter and resources they had so little of to offer at all.

Noah was among that number. Though Ana had been made to be a soldier for their Father, Noah was *carved* into a soldier by the life he'd led. He'd shown them a kind of self-possessed strength, a quiet power, that flipped Ana's stomach and turned their world on its head. And for some reason, he loved them.

If they were righteous, they would have taken that love and used it against him. They would have twisted the trust in the hearts of all their human companions and led them to the shores of their own damnation. But they couldn't bring themself to. Because, instead, they came to love them, too.

That was Ana's first sin. Angels are not meant to love humans. Angels are meant to love no one but Him. The human experiment, the Father's messiest creation so far, was never intended to live forever. He will wipe clean any record of their existence, and then He will begin again. And the angels will one day return to eradicate the next of His designs, just as they have many times before now. They cannot do that if they come to love the thing they are meant to destroy.

The angels are His chosen creation. They alone will outlive the others. And for that, they must obey.

Ana has not been obedient, and they will suffer the consequences.

Especially because, though loving humans was their original sin, they have never committed an act so wicked as their union with Noah. To love a human is to enact heresy. To *lie* with a human is to give rise to abomination.

Especially if it begets a child.

"Don't apologize," Ana manages to say, uncannily calm on the exterior despite the incandescent undoing beneath the surface. Like the quiet streets of Brooklyn, who know naught of the hurricane that will wash them away. They cannot actually feel their mouth when they form the words, "I should have been more careful."

Ana's understanding of human sexuality, before Noah, was entirely theoretical and wholly biological. It wasn't as if there were a sex-ed class in Father's kingdom, nor anyone with whom Ana might have experienced such a relationship. Sex, in its entirety, is earthly. And having a powerful grasp on the *principles* of the thing ended up meaning very little when it came to actually experiencing it for themself. The first time they'd had sex with Noah—seventeen years old, two weeks into their relationship, and the very night they moved into the underground city—they'd been so overwhelmed by the unexpected sensations, they hadn't been *capable* of remembering any principles.

They got lucky that night. And they've tried—Ana *and* Noah—to be more careful every time since. They source condoms the same way they source other medicine. If there isn't one to be used, they promise things won't go *that* far, that they'll stop before one would be needed. And it's always true when they say it. It's just that it doesn't always stay true till the end, is all. They've both slipped up countless times.

Eventually, their luck had to run out.

"*We* should've been more careful," Noah pushes, reaching up to scrub the sleeve of his hoodie over one tawny cheekbone. "I knew this was going to happen."

Noah is not psychic. He just always assumes the worst—a trait Ana has found both validating and irksome for different reasons, in different moments—and they live in a world where the worst-case scenario is almost always a safe guess for a charlatan prophet.

This, though, is a different kind of worst. This is *the* worst.

"There's no use blaming anyone," Ana offers, by which they mean, there's no use in *Noah* blaming himself. They will continue to quietly blame *themself,* of course. They reach up to rest a hand on his shoulder, welcomed by the familiar spark of warmth that spreads from his body to theirs. It's usually more comforting than it can be right now, but they still lean into it. "What's done cannot be undone."

"Well, *that's* just not true." Noah huffs, swiping his fingertips under his eyes. "There are *ways* to undo this. I mean, probably not right now, right before we all drown—but I mean, hey, if we're all dying anyway, I guess it doesn't matter, right? I mean—"

"Ways?" Ana asks, their heart stumbling up the cobblestone drive of their throat. "What do you mean?"

Noah blinks at them, tugging his hands away. He says nothing, expression too contorted with grief to appear truly frustrated, though there is clearly *something* irritable tucked into the corners of his eyes.

A moment ticks by. Of course, Ana lacks the internal clock of humans, and *time* continues to make no sense. It might be a moment. It might be an age.

Finally, they ask, "An abortion?"

"Well," Noah huffs. "I mean, we know where Lu is—it wouldn't be the first time someone's gone to see her. I mean . . . you're not, like, getting all . . . God-y on me, are you? Cause, like, I really didn't—"

"I'll take you to Lu." Ana's hand falls from Noah's shoulder, and they nod, heart racing as something like hope begins to thread into their spine, making them stand taller. "We'll go now—if we hurry, we can beat the storm."

Lu is Doctor Lucy. Most people left in Brooklyn know her name. Ana isn't sure if she was a doctor *before* the world ended, or if she just made herself one after. She has a whole collective living in the heart of Prospect Park, with seemingly endless supplies raided from NewYork-Presbyterian and University Hospital in those first days of reckoning. She and her ilk trade treatment for favors. And Noah's right. It wouldn't be the first time their own group took someone to her for abortion care.

"I—what?" Noah shakes his head, clearly struggling to catch up with Ana's line of thinking. "What do you mean? How did we jump from antiabortion to you taking me to get it done in the next couple of hours?"

"I am not antiabortion." Actually, in this case, Ana is incredibly proabortion. Ana is an abortion superfan, as far as this moment is concerned. "I know you cannot bring that *thing* into the world."

Noah flinches as if he's been struck, eyes widening.

Ana knows they'll need to circle back to that later. But there's no time now. "Come on. We have to leave now if we're going to make this happen."

"Why—why?" Noah shakes his head. "I just . . . like, doesn't that feel kind of fast to you? I mean, why can't we just wait until the storm's over? I'm being serious, there's like . . . there's no point doing it if we're just gonna die anyway, and I don't really wanna spend my last night with you doing *this*."

Ana hesitates.

They know they should be honest with him. It has to happen now because, as soon as it's over, they're going to take him to Rikers Island, to the stronghold of the angels, to survive the hurricane. And there's no way the angels will let him inside if he's carrying one of these monsters in his womb. They're already going to be displeased to see Ana dragging a human along with them. Expecting them to accept the presence of a Nephilim—even a fetal one—is expecting far too much.

But Noah is not going to be happy about that plan. And if they stand here arguing for much longer, they're going to run out of time.

And so, instead, Ana says, "We have no idea how long this is going to last, or what the world is going to look like when it's over. What happens if we get stuck underground for weeks, or months? What happens if you can't just go out after the storm— if you have to see this pregnancy through because we're trapped down here?"

Noah swallows, face paling. Another moment that might be a year drags past before he nods. "You're right. Okay, you're right—we have to go now."

It is exactly what Ana wants to hear, and they feel like they're going to be sick.

The first gray clouds have begun their creeping descent on the dead city, filtering sunlight now through a bleak haze that makes it feel like smoldering electricity in the air around them. The hair on Ana's arms rises to attention, gooseflesh pimpling along the back of their neck. Noah's hand in theirs is the only source of warmth in the bloated corpse of what was once Crown Heights, and he clutches their fingers so tightly, Ana worries their own hand might shatter. But it would be worth it, they think, as the two of them make their way toward the park.

Ana's heard stories of what Brooklyn was like before the reckoning, but their own firsthand account is too littered with trauma to make much sense. The city was an anchorage, once, for artists and immigrants and people whose lives existed at the intersections of hope and lament. By the time the legion of angels descended on Earth, the world was already upturned, the preamble to Revelation lurching any illusion of social order off its axis. The rich and powerful who'd once owned this city had either fled to some new harbor far away from the hands of accountability, or had themselves fallen from their towers of influence, spewing vitriol to anyone in the ooze with them who might listen. The cruel foundations of human civilization, empires built by the worst of Father's ill-designed offspring, were already cracked wide open.

Whatever it once was, it isn't now. The Eastern Parkway, long and skinny and winding its way through the city toward the park, reminds Ana of a serpent, its abandoned cars like the exposed ribs of a reptilian corpse. Is this their Eden? Is Father watching them even now, as they navigate this ultimate sin? Or perhaps He's sent one of His soldiers instead.

The thought makes their spine tingle uncomfortably, and they pull their hand free from Noah's to rub their moist palms over their thighs.

He watches them through a side-eye, round face soft and downturned.

"Sorry," Ana mumbles, and offers him their hand again, but Noah doesn't take it.

Instead, he says, "I want to talk about something you said. About bringing a *thing* into this world."

Ana does not want to have that conversation.

And they're saved, it would seem, from actually having to endure it. Because just as they open their mouth to ask what Noah wants to say about it, the angry blaring of a car alarm makes them jump out of their skin.

Like a perfectly synchronized team, as if they'd practiced it, Noah moves to stand in front of Ana at the same moment Ana steps behind him. He pulls the shotgun strapped across his back into his waiting hands, barrel aimed in the direction of the sound. There's something sickening about it, the high-pitched blaring that floats over the memory of the highway. An alarm in a world where there's no one *left* to alarm sounds a lot like a ghost screaming to be heard by the living—only the living, in the days of reckoning, *are* the ghosts.

"Who's there?" Noah demands, raising his voice to be heard over the siren.

Ana can hardly breathe. They press tight to his back, frenzied eyes flicking back and forth along the line of cars, searching for any hint of movement.

There. A shadow stumbling over the pavement. The sharp angles of a man's face coming into view.

The cavernous sockets of his endless black eyes.

Ana's heart flips and flips and threatens to come sliding off their tongue. Their fingers curl into Noah's shoulder.

"Get down, close your eyes, and whatever you do—do not look at me."

"What? I—"

"It's a demon."

And they're lucky a demon is all it is. It could've been worse. It could've been another angel.

In their first days on Earth, confused and afraid and wanting so badly to follow Father's commands, Ana spent every night in fevered prayer. They would hide behind dumpsters, under bridges, in the backs of subway trains, and they would try to pray until they could no longer hear the aching grumbles of their empty stomach.

Food, of course, was hard to come by, but the problem went deeper than that. The concept of eating at all was still fresh for Ana back then, a mysterious abstraction that didn't make any sense. It was a monotonous task, any time-consuming attempt at securing sustenance for their new human body, and even when they were successful in finding *something*, they found themself confused by their *reaction* to different foods. *Why* did humans need calories—and calories of the right sort, even—in order to function properly? And *why* did so many vessels for these calories have textures or tastes that made them impossible for Ana to consume without gagging? Another flaw in Father's human design. Another reason for the Revelation.

Having to eat wasn't the only upsetting new reality about this body. Its need for sleep was bizarre—spending one-third of their time unconscious, vulnerable, in some stasis where they recharged by simply doing *nothing* at all . . . well, no one could possibly argue that made any sense. And so they didn't. In the beginning, they didn't sleep until they couldn't *not* for a moment longer. Instead, they prayed.

So many mistakes in the human body, and yet living in their own was not an option. Their *true* form—though Ana hasn't thought of their celestial body as *their* body in a long time—was never to be seen by humans. Too much for them to behold, too terrifying and grotesque, the angels could not walk this earth as they truly were. Doing so would work against their purpose, after all—no humans would follow them if they recognized their monstrousness for what it was.

They could recognize one another, though. Not by physical feature, but by the crackling air around their bodies, the emanating light that no truly mortal eyes could ever distinguish for what it was. They were called to one another, even if they chose not to answer.

And they weren't the only ones. Demons walked the earth long before angels did—they have never been bound to *their* father's kingdom—and they'd long since learned to blend in.

There are still signs, though, if one knows what to look for.

Ana's body tears itself asunder.

There is pain in this, they know, but it hardly registers. Not because it is insignificant, but because it is *so* unbearable, the shedding of their skin and gnarling of their bones, that the messengers in their nervous system simply cannot get the point across to their brain. They know it hurts in the same way they once knew they were hungry—only, instead of waiting to *hear* the sound of their stomach, they *watch* as ivory shards of bone, like an armory of blades, slice them open and flare out around the shredded strips of their skin. One might look at them and think they saw wings.

"YOU WILL TURN AND LEAVE US BE!" Ana's voice—not theirs, deeper and more powerful than theirs, but somehow, still theirs all the same—booms across the highway, making the pavement rumble, shaking the parked cars. Their feet begin to lift away from the asphalt, body levitating inch by inch over the ground.

"Okay!"

Wait.

Ana hits the earth once more and frowns. "What?"

The demon, wide-eyed and trembling, his hands raised with palms facing them, shakes his head. "I don't want any trouble. I don't want any trouble. I don't—"

"You *are* trouble," Ana reminds him.

"I was just trying to find a car that had gas." The demon shakes his head, motioning behind him in the direction of the blaring alarm. "I'm just trying to get my family out of the city."

An obvious lie. No demon has a family. Clearly, he's trying to—

Across the street, peeking out from over the side mirror of one parked car, a crouching child watches from their hiding spot. *That* is what the demon was pointing to.

Something squirms in Ana's chest, threatening to tighten around their lungs. They can hardly breathe, and certainly can't speak.

In their silence, hesitant, as if he thinks he still might be struck down, the demon begins to back away. Slowly, at first, and then as quickly as he can move, racing back to the sidewalk. He and the child disappear around the corner.

Mind frayed, Ana is silent and still as their body restitches itself back into the semblance of humanity. They turn toward Noah, on his knees behind them, head bowed, eyes closed.

Tenderly, they press their fingers to his shoulder.

He looks up. The weight in his dark eyes tells them he heard every word exchanged.

"That isn't what I would've expected from a demon," he says, dragging the obvious into the light as he stands and brushes off his knees.

"I'm still unconvinced it isn't a trick." Ana sniffs. "That isn't a typical demon."

"How would you know? Have you ever actually talked to one?"

Ana doesn't answer.

Noah takes that for the answer it is. "Have you ever considered you've been lied to? A lot? About everything?"

He keeps the course toward the park, one hand on the strap of his gun, just in case.

Ana watches him go for a breath too long before following. They do not think of how many nights they once spent praying. They do not think of how every prayer went unanswered.

It starts to rain just as they reach their destination. The massive white boathouse sits on the shore of the lake, its white columns reflected in the water's surface made unrecognizable by the drizzle. Noah is the one to approach the front door, where a sign has hung for the last few years, reading,

DOCTOR LUCY
AND ASSOCIATES

It feels remarkably mundane for the apocalypse. Ana swallows and shoves their hands into their pockets, while Noah uses his fist to knock three times.

When no one answers, he tries a fourth.

On the fifth, the door finally cracks open. Only the hint of a man can be seen through the slot, frantic blue eyes and a thrumming energy, like he's had too much caffeine. Ana instinctively steps closer to Noah.

"No patients today," he snaps. "Come back tomorrow if we're still standing."

He goes to slam the door closed again, and Ana moves without thinking, pressing their palm to the wood so it remains unmoved. He glares at them.

Between them, Noah says, "Please. I need to see Lu."

"Yeah." The man rolls his eyes. "So does everyone else. And just like everyone else, you can wait."

"I don't know if I can, though."

"You don't look like you're dying to me."

"Does he look like he's pregnant?" Ana demands.

Anger is not an emotion they understand, made of some strange dichotomy. It seems to seep from the things they love, surrounding them like water. But inside Ana's body, it feels like it's burning.

A flicker of what might be surprise dusts the man's expression, and he looks Noah up and down. "Huh. That sucks. But it also doesn't mean you're dying. Go away now."

"Please," Noah groans. Ana notes the way his shoulders tremble. They think of how little effort it would take to destroy this house of healing. They don't like thinking that way—but it *is* what the sword of God would do. "None of us knows what tomorrow's going to look like. You have no idea when I'll be able to make it back here. But I'm not ready for this—I *can't* do this right now."

Ana's chest tightens. Ready. Right now. White lies that Noah is telling himself. They try not to think about it.

"Like I said, that's not my—"

"Let them in."

The man looks over his shoulder and balks. "I was just—"

"I heard. Now let them in. There's still time."

While the man just stands there, looking as if he might cry, Ana uses their flattened palm to force the door open.

Inside, a woman in a denim jacket and a trucker cap, with a fanny pack around her waist and a stethoscope around her neck, inclines her head at them. Doctor Lucy raises her hand and points down the hall, toward a set of double doors. "Wait for me there. Do you know how far along you are?"

"Can't be more than . . . eight weeks?" Noah's voice shakes as he tries to sound certain. Ana slips their hand into his.

"Okay. I'll grab what you need."

She disappears in one direction, and they disappear in the other.

The room beyond the double doors is some kind of office. There's a cot to one side and a desk to the other, and every other available surface is covered in books—textbooks and notebooks, mirrors of one another.

Noah sits down on the cot and twists his hands in front of his stomach. Ana hovers near his elbow, bones tight, gut hollowed out.

The quiet in the room is enough to make their skin crawl. It feels like being buried alive. They watch the rain pelt the office window and realize they've stopped breathing only when Noah speaks and the surprise of the sound forces their lungs to inflate.

"I want to have kids someday, you know. I've always wanted kids." He sniffs, shifting in his seat, rubbing his hands over his wide thighs. Noah isn't a *small* person, taller and broader and rounder than Ana, but the cramped confines of the room make him look even bigger than he is.

Ana swallows. For all the space he takes up, they have to look away from him. They focus on one particular stack of books when they answer, "There are many ways to make a family. Many children have lost their parents."

"Yeah, and we can take care of them, too. But I want *us* to have a *baby*, Ana." He sighs. "God, I mean—not now, right? Obviously. Not now. The world is just—but—you know, what if it isn't always like this? I mean . . . maybe it will be. Maybe everything's just . . . this, forever, until we're all dead. But maybe it isn't. And maybe someday we'll be able to like, fucking, I don't know, repopulate the Earth or some shit, and—"

"Not with me." Ana gives a single jerk of their head. "If you want a baby, Noah, it won't be with me. I'm sorry."

Whatever look is on Noah's face, his eyes burn the back of Ana's neck. But they are a coward, and they don't turn to look at him. Eventually, he continues, "I mean—if you don't want kids, like, okay, fine. That's . . . that's a whole conversation we can have, you know? I get that. But I don't—I don't think that's what's going on here, is it?"

Ana does not answer.

"You called it a *thing*."

"It would not be human."

"Neither are you," Noah reminds them.

"It would be a monster."

"According to *who*?" Noah demands.

And again, Ana does not answer.

The door opens, and Doctor Lucy steps inside, and finally Ana raises their head to watch as she moves toward Noah and presses three pills into his palm. Pointing to each individually, she explains, "This will stop the pregnancy from continuing to develop, but it won't expel the tissue. You shouldn't experience any pain. You can take it now, if you'd like. *This* will start the process of expulsion—you need to take it within two days after the first. If you wait any longer, you could get sick, or worse. When you take it, you'll begin cramping—it's your body working to push the tissue out. There will be blood, including clots big enough that they might scare you. But it's normal, and so is pain. That's what the third pill is for. Any questions?"

Noah's whole body shakes, like a tree caught in the whipping wind, threatening to be uprooted by the storm outside. Ana reaches for him, pressing their hand into his shoulder and squeezing.

When he does not speak, they ask, "How long will it take?"

"A few hours. Once the tissue is passed, the pain should ease, but he might be uncomfortable for another couple of days."

"Will he be okay?"

"Adverse reactions are rare, but they happen. The biggest concern is excess bleeding. I can make room for you to stay here, if—"

"No." Noah finally speaks, shaking his head. He closes his fist, pulling the pills closer to his chest. "No, I have to go. I can't—with the storm, I can't leave my people."

Ana is *calm*. Inside, another scream is added to the choir.

"What do we owe you?" they ask.

Doctor Lucy shrugs. "If you're still alive when the streets are usable again, come and see me. We'll figure something out."

With a trio of abortion pills in Noah's pocket and the doctor's cryptic words hanging over their heads, Noah and Ana make their way back into the park. The storm has gotten worse since they went inside, rain pelting the ground now.

Noah tugs his hood over his head and reaches for their hand. "Come on. We should get back before they have to close up."

Ana brushes the pad of their thumb along the back of his. They take a deep breath to savor the feeling of his touch, the vitality of him, the grounding nature of his presence. They don't know how much longer they'll be able to tether themself to it.

"We aren't going back, Noah."

A beat passes. His hand slips from theirs.

"What the hell does that mean, Ana?"

"I'm not going to let you die like some drowned rat." They swallow and look away. Coward. "We're going to Rikers."

"Ri—" Noah begins, but comes up short. "You can't—there's no way. That's where you expect me to go, to the *angels*?"

"They are our best chance of surviving," Ana warns. "They *are* divine intervention."

"They're monsters," Noah reminds them, as if Ana could ever forget.

"Yes. Just as I am."

"No. Nothing like you are." Noah groans, pacing in front of them. They can't bring themself to look at his face again, so they watch his boots squelching in the mud. "They won't let me in, anyway. Right? Because I'm—I'm human. And they—well, they *kill* humans, right? God's little mistakes? How is my best chance of survival walking into the one place where everyone inside actively wants me to die?"

"They don't think of themselves as killers. They are just following our Father's path. I thought, if I could show penance, if I could make them believe you were one of His chosen few—"

"*Me*?" Noah laughs, and it stings. "Handpicked by God to survive the apocalypse? I'm fifteen slurs in a trench coat. I don't think your dad gives a *shit* about me, Ana."

"I just *thought*," they press on, "they could be persuaded to give you a chance, if I begged. There is little they enjoy more than watching one of their own grovel, or having the opportunity to make themselves look pious. As long as they didn't find out about our relationship, I thought it was worth trying. Your life is worth—"

"As long . . . as they didn't find out . . . about our relationship . . ."

Ana scrubs their hands over their face, heart sinking into their empty stomach.

"That's why you were so eager to get me here. So we could take care of our little monster problem before we went home to see your family."

"That is unfair," Ana whispers. "Every choice I have made has been out of love for you. It wouldn't have mattered where we spent the storm—the pregnancy was going to end, either way."

"Yeah, okay. I would have wanted the abortion no matter what; you're right. But who's calling our maybe-someday child a *thing*? Is it actually you? Or is that just their gospel coming out of your mouth?"

"Tell me I'm misunderstanding what I just heard," another voice rises over the rain.

Ana's head snaps up, and they twist their neck to look toward the sound. The world seems to fall away—they forget they need to breathe.

A dozen feet away, the archangel Uriel approaches.

God's most loyal weapon, the sharpest sword in his armory—sauntering straight toward Ana and everything that means anything to them.

"Tell me there is not an abomination growing in the human's womb."

"Noah, look away! Now!" Ana roars as they begin their transformation once more.

They cannot win against an archangel. They know this. And even as they know it, they know they will die here, die to give Noah a moment longer to run. Ana was always going to die for love. This has been true since the moment they landed on Earth.

Through the pain of their shift, the screaming of their own bones as they rip themself apart, they hear Uriel's laughter.

"Pitiful creature." He tsks. "You think I would give you the mercy of an early death? When your suffering at His hands will be so decadent?"

"You will not lay a hand on him," Ana growls. "I won't let you."

"*I'm* not the one with a penchant for laying hands on humans, little Judas." Uriel smirks, eyeing Noah over the bone shards erupting from Ana's shoulder. "He will succumb to eternal agony soon enough. And your unborn shall burn along with him."

Ana screams. Fire erupts in their hands, a sword of flame appearing from nothing. They swing for Uriel's throat and miss by a humiliating margin.

"Run along now, children. You'll catch your death out here." Uriel grins, flashing canine teeth a fraction too sharp to be a human's. "Tell my brother I send my regards."

And as quickly as he appeared, the archangel is gone.

Ana stands there burning in the rain, staring at the empty space he left behind.

"Ana?" Noah asks.

They take a deep breath, turning to tell him to keep his eyes closed for a moment longer—only for the words to turn to ash in their mouth.

Noah is staring right at them.

"No!" Ana wails. "Look away! You will surely—"

"Babe, I'm fine."

And . . . it would seem that was true. The expression on their boyfriend's face is one of awe, sure, but he isn't . . .

Actively melting or turning to a pile of salt or anything.

Noah is looking directly at their celestial body, unflinching and unharmed.

"How is this possible?" they demand, voice cracking on an unreleased sob.

Noah steps forward. At his approach, Ana extinguishes the flame in their palm, the sword turning to smoke. When Noah is close enough that he stands within the circle of their porcelain wings, he reaches up to press the pads of his fingers to their cheek.

"Because you have been *lied* to," he whispers, barely audible over the downpour. "There is nothing monstrous about you. And your day of judgment is *not fucking coming.*"

That cannot be true. If it were . . . nothing Ana knows could be true. They don't know if that would be better or worse.

Noah presses his hand into theirs. "Let's go home."

When the latch closes behind them, sealing away the rain from continuing to pour down with them into the underground city, they know it is the last time that door will close for a while. How long exactly, they can't be sure. But this storm is not going to end in a single night. That much, they can feel in their bones.

The tunnel is quiet and empty, and Ana might have a brief moment of panic that they'd been abandoned if it weren't sort of nice, one last moment alone with nothing to focus on but the warmth of Noah's hand in theirs. But any opportunity for panic is short-lived, regardless, when they come upon the broken-down corpse of an old train, dragged from the belly of the underground city.

The others are inside, people and animals and food and water and blankets and medicine, as much as possible, crammed into the train like one extra layer of protection from death by drowning. Noah enters in front of Ana and makes his way toward the back, checking in with others as he goes. They hover by the door, watching him walk away.

"I saw Uriel," they say.

At the front of the train, appearing to be asleep, the archangel Gabriel sits with his head tipped back and his eyes closed. He opens one at Ana's words, an unfamiliar spark of interest in his expression. "Oh?"

"He told me to tell you hi."

"Of course he did." Gabriel yawns, rubbing a hand over his face, and sits up straighter. "Where were you two?"

"It's a long story." And it isn't. Ana rubs a hand over their aching chest. "Can I ask you something?"

"Mm," Gabriel grunts, neither a yes or a no, but probably a no.

Still, Ana has to try. They have to know.

"I know I'm nothing in the big picture, but you're an *archangel*. He loved you more than any of us. How . . . how does the hand of God fall from His path?"

Gabriel tilts his head at them before turning to look back into the train car. He smiles. "I didn't."

That isn't actually an answer, and it definitely doesn't make any sense. Frustration begins to knot in their chest, until they follow Gabriel's eyes, turning to the others underground. The community huddled together. The families and friends. The sick and their caretakers. The weeping and the comforting.

Noah's made himself a spot in one back corner, head tilted against the cool metal, eyes half-closed so he can keep an eye on Ana. When their gazes meet, he offers the sad whisper of a would-be smile.

What if they've been lied to? The question is terrifying, forcing Ana to reconsider everything they have ever known about this world and the one beyond it, about themself and the humans and every creature of His design. But along with it comes another question, one just as capable of shattering the world beneath Ana's feet, in another way entirely—

What if they never stepped off their path? What if this is exactly what they were made to do?

Gabriel has gone back to feigning sleep, so Ana leaves him to it, slipping through the train car to join Noah. When they settle down next to him, he leans his head on their shoulder.

Over his thigh, he opens his fist. The first pill is pressed into his palm.

"Well," he says. "Here we go."

In the world above, the ground begins to shake under the weight of the hurricane's approach.

And even as their bones go cold and their stomach rolls with fear of what may follow in the days to come . . . the very first seeds of something like hope begin to take root.

"Yeah." Ana kisses the top of his head. "Here we go."

MONSTER REFLECTION

Growing up, I didn't have much access to what you might think of as traditional "monsters." I was born and raised in the rural south. When I was still too young to really start unpacking the religion I'd been raised in, and all the hypocrisy and trauma that came along with it, I didn't *mind* being dragged into the pews every Sunday. Actually, I found the stories fascinating—little me was enthralled with the tall tales of biblical heroes and villains, the epic mythology of ultimate good and evil. It was a good *story*.

Of course, eventually I realized I was developing a very different relationship to the Bible than all the adults around me were. At the same time, it started to click that I was different from them in other ways, too—notably, I knew I was queer, even if I didn't have the language to explain exactly how. I still loved Bible stories, but I started gravitating to the more obvious monsters the books provided. I read about Lilith, Adam's possible first wife, whispered to be the mother of vampires. I dived deep into the dragons and sea monsters of Revelation. I was fascinated with Lucifer himself. I saw myself there, in the shadows of Christianity.

Today I no longer feel the need to stick to shadows. My relationship with the church has long since died, but my affinity for stories remains, including those first Bible stories that sparked my love of the fantastical. Today I'm interested in reclaiming those stories from a new lens—namely, to ask who the *real* monsters have been all along.

WORLD-WEARINESS

BY NAOMI KANAKIA

I was sitting on a park bench, eating frozen yogurt, and Linnriel, my best elf friend, had gone to the bathroom, and the moment Linn was out of sight, a human woman stopped and sneered at me. The woman was tall and pinched, with her hair pulled back and a stroller that had a baby so covered up you could see only its pink nose and forehead.

"Stay away from our kids, troll."

I said, "Uhh, what?" The teraphobia was bad enough; even elves got plenty of hate. But she'd also mistaken me for a troll! I wasn't a troll. I didn't look anything like a troll.

"If we see you around any kids, you won't like what happens."

Then she pushed her stroller onward, just like that. And I already knew I wouldn't mention this to Linnriel. My friend had trauma, and she absolutely hated humans—way more than I did—and she would've wanted to hunt down the woman and shout at her.

Linnriel floated toward the park bench, in a cloud of sunlight and flowing silk. She had blond hair that shone. She wore only flowing white tunics and dresses, loosely belted at the waist, which never got stained, even if she ate a sandwich with mustard (elves tend to like strong sauces, since their food is mostly made of bitter leaves). Her lips were wide and pink; her eyes were green. And her skin, of course, was pale, with her blue veins set off by the healthy, vibrant color of her lips and hair and nails.

"How does Earnath's song find you?" she said. "Does she call you to consume her frozen bounty? In yogurt form, I mean?" Yes, Linnriel could make fun of herself, too, if she needed to.

"Do you know any trolls?" I said.

Linnriel looked around warily, and she put one knee on the bench, ready to spring off if any humans came near.

"I have thought deeply on this matter, ever since it started to concern you, my sister. And I've been reading in the ancient scrolls—well, on my phone, actually, but whatever—I have been reading that *troll* and *elf* are just labels. What matters is that we're all magical."

"So then is *human* just a label?"

"Mankind means nothing to me. They are forever outside Earnath's song, doomed to a lifetime of suffering and despair."

Her eyes were hard now. Linnriel had gone through some bad stuff early in her transformation, before the other elves came and took her away from her parents. I'd heard her talk about that stuff but never in public. It's a good thing elves were sworn to nonviolence, or she'd probably have killed a few people by now.

"But . . . being a troll seems worse than being a human. . . ."

"Oh, my sister . . ." Linnriel lifted a hand to my cheek, holding her fingertips just a hair's breadth apart, so I could feel only the wind from the passing hand, without feeling the touch itself. The elven ethos was to leave the world untouched; elves refused even to keep pets, and there were great formal rituals before they felt pure enough to shake hands, much less kiss. Linnriel was my age—fifteen—but she'd already gotten those graceful, ageless gestures that elves get. And she was working on that detached, airy-fairy elven "manner of speech." She would be immortal, of course. Elves were the longest lived of Earnath's creations. Then dwarves, giants, sentient trees, etc. The further you got from Earnath's song, the shorter your life. Which meant trolls didn't live very long, maybe just fifty years on average.

"It'll be okay," Linnriel said. "I wouldn't say this to anyone else, but we both know trolls are almost always people who realize they're magical only when they're, like, thirty years old. I mean, it's not their fault: it's our society, and the way it blocks people from hearing Earnath's song. Or sometimes if an elf turns evil and violent, and they spill blood, they'll become a troll. But still . . . you're so young. Believe me, you're going to have so many more centuries and millennia ahead to laugh about this. Ten thousand years from now, when this park bench has returned to Earnath, we'll sit in the trees and laugh about these worries."

I smiled. She'd dropped her accent and for a second started talking like Lily, the girl I'd grown up with.

"You will find Earnath's song soon," Linnriel said. "I know this to be true."

Earnath was the elven name for the Earth. Fifteen thousand and fifty-two years ago, the first Men coerced her into submitting to their will, and that's why human beings have dominated the Earth ever since.

"Okay," I said.

But Linnriel wasn't totally right. There were plenty of younger trolls. Although I'd never admit this to Linn, I actually had one troll friend. Amanda had tried to modify her germ by herself, using a ritual she learned from the internet. Her parents found out only when the IT guy at our school noticed someone was visiting forbidden forums. They confronted her, and then we all needed to have an assembly on safe magic. Her parents took her to doctors, trying to get the "damage" reversed. But she changed quickly after that, growing to around eight feet and developing big claws, green skin, and bloodshot eyes. She got sent home a few times because her clothes didn't fit, and people used to mock her because she was always half-dressed in sheets and curtains that rode up, showing her butt, so she looked really indecent. After leaving school, she just started going naked— now she was a mass of muddy hair and wrinkled skin.

I'd heard that she lived under one of the bridges that led to the Eternal Forest, and she collected tolls from people who crossed. Usually people paid up willingly—a lot of people honored the old ways and thought paying a troll was good luck—but sometimes they didn't, and she attacked them, tearing up their clothes, destroying their cars, and generally making them regret being alive.

After the woman called me a troll, I went home, and I went to my room to say my prescribed incantations—I was careful never to miss them, because if I did, then I'd for *certain* turn into a troll.

My parents had taken the mirror off the wall because they'd read somewhere it was bad for magical kids to look at themselves too much. The websites are like, *When you were in the womb, you spent some time as an egg, some time as a tadpole, and some time as a fish, and if you'd looked at yourself during any of those stages, you'd have thought, "I look nothing like a person." So don't waste time now. Wait until the rebirth is complete.*

But I took pictures of myself in my underwear, with my fingers splayed, pictures from odd angles, so I could run my limb lengths through a calculator (result: inconclusive). And then I posted the pics on Reddit, and they were like, *Huh, in certain light, yeah, you do look trollish. I see it.*

So I sent a message to Amanda, being like, *Hey, remember me? It's Niyal? We were on the wrestling team together? Do you have time to talk? I guess, uhh, I guess I'm transforming, too. . . .*

Amanda answered my message a few weeks later. *Still interested? Been long. Only check messages when at library. If need, come to bridge.*

I wrote back, *When?*

But I didn't get a response. I guess she'd already left the library. She lived to the west, near the Darklands. (I was using the human names, of course, since the elven names are all from fifteen thousand years ago and mean stuff like "Shining Forest of Happiness" and really don't reflect the current feel of the places.) It wasn't too far away. I could bike there, if I wanted, though I never had. So today after school, I headed west, across cracked pavement toward the tall white sails of the ships that no mortal had ever visited. Beyond the Eternal Forest was a cove where the elven fleets docked eternally, singing their songs and mourning their lost homeland.

The ground was cracked and overgrown, and eventually it was too hard to bike. Cars were sputtering nearby—technology failed more often as you went farther west. I ran into a checkpoint, where a little dwarf was waving cars into a big, empty parking lot. Several giants were standing by with huge packs, and one baby cried as he and his family got heaved up into the air: "No, no, no! Dun wanna, no!"

I took a right, taking a little trail to the Darklands, and soon I was on a muddy embankment that was covered in giant red-and-white mushroom caps, like in a video game. We were still technically in the mortal realm right now, and the water was slow and choked with paper wrappers and glass bottles.

"H-hey," I said as I got to the dirt piled up against the under-side of the bridge. "Ah—Amanda?"

The pile of dirt shifted, and then the great muddy mass moved, all at once. Arms and legs appeared, and a big foot splashed into the stream. I saw now the several sealed crates piled up against the concrete, and beyond the mass of moving dirt, I saw the little burrow—crude and animalistic, with long scratches along the sides, like a giant mousehole.

The creature was clothed in mud. Even its hair and forehead were a mass of mud. The creature took a long breath. It looked like a gigantic naked sloth, with immense claws and wide-open sleepy eyes. When its mouth opened, the little tongue poked out, embarrassingly short and human and out of proportion to the rest of its giant body.

"Niyal?" she said. "You came. Sit. P-please. S-sorry. Do not get visitors much. Sit p-p-p-please."

I nodded.

She made a peculiar, unforgettable noise, something like the purring of a cat—except she made it with her tongue and lips. Then she reached down with her massive hands, and she patted some of the dirt into a little pylon, shaping it with her broad palms, then flicking away the excess with her claws. She splashed the mud with water, then she breathed slowly over it, and the mound got dry and developed little cracks and a hard surface.

"Sit," she said, patting the mound. "Sit down."

Creeping up to it, I took a seat on the warm, dry dirt. My whole body was drenched in sweat. I couldn't look directly at her. Her legs were hinged backward, like a kangaroo's, or maybe it was only that her feet were so incredibly broad that she didn't put her full foot on the ground and walked on her toes all the time. Either way, she settled back on her haunches, and she kept making that catlike noise as she looked at me.

"Good magic. Clean magic. Have not smelled that in many moons. I mean months, sorry. I no good code-switcher."

"You can talk natural," I said. "I mean, the way you normally do."

"No, no, troll need speak human good," Amanda said. "Or troll die. Et cetera. Also you sound stupid if you speak troll, which is silly, since it 'nother vernacular English, but still, cannot help human prejudice. Sometime I think prejudice make sense. When you are in the rock trance, you forget how human beings think and speak. You become dangerous. Unclean."

"You're not dangerous!" I said.

"How you know?" She cleared her throat. "Don't be fool. *A* fool. Articles are what was missing. Pronouns, too. Okay, I remember. Don't be a fool. I am very, very dangerous. I could tear apart this bridge with my hands. Bullets cannot stop me. I am very dangerous."

"Humans are the dangerous ones. That's just . . . you don't . . . like they're the ones that built capitalism! And . . . and strip mining! And . . . global warming?"

"Yessssss . . ." Amanda said. "I like elves. Silly elves. So amusing. What did you want? I forget how elves think. Very flowery thoughts, I think. My social worker is an elf. Still visits me sometimes. Good person. I like her. But you stay? I build a burrow? Nice to have visitor. You test out being a troll. Maybe you like it? Or else doomed to elfdom, I suppose."

She trailed off, looking into the stream. She was a little scattered. Very, er, trollish. She talked to herself a lot. She broke into houses, and she stole, and she could be cruel—she always said what she thought—but I'd learn all that later. For now, I told her that my parents were expecting me home tonight.

"Parents? Sure? Are you stupid? Of course not. Of course not. No, of course. No. Well, come on, then; I'll clear space for you in the burrow. We'll have a nice—nice few months."

I asked my parents for permission to spend a few nights with Amanda, and they said, "Who is this person? Should they be speaking to children? Where do they live?" So I backed away and told them it was just a joke.

Let's be honest; I was a good kid. I wasn't a rebel. Until I started my transformation, I hardly talked, didn't have lots of friends. In fact, for six months I was like, this can't possibly be me. I can't be magical! I'm definitely not interesting enough to be a magic creature.

Once my mom asked me, "Are you just doing this because you think your life will be more interesting and special if you're magical?" And I was like, "Yeah, of course, that's the reason. Why would any person *not* want to be magical?" But I worried for a few months that I was just doing this because I thought it was cool, or that I was suffering from Rapid Onset Magical Ideation. But then I read a blog post that said, *You know, if you want to, if you're willing to take the risk, that's reason enough.*

I don't know; it was all confused. Sometimes I felt the idea of being magical was like a virus. It just took hold of me, started obsessing me. I browsed websites, looked up rituals, just thought about it, night after night. Thought about being an elf, living forever, tending to the trees, doing everything I could to keep Earnath alive and singing. I honestly was surprised *everyone* didn't transform.

But now that I was doing it, I wasn't sure. Everything was just . . . scarier. More uncertain. One day, a few weeks after I saw Amanda, my mom looked at me and her eyes were full of tears, and I asked her why, and she said, "You would . . . do you remember when you first *heard* about being magical? Did your friend Linnriel . . . you knew her as Lily, right? Did she ever . . . did she ever glamorize it? Make it seem cool or fun?"

"Mom, what is happening?"

"I've just been reading some things about . . . about recruitment. About how the elves want . . . well, they have aims. They hate humanity."

"But they're pacifists. And vegans. They're sworn to, you know, nonviolence."

"So they say," she said. "I just . . . I don't want to lose you!"

What's there to say? We argued. I got mad and stomped upstairs, and she didn't come to comfort me.

Amanda was absolutely no help with any of this, by the way. She somehow wasn't very reflective. Not very conversational, either. She spent a lot of time hunched over books in her little hovel, reading them slowly out loud in a monotone as her finger ran through the lines. They were all kinds of stories, almost as if she was picking out books at random. I remember one of them once was a physics textbook, and she couldn't pronounce half the words.

The day after the fight with my mom, I came back with a sleeping bag and tent, and Amanda said, "I help."

We were in the process of setting it up, when suddenly I heard a splintery snap. Amanda held up one of the rods, which was thrust through the fabric of the tent. "Oops," she said.

"Fuck!" I said. "That was my only tent!"

"Trolls no need human things."

"But I get cold," I said.

"No. Untrue. Human lie."

I was going to ask, *What does that mean?* But suddenly I understood. Do I actually get cold? Or was that just something I'd been told? I sat on the dirt podium, which Amanda had never taken down in the weeks I'd been coming here, and I slipped off my shoes and socks. Wiggling my toes, I saw the yellowish tinge of the nails. Then I rolled my jeans up to my calves, and I stepped into the stream. It was cold. I could feel that. It was absolutely very cold, glacially cold. But the coldness didn't hurt. Cold or hot were like red or blue—just information. Not something to worry about. Above us, I heard the tromping of giants over the bridge. Amanda yelled something, and she grabbed a concrete handhold, swinging up top, and I heard her yelling at some passersby.

Afterward, she came down, and she flung two golden coins into the mud.

"See," she said. "No cold."

"No," I said. "What does that mean? Am . . . am I a troll?"

"It means no need for tent."

She helped me dig a burrow. It wasn't hard. I could see that other burrows had existed here before. There were claw marks in the concrete. And I could smell old smells in the dirt.

Then I crawled into the space, and I felt the earth breathe around me: I heard its heaviness and its impossible age. And, most of all, its mute, uncaring force. The earth was alive, and it didn't care one bit whether we were here or were absent. Compared with its terrible power, we were nothing. And I enjoyed the feeling of being nothing. Time stretched onward, and I lived an eternity, frozen inside that empty moment. I was face-to-face with the Goddess, and I was discovering that she didn't care about me. I was totally irrelevant to the functioning of the world, and the idea was oddly comforting.

Eventually, something woke up—something called Niyal— something that walked around and talked. But something also stayed behind in that burrow, something brown and green and furry, something that was ugly and short-lived and didn't care about what anyone thought. And every time I went back into that burrow, I crawled into the cocoon of that old skin, and I didn't sleep—I wouldn't call it sleep—because it was above being awake, in the same way that being awake is above being asleep. Inside those moments underground, I truly lived.

I slept out there for a few nights. I texted my parents, before my phone ran out of battery power, but when I came home they were furious.

"You have your future to think of!"

"Think, do, myself." The words were sluggish on my tongue. I knew exactly what I was saying: the future didn't exist. I'd only done what I needed to do. But I'd been underground so long that I'd forgotten how other people think.

"This isn't good for you! You're withdrawn; you don't care about school anymore. Niyal, please! We can pause this. We could even . . . we could even go backward."

"I . . ." But the word sounded strange. Even the concept of "I" didn't make sense anymore. My real self lived underground, was inextricable from the underground. To ask me why I visited Amanda was the same as asking someone, *Why did you go home?* Well . . . because that's what a home is: it's the place you go.

They took my phone and sent me to my room and said we were gonna have a long talk in the morning. That night I sat down and said my incantations—feeling for the first time in ages that everything would be fine, no matter what happened with my rebirth.

The next morning I was upstairs for a long time, until finally my mom barged into my room. I still remember the exact moment she saw me. Her jaw dropped. Her eyes went wide. "Niyal," she said. "You're . . . you're . . ."

And I knew. Without even seeing a mirror, I knew that the rebirth was complete. I looked down at my fingers, and they were white. My hair was smooth and silky. My face felt different, sharp and jagged, not soft like before. My clothes hung loose around me. The air tasted like flowers—it tasted like a food that I could take or leave as I wished—and I experimented with holding my breath, and I experienced no discomfort. My mind expanded, zooming outward, until I was way above us, up in the clouds, looking down from a great height.

"I'll need new clothing," I said.

"We . . . we'll shop. . . ."

"Don't worry; I can handle it. Do you have the car keys?"

I put up my hand, and she dug through her pocket. Then she tossed them to me, and I caught them in midair, even though I only had my learner's permit. This woman was no longer my mother. I belonged now to eternity.

Everything was different. I was an elf. I was a freaking elf. Normally I could be a bit detached and philosophical about it, but sometimes my consciousness plummeted back into my body, and I saw the way everybody looked at me, inside my forest-green tunic, with my silken trousers, Linnriel sitting by my side braiding flowers into my hair. We were underneath a tree, and I could hear it speaking to me. Trees were anxious creatures, and they felt safe only when elves were around to comfort them.

"It's almost unfair," I said. "This is absolute perfection. I don't feel hungry. I don't need to breathe. Do we sleep?"

"If we want." Since my rebirth, she had toned down the elf-speak.

"I thought that I was going to be a troll."

"Honestly?" she said. "I feared it, too. Not that you would have despaired."

"No, I'd have survived."

"Exactly," she said. "Trolls don't all live under bridges. Many have good lives. But still . . ."

"Nothing like this."

A human boy spit at our feet. "Freaks," he said.

Our eyes pierced his body, and we stared unblinking. He muttered the word again, and he said, "If you were alone, you'd be dead."

"Do you own a knife?" Linnriel said.

"Er . . . no," I said.

Linnriel slid something into the pocket of my tunic. Warm and glossy, covered in runes. I slid my hand over the leather scabbard. Pulling out the knife, I felt no fear. The elves hadn't mined this metal, extracting it by force—they'd sought it out in naturally exposed veins, and they'd spoken to the lode-bearing rocks for years, sometimes dozens or hundreds of years, until they found some ores that willingly consented to be smelted and transformed and worked, until they'd turned into this knife. Nobody knew why the elves made knives and swords and other implements of war. Elves were sworn to nonviolence, and it was well-known that if they spilled blood, their germ would become polluted, and they would transform into a troll. But still they sometimes carried these blades that they never used.

The gleaming metal reflected my perfect face: the slender nose and pale skin and long ears. I'd been a dark-skinned human being, but as an elf I was much lighter. The knife sang to me, sang not in words but in something deeper than words, sang in concepts and feelings, sang using pure experience, pure reality—the thing that mankind had dominated and conquered and segmented into words, languages, species, races.

"The metal is wiser than you are, at least for now," Linnriel said. "I am so excited for you to meet the rest of our clade!"

"W-wait, I thought elves were nonviolent."

"We are," Linnriel said. "The moment we draw blood, we turn into trolls. But still, you can scare people off sometimes. And . . . I don't know. We elves are *so* powerful: maybe the blood thing isn't true. Sometimes I think it's just a *Homo sapiens* myth designed to maintain *Homo-sap*-remacy."

As twilight approached, we saw other figures in the trees. And Linnriel lost something, some guardedness, some artificiality. She let out a breath, and she stood up, putting out a hand. Suddenly other figures appeared around us, and they arranged themselves naturally in the boughs of trees and on the grass. One of them looked at a park bench and grimaced, then ran a hand over it, speaking to the wood.

Linnriel stood next to him, and the other figures, all in their simple, dark tunics and cloaks, stood near. My phone chimed, and one of them smiled at me.

Will you be out late? my mother wrote. *Remember you still have a curfew!*

The new face had a sly grin. He said, "May I make your acquaintance? I am Cevemen. Earth-husband, in your language."

"Sure," I said. "I'm Niyal."

Then he took the phone, turned it over in his fingers, and traced the contours of the gleaming metal. "It's so odd. Human beings strain so mightily to achieve elven craft, and they come so close. The device is so delicate—an elven creation would never crack or scuff—but they have made hundreds of millions of these in just a few years. It would take elves a thousand years to make just one phone. It's violent, of course, an act of violence, this device, but still . . . it possesses a certain beauty, even in its ephemerality."

"Yeah, and wait till you see next year's model. It's gonna be three millimeters bigger."

He smiled. "You'll lose your humor, but it's a pleasant thing while it lasts."

We stood silently in the trees, and I could feel the elven senses go out, could feel them speaking to the forest and healing the land, easing the scars of the pathways dug into it, the electric lines crisscrossing it, the pipes running through it. Linnriel's voice rose, joining them, speaking in that same wordless tongue, and I felt the song inside me, too. I felt ancient senses awaken, and I let the music come out of me. We spun a vision of a world without mankind, a world without violence, a world of endless laughter and light, living on the thin envelope of habitable atmosphere where Solien—the sun—warmed Earnath. I saw the ancient civilizations buried on this Earth, and I saw the faraway stars, glittering in the dark, yearning to speak with us, and yet afraid of touching mankind's darkness.

When it was done, Linnriel leaned close. "Do you see?" she said. "Did you hear it?"

"Mm-hmm," I said.

"Earnath's song," she said. "You joined in so beautifully."

"You are a true elf," Cevemen said. "One more song-circle, I think, and your transformation will be complete."

"It's too soon," Linnriel said. "She's been an elf for three days."

"But she is fully in tune with Earnath nonetheless," Cevemen said. "It's like all the evil in you has been purged and hidden underground." He winked. Did he, did he actually? It was as if he _knew_ a part of me was still buried under Amanda's bridge.

Cevemen, his palm an inch above mine, told me softly about the White Fleet, and about the day far in the future when it would sail again. His voice got husky and low, and he was filled with the glorious sadness of his lost homeland and of the unpolluted Earnath that'd once existed and that would never come again. And before he left, he said I'd be a worthy witness to Earnath's love, and that he looked forward to showing me the White Ships someday. At the end he said, "Don't worry, little one. After the next song-circle, your buried trollskin will fade away."

Afterward, I whispered to Linnriel.

"So . . . was I supposed to feel some connection with Earnath?" I said. "Because I really didn't. It felt totally just like something *we* were doing, all of us. Like the magic was coming from us, and not from the earth. It was a beautiful vision, though!"

"*Not* a vision," Linnriel said. "You're still thinking in *words*. I won't get offended, because you're not fully reborn yet, but don't talk that way around the rest. It's offensive."

"I'm just saying, when I was a troll, I felt something really different from the earth. As a troll, I could actually see and feel the earth. Today didn't feel that way. I'm not saying it wasn't beautiful, but we weren't channeling the earth; we were doing it ourselves. That's all."

"That is literal blasphemy," she said. "You would be stoned to death for that in the old days. It takes *millennia* to make direct communication with Earnath. That's what we call it, not Earth, by the way. Earth is a *human* abomination, just like everything human is an abomination. Don't think you're great just because Cevemen anointed you, by the way. It could still be a long time before you become a full elf. What he says doesn't *matter*. He's not the *boss* of all elves. He's just some guy."

She pulled her hand away, and we walked in silence. We both lived in a little development that had no sidewalks, and we made our way on silent feet over rooftops, jumping from house to house, our footsteps so light that we didn't even arouse the barking of dogs.

We needed to stay off the street, because a gang had formed recently that gave beatings to magical creatures if they were caught alone: a gnome was found dead just the other day, and the police weren't even bothering to investigate. Magical creatures hunted one another all the time, the cops said; everyone knew that. It probably hadn't been a human at all.

Linnriel peeled away, going to the abandoned tree house she'd found far off in the woods, distant from any human being. As I approached my house, I saw my mother waiting for me in the darkened kitchen, squinting through the window, scanning the sideways for my approach. I didn't hate her anymore. I'd expected that human beings, as strange as it might seem, simply didn't feel the pull toward magic that I did. Perhaps they were afraid of it, or maybe the elves were right and humans truly were dead inside. I simply did not know.

I texted my mom that I was spending the night at Linnriel's house—she would know enough to cover for me—and I raced onward, heading for the Darklands.

Amanda wasn't in her burrow. I rooted around in the ground, looked in several of her treasure chests—one was filled with golden coins, but most had muddy books, often with the markings of human libraries or with little scraps of paper tucked in, showing due dates long past.

Morning came, and she hadn't returned. I didn't know if she had friends or anyone I should talk to. I'd messaged her a few days ago that I'd turned into an elf, and she'd written back: *Congratulations. Amanda eat your leftover skin if Niyal no come back.*

That was the problem with being magical—people didn't talk enough. You wondered whether maybe humans had the right idea. Language was imprecise, but it was *useful*. Amanda and I had never even talked about what I'd felt in the burrow— how the earth was uncaring and even hostile to life. It was so different from how the elves thought about the world.

Halfway through the day, Amanda came walking along the line of the stream, carrying a big carpet over her shoulder. When she saw me, her face turned. "No time right now for elf-people."

"But I just want to talk about . . . about what I saw. About that other vision of Earnath . . ."

She dumped the carpet onto the bank of the stream, and the body flopped out like a fish. The boy. The boy who'd called us freaks. His body was rigid and his eyes wide open.

"Wha—"

"No pacifist here," Amanda said. "This boy was killer. Killed gnome. Now go, elf. Go."

Then I noticed her revolting smell. The sulfur and rot on her breath. And I thought, the forest isn't all singing and lounging and sunshine. There is another part of it, an ugly part, that never stops eating and killing.

"I . . . I just came to ask. I sang with the elves the other night. I sang with them, and they . . . they said I was feeling Earnath, but it didn't feel like what I felt with you, what I felt underground. What . . . what is that about?"

"Elves good," she said. "And good b—good do not exist. Good is an illusion. They take what—what's bad and put it away from them. Put it—put it into Man. And they pretend it never was. Elves are . . . elves are . . ." I thought she was going to say something really cutting, but instead she smiled. "Elves are *silly*. Just like you."

And with that, she started to dig a grave for the boy she'd killed.

Another song-circle was tonight. But when I got there, the elves were keening. The song was composed of long, undulating noises, and this time it was no celebratory vision: it was a lament. I got closer, and I saw they had gathered around a body laid out on a bed of flowers. My heart lurched at the blond hair: Linn—no, thank God, no. But someone else I knew: Cevemen. And thank God, his chest was rising. He was alive, breathing.

I crept closer, and one of the elves ushered me into the circle, told me to bow next to him. A gang had been brutalizing two pixies, and he'd stopped, put out his hand, and tried to ward off the Men, to tell them we were all children of Earnath. But they'd outnumbered him, and he'd refused to run or fight back as they beat him into the ground.

Even bruised and bloody, his body was artful, like the wounds had been dabbed on by a makeup brush.

"What are we doing?" said a voice. "We can't just *sit* here waiting to die!"

One of the elves said, "We are mourning. We are feeling. You are young, Linnriel. But you should know that anger is only a way of avoiding the fullness of our grief."

"We can't do nothing!"

"The world is fallen," the elf said. "It can never be restored. All that is left is to love, to live, to make song, and to remember the glories that once were. It is hard for you, who never saw the old lands, but if you had—"

"Screw you!"

Linnriel stalked off, knife in hand. After she was a few feet away, she started loping like a deer, covering a long stretch of grass.

"Go find your friend," the elf said to me. "None of us should be alone now."

So I walked toward Linnriel, but she sped up, darting suddenly toward the forest at the edge of the park and disappearing into the trees.

I walked into the boughs of the trees, inhaling the sweet fragrance of the flowers and, underneath them, the clean, dry smell of the dirt underfoot, and then I saw a pair of slippers attached to two long legs. I'd heard about her tree house, but she'd never allowed me to visit. The wood was scabrous and peeling. I hopped up, grabbing the broken rung of a ladder.

Even the sound of Linnriel's sobbing was gorgeous. When she turned toward me, I saw three tears artfully decorating her face. Her body was half-turned, so she looked over her bare shoulder, and it took a moment for me to realize: I looked like this, too. Tall and pale-skinned and impregnable. My mother had gotten weird lately, hugging me and talking about the long life I'd have and the things I'd do. It came up virtually every time we got together.

"What's wrong?" I said.

"Someone's *dead*. We'll all be dead if the humans get their way."

"But Linn, you'll turn into a troll if you fight back. You know that."

"That's a myth. Probably . . ."

I sat in a corner of the tree house, at the edge of the bed of withered rose petals where I assume she slept. Whenever two elves come together, the forest is heightened. Birds stand at attention in the trees, and where normally they don't care what people do, now we could see them admiring us, preening themselves to please us. An old owl was in a branch just opposite, its eyes very wide and yellow, and I smiled at the permanent snarl of its beak. Lifting a hand, I pointed to the spot between us, and the owl took flight—more of a hop, really, than a flight—beating its wings a few times, and then it was between us. Linnriel smiled through her tears and put out a hand to scratch its cheek, keeping her fingertip just a bit away. The owl pulled closer, trying to be touched, and her hand moved, instinctively.

"You can touch it," I said.

"N-no, we shouldn't interfere—" Elves could be so stupidly delicate sometimes.

I took her hand, put her finger on its beak. The owl still looked very serious as she scratched it softly with her index finger.

"Did something happen?" I said. "Or just Cevemen? He . . . he'll live. Elves heal. . . ."

"I just . . . my parents are religious. And I went to them—I know I shouldn't—but I was like, I'm going to live forever. Look at me, Mom. Look at me! You thought I was brainwashed, but now look at me!"

She couldn't meet my eyes. I said, "And I bet she said, you're going to hell. And stay away from your brothers or sisters or any other children, because I won't let the devil claim them, either."

"Kind of," Linnriel said.

"I'm sorry."

"But, you know, I told her, I've heard the real God," Linnriel said. "I've spoken to her. My power came from her. And she's more beautiful and loving than you can imagine." Now Linnriel looked at me. "And I *have* heard her. I've heard *something*, right?"

"Sure."

"I wanted to burn their house down. Stab them a hundred times. I want *all* of them dead. And we could do it, Niyal. That's the crazy thing. We could do it. We're strong enough and fast enough."

"But there's no *reason* to."

"If humans understood how *weak* they were, maybe they'd leave Earnath alone. . . ." She shook her head. "I know my anger is keeping me from full transformation. Why . . . why aren't you angry? Is it you're just so glad to not be a troll?"

338

"Why be angry? Being an elf is just a thousand times better than being a human. They're stupid. We should pity them."

"I guess . . ."

The hairs on her neck twitched. She didn't see it. She was beautiful, and she'd live forever on the distant ships, blessed by fate to experience life in every possible form, with every possible emotion—she would feel things that were so ephemeral and delicate that human beings didn't even have names for the emotions. But she'd always wonder—could it be better? Could it be different? In her mind, there would always be something wrong with the world, some pollution, some insult, some lost homeland or some darkness. And that was fine. That was her fate.

And it could be mine, too. I knew that Earnath didn't care whether I chose to become an elf or to become a troll. If I chose one thing, I'd experience endless millennia of frolicking—but if I chose the other . . .

I'd live apart even from other magical creatures. And they'd think I was vicious and bloodthirsty and stupid and polluted. And why suffer through that? Being a troll wasn't *better* than being an elf. It wasn't.

But it also wasn't worse. Because the truth—the truth was that the world was neither good or bad. It simply existed. And if you couldn't see and grapple with that, then you couldn't ever truly live.

And that's when we heard shouting from the park.

They looked like soldiers. People in camo gear and bandannas, holding guns. They drove toward the elves, screaming through megaphones, "Humanity forever!"

The trees bent toward them, holding one of the cars in place. But another swerved to the side and kept going. Most of the elves had disappeared, but a few were struggling with a white form. Cevemen.

Linnriel and I were running, and both our knives were out. Our legs went so fast that we could almost but not quite keep up with the car. Then the knife sang out to me, and I knew why the elves had forged it. Not for cutting our enemies, no, but for making a sacrifice, so that others could remain happy and untouched.

The line of blood appeared on my hand, then it was swallowed by my expanding, hardening skin. The knife fell into the grass, ready to be used by another elf, in some long-distant future perhaps. My back and legs and arms all grew as I ran, and I let loose a roar. I stopped and bound forward, making contact with the car, shattering its side doors. The car swerved, and I felt a pinprick, the discharge of a gun. Then my hands tore through the metal roof, and in a few moments it was done.

The human beings were dead. The car was overturned. The grove was quiet again. And Linnriel stood aghast before me: "Niyal," she said. "What did you do?"

"You don't want this, Linnriel. Go west. Go west, Linn. Go west and forget."

The other elves wouldn't look at me. Only Cevemen gestured me close as they carried me away. "You're braver than I was," he whispered. And that's when I knew Cevemen himself had once faced the choice between elf and troll, and that he'd regretted the decision ever since. And would perhaps continue to regret it for many thousands of years to come. But that was no longer my concern.

After the elven procession reached the edge of the Eternal Forest, I turned south, taking the trail to Amanda's bridge.

I was headed home.

MONSTER REFLECTION

When I was about ten or eleven years old, I read a story about an elven kid who's bad at magic, so the other elves make fun of him. His only friend is a girl named Greta, but even she's ashamed of the friendship and hides it. Eventually his teacher sends him to the furnace for some reason, and he makes friends with the troll who lives down there, stoking the furnace. The troll is the only one who makes him comfortable. And at the end the troll helps him *kill* and *eat* all the other kids, including Greta, and the kid turns into a troll himself and, I guess, lives happily ever after. This story is so twisted that I couldn't believe it appeared in a kids' anthology, so a few years ago I hunted it down: the story is called "Timor and the Furnace Troll" and it's by Bruce Coville, appearing in an anthology he edited.

I went to an all-boys middle school and high school, and I was bullied about an average amount, and somehow I just never felt quite right. I always had that ugly-duckling feeling, that I didn't belong among these people. That I was *bad* and *wrong* somehow. It's taken me twenty-five years to accept that the source of that feeling was gender dysphoria. Even now, it seems absurd that something so deeply formative could've been so easily fixed.

When I go online in trans spaces, I often see trans kids asking anxiously "Will I pass?" or "Is it too late?" or "Will I be ugly?" I don't know the answer to their questions, but I do know that, in their eyes, I am the furnace troll (I am six-foot seven and don't come anywhere close to passing), and yet I enjoy being a furnace troll much more than I ever enjoyed being an elf. The appeal of trolldom is not something you can really explain, since to most people it's their worst nightmare, but with this story I've at least made the attempt.

HOW WE FOUNDED CLUB FEATHERS AT THE DISCARD DEPOT

BY SARAH MAXFIELD

Whoop-de-freakin'-PROM.

Serving electric-pink punch in this wasteland of crepe paper and balloons is crushing my soul. The gym is packed with bubbly girls modeling sculpted hair and shiny smiles as they bounce around puffed-up boys in preposterous jackets and slippery shoes. Bright candy dresses paired with plain wrapper suits. And no one's allowed in between. We're required to attend this monstrosity dressed as a personification of the gender-reveal party our parents threw for us before we were even born, let alone able to protest. Not that it's gotten much easier in the years since to register any objections.

I heard that some other schools aren't still stuck in the Stone Age with stuff like this, but we're positively Paleolithic here. They even make us turn in our phones at the door to ensure a *traditional* prom experience. Traditionally brutal. If I had my phone I could at least surf pictures online of queer couples at other proms and pretend I lived there. Can you imagine? Dressed as you want with the date you want? I wish. You can't even say the word *queer* in this town without getting the pulp beaten out of you—or worse.

I'm here (alone) because my parents insist that participating in these *rituals of adolescence* (or whatever they read in *The Atlantic* last month) will finally turn me into the perfect daughter they were promised with that ultrasound. Sorry, folks, still a misfit who prefers pants to pantyhose (I can't even) and girls to pretty much anything else.

But I'm not here in pants or with a girl. I'm here in a green-taffeta catastrophe serving punch to avoid having to dance with any of the Jackets. If this town didn't suck, I'd be here with Em. If it were up to me, I'd be everywhere with Em. Look, I've been crushing on girls since at least the second grade, but I never did anything about it. I learned a long time ago to lock that part of myself into a box and shove it under a pile of jokes. Mostly it works. Mostly.

But Em just . . . found me.

She's a year below me, but we're the same level in French (shut up!), which is where we met. Study hall vocab practice somehow led to a library meetup one weekend, which led to her walking me home, which led to me temporarily dissociating from my shame and kissing her behind my parents' garage. She kissed me back. It was amazing. *She's* amazing. She's obsessed with outer space and watches scary movies with her hands over her eyes. She's also—to my constant surprise—somehow as interested in me as I am in her. But: we have to be careful. We can't exactly date in the open, and we certainly can't attend this watered-down cotillion together.

Instead, the best Em and I can do is roll our eyes at each other across the room while I ladle out Kool-Aid and she counts the ballots to crown Nowheresville's Straightest Couple.

Ironic, right?

Chad and Brad (really their names) come by to grab punch for their dates. They take two crystalized plastic cups each while paying me about as much attention as the furniture. Chad elbows Brad, spilling some of the punch.

"Ow, what's wrong with you, dipshit!" Brad snarls.

Chad nods with an evil smirk toward the ballot table. "Check it out. That freak Emily is counting the votes for Prom Court. I'll pay you ten bucks if you can get her to take off her sweater."

"What? No way! My girl Kelsy told me last week after gym that Emily doesn't even shave her pits. She's disgusting, man."

"I know, but she's got a great rack."

They laugh and walk back over to Kelsy and whoever, and I just stand there, gripping the handle of the punch ladle so hard it's leaving a mark on my palm, but I don't care. Why do the Chads, Brads, and Kelsys of the world get to be in charge? Why do we always have to be around them hating us? I'd like to throw an actual punch in Chad's actual face, but I know I'd probably end up in the hospital if I punched Chad or Brad. Plus, when they'd found out I'd done it to defend Em, I might never wake up. So they win. Again. This time.

The rage of righteous vengeance must be emanating from me in waves because my punch table has cleared, while a small crowd jostles around Em to cast their pointless votes before the nine o'clock deadline. All I can see is the top of her head. I hope she's managing okay in that swarm.

"Penny for your thoughts?" Kevin, from my art class, asks as he picks up some punch.

"Sorry, I only work for union rates."

"Ha, good one. I just always wanted to say that. How's your night?"

"Living the dream. You?"

"Yeah, same. I've been staffing the photo area. It's . . . uh . . . entertaining. I better get back before all the props disappear. See you around, Ashley."

"See ya." I remember freshman year somebody put a bunch of cut-out magazine photos of naked men all over Kevin's locker to spell out the word *SICKO*. Everyone remembers. Kevin was the only one who got in trouble for it, though. As if anyone would do that to their own locker. It's always seemed obnoxious to me that when people do stuff like that it's called *phobia*, like they're the ones who have a reason to be scared. I toast Kevin across the distance of the gym with the punch cup I've just refilled, and he waves a cardboard scepter back at me from the photo stand. Two more hours, and we can all go home.

The music shifts to something slow, and the lights dim. You can feel the room split between panic and delight. Panic creeps to the corners and leans against the walls, attempting to fade into the bricks of the gym. Delight crowds to the dance floor. Candy arms circle around Jacketed necks. They step-touch toward a future of board meetings and soccer practices. I glance back at Em, and she catches my eye to pull a face. I make one back, which instantly becomes a battle of who can be the most ridiculous from across the room.

I fashion my hands into winged glasses. She smooshes her mouth into a duckbill. I pull my cheeks down to reveal red rims under my eyes and flutter my lashes, and she sticks out her tongue while baring her teeth. Other oddballs ringing the perimeter spot our antics and join in. Kevin puts on a tiara from the photo props and fakes a selfie, miming his confiscated phone. We build a wave of goofiness around the oblivious step-touch zombies. Bent double, hands covering mouths, breaths held, we make an enormous effort to stifle our laughter, but it's too much and eventually our cackles escape. It sounds like a collective *I wish*, and it bursts into the room like an explosion.

Except that it's not *like* an explosion. There is an *actual* burst of flame and puff of smoke dominating the center of the room.

Record scratch.

Dahhhlings. You've called me, and I am hhhhere.

From the smoke emerges a pair of giant wings, like a hawk or an owl but massive, spanning the entire gym. The Candies and their Jackets scramble out of the way as the wings expand to fill the space. Smoke hangs like a mist around the room. Attached to the wings is a figure who is dripping in draped smoke like a living garment, which curls and snakes in a curvaceous hug from shoulder to floor, wings spreading out behind. More smoke curls like hair above a mountainous forehead. The creature speaks from a mask of makeup—eyebrows too high and tinged with blue, lashes that extend like insects, and a mouth smeared across like an open wound.

What. A. Boss.

One of the chaperones rushes to take charge, grabbing for the end of a wing with his fists.

"Go back to wherever you came from! We don't—"

I've heard rants like this a million times before, and they're usually lengthy, so it's striking that he cuts out midsentence, slumping to the ground as if asleep. His hand rolls open on the floor, revealing the quill end of a giant feather embedded in his finger.

The new voice echoes from everywhere, "How disappointing. But we mustn't fret, mes petits choux. There will always be those who prefer to slumber in lullabies than awaken to their strangeness. No matter. I'm not here for them."

Angela Danvers, the likely front-runner in Em's ballot count for Candy Queen, shrieks through the haze, "I am *not* letting some dry-ice *Carrie* ruin my senior prom!" Then she turns and pouts to her likely King Jacket. "Sweetie, can you get rid of it, please?" as if this force of nature that has just burst into the room is nothing more than a spider in the shower.

King Jacket dutifully lunges for a wing, pulling out a hand-ful of feathers before also collapsing into sleep. Candy Queen screams and runs to remove the feathers from her king's hand, only to land in a snoring heap next to him.

"Tiresome. Any others of you who are satisfied with *this*"—the monster sniffs dismissively and gestures to the room—"by all means please join them quickly and stop wasting my time." Smoke furls in all directions, blowing through the room like a gust of opaque wind.

I cough and sputter as folks flop into a tangled doze on the floor all around me. Even in the middle of this absolute chaos scenario, I'm more scared of my classmates finding out that I'm one of *those alphabet-soup people* than I am of this sentient winged smoke with the awesome makeup, so I keep my voice to a whisper as I tumble toward the ballot table. "Em? Em, are you all right?"

The smoke is suddenly sucked back toward the towering figure, and the room immediately clears. I see Em on the other side of the dance floor, searching for me at the punch table. We catch each other's gaze again, and I giggle before remembering that more than half the room is asleep, and I have no idea what this terrifying creature wants from the rest of us.

The voice booms from the curling smoke, "Now that it's just us chickens, let's have a proper introduction, shall we? Most of you plebeians associate me with a certain so-called Sleeping Beauty from the fourteenth century, give or take. Honestly, the whole situation was dreadfully reported and not nearly my most interesting nor recent activity. Just the same, one does enjoy an air of mystery much more than the hustle and bustle of common celebrity."

Kevin pipes up from the photo booth, "Wait, you're Maleficen—"

"SILENCE! First of all, I'm not interested in being sued *again* by that *mouse* for daring to assert *my own* identity. Second of all, I'd eat that glamazon version of moi for breakfast. The name is—and has always been—Carabosse."

Carabosse. The name catches like fire, spreading sparks through the crowd in awed whispers. None of us have heard it before, but it carries a power that's deeper than fame. We all feel it.

"So you see, my little moths, I am here because you wished for me. Intentionally or not, you wished for me to whisk you away from this dull disaster. Not to brag, but there are many who call me the fairy godmother of the ostracized, a sweet soul dedicated to saving you wee weirdos from the clutches of a colorless life. I do enjoy that one, though, to be frank, I'd say that particular description has less to do with me than it does the considerable 'God and Mommy' issues you humans seem so desperately obsessed with. Perhaps, though, you're more familiar with the story that I'm a cruel, wicked fairy who snatches futures from beautiful royals. I hear that one a lot, too, but come now, kumquats; we're all used to being called horrid names here, right? And may I say, the royals usually have it coming."

Carabosse jabs the snoring Angela with a pointed shoe.

"In any event, since I'm running my own press today, I'll tell you the truth: I am an uncanny presence who lives beyond the limits of others' expectations, one who delights in humiliating the powerful and energizing the humiliated. Sounds fun, right? It is, but *you* still have a choice to make. You wished for me, but lives are not built on wishes, bijoux. If you'd like to join these pitiful lumps in their slumber party, simply close your eyes and do so. You'll all wake up soon enough—give or take a century—and it will be as if I was never here."

The Uncanny Presence pauses to frown in mock empathy for those who will have the misfortune to forget this encounter, before continuing, eyes aglow. "If, on the other hand, you'd prefer *not* to sleepwalk through your life, I invite you to come with me. Oooh, I know it's *risky*, but *real talk*, my dears: you're here, you're queer, wouldn't you like to get used to it?"

Nervous murmurs now fill the crowd. Questions like this are usually hurled at us as accusations, and we instinctively scan the room for threats. Gradually we register that, for this one precious moment, all the threats are asleep.

Carabosse sweeps a dramatic arm toward us. "If you choose to sleep on yourself, close your eyes. If you'd prefer to wake up and *live* ... please raise your hand." The smoky arm drops, deadpanning, "I know it's a bit pedestrian, poppets, but the classics are effective, and I have things to do."

Those of us who remain awake and standing look around awkwardly at one another. It's likely we're each doing a similar calculation as to how much protective power we can actually count on from this creature when the rest of the place wakes up. Can we really afford to be ourselves, or is it safer just to go to sleep?

All the chaperones are out cold. I briefly wonder what would have happened if Mr. Fynch had been here. He was our drama teacher who got fired last year for posting a picture with his boyfriend online. After getting rid of Mr. Fynch, the school board decided it was probably better to cancel theater, too, so no more Mr. Fynch *and* no more drama department. Predictably, any other adults I've thought might be like me are using their grown-up privileges to avoid things like suffering through the prom. It's just us kids standing awake now, with Carabosse requesting volunteers to out ourselves for an ominous journey to an undisclosed destination. Definitely sus.

I'm shocked to see a hand shoot up from among the Jackets. It's Angela's brother Danny, whose date sleeps peacefully at his feet. His face turns beet red as he realizes he's the only one with a hand up, but he doesn't take it down. Wow, I had no idea that guy was so brave. I guess with a name like Danny Danvers, he's had some practice toughing things out.

"Ticktock, chickadees," Carabosse prods. "Thirty seconds till liftoff."

The crowd shuffles, and a few more hands dart up, including Kevin's. Other kids crumple to the floor, having chosen to close their eyes, I guess. Em bites her lip in that cute way she does when she's excited. Like that time the power went out, and it was dark enough to see the whole Milky Way from her old tree house. *That* was a great night. She shrugs at me and cautiously raises her hand.

Holy crap. Is this real? What is even happening right now?

"Fifteen seconds, and the bus is leaving," Carabosse hisses in our ears.

My brain scrambles. Em is staring at me with increasing urgency. I look at all the brave kids with their hands up. I look at all the blissful kids sleeping on the floor. For a gaping moment, I can't decide. Who knew it took so much freaking guts to say yes to everything you ever wanted?

"Ten . . . nine . . . eight . . ."

Crap. Now Em's making a face that means she's either gonna cry or murder me, and neither is good. I consider the wings, following their arc to the glowing eyes surrounded by curling smoke. I'm overwhelmed by the utter aliveness of this creature, and all at once I just get it. I want to be awake to myself more than I want safety, more than I want anything else in the world. My hand flies up.

"Time's up; we're off!"

The smoke swirls again to fill the room, pulling those of us with our hands raised into a weird group hug surrounded by those huge wings. In a flash of light and a final puff of smoke, we disappear from the gym.

The wings unfurl from us. The light fades, and the smoke clears. We're in the old school-bus depot that's been abandoned since all the zoning routes got changed. Fairy lights twinkle along the walls, and music is piped in from somewhere. The taffeta dress my mom picked is nowhere to be seen, and I'm wearing blessed, wonderful, miraculous pants and a tuxedo T-shirt. The classics are effective; I smile.

I don't see our winged benefactor anywhere, but I notice Danny, who is still wearing his suit. He reaches his hand out to Kevin, who is beyond stunning in perfectly placed eyeliner, four-inch heels, and a backless red satin dress. (Like, whoa.) Kevin takes Danny's hand, and they walk to the dance floor, swaying with their arms around each other. I mean, okay, to be fair, it's not much more than a step-touch, but there is nothing zombified about Danny or Kevin as they dance together.

The atmosphere is palpable with relief and excitement. Everywhere shoulders relax, eyes float up to meet each other. Ivy Collins rocks the floor in a purple minidress, her forearm crutches transformed from their usual medical-grade silver to an iridescent rainbow print. She joins T. Mathers and Sawyer Lennon in some serious choreo, as a disco ball reflects its mirrored confetti over them like pixie dust.

More kids flood the dance floor while others chat in corners. However they choose to spend this moment, no one here is alone anymore. The discarded depot fills with dancing and laughter, overflowing with previously unexpressed joy. It's glorious, magical.

And finally, amid all this sparkle and sass, I spot Em, gorgeous in a gold V-neck pantsuit standing by our own glittering punch bowl. She waves to me, sleeveless and unshaven, confident and comfortable. Jaw-dropping. I can't cross the room fast enough.

"Nice shirt, Ash." She grins, and I die.

"Em, you look . . . wow."

She blushes. "Do you think this will all last?"

"Either way, I'll take my chances."

I take Em's face in my hands and kiss her fearlessly in the middle of the crowd. She puts her arms around my neck and kisses me back in front of everyone.

It feels like sprouting wings.

Maybe everyone else will wake up in a hundred years; maybe they'll wake up tomorrow. Either way, we'll take our chances. Happily or otherwise, we're gonna *live* ever after.

MONSTER REFLECTION

I spent a lot of my childhood in pink tights and ballet slippers. In a world of tutus and rhinestones, the wicked fairy Carabosse was a revelation. I don't remember exactly how old I was when my studio first presented *The Sleeping Beauty* ballet, but I do remember exactly how I felt watching an older girl embody this powerful character full of an unburdened wildness. She was unafraid to be ugly and strange, to take up space, to howl and roar. Watching this force of a performance was the first time my heart understood its queerness. Before I even knew that there were words to describe my identity, I saw myself mirrored in a monster, and she was the coolest thing I'd ever seen.

ACKNOWLEDGMENTS

The first people I need to thank are our brilliant contributors, who entrusted this first-time anthologist with their stories and enthusiasm. You guys have made magic happen here, and I couldn't be prouder of the result.

Thank you to the team at Running Press Teens for delivering this beautiful beast of a book to the world: Leah Gordon, our production editor; Rebecca Matheson, our marketing lead, plus the entire Running Press marketing and publicity team; our genius designer, Frances Soo Ping Chow; and finally, our kick-ass illustrator, James Fenner, who brought all our monsters to life. Special heartfelt thanks to my phenomenal editor, Britny Perilli, who has made every single page here—and the experience of assembling them all into this collection—better. You are amazing!

Endless thanks to my publishing guardian angels, Jennifer De Chiara and especially Marie Lamba, my intrepid agent. Marie, I can't decide whether your middle name is Persistence, Optimism, or Kindness. Maybe all three?

Special thanks to Nora Shalaway Carpenter for being my anthology guru and chief inspiration. This book literally would not exist without your encouragement and example.

Finally, all my love and gratitude to my husband, Werner Sun, whose support, advice, and cheerleading mean everything to me. You are the queer little beastie of my heart. XXOO

AUTHOR BIOGRAPHIES

Kalynn Bayron (she/her) is the *New York Times* and Indie bestselling author of the YA fantasy novels *Cinderella Is Dead* and *This Poison Heart*. Her latest works include the YA fantasy *This Wicked Fate* and the middle grade paranormal adventure *The Vanquishers*. She is a CILIP Carnegie Medal Nominee, a three-time CYBILS Award nominee, a LOCUS Award finalist, and the recipient of the 2022 Randall Kenan Award for Black LGBTQ fiction. She is a classically trained vocalist and musical theater enthusiast. When she's not writing, you can find her watching scary movies and spending time with her family.

David Bowles (he/him) is a Mexican American author and translator from South Texas. Among his multiple award-winning titles are *The Sea-Ringed World: Sacred Stories of the Americas, Feathered Serpent, Dark Heart of Sky: Myths of Mexico, They Call Me Güero*, and the Clockwork Curandera graphic novel series. David presently serves as the vice president of the Texas Institute of Letters.

Shae Carys (she/her) has spent her entire life being weird. It's her firm opinion not only that being normal is vastly overrated, but also that normal doesn't exist. Shae identifies with all weirdlings and encourages them to find their own people and their own joy. It's not easy, sometimes, but it's worth it. Shae has contributed short stories to the anthology *13 Candles* as well as *Rural Voices: 15 Authors Challenge Assumptions*

About Small-Town America. Her writing also includes a variety of articles for *HorrorHound Magazine* as well as work for Anne Taintor. She has two small, feisty dogs.

Rob Costello (he/him) writes contemporary and speculative fiction with a queer bent for and about young people. He's the contributing editor of *We Mostly Come Out at Night: 15 Queer Tales of Monsters, Angels & Other Creatures* and author of the short story collection *The Dancing Bears: Queer Fables for the End Times.* His stories have appeared in *The Dark, The NoSleep Podcast, The Magazine of Fantasy & Science Fiction, Hunger Mountain, Stone Canoe, Narrative,* and *Rural Voices: 15 Authors Challenge Assumptions About Small-Town America.* An alumnus of the Millay Colony of the Arts, Rob holds an MFA in writing from Vermont College of Fine Arts and has served on the faculty of the Highlights Foundation since 2014. He lives in upstate New York with his husband and their four-legged overlords. Learn more at www.cloudbusterpress.com.

H.E. Edgmon (he/they) is a questionable influence, a dog person, and an author of books both irreverent and radicalizing. Born and raised in the rural south, he currently lives in the Pacific Northwest with his eccentric little family. His stories imagine Indigenous futures and center queer kids saving each other. H.E. has never once gotten enough sleep and probably isn't going to anytime soon. His other works include *The Witch King* duology and *Godly Heathens.*

Michael Thomas Ford (he/him) is the author of numerous books for both young readers and adults. His novels for teenagers include *Every Star That Falls, Love & Other Curses*, and *Suicide Notes*. A five-time winner of the Lambda Literary Award for LGBTQ books, he has also been a finalist for the Shirley Jackson Award, the Bram Stoker Award, the Ignyte Award, and the Firecracker Alternative Book Award. He lives in rural Ohio with his husband and dogs, where he gardens, collects flannel shirts, and waits impatiently for Mothman to pay him a visit. Find out more at www.michaelthomasford.com.

Val Howlett (they/them) is a folktale lover, a curious researcher, and a bookish florist. Val is a recipient of the Katherine Paterson Prize for YA. Their fiction has appeared in *Lunch Ticket, Hunger Mountain*, and the anthology *Ab(solutely) Normal: Short Stories That Smash Mental Health Stereotypes*.

Brittany Johnson (she/her) is an author, TV writer, performer, and karaoke enthusiast originally from Florida and New Jersey and currently based in Southern California. She writes stories and essays surrounding love, connection, and emotional authenticity for queer Black girls and women. She believes Black people deserve more than just a happily ever after, but a beginning and middle, too. You can connect with her on Instagram @ByBrittanyJohnson or on X/Twitter @ByBrittanyJ.

Naomi Kanakia (she/her) is the author of three contemporary YA novels. She also has a literary novel coming from Feminist Press and a work of literary criticism from Princeton University

Press. She also writes stories, essays, and poetry, which've been featured in, you know, a bunch of different journals and anthologies.

Claire Kann (she/her) is the author of several novels and is an award-winning online storyteller. Her favorite stories are the kind about everyday life with just a touch of magic hidden in the details. She lives and writes in dreamy California with her cat, Bebe. Visit her website at www.clairekann.com and keep in touch everywhere else @KannClaire.

Jonathan Lenore Kastin (he/they) is a queer, trans poet with an MFA in writing for children and young adults from Vermont College of Fine Arts. His poems can be found in *Mythic Delirium*, *Goblin Fruit*, *Liminality*, and *Abyss & Apex*. His short stories can be found in *Cosmic Roots and Eldritch Shores*, *On Spec*, *Galaxy's Edge*, *Ab(solutely) Normal: Short Stories That Smash Mental Health Stereotypes*, and *Transmogrify! 14 Fantastical Tales of Trans Magic*. He lives with two mischievous cats, more books than he could ever read, and a frightening number of skulls. He is trying to write a novel. Pray for him.

Sarah Maxfield (she/her) is a queer/bi+ disabled storyteller with deep roots in dance. Her work has taken many forms, and she's currently writing a series of comic scripts and a flurry of flash fiction. Her story "Buried Treasure" recently won second place in *Voyage YA*'s flash-fiction contest, and she was also selected as a semifinalist in a flash-fiction contest hosted by

Cast of Wonders. Sarah lives in Lenapehoking (Brooklyn) with her family and their imaginary cat.

Sam J. Miller's (he/him) books have been called "must reads" and "bests of the year" by *USA Today*, *Entertainment Weekly*, NPR, and *O, The Oprah Magazine*, among others. He is the Nebula Award–winning author of *Blackfish City*, which has been translated into six languages and won the hopefully-soon-to-be-renamed John W. Campbell Memorial Award. Sam's short stories have been nominated for World Fantasy Awards, the Theodore Sturgeon Memorial Award, and Locus Awards and reprinted in dozens of anthologies. He's also the last in a long line of butchers. He lives in New York City and at www.samjmiller.com.

Alexandra Villasante's (she/her) debut young adult novel, *The Grief Keeper*, was a Junior Library Guild Gold Standard Selection and the winner of the 2020 Lambda Literary Award for LGBTQ Children's/Young Adult. Alex is a member of the Las Musas collective of Latinx children's book creators and a cofounder of the Latinx Kidlit Book Festival. Alex's short stories appear in the young adult anthologies *All Signs Point to Yes* and *Our Shadows Have Claws*. She is the program manager for the nonprofit Highlights Foundation, which supports children's book writers and illustrators, and lives in the semiwilds of Pennsylvania with her family.

Merc Fenn Wolfmoor (they/them) is a queer nonbinary writer from Minnesota, where they live with their two cats. Merc is the author of several short story collections as well as the novella *The Wolf Among the Wild Hunt.* They have had short stories published in such fine venues as *Lightspeed, Fireside, Nightmare, Apex, Beneath Ceaseless Skies, Escape Pod, Uncanny,* and multiple Best American Science Fiction and Fantasy anthologies. Visit them online at www.linktr.ee/mercfennwolfmoor.